SHARPE'S ASSASSIN

BOOKS BY BERNARD CORNWELL

1356
THE FORT
AGINCOURT

Nonfiction

WATERLOO

The Saxon Tales

THE LAST KINGDOM
THE PALE HORSEMAN
THE LORDS OF THE NORTH
SWORD SONG
THE BURNING LAND
DEATH OF KINGS
THE PAGAN LORD
THE EMPTY THRONE
WARRIORS OF THE STORM
THE FLAME BEARER
WAR OF THE WOLF
SWORD OF KINGS
WAR LORD

The Sharpe Novels (in chronological order)

SHARPE'S TIGER
Richard Sharpe and the Siege of Seringapatam, 1799

SHARPE'S TRIUMPH
Richard Sharpe and the Battle of Assaye, September 1803

SHARPE'S FORTRESS
Richard Sharpe and the Siege of Gawilghur, December 1803

SHARPE'S TRAFALGAR
Richard Sharpe and the Battle of Trafalgar, 21 October 1805

SHARPE'S PREY
Richard Sharpe and the Expedition to Copenhagen, 1807

SHARPE'S RIFLES
Richard Sharpe and the French Invasion of Galicia, January 1809

SHARPE'S HAVOC
Richard Sharpe and the Campaign in Northern Portugal, Spring 1809

SHARPE'S EAGLE
Richard Sharpe and the Talavera Campaign, July 1809

SHARPE'S GOLD
Richard Sharpe and the Destruction of Almeida, August 1810

SHARPE'S ESCAPE
Richard Sharpe and the Bussaco Campaign, 1810

SHARPE'S FURY
Richard Sharpe and the Battle of Barrosa, March 1811

SHARPE'S BATTLE
Richard Sharpe and the Battle of Fuentes de Onoro, May 1811

SHARPE'S COMPANY
Richard Sharpe and the Siege of Badajoz, January to April 1812

SHARPE'S SWORD
Richard Sharpe and the Salamanca Campaign, June and July 1812

SHARPE'S ENEMY
Richard Sharpe and the Defense of Portugal, Christmas 1812

SHARPE'S HONOR
Richard Sharpe and the Vitoria Campaign, February to June 1813

SHARPE'S REGIMENT
Richard Sharpe and the Invasion of France, June to November 1813

SHARPE'S SIEGE
Richard Sharpe and the Winter Campaign, 1814

SHARPE'S REVENGE
Richard Sharpe and the Peace of 1814

SHARPE'S WATERLOO
Richard Sharpe and the Waterloo Campaign, 15 June to 18 June 1815

SHARPE'S DEVIL
Richard Sharpe and the Emperor, 1820–1821

SHARPE'S ASSASSIN

Richard Sharpe and the
Occupation of Paris, 1815

BERNARD CORNWELL

HARPER

An Imprint of HarperCollins*Publishers*

SHARPE'S ASSASSIN. Copyright © 2021 by Bernard Cornwell. All rights reserved. Printed in the United States of America. No part of this book may be used or re-produced in any manner whatsoever without written permission except in the case of brief quotations embodied in critical articles and reviews. For information, address HarperCollins Publishers, 195 Broadway, New York, NY 10007.

HarperCollins books may be purchased for educational, business, or sales promotional use. For information, please email the Special Markets Department at SP-sales@harpercollins.com.

Originally published in Great Britain in 2021 by HarperCollins Publishers.

FIRST U.S. EDITION

Library of Congress Cataloging-in-Publication Data has been applied for.

ISBN 978-0-06-256326-2

21 22 23 24 25 LSC 10 9 8 7 6 5 4 3 2 1

Sharpe's Assassin
is for
WHISKEY
My wonderful dog
who kept me company
as I wrote eleven books and
who died just as this one was finished

PART ONE

The Fortress

CHAPTER 1

There were three men on the ridgetop. Two were alive.

One of the two, a tall, lean man, his face darkened by sun, was wielding a pickaxe, slamming the blade down into the stubborn earth. The top twelve inches of digging had been easy, but the hard rain of two days before had not loosened the thick clay soil beneath and the pick was striking hard, but not deep. "This'll take all bloody day," he grumbled.

"Let me do it," the second man said. He was even taller, a burly hard-muscled man who spoke in an Irish accent. "You take the shovel."

"I want to do it," the first man said surlily and slammed the pick down again. He was stripped to the waist, wearing only a crude straw hat, calf-length boots, and French cavalry overalls. His shirt and his green rifleman's jacket were hung on a nearby tree, together with his heavy cavalry sword, a tattered red officer's sash, and a rifle.

"I told you to dig the hole in the valley," the bigger man said. "Ground's softer down there."

"It has to be up here, Pat. Dan always liked the high ground."

"I'll miss Dan," Patrick Harper said wistfully.

"Bloody Frogs." The pickaxe hammered down again. "Give me that shovel."

"I'll shovel it," Harper said, "make room." He jumped into the shallow grave and scraped out some loose soil and stones.

The officer walked to the tree and took down his rifle. "I'll bury this with him," he said.

"Why not his own rifle?"

"Because his is better than mine. Dan won't mind."

"He looked after his rifle, that's for sure."

Dan Hagman's corpse lay on the grass. He had been killed by a French voltigeur in the battle that had been fought on the ridge just one day before. Most of the battalion's dead were being buried in a shallow grave on the lower ground close to the château of Hougoumont that still smoked from the fire that had destroyed the main house. Another fiercer and larger fire burned closer to the château, and the stink of it wafted up the ridge.

The officer crouched beside Hagman's corpse and gently touched the dead man's face. "You were a good man, Dan," he said.

"He was that."

The officer, whose name was Richard Sharpe, flicked a piece of dirt from Dan Hagman's green jacket that had been cleaned and mended by one of the battalion wives. Sharpe had washed Hagman's face, though no amount of washing could erase the rash of powder burns scored into Hagman's right cheek, each burn thrown up by the explosion of powder in his rifle's pan. "We should say a prayer," he said.

"If we ever make his grave deep enough," Harper grumbled.

"You can say it. You're a Catholic?"

"Christ, I haven't seen a church in ten years," Harper said. "I doubt God listens to me."

"He doesn't even know I exist. I wonder if Dan prayed?"

"He sang a nice hymn, so he did," Harper said. He took the pickaxe and drove it deep in the ground. "We'll soon have this done," he said, loosening the hard-packed soil with a heave.

"I don't want the foxes digging him up."

"We'll put rocks on top of him."

Sharpe had made a wooden cross from the shattered backboards of an artillery wagon. He had used a red-hot bayonet to burn Dan Hagman's name into the crosspiece, then added "Rifleman." He arched his back, trying to work the pain from his muscles, and stared across the shallow valley where the battle had been fought. There were corpses everywhere, men and horses, while the crops were flattened and scorched by artillery fire. "God, that stinks," Sharpe said, nodding down the slope to where the fiercer fire was being fed with timber cut from the wood beyond Hougoumont. Men were also carrying French corpses to the fire and throwing them onto the flames. The British dead were being buried, but the enemy would burn their way into eternity. Sharpe dropped the wooden cross and picked up the spade.

"Officer coming," Harper said in warning.

Sharpe turned to see a cavalry officer coming toward them. "Not one of ours," he said dismissively, turning away to scrape at the soil Harper had loosened. The approaching officer had sky blue trousers and a dark blue tunic crossed with a golden sash. To Sharpe's eyes the uniform looked unnaturally clean. The men who had fought on this ridge were filthy, their uniforms stained with mud, darkened by blood, and scorched by powder burns, but the young cavalry officer appeared elegant and polished.

"The bugger's talking to Sergeant Huckfield," Harper said, eyeing the horseman, who had stopped beside a group of redcoats who were cleaning muskets gathered from the battlefield. One of the redcoats gestured toward Sharpe, who swore under his breath, making Pat Harper laugh. "Trouble will find you," he said.

The elegantly uniformed officer turned his horse and spurred toward Sharpe and Harper. He saw what they were doing and grimaced. "I'm told you men know where I can find Lieutenant-Colonel Sharpe," he said. He had a crisp voice that, like his well-groomed horse and expensive uniform, spoke of money.

"You've found him, your honor," Harper said, exaggerating his Irish accent.

"You?" The officer stared at Harper with disbelief.

"I'm Colonel Sharpe," Sharpe said.

If the cavalry officer had found the thought of Harper as a colonel unbelievable he seemed to find Sharpe even more preposterous. That could have been because Sharpe had his back turned and that back was crossed with the scars of a flogging. Sharpe tipped back his straw hat as he faced the newcomer. "And you are?"

"Captain Burrell, sir. I'm on the Duke's staff."

"Lord Burrell?" The scorn in Sharpe's voice was unmistakable.

"A younger son, so no, sir."

"What can I do for you, Burrell?"

"The Duke wants to see you, sir."

"He's still in Waterloo?"

"In Brussels, sir. We rode there this morning."

"I'll have to finish here first," Sharpe said, and drove the spade into the earth. "And I need to shave." He had not shaved in four days and the stubble was dark on his cheeks.

"The Duke says it's important," Burrell said nervously. "He insisted on the utmost haste, sir."

Sharpe straightened. "You see that dead man, Captain?"

"Of course, sir."

"He was a damn fine soldier and a good friend. That man marched with me from Portugal to France, then came here, where some bastard voltigeur killed him. I owe him a grave, and I pay my debts. If you're in such a hurry then you can climb off that bloody horse and help us."

"I'll wait, sir," Burrell said uncertainly.

It took another hour to deepen the grave sufficiently, but then Dan Hagman was laid in the earth and Sharpe put his own rifle at the side of the corpse and hooked one of the dead man's fingers through the trigger guard. He touched Hagman's powder-scarred cheek. "If you go to the wrong place, Dan, take a shot at the devil. Tell him it's from me."

He climbed out of the pit and helped Harper shovel earth and stones onto the corpse. "You want to say a prayer, Pat?"

"Not me, sir. We want someone who has God's ear. I might as well fart as pray."

Sharpe grunted. "Find someone who can give him a prayer, Pat, but not Huckfield or any other bloody Methodist." He looked up at Burrell, who had been walking his horse up and down the ridgetop as if impatient to leave. "So what does the Duke want?"

"Best for him to tell you himself, sir. And he did urge the utmost haste." Burrell hesitated. "You don't like Methodists, sir?"

"I hate the bastards," Sharpe said, "all they do is preach at me. I already know I'm a sinner, and don't need them telling me. No, I just want a good prayer said for a good man." He shoveled more earth to make a mound over the grave, rammed in the crude wooden cross, and was just finishing as Pat Harper returned leading a pale and skinny youth. "Who the hell are you?" Sharpe asked him.

"Private Bee, sir," the youngster said nervously. He looked scarcely a day over seventeen, was as thin as a ramrod, and had long black hair. His red coat was bright, unstained by mud or powder burns.

"We got a draft of new troops this morning," Harper explained, "thirty-six men. Young Bee was one of them."

"So you missed the battle?" Sharpe asked the lad.

"We did, sir."

"Then you were lucky," Sharpe said, "and you know a prayer, Bee?"

"I do, sir."

"Then say it, lad. This was a good man who fought hard and I want him to go to heaven."

"Yes, sir." Bee sounded excruciatingly nervous as he stepped to the grave's edge and clasped his hands. "*Dormi fili, dormi,*" he started uncertainly, then found his voice, "*mater cantat unigenito. Dormi, puer, dormi. Pater nato clamat parvulo.*" He stopped.

"Amen," Burrell said solemnly.

"Amen," Sharpe said. "That sounded good, Bee."

"There's more, sir?"

"I'm sure that's enough. It sounded like a proper prayer."

"My mother taught it to me," Bee said. He looked so frail that Sharpe was surprised the boy could even heft his musket.

"You did well, lad," Harper said, then took a bottle from his pack and poured half the contents onto the grave. "A wee drop of brandy to see you to heaven, Dan."

"God damn it," Sharpe said angrily, cuffing at the tears in his eyes, "but he was a good man."

"The best," Harper agreed.

"Fetch my horse, Pat," Sharpe said, and saw Private Bee look confused.

"Your horse, sir?" the boy asked.

"Is your name Pat too?"

"It's Patrick, sir."

"Pat Bee," Sharpe said, amused, "Sergeant Pat Harper can fetch the horse." Harper had already left and Sharpe looked up at Burrell. "I'll be with you in a minute, Captain." He pulled on his shirt and then the ragged rifleman's green jacket, stained with blood and burned powder. He tied the ragged red sash at his waist, strapped on his sword belt, then slung Hagman's rifle on his shoulder. He exchanged the straw hat for a battered shako that had a ragged split where a French musket ball had hit. He cupped his hands. "Captain Price!"

Harry Price ran from the field behind the ridge where the battalion was camped. "Sir?"

"You're in charge. I'm going to Brussels and Lord only knows when I'll be back. Set picquets tonight."

"You think the French will be back, sir?"

"The buggers are still running away, Harry, but it's regulations. Picquets." He looked at Bee. "What company are you in, Bee?"

"Haven't been told, sir."

"Take him, Harry, he looks like a light infantryman."

"About as light as they come, sir," Price said, looking at Bee's frail body.

Sharpe gave Bee two shillings for what had sounded like a good prayer, then hoisted himself into his saddle. The horse had been captured from a French dragoon and had a green saddlecloth embroidered with a wreathed N. "Look after Nosey," Sharpe told Harper.

"Nosey will be eating fresh horse meat tonight, sir," Harper said. "And Charlie Weller can look after him. I'm coming with you."

"There's no need, Pat."

"I'm coming," Harper said obstinately. He ran to find his own horse, then joined Sharpe, who was trotting west to catch up with the elegant cavalryman.

9

"Nosey?" Burrell asked, amused.

"My dog."

"The Duke might not like that name, sir."

"The Duke doesn't have to know. Besides, he's spent a lifetime giving me orders, so calling my dog Nosey is payback. So tell me what the Duke wants?"

"He insists on telling you himself, sir."

The three horses walked along the road, which ran the length of the ridge. They passed a group of captured French cannon, their muzzles dark, and Sharpe looked to his right to see where the Imperial Guard had attacked up the slope. The bodies were still thick there, most of them stripped naked by the peasants who had crept onto the battlefield after dark to pillage the corpses. "Were you here?" he asked the captain.

"I was, sir. I watched you lead your battalion down the slope. It was well done."

Sharpe grunted. His memory of the battle was confused, mostly images of thick smoke through which the blue-uniformed French had loomed menacingly, but he did remember the battle's end when he had swung the battalion out of line and wheeled it onto the flank of the Imperial Guard before unleashing a murderous volley of musketry. "It was bloody desperate, Captain."

"And the Duke named you commanding officer," Burrell said admiringly.

"Maybe he's about to take that away," Sharpe said grimly.

"I don't think so, Colonel," Burrell said, though he sounded anything but certain, "it didn't sound that way. What happened to Colonel Ford?"

"He lost his wits," Sharpe said. "Poor man."

"Poor man, indeed." Burrell steered his horse around the corpses of a dozen French horses that were bloodily heaped where a blast of canister had ripped the heart from the French cavalry assaults.

"What's this place called?" Sharpe asked.

"Well, the farm here is called Mont-Saint-Jean, but the Duke is naming the battle after the closest town, Waterloo."

"The battle of Waterloo," Sharpe said, thinking how odd that name sounded. "Let's hope it's the last battle we ever fight."

"Amen to that, sir," Burrell responded, "but who knows what will happen before we get to Paris."

"Paris?"

"We march tomorrow." Burrell sounded almost apologetic.

"To Paris?"

"Indeed, sir."

The track along the ridge met the high road to Brussels, where they turned left, trotting their horses past the farm of Mont-Saint-Jean, outside of which two redcoats kept marauding dogs away from the pile of amputated arms and legs tossed from the farmhouse where the surgeons worked. "Most of the wounded are back in Brussels," Burrell said, flinching at the sight of the blood-streaked heap. "Poor fellows."

"A lot are still out on the field," Sharpe commented. At dawn he had sent four companies to rescue wounded men from the valley. The other companies had been digging graves.

"It was bad," Burrell said.

"Worst I've seen."

"And the Duke tells me you've seen a lot, sir?" The young cavalry officer made it sound like a question.

"The Duke said that?"

"He says you're a remarkable man, sir."

Sharpe hid his surprise. "Nice of him," he grunted.

"You were a ranker, sir?" Burrell asked cautiously.

"You saw my back, Captain. You ever saw an officer flogged?"

"No, sir."

"I enlisted in '93," Sharpe said, "into the Havercakes. Made sergeant in '99 and was commissioned four years later."

"And you captured an Eagle," the captain said admiringly, "at Talavera?"

"Aye," Sharpe said.

"How did you do it?" Burrell asked.

Sharpe looked at him. A youngster, he thought, fresh-faced and blue-eyed, and to Sharpe's eyes he looked as if he was only two or three years out of school. But he was a lordling and so already a captain and enjoying the patronage of the Duke. "Patrick and I did it," Sharpe said harshly, gesturing at Harper, "by cutting our way into a French column. Damn nearly did it yesterday too, but there were too many of the buggers."

"And now you command a battalion," Burrell said.

Sharpe was not so sure. His promotion to lieutenant-colonel had been purely to give him suitable rank as an aide to William, Prince of Orange, a young and idiotic princeling who had been wished on the Duke as the price to be paid for the Dutch troops who had helped defeat the Emperor on the low ridge. Orange, who had done more harm than good to the allied cause, had dismissed Sharpe during the battle and Sharpe had rejoined his battalion and taken command of it when Ford, the colonel, had fled in panicked confusion. The Duke, seeing Sharpe lead the Prince of Wales's Own Volunteers against the Imperial Guard, had called out that the battalion now belonged to Sharpe, but whether that was permanent Sharpe did not know. He wanted the command, but feared and expected that the Duke would now demote him and appoint another man.

The road led into the forest of Soignes, where scores of men bivouacked beneath the trees, their campfires sifting smoke into the leaves. Beyond the forest was the small town of Waterloo and then the road led between peaceful fields to the smoke-crowned city of Brussels. "I suppose the war really is over," Burrell said when they saw the great smear of gray rising from Brussels's chimneys.

"Aye, you can go home, Captain."

"Paris first," Burrell said eagerly.

"We might have to fight for that," Sharpe warned.

"You think so, sir?"

"What do I know? I hope not, but we'll do whatever we must. And the sooner it's over, the better, then we can all go home."

"Where is home for you, sir?"

"Normandy."

Burrell looked at him in astonishment. "Normandy, sir?"

"I have a French woman," Sharpe explained, "and she has a farm in Normandy." He smiled at Burrell's expression. "It's not what I expected, Captain. I spend a lifetime fighting the buggers, then end up living with them. Life is never what you expect."

"I do have some good news," Burrell said suddenly.

"What?"

"The Prince of Orange is recovering well, sir, I thought you'd like to know."

Sharpe grunted. The prince had taken a bullet in the shoulder and Sharpe would have been happy if the ball had struck lower, straight into the heart, because in three days the prince had destroyed four or five battalions with his idiocy. "The surgeons removed the bullet," Burrell said, "and the wound is clean."

"Good," Sharpe said unconvincingly.

"But the Duke said the bullet was one of ours!"

13

"One of ours?"

"It still had scraps of leather, sir, and don't our riflemen wrap their bullets in a leather patch?"

"We do," Sharpe said. "It helps the barrel grip the bullet."

"The Duke surmised that one of our men shot the prince," Burrell said.

"Why would they do that?" Sharpe asked, and wondered if that was why the Duke had summoned him. When Sharpe had fired at the prince he was scarcely a hundred paces beneath the ridge from which the Duke had been watching the battle. Damn it, he thought, but the ball should have hit the prince plumb in the middle of his chest to explode his heart, but instead had gone high. And had the Duke seen him fire the shot? In which case, he thought, he no longer commanded a battalion, indeed he would be lucky to escape a court-martial and disgrace. What was the penalty for shooting royalty? The rope? Or a firing squad? "Some Frogs use our captured rifles," Sharpe added, sounding unconvincing even to himself.

Burrell said nothing more, just led Sharpe into the city, and then it was time to hand the horses to waiting orderlies and climb the steps to the Duke's headquarters.

Captain Burrell showed Pat Harper the door that led to the kitchens, assuring the big Irishman there would be food and drink, then led Sharpe through a maze of corridors. "The Duke is in the library," he told Sharpe as he rapped on a large door. A stern voice responded and Burrell accompanied Sharpe into the library, which was lit by a huge north-facing window. The walls were lined with shelves holding leather-bound books, and the Duke was seated at a round table covered in papers. But most worrying, Rebecque was seated beside him.

Baron Rebecque was a good man who served as the Prince of Orange's chief aide and adviser. He smiled as Sharpe entered, nodding a greeting. The Duke, however, looked at Sharpe coldly and grunted his name.

"Your Grace," Sharpe responded awkwardly, wishing he had taken time to shave before leaving the battalion.

"Rebecque tells me the Prince of Orange will live."

"That's good news, Your Grace."

"The wound is clean, Sharpe," Rebecque said, "though His Highness is still in considerable pain, but the surgeons are certain he will recover."

"I'm glad," Sharpe said.

"Are you, Sharpe?" the Duke demanded.

"Of course, sir."

"The ball was one of ours," the Duke said, "rifle caliber. The French don't use that size ball."

"They use captured ammunition, my lord," Sharpe said. "And a rifle ball fits their musket almost exactly."

"Then how do you explain the scrap of leather found around the bullet? The French won't wrap a bullet!"

"They won't, my lord, but I remember that the prince was wearing a leather strap over his shoulder. It was probably from the strap." In fact he was sure of that because, in his haste, Sharpe had not wrapped the bullet in its greased leather patch, which might explain why it had struck too high. "And our patches burn up, my lord." He knew he should call the Duke "Your Grace," but he found it awkward.

"We ask, Colonel," Rebecque said gently, "because you were seen on the slope beneath the prince's position shortly before he was wounded."

"I was there, sir. I went to help Major Dunnett's riflemen."

"Who were fighting the French," the Duke said pointedly.

15

"Of course, my lord."

"Of course," the Duke said, and gazed at Sharpe for a few silent seconds. "So you don't know who fired the shot that almost killed His Royal Highness?"

"There were scores of voltigeurs there, my lord. Could have been any one of them."

"It could indeed," the Duke said, "and I think we're done here, Rebecque. Your men will march midmorning."

"Of course, Your Grace." Rebecque stood and collected some papers, presumably the marching orders. "It's good to see you, Sharpe," Rebecque said, then left the library.

"A bullet in the shoulder," the Duke said, "which takes the young fool off the battlefield and stops him from committing more idiocies, but doesn't kill him. I would call that a very fine shot indeed."

"Pure bad luck for the prince, my lord. There were a lot of voltigeurs firing up that slope."

"As I said, a very fine shot." Was there a trace of a smile on the Duke's face? If so it vanished quickly. "How's your battalion?"

"As good as can be expected, my lord."

"Casualties?"

"Too many, my lord. We buried a hundred and eighty-six men."

The Duke flinched at the figure. "And officers?"

"Five killed, my lord, eight are still in the surgeons' hands."

The Duke grunted. "You lost a major at Quatre Bras."

"Major Micklewhite, my lord."

"Because of that young fool's incompetence," the Duke said bitterly, talking of William, Prince of Orange. "Who's the other major?"

"We don't have one, my lord. Major Vine died yesterday."

"You have adequate replacements?"

"No, my lord. Peter d'Alembord is our best man, but he was

16

wounded." Sharpe needed a good major to be his second in command, but both the battalion's majors were dead and he doubted any of the surviving company commanders were ready for the higher rank. He had taken Captain Jefferson from the Light Company and put him in charge of the Grenadiers, hoping that would give him more experience, and put Harry Price in charge of the Light Company, but he doubted that either man would know how to fight the battalion as a single unit. "Peter d'Alembord is my best captain, my lord."

"But you say he's wounded? He's hors de combat? Pity. Then I'd better find you someone," the Duke said. "Probably not by tomorrow, Sharpe, and you march at dawn tomorrow. Yours will be the first battalion in the line of march."

"An honor, my lord."

Again the Duke grunted. "Don't count on it, Sharpe. Look at this map." He unfolded a vast map that he spread on the table and half turned toward Sharpe, who moved to the Duke's side.

"The Prussians are marching south as well," the Duke said, sounding disgruntled. "They'll take the easternmost route, while we march to the west. Here." He put a finger on a town called Mons. "We cross the border just south of Mons. Next town is Valenciennes, garrisoned, but if they don't trouble us, we won't trouble them. Then Péronne, another fortress, and note this road, Sharpe," the finger moved south and east from Péronne, "to a town called Ham."

"Ham, sir?"

"As in eggs. You're going there with your battalion."

"Yes, sir," Sharpe said, for want of anything else to say.

"There's a citadel in Ham, Sharpe. You capture it." The Duke rapped out the last three words, then fell silent.

"What do we know of the citadel, my lord?"

"Damn all. It's ancient, I do know that, and it's almost certainly garrisoned, and Bonaparte has been using it as a prison. That's why you're going. To free the prisoners."

Sharpe peered at the map and saw that the direct route to Paris from Péronne went well to the west of Ham. "I assume, my lord, that the rest of the army doesn't go to Ham?"

"It does not. From Péronne we march straight on for Paris. But there might be Prussians in Ham. The place is close to their line of march, but the prisoners come to me, Sharpe."

"Of course, my lord." Sharpe hesitated. "And the prisoners? Do we know who they are?"

"They're whoever irritated Bonaparte enough to shut them away," the Duke said unhelpfully, "but we know of at least one Englishman there, and he's the fellow you bring back."

"Yes, sir."

"I'm sending an officer with you, Sharpe, Major Vincent. He speaks German and French, and he knows the prisoner we want. Listen to him, he's capable. He's one of my best exploring officers. You're familiar with them?"

"I am, my lord," Sharpe said. Exploring officers were men who rode fast, well-bred horses far behind the enemy lines to scout their positions and strength.

"Vincent has been to Ham before," the Duke went on, "so he'll be valuable to you. But he won't interfere with your conduct of the battle, and you make that battle fast! Understand me, Sharpe? Fast! The French are more than capable of executing their captives, so you have to be in there quicker than they can line them up against a wall."

"I will, my lord," Sharpe said, wondering how in hell he was supposed to capture a fortress. He had no cannon so could not batter it down, and from all the Duke had just said there would not be enough time to make ladders and escalade the citadel's walls.

"Where and when shall Major Vincent meet you tomorrow?" the Duke demanded.

"Four thirty a.m.," Sharpe said, "at the Hotel Vlezenbeek."

"You're staying in the city overnight?" The question was a reprimand, suggesting Sharpe was choosing comfort over duty.

"I am, my lord, but the battalion will be ready."

"Make sure it is. You'll inform Major Vincent?" the Duke inquired of Captain Burrell, who had been listening.

"Of course, Your Grace."

"March hard and fight fast, Sharpe. Don't let me down."

"Of course not, my lord."

"Show Colonel Sharpe out, Burrell."

The captain escorted Sharpe to the front door, where Harper waited and where he offered to shake hands. "I wish I were going with you, Colonel."

"It's a fool's errand," Sharpe said, but shook Burrell's offered hand. "Hotel Vlezenbeek, four thirty."

"I'll tell Major Vincent, sir."

Burrell watched the rifleman mount his captured horse, then returned to the library, where the Duke was standing at the street window, evidently watching Sharpe.

"He's a remarkable-looking fellow, don't you think, Burrell?"

"To quote you, Your Grace, I don't know what he does to the enemy, but by God he frightens me."

"Ha!" the Duke said without a trace of amusement. "Did he make any comment?"

"He said it was a fool's errand, Your Grace."

"And so it is, Burrell, so it is. But Sharpe's no fool. He's a rogue, a damned rogue, but he's my rogue. He also has the devil's own luck and he wins his fights. And pray God he wins this one, otherwise . . ." The Duke's voice trailed away, because the alternative was unthinkable.

Captain Burrell hesitated, then dared offer the Duke advice. "You could send another battalion, Your Grace?"

"You mean send a gentleman instead of a scoundrel?"

"Maybe an officer with more experience, Your Grace?"

"Ha!" The Duke snorted. "Sharpe's no gentleman, but he has more experience of battle than all my other colonels put together. No, for this job we don't need a gentleman, we need a ruthless bastard. And just pray he wins, Burrell, just pray he wins."

Sharpe sent Harper south again, taking orders that the Prince of Wales's Own Volunteers must be ready to march at dawn. "And I mean ready, Pat. As soon as I get there tomorrow we march."

"They'll be ready."

"And we don't wait for the rest of the army," Sharpe said, "we go at dawn and we go on our own."

"Us against France?"

"The wounded have to stay behind. The bandsmen stay with them. And if anyone argues with you, tell them it's the Duke's orders."

Pat Harper had no true authority, other than his size and his reputation. He had left the army after the victories in southern France and gone home to his beloved Dublin, but the Emperor's return from Elba had brought Harper to Sharpe's side. At least the officers in the Prince of Wales's Own Volunteers recognized his worth. He had been the battalion's regimental sergeant major, and though he was now officially a civilian, he wore his uniform jacket and everyone in the battalion knew he spoke for Sharpe.

Who found his way to the cheap hotel where he had taken rooms for Lucille. He half expected she might be with the friend she had made in Brussels, the Dowager Countess of Mauberges, an elderly Frenchwoman who was a fierce supporter of Napoleon, but who had nevertheless taken Lucille under her generous wing. "Madame is here." Jeanette, the maid, opened the door and offered Sharpe a curtsey.

"How are you, Jeanette?"

"We are all well, monsieur."

"The baby?"

"He eats, he sleeps, he demands food."

"You look tired," Sharpe said, using French.

"You too, monsieur."

Sharpe smiled. "The English have a saying, Jeanette; no rest for the wicked."

"The English would certainly know about that, monsieur."

He laughed and went into the bedroom that opened off the small hallway. Lucille, sitting up in bed, looked pleased, but put a finger to her lips. "Patrick is sleeping!"

Patrick was their son, and, like Sharpe, born out of wedlock. Sharpe bent over the crude cot, made from a fruit basket, and touched a gentle finger to the baby's cheek, then sat on the bed and kissed Lucille. "This is a surprise!" she said.

"The Duke wanted to see me."

"And the battle," she gripped him fiercely, "was it bad?"

"Worst I've been through. You don't want to know."

"And the Emperor is gone?"

"He's gone," Sharpe said. He kissed her again, marveling as ever at her delicate beauty and his own good fortune in finding her. "Boney's running south as fast as his legs can carry him."

"So we can go home."

"Paris first, then home. And no more soldiering."

"What did the Duke want?" She sounded wary.

"Marching orders, love. We leave tomorrow."

"You go to Paris?" He nodded. "Then we come too," she said. "The Countess wants to get home!"

"You can't come with us," Sharpe said. "We're marching at the front of the army. But there'll be a crowd of carriages in the army's baggage train. You'll be safe there."

"And tonight?"

"You're not safe tonight," Sharpe said, "I'm coming to bed."

"Tell me there'll be no more fighting," Lucille said some time later.

"There'll be no more fighting," Sharpe said.

"Truly?"

"Not much more fighting," Sharpe said, hoping he was right. "We beat the bastard. Now we just have to sweep up the pieces."

Including whatever pieces waited at Ham, a citadel that Sharpe had to capture. And he had no idea how.

CHAPTER 2

Major Vincent was waiting outside the hotel next morning. He was a tall, rangy man mounted on a powerful black stallion. "He's called Satan!" Vincent told Sharpe happily. "Bred in County Meath. He flies over hedgerows and can outgallop any French nag."

"Let's hope he doesn't have to." Sharpe hauled himself into his saddle, then offered Vincent a half loaf of bread that had been hollowed out and stuffed with bacon. "Breakfast, if you want it."

"What a good fellow you are. Bread and bacon?"

"With butter," Sharpe said, "and that's the last of our bacon. From now on it's salt pork. Shall we go?"

"The sooner the better." Vincent was wearing the dark blue double-breasted coat of the Royal Artillery, though Sharpe suspected the major had been nowhere near a cannon in the last few years. "The Duke tells me you're a rogue," Vincent said cheerfully as they started their southward journey.

"Aye, probably."

"Tell me about yourself."

"Not much to tell."

"Oh come, Sharpe, don't be modest. You took an Eagle at Talavera, yes?"

"Me and a sergeant, yes."

"And doubtless you'll claim it was just good luck?"

"No, it was bloody hard fighting. But I was angry. A bastard called Henry Simmerson had lost our King's Color a few weeks earlier, so I wanted to square accounts."

"Yes, I've met Sir Henry. He's useless."

"Worse than useless. He was malevolent."

"He works for the excise now. A taxman!"

"Then God help England."

"You're the one who'll help England, Sharpe, by capturing the citadel at Ham."

"Which you've seen, sir."

"I have indeed, not three weeks ago!"

Sharpe looked across at the lean officer. "You were deep in France? I heard that exploring officers weren't allowed across the frontier?"

"Nor were we, because officially we weren't at war with France, only with the Emperor, so were ordered not to provoke him, but some orders are made to be disobeyed. The Duke tells me you're very good at that too." He sounded amused.

"And if you'd been captured?"

"Death, I suppose, but that would never happen with this horse beneath me. Some of their lancers gave me a run, but Satan saw them off, didn't you, boy?" He patted his stallion's neck. The major looked as if he might be a year or two older than Sharpe, who thought he was thirty-eight. Like many children raised in the poorhouses, he had never been entirely sure of his age, nor did he know his birthday, but the estimate was close enough and he had long ago decided that his birthday would be August first because it was an easy date to remember. Major Vincent, Sharpe thought, would have no such problems. His horse was obviously expensive and his uniform was elegantly cut, and he affected a cavalryman's pelisse edged with fur. Sharpe half smiled. "When did you last fire a cannon, Major?"

Vincent understood the question's real meaning and smiled. "Thank the good Lord I've never got close to one, Sharpe. Nasty things, cannon. They make far too much noise."

Vincent was one of Wellington's exploring officers, and that made sense. Sharpe had worked with them before and knew them to be subtle and clever men whose job was to determine the enemy's dispositions and plans. They rode good horses far behind the enemy lines and always wore uniform so that if they were captured they could claim they were not spies. "So what can you tell me about Ham?" Sharpe asked.

"It's a nice little town on the River Somme, Sharpe, with a citadel in a bend of the river. And the citadel is a bloody great stone fortress. Big corner towers, high walls. You've seen the Tower of London?"

"Many times."

"Think of the White Tower, only twice the size."

"Jesus!" Sharpe said. "And it's well garrisoned?"

"Oh, indeed, but usually garrison troops aren't the best fighting men."

"They might have been reinforced, sir," Sharpe suggested.

"Reinforced?"

"Men fleeing the battle, sir."

"I suppose a few might have reached there, yes, but most of the French will be retreating to the east of Ham, and the Prussians will be on their heels."

"The Duke suggested the Prussians might reach Ham first, sir."

"God, I hope not! The prisoners will be scattered across half of France if they do. No, Sharpe, we get there first, we release them, and we take our fellow back to the Duke."

"Our fellow, sir?"

"Rather an important man. Pity he was captured."

"Who is he?"

"No need for you to know until you meet him."

Sharpe bridled at that curt response, but did not argue. "The garrison will have learned about the battle soon enough," he said, "so why wouldn't they just take the prisoners south, out of our way?"

"Don't even think about that," Vincent said. "They should do that, but will the garrison's commandant be astute enough to act without orders? My guess is that if we hurry we'll get there in time."

"The Duke should have sent cavalry," Sharpe grumbled.

"Can you imagine cavalry capturing a fortress? The poor darlings wouldn't know how to begin."

"And you think I do?"

"The Duke has faith in you, Sharpe," Vincent said sternly. "Will your fellows be ready to march?"

"They'd better be," Sharpe growled, and the Prince of Wales's Own Volunteers were indeed ready, drawn up in ranks on the road that led along the ridge where the battle had been fought. The fires in the valley still smoked, their stench of burning flesh carrying up to the road. The wounded were still in their encampment, tended by the bandsmen, all but for the six drummers, who would march with the battalion.

"What about the women, sir?" Harry Price accosted Sharpe.

"What about them, Harry?"

"Can they come?"

"Of course not!" Vincent put in brusquely.

Sharpe leaned down. "Listen, Harry, we're going to be marching fast, really fast. The women will have to keep up. If they don't? We abandon them. Let them know."

"Of course, sir."

"Is that wise, Sharpe?" Vincent asked.

Sharpe turned to him. "You want these men to fight hard, and they're not going to be happy if their wives are left with the rest of the army. Happy men fight a damn sight better than a battalion of miserable buggers. Besides, the wives will make up their own minds. Some will come, some will stay with the wounded, and some will decide their children can't stand the pace."

"Children too!" Vincent sounded alarmed.

"They happen when you put men and women together," Sharpe said, then spurred his horse to the center of the battalion's line. Harper rode with him. "'Talion!" the Irishman bellowed. "'Ten'shun!"

"Stand easy," Sharpe called. "Now listen, you rogues! The Duke has given us a special task, and he did that because we're special! He reckons we're one of his best battalions! So we're marching into France, and we're going on our own." He let that idea settle, hearing the murmurs in the ranks. "Quiet!" he called. "We're going on our own and we're also going fast! If you can't keep up you'll be left behind, but the Duke trusts you to march hard and we will not let him down!" It was not much of a speech, but Sharpe had wanted to warn them that they faced a hard slog. "Right, Pat, lead them off."

"Where to?" Harper asked, amused.

"Center of the ridge, then turn right. And reverse the company order."

The battalion had lined up facing north, so the Grenadier Company was on Sharpe's left, the direction they would march. They were a good company, but the Light Company, on his right, would set a quicker pace and Sharpe intended to march fast. The Grenadiers wouldn't like it, reckoning that they should always lead the battalion, but a Light Company marching pace would leave them too tired to grumble. "Drummers!" Sharpe bellowed. "I want to hear you!"

He rode to the head of the column, accompanied by Harper and

Vincent. They marched along the ridge, past the corpses of the French horses that had charged so gallantly and been cut down ruthlessly by canister fire from the cannons and by the relentless volley fire from the British squares. A little farther on Sharpe passed the spot where his rifle bullet had struck the Prince of Orange's shoulder and he felt a pulse of pleasure in the memory, along with a wish that the bullet has struck a hand's breadth lower. Then they were at the crossroads where the farm track joined the main road, and Sharpe turned right, leading his battalion past the walled farmyard of La Haye Sainte, where the King's German Legion had fought and died. Dead horses lined the road and there were still dead men who had not yet been collected for burial or burning. Among them were too many green-jacketed riflemen. "God," he said to Harper, "this was a bloody slaughter."

"Worst I've been in," the Irishman said.

"Badajoz was worse."

"Aye, that was a proper fight too."

"You were at Badajoz?" Vincent asked, then looked at the wreath of oak leaves sewn onto Sharpe's sleeve. "Is that—" he began, then stopped.

"That's Badajoz." Sharpe had seen the major's glance. "We were both there." The oak wreath marked a man who had survived a Forlorn Hope, the suicidal group that went first into an enemy breach. Sharpe and Harper had climbed the Santa Maria breach, clawing their way up blood-soaked stones into the fire of the defenders, while behind them the deep ditch had been filled with the dead. There were nights when he still woke in a sweat, dreaming of that fight, wondering how he and Harper had survived, and to this day he did not know by what miracle they had lived, let alone won. "And I hope," he continued to Vincent, "that we never have to fight again."

"Amen to that," Harper said.

"The damned Frogs haven't surrendered yet, Colonel," Vincent said.

"They're well beaten though."

"Maybe." Vincent sounded dubious. "Marshal Grouchy led his Corps south, and Davout has at least a hundred thousand men in and around Paris. And the Emperor don't give up easy! He'll fight to the end."

"Then we'll just have to beat him again," Sharpe said. They had reached the floor of the valley where there were fewer corpses, though the foul smoke of the fires still soured the air. A woman with a baby strapped to her back was busy pulling teeth from a French corpse. She grunted as her pliers dragged another free, then grinned at Sharpe. "Need new teeth?" She pushed the extracted tooth into a bag and went back to work.

"Teeth?" Vincent asked with a shudder.

"She'll get good money for them," Sharpe said. "They make the best false teeth."

"We collected a sackful after Salamanca," Harper said cheerfully, "sold them too!"

Sharpe nodded a greeting to a dozen artillerymen who were guarding a group of captured French cannon, then climbed the slope toward the ridge where Napoleon had arrayed his army, and where the French attacks had started, only to die under the flail of British musketry. There was a tavern at the top of the slope and not far away a rickety tower made of slender tree trunks lashed together to support a platform reached by a ladder. "Boney spent much of the battle up that contraption," Vincent said, "watching us through his glass."

"And where were you?" Sharpe asked.

"I spent most of the day out there," Vincent waved eastward, "looking for the Prussians."

Sharpe spurred his horse toward the head of the column. He noticed two or three soldiers wearing new bright redcoats, meaning they had come with the new draft. Private Bee was one of them, and Sharpe beckoned the lad. "Can you ride a horse, Bee?"

"Never ridden one, sir."

"Time you learned then, Pat Bee." Sharpe gave the boy the horse's reins. "He's an easy horse, just don't kick him too hard, and try to stay close to me." He helped him into the saddle. "How old are you, Bee?"

"Seventeen, sir?" the boy sounded uncertain and, to Sharpe's eyes, appeared little more than a boy, no taller than his musket, which looked too heavy for him to carry.

"Where are you from, Bee?"

"I was born in Balham, sir, but live in Shoreditch now."

"I'm from that part of the world," Sharpe said, "and why did you join up?"

"Magistrate, sir."

Sharpe laughed. "Me too. What did you do?"

"Pickpocket, sir." Bee sounded ashamed.

"You were a clouter!" Sharpe said, using the Londoners' word for a pickpocket.

"Not a very good one, sir."

"Then be a good soldier, Bee," Sharpe said, then strode to the front of the column. He would set the pace and it would be a fast one. They were south of the battlefield now, though the fields on either side of the road were littered with muskets and knapsacks that had been discarded by French soldiers fleeing the carnage. Harry Price caught up with Sharpe and fell into step. "Showing the men you can march like them, sir?" Price asked, amused.

"Exactly, Harry."

"So what are we doing, sir?"

"Following the Duke's orders, Harry."

"Which are what, sir?"

"Not very much, Harry. Get first into France, capture a fortress, release some prisoners, and then rejoin the army."

Price marched a few paces in silence. "I knew you wouldn't tell me."

"You shouldn't have asked, Harry. Oh, and once we do rejoin the army I want you to detail half a dozen men to accompany the Vicomtesse." Lucille was the Vicomtesse de Seleglise, a title she rarely used and that never ceased to astonish Sharpe. "Reliable men."

"That I can do, sir, but capturing a fortress? Ha ha."

The dawn was obscured by clouds and by the time the battalion reached the crossroads called Quatre Bras a light rain was falling. Sharpe turned right at the crossroads, leading the battalion through yet more unburied corpses of men and horses killed in the battle two days before the bigger conflict at Mont-Saint-Jean. The corpses were mostly naked, having been stripped by villagers. He looked left to where the French heavy cavalry had hammered three battalions of good infantry that the Prince of Orange had insisted stay in line despite Sharpe's warnings that enemy horsemen were lurking in the fields of rye.

They stopped beyond the battlefield to rest for a few minutes and to let the men fill their canteens from a small stream. Major Vincent unfolded a map and ineffectually tried to protect it from the rain with his pelisse. "A good start, Sharpe!" he said happily. "On to Mons, eh?"

"How far's that, sir?"

Vincent traced the route with a finger. "Oh, about thirty miles."

"We'll not make it today," Sharpe said.

"Then we'd best press on!"

They marched through the fortress town of Mons next morning, assailed by folk wanting news of the battle. Sharpe purchased bread and salt pork in the town and ignored the ale that his men bought. They deserved it after their hard marching. He had marched with them, setting a brisk pace.

31

That afternoon they crossed into France. The road, which was gravel over stone, suddenly deteriorated. "Boney ordered it plowed up," Vincent explained. "He didn't want to make it easy for an invasion." Any invasion of France must follow the main roads and, while infantry and cavalry could move easily through the fields on either side, the big guns and the supply wagons must stay on the road, which was now a churned mess. They passed through villages where sullen folk watched them. Sharpe had spoken to the battalion the night before, warning them that the Duke had ordered that there was to be no pillaging. "The bloody Frogs aren't going to like us, but we don't want them angry enough to fight us. If you want bread or beer you pay for it! And not with buttons either." In Spain the British soldiers had learned to detach their uniform buttons and hammer them flat, then persuade villagers that they were genuine coinage. "I'm not a flogger," Sharpe had told his men, "but if you mistreat French civilians I'll beat the shit out of you myself."

"Or I will!" Harper put in.

They marched on. Sharpe had decided to start early each morning, before dawn, and march through the morning and early afternoon, then stop long before sundown to give the men time to make shelters. The rain followed them, but never fell hard. Major Vincent had a hoard of French currency that Sharpe used to buy bread, wine, eggs, and meat. A half-dozen men, their feet blistered or bleeding, had to drop out of the marching column, and Sharpe left them behind with a scribbled note that listed the men's names and testified they were not deserters. Vincent countersigned it. "Wait for the army," Sharpe told them.

Vincent reckoned they must be at least twenty miles ahead of the rest of the army, which would be slowed by the heavy guns and baggage wagons. That afternoon they passed Condé, a fortress town, and blue-uniformed men watched them from the walls, but made no effort to oppose them. "Valenciennes next," Vincent said, "a much bigger garrison."

The rain had stopped and a weak sun lit the flat countryside, and Sharpe kept the column moving. "We'll stop close to Valenciennes," he told Vincent. "You think there'll be trouble there?"

"Garrison troops gone soft," Vincent said scornfully. "They'll leave us alone if they've a scrap of sense."

"How many in the garrison?"

"Lord knows," Vincent said airily, "maybe a thousand?"

They skirted Valenciennes, again watched by troops on the town's ramparts. Sharpe wanted to stop, but not so close to an enemy fortress and so they marched on, following field tracks to the west of the town.

Then the enemy opened fire. Two cannons shot from a bulwark, their balls searing across the damp fields to throw up sprays of earth and water some fifty paces to the right of the column. "Cold barrels," Sharpe said.

"Cold?" Vincent asked.

"Cannons fire farther with hot barrels," Sharpe said, "so the next shots will be closer."

The next shots screamed overhead, missing the Light Company's shakos by less than a yard. Sharpe hurried the pace.

"Sir?" Private Bee said nervously.

"What is it, Bee?"

"Horsemen, sir, behind us." Bee, with the added height of being on Sharpe's horse, could see farther. Sharpe turned and saw three blue-uniformed horsemen following them. The cannons hammered again, their sound bellowing across the damp fields, but the artillery-men on the wall had overcompensated and their shots again fell short and were stopped by the soggy ground. The horsemen stayed well back. Sharpe thought of leaving riflemen behind to ambush the followers, but decided it was best not to provoke an enemy that could outnumber them.

He finally stopped some five miles south of Valenciennes in a wood that gave them timber for shelters and fires. The three horsemen left at dusk, spurring back to the town. "I don't like it," Sharpe said, peeling a hard-boiled egg.

"What?" Vincent asked.

"Maybe I should have shot those three. Some ambitious bastard back in the town might be reckoning we're easy meat."

"They'll have heard of Boney's defeat," the major said, "and won't want trouble."

"And they'll have counted us as we went past," Sharpe insisted, "and they'll know we're on our own. Harry!"

Price ran to Sharpe's side. "Sir?"

"Picquets, Harry, strong ones, watching the road back to town."

At nightfall Sharpe walked the picquet line that was strung between the road and the River Scheldt that ran to the west. The small rain had stopped and the sky was ragged with clearing clouds. "You really think they'll come, sir?" Price asked him.

"I've no idea, Harry, but we're a tempting target. One badly under-strength battalion all on its own? I'd attack us."

"They must know the war's lost!"

"Must they? Major Vincent assures me Davout has over a hundred thousand men around Paris, and Marshal Grouchy escaped Waterloo with a whole army corps."

"And we're all alone in France," Price said dourly.

"Don't worry, Harry, you've got me." Sharpe clapped him on the shoulder. "And if they do come, Harry, you'll command the skirmishers."

"Of course, sir."

"The lads know what to do," Sharpe reassured Price, who was new to the Light Company, "your job is to pull them back before the enemy skirmishers overwhelm them. Best job in the army, Harry, commanding a Light Company! You'll love it!"

Sharpe went back to his bivouac, where Harper was making tea. "How's Mister Price?"

"Nervous, but he'll do. He's a natural Light Company officer."

"Irresponsible?"

"Daring and quick-thinking."

Harper broke a double-baked biscuit in two and handed one piece to Sharpe. "You think they'll attack us?"

"For the glory of France, it's possible. But get some sleep."

"They won't come, Sharpe," Vincent broke in. "Their job is to defend the town, not sally out for a fight."

"We're too tempting a target," Sharpe said, "and all it needs is one ambitious bastard who wants an easy victory. They'll come."

"Five guineas says you're wrong. The garrison will be tucked up in their beds by now."

"Five guineas," Sharpe agreed, drank his tea, and went to bed himself.

The sound of musketry woke Sharpe, though it took him a few seconds to realize where he was. Then he swore, rolled out of the cloak that served as a blanket, and reached for his rifle. The moon was nearly full, and high in the eastern sky, its light filtering through the thick trees where the battalion was camped. He kicked a sleeping lump. "Wake up! We've got visitors."

"God save Ireland," Harper groaned.

Another spatter of musketry sounded from the north of the trees and just then one of the picquets came running back. "Mister Sharpe! Mister Sharpe!"

"Calm down, lad, we're awake."

The picquet was Rifleman McGurk. "Mister Sharpe! There are hundreds of them! Coming up by the river!"

"Then we'll just have to send them home," Sharpe said. Harper was fully awake now. "Pat, stir the damn lot. I want the battalion at the northern edge of the trees, but in cover. Grenadier Company on the right."

Sharpe plucked McGurk's elbow. "Show me," he said, and followed the rifleman through the trees, which grew dense at the top of a low hill. He stopped at the northern edge where the land fell very gently away toward the town of Valenciennes. To his left, the west, was the River Scheldt, beside which a rutted farm track came toward the woods where the Prince of Wales's Own Volunteers had bivouacked, and on that track was what looked like a large battalion of enemy troops. The moon, glowing between two heaps of cloud, was bright enough to show that the advancing men were carrying muskets. "About a thousand of them," Sharpe grunted, having done a swift count of the approaching ranks. "Where's Captain Price?" Sharpe asked McGurk.

"Out there, sir," McGurk pointed toward a hedgerow some two hundred yards north.

"Go find him," Sharpe said, "and tell him to suck the buggers in to us."

Sharpe, who had led a Light Company, trusted Price to know what he meant. Price's picquets were firing at the approaching troops from the cover of the hedgerow. The leading French were a hundred paces beyond them, advancing in a long dark column. "No voltigeurs." Pat Harper appeared beside Sharpe.

"None that I can see, Pat."

"So what will they do?"

"Die," Sharpe said nastily. "As the men arrive, make them lie down at the wood's edge, and send Captain Jefferson to me."

Harper vanished in the shadowed trees where men were hurrying. Vincent found Sharpe. "What's happening, Colonel?"

"You owe me five guineas."

"Damn." Vincent stared at the approaching column. "Why are they bothering?"

Sharpe sighed. "There's a French officer over there, Major, who wants to make a name for himself. He's been stuck on garrison duty while other men do the fighting, and he knows how few we are and he thinks he's got an easy victory. He's a bloody idiot!" Sharpe saw Captain Jefferson, who commanded the Grenadier Company, coming. "Captain! Take your company out to the right flank. There's a ditch there. Go halfway down the slope, then hide in the ditch. When we start filleting the buggers, join in, but wait for us to thin them out."

"With pleasure, sir," Jefferson said and turned away.

Major Vincent knelt beside Sharpe. "You think the enemy is led by an idiot?"

"I've got a line of skirmishers out there, and they're hurting the buggers, and the idiot hasn't thought of putting out his own skirmishers. So his men are dying and mine aren't. I reckon the idiot is planning a direct assault on the wood. It'll fail."

Vincent looked at Sharpe. "You sound confident, Colonel."

Sharpe grimaced. "Garrison troops, Major, don't know their arses from their belly buttons. We'll suck them in, kill a few of them, then go back to sleep."

"There's a lot of them," Vincent warned. He sounded nervous.

"I've got just under four hundred and fifty men and he's got about a thousand," Sharpe said, "but a thousand isn't enough. Now excuse me, Major."

Sharpe walked along the treeline, noting that his men were lying flat at the edge of the trees. "It'll be a battalion volley first, lads," he told them as he walked. "Wait for my orders. Don't fire till I tell you! And aim low! You'll hear rifle fire, ignore it! Wait for my order! This is nothing to get excited about!" The last men were arriving from the encampment where the fires glowed dully. The French could presumably see that faint glow through the trees and would aim for it, which meant they must climb the shallow rising field directly in front of Sharpe's battalion. "They're bloody idiots," he grumbled to Harper. "Want to be heroes."

"I'm not complaining," Harper said.

"It annoys me," Sharpe said. "The bloody war is over and they want to die? It's a waste of men."

"Frenchmen."

"They're good men, Pat. They deserve better." Sharpe took the rifle from his shoulder, eased the cock back, then primed the gun with finely mealed powder from the horn every rifleman carried. The barrel was already charged with powder and a leather-wrapped ball.

"But you'll shoot one of the good men?" Pat Harper asked, amused.

"With any luck the bastard who's leading them," Sharpe said.

Harper walked to the edge of the trees and gazed northward past the approaching enemy. "Where's the rest of our army?"

"Long way north. Probably haven't crossed the frontier yet."

"So we're all alone?"

"Just us, no one else," Sharpe said. A crackle of muskets and the crisper sound of rifles sounded from the hedgerow where Harry Price's hidden skirmishers were firing at the leading ranks of the French troops. Men were falling there, but the French kept coming, following the track that curved away from the river and led toward a gated gap in the hedge. From there the track arrowed straight to the moon-shadowed woods where Sharpe's battalion waited with loaded muskets. Sharpe strolled back to join Vincent. "You think they know Napoleon lost the battle?" he asked.

"They'll know," Vincent said confidently. "Some fugitives must have come this way. Not many, probably, but some."

"Then why fight?"

"Duty?" Vincent suggested. "Honor?"

"Stupidity," Sharpe snarled, pulling back the rifle's cock. He was tempted to add that what the French were doing was almost as stupid as the orders that had sent his battalion so far ahead of the British pursuit of the defeated French, but he suspected that Major Vincent had been the inspiration for those orders, which left Sharpe only one option; to obey them.

And to obey them he had to end this nonsense. "Not long now," he said quietly. He was watching the first French ranks advance toward the gated gap in the hedge. Price's Light Company was hitting those forward ranks hard, dropping more men as the range decreased and the muskets became more accurate. Then a bugle sounded from the French ranks and the column started to run.

"Now," Sharpe said, "now!"

"Now?" Vincent asked.

"We suck them in, Major. Come on, man! Move!" the last words were directed at Captain Price, who was far too distant to hear them, but almost immediately the Light Company began to retreat across the field. An ill-aimed scatter of shots pursued them, the musket balls tearing noisily through the leaves above Sharpe's head. "They're firing high," Sharpe said. "Badly trained troops, Major."

"Garrison troops?"

"And the *Garde Nationale*," Sharpe said, meaning the French equivalent of the militia. "They've been stuck in that town for years while real soldiers fight. Probably get two days' training a month."

"Then why attack us?"

Sharpe had already answered that question more than once, but he knew it came from Vincent's nervousness. The major was a brave man, as all exploring officers had to be, but he was not accustomed to the carnage of battle. "They'll attack us," Sharpe said patiently, "because their damned commanding officer wants to get a *Légion d'honneur*, or more likely wants to impress his poxy mistress."

The French had reached the gap, pushed open the big wooden gate, and were now filing through.

"Someone's got a lick of sense," Sharpe commented as he watched the enemy troops spread across the field's lower edge. "They'll attack in line."

"Don't they always?" Vincent asked.

"Buggers usually attack in column," Sharpe said, "which makes it easier to kill them. But this idiot," he gestured toward the French, "must have read his bulletin."

"Bulletin?" Vincent asked.

"The columns always lose," Sharpe said, "because only the men in the front rank and the side files can fire their muskets, while every man in a line can pour musketry into them. But last Sunday they were trying to deploy into line, which suggests someone ordered them to stop committing suicide by attacking our lines with columns."

"It didn't work for them last Sunday, though."

"Of course not. They fire too slowly, and we're better." Sharpe grinned at the major. "Don't worry, we'll beat them."

Harry Price found Sharpe. "Can my boys keep firing?" he asked. His Light Company was now back among the trees.

"Your riflemen can pick off the officers, rest of you wait for the battalion volley. And well done."

"We ran away well?" Price asked, amused.

"Couldn't have done it better myself, Harry. Those idiots think they're winning. Tell your riflemen to look for the officers."

Price took the redcoats of his company to the left of the line, while his green-jacketed riflemen spread themselves among the remainder of the battalion. The riflemen kept firing as the French arranged themselves in three ranks. Sharpe reckoned the field was some two hundred paces deep, and he would wait till the enemy was halfway to the trees before he opened fire with his muskets. Vincent was still at Sharpe's elbow. "Are we going to be saddled with our wounded?" the major asked, plainly worried that coping with injured men would slow the journey.

"We'll put them in the nearest farmhouse, leave some money to pay for their care, and let the army deal with them when they get here."

The French had brought some drummers, who now began beating their instruments, provoking the whole line forward. They stumbled on the uneven turf. The bright moonlight glinted from shako badges and the metal furniture of the muskets. No bayonets were fixed. The drumbeats were slow, which meant the advance was slow. Sharpe stepped back into deeper shadow and unslung his rifle. He could see an officer at the center of the advancing line, a man wearing a bicorne hat with a white plume. The man carried a sword, and Sharpe guessed he was the commander of the garrison. He steadied the rifle against the trunk of an oak and folded up the rear sight, then saw there was not enough moonlight to show the sights clearly, so folded it down again. "By guess and by God, Dan," he muttered, then peered along the barrel. He aimed at the officer's moonlit plume, reckoning the ball would drop to hit the man in the chest. He heard the other rifles firing, saw a man stumble and fall, then pulled the trigger.

The flint fell on the striker, ignited the priming with a small shower of sparks and, a heartbeat later, the rifle fired, kicking back into

Sharpe's shoulder as a fleck of burning powder landed on his cheek. A billow of smoke hid the enemy, and Sharpe moved sideways until he could see again. The officer had vanished, and Sharpe reloaded the rifle.

He reloaded without thinking what he was doing, nor did he need to think. Sharpe had begun his career in the ranks of the 33rd, a soldier who had been taught how to load and fire a musket and, though it was ten years since he had been commissioned as an officer, he still carried a longarm. For Sharpe a rifle was a soldier's proper weapon, even more so than the heavy cavalry sword he wore at his left hip. The sword denoted that he was an officer, but the rifle said he was a soldier, one of the green-jacketed killers who had haunted the French through the long wars. He rammed the leather-wrapped ball hard down the rifled barrel, slotted the ramrod back in place, and saw the French were halfway up the field.

"South Essex!" he bawled, using the battalion's old name. "Stand!"

The French stopped instantly when they saw the soldiers suddenly appear from the shadows of the wood. The redcoats made a line of two ranks that was almost as wide as the French line. "Present!" Sharpe bellowed. "And aim low!"

The muskets came up to the shoulders. A few French muskets fired, the shots whipping overhead.

"Fire!" Sharpe bellowed, and the long line of muskets flamed and belched smoke. "Reload!"

The last command had been unnecessary because the Prince of Wales's Own Volunteers were as well trained as any battalion in the army. And they could fire three shots a minute which, Sharpe guessed, was at least twice the rate of the opposing Frenchmen. "Platoon fire!" Sharpe bellowed. "Number Two Company first!"

A small night wind drifted the smoke toward the river and, as it cleared, Sharpe saw his opening volley had struck the French hard. There were gaps in the line and dark shapes heaped on the grass. The attackers, bereft of orders, had not continued their advance, but were now reloading muskets. Sharpe's men began the platoon firing from the right, the half company volleys following each other in a deadly rhythm.

The French, staggered by the initial volley, began advancing again, but unsteadily. Portions of their line came forward, others hesitated. Sharpe saw men still reloading their muskets, and just then Jefferson unleashed a volley from the Frenchmen's left flank. Sharpe saw the enemy recoil, but knew he dared not leave his Grenadier Company exposed for too long. The platoon volleys were still firing, hammering a steady rhythm of musket balls into the moon-shadowed enemy. Sharpe slung his rifle and took a step forward. "Cease fire!" he shouted. "And fix swords!"

The command was a rifleman's order, because only riflemen carried the longer sword-bayonet, but the Prince of Wales's Own Volunteers were accustomed to Sharpe's ways and they obediently slotted their bayonets onto their muskets. "If you're loaded," Sharpe bellowed, "present!"

About half of the battalion's muskets were raised to shoulders. "Fire!" Sharpe paused to let the sound of the volley fade. "Battalion will advance! March!"

Another volley crashed from the grenadiers as Sharpe drew his sword and took his place between companies Four and Five. Major Vincent fell into step beside him. "Careful, Major," Sharpe growled, "I'm supposed to keep you alive."

"They're shooting high," Vincent said.

"Not all of them." Sharpe had seen some of his men fall and heard the sound of enemy balls striking musket stocks.

43

The battalion went forward in line while the enemy's progress stopped entirely. The few French drums had gone silent, but Sharpe could hear their remaining officers urging their men forward, but the sight of a long line of bayonets advancing on them had taken away the enemy's resolve. Sharpe still kept the battalion at a walk, and it was not till he had halved the distance that he shouted his next command. "Charge!"

The Prince of Wales's Own Volunteers let out a cheer as they began to run, and the sound, or else the sight of the closing bayonets, decided the enemy. They turned and ran, a mob streaming for the gate in the hedge, some even throwing down their heavy muskets. Sharpe ran ahead of his advancing line and waved them to a stop. "Let them go!" he bellowed. "Let them go!"

"'Talion, halt!" Harper roared, and the Prince of Wales's Own Volunteers came to a stop.

The French nearest the redcoat battalion gate turned and stared at their enemy, apparently puzzled. Sharpe walked toward them, sword in hand. "Who commands you?" he shouted in French. "Tell him to come here!"

He shouted it again, then stood amid the French casualties, waiting. Eventually two officers came from the enemy still crushed about the gate. Sharpe pointedly pushed his sword into its scabbard, then nodded a curt greeting as the two stopped a few paces away. "You can rescue your wounded," he said. "There's a hospital in Valenciennes?"

"Oui, monsieur," one of the two said. Both were young, and both looked nervous.

"Then carry the wounded back. The dead you can bury later. And if you disturb our sleep again you'll have more dead to bury." He turned away and began to walk toward his men.

"Monsieur?" one of the French officers called.

Sharpe turned back. "Yes?"

"Is it true? The Emperor lost the battle?"

"He lost it," Sharpe said curtly. He went on walking, and saw Private Bee gaping at a dead Frenchman. "Bee!"

"Sir?"

Sharpe pointed at the dead man. "Steal that bugger's knapsack. Leave yours here."

"His knapsack, sir?"

"It's more comfortable than the one the army gives you," Harper explained. The British knapsack with its narrow shoulder straps and tight chest strap was famously painful to wear. "And search his pockets for coins," Harper added.

"Back to the bivouac," Sharpe told Harper, "and we march at daybreak."

"That's not long," Harper said, looking at the eastern sky.

Sharpe beckoned Major Vincent. "How many miles to Ham now, Major?"

"About sixty, Colonel."

Sharpe grunted. "Two days, then."

"Hard marching," Harper added grimly.

"The Duke wants us there fast," Vincent reminded Sharpe, though the reminder was hardly necessary. "And we'll be on good roads."

"And doubtless we'll meet more idiots on the way," Sharpe said. "We rest till dawn, then go."

Deeper into France, and still on their own.

CHAPTER 3

The battalion marched in a misty dawn under a gray sky. "Pray it doesn't rain again," Sharpe grunted to Major Vincent. "Rain will slow us down."

"It doesn't look good," Vincent answered, looking up at the clouds.

They stopped at a farmhouse not far from where they had bivouacked, and Vincent, whose French was fluent, paid the farmer to let the wounded stay in a barn. "The British army will be here in two or three days," he told the man, "and they'll take these poor fellows away." He gave the man coins. Sharpe left three men with blistered feet to look after the fourteen wounded, then rousted the battalion that rested on the road's verges. "Up, lads! Long day ahead!"

Major Vincent watched the men form into their companies. "They're not happy," he remarked.

"Would you be?" Sharpe retorted. "They're way ahead of the army, alone in France, but they'll fight, Major."

"So the Duke said," Vincent answered as the column started marching.

"Tell me more about Ham," Sharpe said. He was riding alongside Vincent.

"A pleasant little town," Vincent said, "with an unpleasant citadel built on the banks of the Somme. Luckily for us the citadel's outworks were destroyed many years ago, but it's still a formidable place."

"Which I'm expected to capture," Sharpe said grimly.

"You are indeed, Colonel," Vincent smiled, "though my hope is that the wretched commandant will simply surrender. He's a vile piece of work called Pierre Gourgand. He's a dyed in the wool Bonapartiste, and he don't like us."

"Vile?"

"He served in Spain, Sharpe, where he made a reputation for brutality. By God's grace he lost a leg at Vittoria, so now he commands the garrison at Ham."

"How big a garrison?"

"Officially no more than seventy or eighty men. Many of them invalided."

Sharpe laughed sourly. "But all trained soldiers."

"And Gourgand might well have more," Vincent admitted. "Maybe even fugitives from last Sunday's battle. In which case God help his prisoners."

"Who are they, Major?"

"Men who deserve to be freed. They're not criminals but enemies of Bonaparte, and among them is a man we desperately need to speak to."

"A spy."

"A gentleman who provided intelligence, Sharpe, and we owe him a debt."

"So who is he?" Sharpe demanded, not expecting a clear answer.

Nor did he receive one. "He is the reason we're marching to Ham, Sharpe. And praying that the gentleman hasn't already been strapped to a guillotine."

"And if Gourgand don't surrender the place?"

"We assault the citadel, but I pray it doesn't come to that." Vincent slapped at a horsefly on his stallion's neck. "The outer ramparts have been slighted, Sharpe, but the central keep is a bastard."

Sharpe grimaced. "We need artillery, Major."

"Which we don't have. There's no time for a siege. We go there, we free our prisoner, and we come back. Then on to Paris!" He rode on for a few paces. "There is one other complication, Sharpe."

"That's a surprise."

Vincent smiled. "The Prussians are advancing on a road to the east, and their line of march isn't far beyond Ham. They might be interested too."

"And we might be grateful for their help," Sharpe said.

"We were never occupied by the French, Sharpe, so we don't hate them as the Prussians do. I suspect that their march south will be a horror story. Rape and thievery," he spat the words. "The natural consequence is that the French detest them. If the Prussians get to Ham before us then there's no hope of the citadel surrendering, not when they realize what fate awaits them."

"So an easy task, Major. Push the Prussians away, defeat the French, and find our man."

"Exactly," Vincent said happily, "and the Duke reckons you're just the fellow."

"What he reckons," Sharpe said sourly, "is that we're an expendable battalion."

Vincent flinched at the words and rode in silence for a few paces. "You're wrong," he finally said. "I asked the Duke to send his best, and he chose you. He assured me that if any man can do the impossible it's Lieutenant-Colonel Sharpe."

Sharpe gave a short dismissive laugh.

"Truly, Sharpe," Vincent said.

"So I'm to do the impossible?"

"Capture Ham's citadel, yes."

They reached Péronne in the early evening and camped to the north of the city. No one troubled them, but next morning, as they skirted the city's eastern side, cannon again fired at the battalion. Yet just as at Valenciennes, the shots either fell short of the marching battalion or seared over their heads. Sharpe rode at the head of the column with Major Vincent. "They seem serious," Sharpe said, nodding at the smoke drifting from the city's battlements.

"The Duke will have to assault."

"Why not leave them?"

"Because whoever rules France now has to be convinced they've lost. If those idiots want a fight, the Duke will give them one."

"And good men will die even though the war's nearly over," Sharpe said sourly, thinking of his own men who were marching toward an enemy-held citadel. He had been fortunate at Valenciennes, losing only a few men to the ill-aimed enemy fire, but he suspected some of his troops would die before Ham was captured.

"The war's not over!" Vincent said firmly. "Napoleon was trounced last Sunday, but he can still gather a sizable army if he has a mind to do it. We have to persuade the French that more fighting is futile, and the only way to do that is to pulverize the bastards every time they resist."

They rode southeast through unremarkable farmland and the sound of the cannon at Péronne stopped as the battalion passed out of sight. There had not been many shots, and none had struck the battalion, but the sound of each had punched across the fields and puzzled Sharpe. The French had been defeated on Sunday, he had watched as the whole of Napoleon's army had fled in disorder, pursued by roundshot, common shell, and cavalry. Yet still the French were defiant. Did the Emperor cling to a hope of a final victory? One last battle that could defeat the British, Prussians, Austrians, and Russians?

The armies of all those countries were now converging on Paris, and surely Bonaparte had no hope of defeating them? Yet still the French were defiant, and Sharpe was beset by the fear that he would be killed in the war's waning days. There would be no return to Normandy, no life with Lucille, no chance to watch his son grow.

Patrick Harper, the only other mounted man in the column, spurred to join Sharpe. "The lads are marching fine," he reassured Sharpe.

"Who is at the rear now?"

"Sergeant Huckfield." Harper wore civilian clothing beneath his green rifleman's jacket, and his appearance plainly puzzled Vincent. Sharpe had introduced him on the day they left the battlefield at Waterloo, but now offered a further explanation. "Sergeant Major Pat Harper," he said, "is an idiot from County Donegal."

"On a good horse," Vincent nodded at Harper's stallion, a big gray.

"I'm a tavern owner back home," Harper said, "and I do some horse-dealing as well."

"Which probably means he's a horse thief," Sharpe put in.

"And according to Colonel Sharpe an idiot?" Vincent asked good-naturedly.

"He left the army a year ago," Sharpe said, "but came back."

"I couldn't let Colonel Sharpe fight without me," Harper said.

Vincent smiled. "And that's a formidable gun you have, Sergeant Major."

"Mister Nock's volley gun, sir."

"I thought only the navy used that weapon?"

"They lost this one, sir, so they did," Harper said happily. "It's a bastard to load, but when you fire the thing? It's a burst from hell." The gun had seven barrels, each shooting a pistol ball and all fired by a single flintlock. Henry Nock had designed his volley gun to scour the rigging of enemy ships, and though it did that effectively, the kick of the gun had broken shoulders. Harper was big enough to fire the weapon without doing himself injury, and now passed the heavy brute to Major Vincent.

"It's not loaded, Sergeant Major?"

"Loaded, but not primed, sir."

Vincent admired the gun and handed it back. "I'm glad you're here, Sergeant. We may need you."

"You'll need me, sir! Colonel Sharpe can't fight without me!"

And Lieutenant-Colonel Sharpe, though reluctant to say it, silently agreed.

The rain held off and the battalion made good time, passing through villages where folk watched them suspiciously. In one village a priest accosted the three horsemen leading the column and asked if they were British.

"We are, Father," Vincent answered.

"And the Emperor, monsieur?"

"Defeated, Father, and running for his life."

"Praise God." The priest crossed himself. "So the boys will come home now?"

"Some of them," Sharpe put in, "but a lot of men died, Father."

"Or were crippled," the priest said, nodding toward a man who had lost both legs and sat by the church wall with an upturned shako in front of him. "He was a forester once, with a wife and three children. Then lost his legs at Austerlitz. How is he to feed his family now?"

"With your help, Father?"

"There are too many to help."

Sharpe kicked his horse to the beggar and dropped coins into the shako, then rode on with Vincent. Harper stayed by the church to make sure no man broke ranks to plunder the small village. "You can buy food, lads," he called to them, "but there's to be no plunder. And I'll check your buttons tonight!"

In the afternoon Sharpe again gave his horse to Private Bee and marched at the column's head. Vincent rode beside him. "I imagine," the major said, "that the garrison at Péronne saw which way we're going and sent a warning to Ham. That's not a reassuring thought."

"I hope they did," Sharpe said.

"You hope . . ." Vincent left the question unfinished.

"I hope they know we're coming, Major. I'm relying on it."

"Good God, Sharpe, we need surprise!"

"We'll surprise them, Major, don't you worry."

"Sharpe—" Vincent began, then quietened as Sharpe held up a hand.

"I can't batter their wall down, Major," Sharpe said, "and I don't have time to make ladders that would probably get us killed anyway, so I have to use deception. I have to make them think all wrong." He stubbornly refused to say more, mostly because he was not sure himself how he could deceive an enemy who was doubtless expecting him.

They came close to Ham that afternoon and stopped a couple of miles outside the town where a large farm had a capacious stone-built barn that offered shelter for the whole battalion. Sharpe paid the farmer in French coins and promised that the farm, its inhabitants, and livestock would suffer no damage. The man was happy enough with the payment and seemed curiously uninquisitive about the reason that had brought a battalion of British soldiers to his farm. "But I reckon he'll send word to the citadel," Sharpe said.

"So we should assault soon," Vincent retorted.

"We're not assaulting the bloody place without looking at it first," Sharpe insisted.

"We'll both go," Vincent suggested. "My uniform's blue, yours is green. And your horse has that enemy saddlecloth. The only problem is your execrable French."

"Execrable, Major?" Sharpe did not even know what the word meant, but it was plainly not a compliment.

"If anyone asks," Vincent said, talking French, "say you're an officer from St. Helier. That will explain your horrible accent."

"St. Helier?"

"On Jersey, one of *Les Îles Anglo-Normandes*, Colonel. Some men volunteered into the French army from those islands. Not many, but a few. Most fought for us, of course."

"And your French, Major?"

"My mother is French, God bless her. I grew up speaking both languages. We'll pretend to be French officers. I shall be Colonel Villon, and you?"

"Lassan," Sharpe said, using Lucille's surname.

"*Capitaine* Lassan," Vincent said, "shall we go?"

"*Capitaine?*" Sharpe asked, amused that Vincent had chosen a lesser rank for him.

"For the moment," Vincent said, smiling, then watched as Sharpe pulled the cloak from his baggage. "Cold, Sharpe?"

Sharpe did not answer at once, but just shook the cloak free. It was made from dark blue wool and lined with scarlet silk, while about its collar were golden threads surrounding woven bees and the letter "N." "Not sure a mere *capitaine* would wear this," Sharpe said, "but if I'm to be French tonight? I will." He slung the cloak around his shoulders and fastened the small golden chain at his neck.

"Good God," Vincent said, "that's an Imperial Guard cloak!"

"It belonged to one once. He died in Russia."

"And you got it?"

"His wife gave it me, sir."

"Ah, the Vicomtesse?"

"The Vicomtesse," Sharpe said, and added nothing more though Vincent was plainly curious.

"The Duke told me about her," Vincent persisted, "he claimed she was proof that you have the devil's own luck."

"I do," Sharpe said, then mounted his horse. The cloak had been Lucille's gift to him on the eve of battle, and the thought of her struck him hard. "Shall we go, Major?"

Sharpe left Captain Price in command, with a stern order that the men were to stay inside the barn, all but the picquets who would watch the road. "God knows how long we'll be, Harry, but we'll be back."

As the dusk faded Sharpe and Vincent rode down the farm track to join the road that led into Ham, which proved to be a large village rather than a town. There was a full moon rising in the south that gave enough light to show small houses and a large church. Lamplight showed in windows, but the streets were empty. Folk peered at the sound of the hoofbeats, but none came out to question the two horsemen. "We shouldn't go too close," Vincent said nervously, still speaking French, "just close enough to let you see the château's entrance."

"I can see enough already," Sharpe answered grimly. Ahead of him, dark in the night, an enormous round tower loomed over the village roofs, and, as they drew nearer, Sharpe saw the tower stood at the corner of immense walls. "Christ, Major! That's a bloody castle!"

"The only approach is from this side," Vincent said, apparently unimpressed by the massive ramparts, "the river runs beyond it."

"God in his heaven," Sharpe said, "we'd need siege guns to get inside that!"

"Let's hope they simply surrender," Vincent answered as he turned his horse into the trees that edged a wide patch of grass that led to the fortress. "That was all defense work once," he said, gesturing at the remnant of a wide ditch and stubs of broken walls. "Vauban built new outworks," Vincent said, "a glacis, ravelins, ditches, all the usual obstacles, but they've been slighted. All that's left is the original castle."

"It's a bastard of a place," Sharpe said gloomily. The glacis, built over a century before, was now just a low ridge in the grassy expanse, in front of which a shallow depression marked where the outer ditch had once been. Beyond the remnant of the glacis were stone walls that now stood only waist high, through which the entrance path led to a triangular bastion, originally built to defend the castle's huge square tower that contained the main gate. The bastion had once stood much higher, but was still high enough to effectively obscure the castle's gate from Sharpe.

He could hear the river now and glimpsed the moon-sheened water through a screen of trees. The château was built inside a bend of the river, which protected its southern and western walls, while he and Vincent were riding across the eastern side where the great entrance loomed. They were over two hundred paces from the château, which showed no lights. The moon was behind it, giving the huge stone walls a dark and forbidding look. "I could die of old age holding that fortress," Sharpe said.

"The Duke has faith in you, Sharpe," Vincent said, sounding amused.

They curbed the horses among the trees by the river. Both men dismounted and gazed at the great castle. "I think we should begin by demanding a surrender," Vincent said.

"No," Sharpe said, "we'll begin by deceiving them."

"How?"

"By making them see what I want them to see." He was deliberately not explaining his thoughts, partly because Vincent refused to discuss the "important" prisoner they had been charged with rescuing, and partly because Sharpe was wondering whether his plan had even a dog's chance of succeeding.

Sharpe was staring at the main gate. He had moved close to the riverbank so he could see past the triangular bastion, and the formidable gate showed clearly now. It was set in an archway of the square entrance tower. He saw the glint of moonlight reflect from metal at the top of the tower and guessed there were sentries there. Those men must have seen the two horsemen come to the woodland near the castle, but they had raised no alarm nor shouted any challenge, which suggested they were used to seeing the townsfolk on the wide grassy space. Yet surely they had been warned by Péronne that British troops were nearby? "They're dozy bastards," he muttered.

"And drunk," Vincent said, amused. A group of men had started singing in the village and slowly came into sight. They were indeed drunk, and sang raucously. They took the path from the road to the main gate and Sharpe saw how that path led first to the triangular bastion that protected the entrance. Originally, Sharpe supposed, the bastion had been a formidable stone fortress, but it had been razed down to scarce more than a man's height. He and Vincent heard a gate or door open, a shouted challenge, and then the drunken men filed into a tunnel that apparently led through the bastion. Another gate opened at the rear of the bastion and the drunks staggered across the bridge that spanned the fortress's inner ditch. A moment later Sharpe heard the creak as the main gate opened. Lantern light spilled onto the stone bridge, there was laughter, then a bang as the big gate was crashed shut. "And that's the only way in?" Sharpe asked.

"There may be a sally port, but I didn't see one."

"So it's the main gate or nothing?"

"Unless you'd prefer an escalade?"

Sharpe snorted at that. The thought of making ladders long enough to scale those immense walls was bad enough, but the idea of climbing the ladders under fire from the towers that stood at the fort's four corners was a nightmare. "No escalade, Major. If we go at all we'll go through the front door." He had an idea how that could be achieved, though God alone knew how desperate an idea that was, and the bastion complicated the problem. The only way to the bridge across the moat was through the bastion's tunnel, and the shouted challenge had confirmed that the bastion was evidently garrisoned.

"Have you seen enough?"

"Too much, Major."

"Then I suggest we go back to the farm."

They rode back to the road and so north through the village. More raucous singing sounded from a tavern and, as they passed the entrance, two French officers came into the road. "*Qui va là?*" one of them challenged.

"Colonel Villon," Vincent answered calmly, "Seventh Infantry Brigade, and you?"

"Lieutenant Brissac, monsieur. Artillery."

"You serve in the garrison here?"

"For the moment, monsieur." The lieutenant hesitated. "You were at the battle, Colonel?"

"We were," Sharpe answered instead of Vincent, "and the British are on our heels."

"Here, monsieur?" The lieutenant sounded alarmed.

"Not far behind. Expect them tonight or tomorrow. Didn't you hear the gunfire today?"

"Yes, monsieur."

"That was Péronne. Didn't they send you a warning?"

"They did," the lieutenant said.

"They're pursuing us," Sharpe said, "and we need refuge."

The lieutenant frowned at Sharpe, whose green rifleman's uniform looked black in the shadows and could have belonged to any army. Besides it was mostly hidden by the great cloak from which the letter "N" glittered in the small light thrown from the tavern door. "Tonight?" Brissac asked.

"We need refuge, and we need it fast," Sharpe said.

"I'm sorry, monsieur?" The Frenchman had apparently misheard Sharpe's answer.

"Capitaine Lassan is from the *Îles Anglo-Normandes*," Vincent put in helpfully, "and wants a refuge for his men."

"How many men?" Brissac asked, evidently satisfied with the explanation.

"I have fifteen," Sharpe said. "The rest are dead."

"They'll be welcome," Brissac said.

"How many men do you have in the château?" Vincent demanded.

"A hundred and eighty, Colonel. And a unit from the *Garde Nationale*." His tone suggested that the men of the *Garde Nationale* would be worse than useless.

"And your artillery?" Sharpe put in.

"We just delivered some old cannon for the *Garde*," the second French officer put in contemptuously.

"We'll join you," Sharpe said, "tonight. Tell your commandant to expect us."

The lieutenant hesitated. "And the battle, monsieur?" he asked. "The Emperor was really defeated?"

"He was torn to pieces, Lieutenant," Vincent answered rather too gleefully, "even the Imperial Guard ran away."

"*Mon Dieu!*" Brissac took a pace back.

"But you're to hold the fortress?" Sharpe asked.

58

"Those are the orders, monsieur."

"Then my men will be pleased to help," Sharpe said, and turned his horse away.

Vincent wished the two lieutenants a good night and spurred to catch up with Sharpe. "Tonight?" he asked sharply.

Sharpe grinned. "I don't have a cannon so I can't blow down their gate, and anyway we can't even reach the gate without going through that bastion. And I'm not going to make ladders and have my men shot down like dogs. But I do have fifteen riflemen."

"How come you have riflemen?"

"We're a strange battalion, Major. We were a company of the 95th Rifles that got attached to the South Essex back in Spain. We've stayed there, and my men, those who survived, wear their green jackets even though they march in a redcoat battalion. Those fifteen will be the only survivors of Captain Lassan's command because in the darkness their uniforms don't look British."

"And me?" Vincent asked.

"You'll still be Colonel Villon, and you'll demand they open the gates."

"Wouldn't it be simpler to demand their surrender?"

Sharpe sighed. "They'll see we've no artillery. They're not going to surrender, Major, and the Duke wants this all done fast. So we go tonight." He paused. "We're going to fight a battle, Major, and we'll win."

"We will?" Vincent sounded dubious.

"We will," Sharpe said firmly.

And if he was right then by morning he would command the Château de Ham.

They were safe enough at the farm. The owner, a dour man, was pleased with the coins Sharpe had given him, and the picquets, who were posted all around the property, reported that no one had left the farm to warn the town that British soldiers were close by. The farmer was even more pleased when three of Sharpe's men had milked his cows. Late in the evening, Sharpe gathered all his men in the barn and talked them through the coming night.

His fifteen riflemen were to one side, joined there by Harper. "You're not coming, Pat," Sharpe told him.

"And how will you stop me?"

"For God's sake, you want to die?"

"I've no mind to do that, Mister Sharpe, but I've no mind to see you die either." He hefted his seven-barrel gun. "I'm coming."

"Dear God, what do I tell Isabella if you die?"

"Tell her there's a wee fortune hidden in the tavern's cellar," Harper said, grinning, "and besides, you know damn well you want me to come."

"I do," Sharpe admitted, "but take care, Pat."

"And don't I always?"

They left close to midnight. The moon lit the road as the riflemen followed Sharpe toward the town. He stopped a hundred paces from the nearest houses and turned to Rifleman Finn, a tall, saturnine Irishman. "You always wanted to shoot a redcoat, Brendan, but try not to."

"How about Captain Price, Mister Sharpe?" The riflemen all knew that Sharpe liked Harry Price.

"You can scare him, but don't hit him."

Finn knelt and brought his rifle to his shoulder. The rest of the battalion was just seventy or eighty paces away and Price was clearly visible leading the column.

Finn fired, the sound sudden and loud in the quiet night. Sharpe saw Price jerk sideways, evidently scared by the bullet's near miss.

"Right, lads," he told his greenjackets, "keep your heads down. Lie flat!"

Sharpe lay on the road, and a moment later the first shots came from the battalion. The musketry came from the Light Company that a startled Price had wheeled into line. The balls flew high over the riflemen's heads, just as Sharpe had ordered. Sharpe waited till he was certain that Harry Price's men were busy reloading, then scrambled to his feet. "Now, boys! Run!"

The riflemen ran toward the village. A scatter of musket shots followed them, all going high, but making enough noise to wake the dead in Ham's graveyard. Sharpe led them past the tavern where he and Vincent had spoken with the French lieutenants. Major Vincent was beside him. "Your fellow almost killed Captain Price!" he panted to Sharpe.

"They're riflemen. They only hit when they intend to."

Sharpe halted his riflemen at the last houses before the open space in front of the citadel. "Give them fire, boys," he called, "but shoot high!"

He aimed his own rifle, waited till the first redcoats appeared at the end of the street, then fired at a rooftop. The redcoats sought shelter as the rifles cracked, and then began returning the fire. Musket balls flew overhead to crack against the citadel's walls. "Fix swords," Sharpe shouted, "and follow me! Come on!"

It took a moment for the riflemen to fix the long sword-bayonets on their rifles, but then they followed Sharpe across the grass toward the door of the bastion. Musket shots flew over them, the crackle of the guns unceasing. Major Vincent, his sword drawn, ran beside Sharpe. All of them were in their dark uniforms. "*Ouvrez! Ouvrez!*" Vincent bellowed for the door to be opened as they neared the bastion. Sharpe drew his sword. It was a long, straight blade, designed to be carried by a heavy cavalryman, but Sharpe liked it. It was reputed to

61

be clumsy, but a strong man could make havoc with the long heavy blade and the very sight of it put the fear of God into enemies.

The bastion's door swung open, letting a shaft of lantern light show on the gravel path. Two blue-uniformed men stood there, beckoning for Sharpe and his companions to run faster. "*Vite! Vite!*" one of them called. He could see the redcoats coming from the trees and waved Sharpe and his men forward. Sharpe, outpacing Vincent, slammed the sword's blade into the man's belly so hard that it went clean through and stuck in the door's wooden jamb. Riflemen thrust past him, their sword-bayonets slashing forward.

Sharpe tugged the sword free, put his foot on the chest of the dying man, and dragged the blade out of his belly. The Frenchman was making a mewing noise and clutching at the wound, so Sharpe finished him with a cut to the throat, then pushed into the tunnel.

The bastion was a triangular wedge with stone walls filled with earth, originally designed to protect the citadel's gate from artillery bombardment. The tunnel inside was a dogleg, entering on one side of the wedge, then turning toward the gate. "Keep going!" Sharpe shouted. He pushed to the front and led them around the sharp bend and saw another door ahead. To its right was a second door that Sharpe guessed was the guardroom. He sensed rather than saw that second door close. "Pat!"

"Sir?"

"Volley gun!"

Sharpe stood by the guardroom door, waited for Harper, then kicked the door wide open. He had an impression of blue-coated men in lantern light, of a table where there was bread, cheese, and playing cards, then Harper pulled the trigger, the volley gun filled the tunnel with noise and smoke, and the blue-coated men were hurled backward. That was stupid, Sharpe thought to himself, the noise of the volley gun was so massive that it must have alarmed the guards on the main gate, but there was no time to worry about stupidity. He hoped they would think it was all part of the pretend battle between the fugitives and the pursuing redcoats. He thrust open the larger door and found himself running across the stone bridge that crossed the dry moat. The gate was huge in front of him. "Open!" he bellowed in French.

The Frenchmen defending the gate had seen dark-uniformed men being pursued by redcoats. They had watched as the fugitives went into the bastion, and now they opened the main gate and beckoned them to safety. "Cooper!" Sharpe shouted.

"Sir?"

"Bugle?"

"I've got it, sir."

"Sound it!" Sharpe shouted, not caring he spoke in English, and ran through the half open gate. A big sergeant waited there and Sharpe ripped the tip of his sword through the man's throat as his riflemen came behind, their bayonets seeking other Frenchmen, while just beyond the gate, Cooper blew the signal to charge. The bugle told the redcoats that the gate was captured and that they should run to reinforce the riflemen. Two or three muskets fired from the citadel's high walls, but there was small resistance in the vast courtyard, where Sharpe stood over the bloodied men who had guarded the gate. "Form line!" he called to his men.

The fifteen riflemen made a line and reloaded their weapons. The courtyard stretched away toward the southern wall, broken only by a solitary tree that grew in the yard's center. There was no enemy in sight, though Sharpe could still hear sporadic musketry coming from the rampart above the gate, presumably aimed at his redcoats who would be filing into the bastion's tunnel. "Sergeant Harper!"

"Sir?"

"Take half a dozen men and finish off those bastards. Must be a way up there!"

"Pleasure, sir." Harper began to reload the volley gun. "Won't be a minute, sir!"

"Any idea where the prison is?" Sharpe asked Vincent.

"God knows," Vincent said. The long courtyard was surrounded on all sides by two-story buildings, three if you included the dormer windows jutting from the slate roofs.

"They're dozy bastards," Sharpe grunted. "We've killed what? A dozen men? The rest of them must be awake by now."

"And there they are," Vincent said. A file of infantrymen had appeared from a door at the courtyard's far end, maybe thirty of them, and were being hurried toward the gate. "Rifles," Sharpe called, "target practice."

The moon cast shadows in front of the hurrying Frenchmen, who scattered as the first rifle bullets struck home. Most sought shelter behind the tree, which was some two hundred paces away, but still the rifle bullets struck mercilessly. Then Sharpe heard a massive shot from above and knew that Pat Harper had fired the volley gun. A spattering of other shots sounded, then silence, before Captain Price was standing beside Sharpe. "All here, sir."

"Lose any men?"

"A couple are wounded. There were buggers on the roof."

"Pat Harper dealt with them."

"Good."

"Cooper!"

"Mister Sharpe?"

"Reveille! Wake the buggers up! Keep repeating it till I tell you."

The bugle sounded over and over as the rest of the battalion came through the gate. They were too many to shelter under the gate's arch, so Sharpe lined them in two ranks across the courtyard. "Prince of Wales's Volunteers!" he shouted, using the battalion's new name. "One volley. Aim at the buggers by the tree." He doubted any of the musket balls would hit. At two hundred paces a musket was notoriously inaccurate, but the sheer weight of the volley would give the French pause. "Make ready!" He paused. "Fire!"

The volley crashed out, the sound echoing back from the buildings. A scream sounded somewhere beyond the thick smoke. "Reload! Rifles, keep firing!"

Cooper was still blowing his bugle, and its sound was answered by another bugle call from the courtyard's far end. "Cease fire!" Sharpe bellowed. "Enough, Cooper! Save your breath!"

The thick smoke slowly cleared and Sharpe saw that French troops, their white crossbelts visible in the moon-shadowed farther end of the courtyard, were being hurried into position. Three officers walked toward the château's entrance. The man in the center had a wooden leg, which made a hollow sound when it struck the courtyard's cobbles. "Gourgand," Sharpe said sourly.

"Let's meet him," Vincent said.

Sharpe and Vincent walked toward the three men, who stopped a few yards beyond the tree and waited for them. Gourgand carried a cane that he tapped impatiently on the ground. He wore a red coat and yellow breeches. "He's a Chasseur of the Guard?" Sharpe asked, surprised at Gourgand's uniform.

"Evidently," Vincent said calmly. "Shall we talk with them?"

"Might be easier to just shoot them."

Vincent smiled. "You forget, Colonel, that we come to bring peace and prosperity to France."

"So we do, Major," Sharpe said. He slung his rifle on his shoulder. "Let's talk."

"You always carry that rifle?" Vincent asked.

"Never without one, Major. I'm a rifleman."

The three French officers stood at attention as Sharpe and Vincent neared them. Lieutenant Brissac was one of the three and was standing beside a plump man who looked nervous. "You are Colonel Gourgand?" Vincent demanded peremptorily as he stopped a few paces away.

"I am," Gourgand replied.

"I am Colonel Vincent," Vincent said, apparently promoting himself again, "of his Brittanic Majesty's army. We have occupied this town and demand your surrender."

Gourgand smiled. It was not friendly. "I serve his Imperial Majesty," he said, "and give you ten minutes to take your forces out of this citadel, and a half hour to leave the town."

Vincent returned the smile. "His Imperial Majesty is defeated, his army broken. What authority he possessed died with his army." He pulled a watch from his pocket and clicked open the lid. He turned the face so the moonlight shone on it. "I give you ten minutes, Colonel, to parade your men. They will pile their arms and march from the citadel. Officers may keep their swords."

"If you are not gone in ten minutes," Gourgand answered, "my men will attack. I have nothing more to say." He turned and stumped away, followed by his two officers.

"He sounded confident," Vincent said when the Frenchmen were out of earshot.

"So did you."

"I'd appreciate it if you could capture Gourgand rather than slaughter him," Vincent said.

"Why?"

"To question him, of course," Vincent said. "If our man isn't here,

God forbid, then Gourgand will know where he's gone. How many men do you think he has?"

"More than us," Sharpe replied, "but we'll find out how many when we fight them." He turned. "Captain Jefferson, to me!"

"What are you doing, Sharpe?" Vincent asked.

"Taking the high ground, Major."

Jefferson met Sharpe as he walked back to the gatehouse. "Split your company into two," Sharpe ordered him. "Half goes to those windows," he pointed to the upper floor of the building that lay on the left of the courtyard, "and half to the other side. Send five riflemen with each half company. The Crapauds think they can drive us out, so your men shoot at them from above. The riflemen take out the officers and sergeants, your boys just keep shooting. But don't show yourselves till the shooting starts, and I want their colonel with the wooden leg as a prisoner."

"You're left with five riflemen," Vincent pointed out.

"They go up there." Sharpe gestured at the high gatehouse. He sent Patrick Harper and five men to the high windows above the gatehouse. "Let the Crapauds shoot first," Sharpe told him, "then start killing the bastards, but I want the bugger with the wooden leg alive. Captain Godwin!"

Godwin ran to Sharpe. "Sir?"

"Split your company into two. One half to that building," again he pointed left, "and the other there. The bastards might try to outflank us by sending men through the buildings. You stop them."

"Yes, sir." Godwin was new to the battalion, having joined a month before, but he had proved steady and sensible, and Colonel Ford, whom Sharpe had replaced during the battle, had put him in command of Number Three Company.

"Captain Jefferson will have men on the top floors," Sharpe told Godwin, "so protect the stairways."

"Yes, sir."

The courtyard was only ninety paces wide, which meant the remaining companies of the battalion could form two ranks across its width. "It will be firing by company when we start!" Sharpe stood in front of the three ranks. "The bastards think they can run us out of here, boys, and we're going to beat them! Don't fire high! A low shot will bounce off the cobbles and cripple a man, so aim low and keep firing! This one's going to be easy!"

"Easy?" Vincent asked quietly.

"They have to think that," Sharpe said. "Can I suggest you join Pat Harper? You'll get a better view from up there."

"And you?"

Sharpe slapped his rifle butt. "I'll join the front rank, Major. Or is it Colonel?"

"One or the other," Vincent said, amused, then edged through the ranks to find the staircase.

Sharpe stood in the front rank. He had considered a swift charge down the length of the courtyard, but there were enemy troops there and he suspected more would erupt from the buildings on either side of the long courtyard to assault his rear. Better to do it the slower way and rely on his men's musketry, which should still be quick enough to keep the prisoners safe. He loaded the rifle, forcing the leather-wrapped ball down the barrel. Once the fighting started he doubted he would bother with the leather patch that made loading a rifle so slow, but just blast away. He was standing among Number Six Company and for the life of him could not recall the name of the soldier to his left. He prided himself on knowing all their names. He knew Jem Carter was to his right, but he could not recall the man on the left, though his face was familiar. "Ready, Jem?" Sharpe asked.

"The buggers won't surrender, sir?"

"They think they can beat us."

"Never, sir."

"Keep your aim low," Sharpe said loudly, "and wait for the order. I'm letting the Crapauds shoot first."

"Why, sir?"

"Because I'm giving them a chance to surrender." He raised his voice. "We'll begin with a battalion volley, lads! Then fire by companies from the right! But wait for it!"

He waited. The far end of the courtyard was shadowed from the moonlight, but he saw men moving there, and the faint sound of boots on the cobbles reached him. This, he reflected, was a rare killing ground, stone floored and edged with stone, a space where musket balls could glance off walls and cobbles to strike the men at either end of the long courtyard. "Can you see how many there are, Jem?" he asked.

"Too many of the buggers, sir."

"Two hundred and forty so far," the man on Sharpe's left said.

"You can count them?"

"Bastards are coming from that door." The man pointed down the courtyard. "Two hundred and sixty now, and still coming."

Sharpe could just make out the white crossbelts of the men filing into the deep shadow. He tried to remember the man's name. A corporal. "Keep counting," he said, "and well done."

"A lot of them," the corporal said.

"But garrison troops," Sharpe said, "not nearly as good as us."

"We hope, sir." The corporal sounded amused.

"Butler, isn't it?" The name suddenly came to Sharpe.

"Tom Butler, sir."

The French must have had close to three hundred men lining across the courtyard's shadowed end. Sharpe suspected that neither their discipline nor their training would match his own battalion, but some of their musket balls would strike home. "Battalion," he shouted, "kneel!"

The movement at the courtyard's far end had ceased. The French were in line, just like Sharpe's men, and he guessed they were in their usual three ranks. Gourgand would be hoping his first volley would decimate the redcoats, which was why Sharpe had made them kneel. Badly trained troops tended to fire high, and the kick of the heavy French muskets exaggerated that fault. He heard a voice call a command. "Wait for it, lads," he said. The French were aiming their muskets.

"*Tirez!*" a voice bellowed, and the far end of the courtyard vanished in a great rill of smoke as the muskets fired. Sharpe heard the balls striking the wall above and behind him. The first rifles were already shooting from the high windows. "Battalion, stand! Present!"

The redcoats stood, brought muskets to their shoulders.

"Aim low! Fire!"

The massive volley flamed and smoked, the balls searing down the courtyard. "Platoon fire!" Sharpe shouted. He heard ramrods scraping in musket barrels. He had not fired his rifle, waiting for the smoke to clear so he could aim the weapon.

"There's a good few of them down," Butler said as he rammed his musket.

Number Two Company fired, then Four, and the musket fire rippled down the redcoat line. This was what the men were trained to do; to deliver an unending fire of musketry. Sharpe's men had already sent two shots each down the courtyard and the French had not yet managed their second volley. Sharpe fired his rifle, not really aiming it, just sending the ball down the courtyard and confident it must hit someone. A few shots came back, but still the French, half blinded by the musket smoke, were firing high. Sharpe slung his rifle and took two paces out of the line. "Fix swords!" There was a pause as the bayonets were latched onto the musket barrels. "Now charge!" Sharpe drew his sword and began running, while behind him the men cheered and ran forward.

This will be messy, Sharpe thought. Maybe he should have let the platoon fire go on for another two or three minutes, but the feeble French response had convinced him that the troops he faced were ill-trained.

He ran past the tree and a musket ball whipped past his face. The smoke ahead was thick, undisturbed by any wind, but he could see the French clearly enough, their white crossbelts standing out in the shadows. Some were reloading muskets, but others, seeing the oncoming glint of moonlight on steel blades, were backing away. Gourgand was there, shouting at his men, and Sharpe saw dozens of dead or wounded on the cobblestones. Some men ran toward the doorways, desperate to escape.

"Battalion, halt!" Sharpe roared the command. "Form line! Present!"

They were twenty paces from the French now. The men lifted their muskets. Sharpe doubted that most were loaded, but it was the threat that would do the job. He looked at the French. "Drop your weapons!" he called in their language. "Muskets on the ground! Now!"

The muskets dropped. One, loaded, fired as it dropped and a Frenchman cried out as the ball pierced his foot. Sharpe could see four officers, betrayed by their sword scabbards, lying on the cobbles, which meant his riflemen had done their work well, but he could no longer see Gourgand.

"That one-legged bugger's getting away, sir," Butler muttered.

"Where?"

Butler pointed and Sharpe saw men filing into a doorway. The prisoners, he thought. "Number Six Company," he bellowed, "with me!"

He ran toward the doorway, clearing the French out of his way with the threat of his sword. He hurtled through the door into a lamplit passageway that turned sharply to the left. A musket shot echoed from within the building and Sharpe kept running. He turned the corner and saw he was in the prison. Cells lay on the left of the long passage that was filled with blue-coated French infantrymen, one of whom had just fired through a barred door. "Kill them!"

Sharpe leaped forward. There was no room to swing the sword in the narrow passage so he lunged with it, skewering a man's belly, then kicking him to free the blade. Butler went past him, his bayonet reaching. A musket fired, the sound huge in the stone passageway, and Sharpe saw that the gun had been fired through the bars, aimed presumably at a prisoner, then Colonel Gourgand shouted at his men to cease fire.

"Hold it, lads!" Sharpe called. His sword was dripping blood and he used the blade to push the French to either side of the passage as he walked toward Colonel Gourgand, who had his saber drawn. He reversed the blade and held the hilt toward Sharpe. "We surrender, monsieur," he said.

"You bastard," Sharpe said, "you'd kill the prisoners?" He took the saber with his free hand, rested the tip on the flagstone floor, then stamped on the blade. It snapped. He gave the broken part of the blade still attached to the hilt back to Gourgand. "Corporal Butler!"

"Sir?"

"Guard this bugger." He looked back to Gourgand. "You have a surgeon here?"

"Oui."

"He can tend your wounded. And Butler?"

"Sir?"

"If this bugger gives you any trouble, shoot his other leg."

"Pleasure, sir."

Gourgand might not have understood the language, but he could not mistake Sharpe's anger, nor the feral expression on Butler's face. He backed against the wall and held his hands wide.

Major Vincent had come into the passageway. "Well done!" he called. Then held up a hand as Sharpe pushed past him. "Where are you going?"

"To see what damage we've suffered." Sharpe leaned down to the first man he had killed in the passageway and cleaned his sword on the skirts of the dead man's jacket. He sheathed the sword. "The prisoners are yours, Major. And that bugger Gourgand was about to kill them."

Sharpe left the prison block and called to Sergeant Huckfield. "What's our butcher's bill?"

"Two dead and six wounded. Sergeant Hoskins and Private Peters died."

"Damn it," Sharpe said. It was a small butcher's bill, very small, but that was no consolation for the two who had died. "The Crapauds have a surgeon," he told Huckfield, "make sure he treats our men too."

Men were detailed to collect the French muskets, while the captured men were ordered to take off their boots, jackets, and belts. "Kick them out the front gate," Sharpe ordered Huckfield, "but warn them there's to be no plundering in the town."

Captain Godwin had discovered the commandant's quarters, which were half of one of the long buildings down the side of the courtyard. Gourgand had a wife there and a daughter, so Sharpe ordered Godwin to put a guard on them. "And find his office. If there's any money there, it's ours."

"Ours, sir?"

"It belongs to the army, not us, but just bring it."

Sharpe suddenly felt immensely tired, the weariness that followed the tension of battle. "Sir! Colonel Sharpe!" It was Captain Yates of Six Company, calling excitedly. "Come and look, sir!" Yates was the youngest captain in the battalion, newly promoted from lieutenant and eager to impress.

Yates was standing by a window of one of the long buildings, the same one that contained Gourgand's quarters. Sharpe crossed to him and Yates gestured through the window that had been broken by a musket ball. The room inside was dark, and for a moment Sharpe could see nothing, but then a door inside the building opened and a wash of lamplight dispersed the shadows. "Christ," Sharpe said.

At first all he had seen were the tall timbers reaching to the room's ceiling. There were two of them and they seemed to spring from a low wooden platform, then the light glinted off metal and he saw it was a guillotine. The slanted blade was in the lowest position.

"Dear God," Yates breathed, "what an awful thing."

"Better than a hanging," Sharpe said. There was a door nearby that led into the room, and Sharpe found a lantern inside, which he lit. The guillotine had plainly been used, judging by the dried blood on the lower platform. Thick leather straps showed where a victim was pinioned to the machine. "It must be a quick death," Sharpe said. "Messy, but quick."

"You've seen one at work, sir?" Yates asked. "In Normandy, perhaps?"

"Never seen one working," Sharpe said, "but I remember there was a guillotine in Yorkshire."

"In Yorkshire?" Yates sounded disbelieving.

"In Halifax," Sharpe said.

"They behead people in Halifax!"

"Used to," Sharpe said. "When I was a lad I worked in a Sheffield tavern and they had a great big picture of the Halifax guillotine on the taproom wall. I always wanted to see the real thing, but I never did get to Halifax. The Crapauds like to say they invented it, but Yorkshire was way ahead of them." He unhooked the rope from its cleat and remembered his disappointment at not seeing a beheading. Fourteen-year-olds, he thought, could be bloodthirsty little buggers. He had been fascinated by the old woodcut of the guillotine, and that old feeling stirred as he gazed up at the ungainly device. He hauled the heavy blade to the top of the frame and cleated the rope off. "Maybe we can try it out."

"Really, sir?" Yates sounded appalled.

"I've always wanted to see if they work," Sharpe said, then noticed the five guns parked at the far end of the big room. "Those must be the cannon brought for the *Garde Nationale*." He crossed to them. "Old-fashioned six-pounders. Thank God the buggers didn't wheel them out."

"What do we do with them?"

"We'll blow the things up. See if your lads can make wedges. There must be a carpentry shop somewhere."

The other long building was a barracks, and some of the defeated French had been married. Their wives now came from the barracks and stood watching nervously. "Keep those women safe," Sharpe told Yates. "When their men leave, they leave too."

Harper had come down from the gatehouse and joined Sharpe as he went back into the building that formed the end of the courtyard, where the prison cells were built. Another door led out into a second, much smaller courtyard, and Sharpe heard voices there. He went through.

"They're starving," Vincent greeted him, pointing to the freed prisoners.

"There must be kitchens here."

There were a score of prisoners, all dressed in white fatigue uniforms. Vincent gestured at a small group, half a dozen men, standing together. "Those are our lads," he said. "I'm not sure they're strong enough to walk back to the army."

"Then we find the stables," Sharpe said, "and if there aren't enough horses, we buy some in the town." He looked at the six prisoners. "Is our fellow among them?" he asked.

"He is, thank God," Vincent said with evident relief. "Gourgand gave orders to execute them all, but they were too slow."

"What do you want done with Gourgand?"

"He's a beast," Vincent said, "he killed one of the prisoners before we stopped him. If it was my decision I'd stand him against a wall and shoot him."

"So you don't want him alive?"

"I don't care what happens to him."

Meaning, Sharpe thought, that it was his decision. "Pat?"

"Mister Sharpe?"

"Take Colonel Gourgand to Captain Yates, he'll know what to do with him."

"Gladly, sir."

"But tell him I'll loosen the rope," Sharpe called after Harper.

"Loosen the rope?" Vincent asked.

"He'll know what I mean," Sharpe brushed the question aside. "Do we take all the prisoners?"

"Just the one," Vincent said, "the other five Britons can come if they want or fend for themselves. But our task now is to rejoin the army quickly. One of those gentlemen," Vincent nodded at the six men standing apart, "has information the Duke needs to hear. Urgently." He stressed the last word.

"We leave in the morning," Sharpe said.

* * *

Next morning they tipped the French six-pounders into the river. The guns were spiked first. They could have been blown apart, but it would have taken time to fashion the wedges that would have jammed the cannonballs in the barrels. There were eight horses in the citadel's stables, four of them carriage horses, and one horse was saddled and given to the man Vincent wanted returned to the army. The carriage horses pulled a wagon with the remaining five released prisoners and Sharpe's wounded. Then, under a light drizzle, they marched. The garrison of the citadel, who had spent a cold damp night outside the fortress, watched them go and doubtless would reoccupy the fort as soon as the British were gone, and Sharpe left them to discover Gourgand's decapitated body still strapped on the guillotine's base. His men had cheered when the blade fell, though some could not bring themselves to watch, and young Pat Bee had thrown up a meal of mutton stew.

"You did well, Sharpe," Vincent said as he rode alongside the rifleman.

"Still buried two men there, Major. They probably thought they'd go home soon."

"I pray we all go home soon, Sharpe, but this war isn't over."

"Damn nearly, Major."

"Let's get to Paris first," Vincent said, then looked at Sharpe. "I'll have work for you there if the Duke allows me to use you."

"Work, Major?"

"To stop the war, Sharpe!"

"I thought we did that last Sunday?"

"Not this war, Sharpe. The next."

They rode on.

CHAPTER 4

The battalion sang as it marched and Sharpe thought ruefully of Dan Hagman, dead and buried on the ridge at Waterloo, poor Dan, he had liked to sing and had sung well.

"I owe you thanks, Colonel Sharpe," a voice said, and Sharpe turned to see that one of the released prisoners was riding toward him. It was the man he had been sent to rescue; an extraordinarily tall man, well over Sharpe's height, who was mounted on a small mare that had belonged to Colonel Gourgand's wife.

"My pleasure, sir," Sharpe said. Major Vincent had made it plain that Sharpe was not to interrogate the freed prisoner, and he kept his voice guarded.

"Alan Fox," the tall man said, holding out a hand. He still wore the grubby white overalls.

Sharpe shook the hand, but said nothing.

"That bastard Gourgand was about to shoot us," Fox said.

"So we thought, sir," Sharpe said, thinking it safest to use the honorific. Fox had a refined accent, sharp as glass.

"The Emperor sent orders that we were to die. Know what saved us, Sharpe?"

"My battalion, sir."

"Before that," Fox said. "The poor bugger couldn't get his guillotine to work! He had it made in the town and the blade got stuck. Poor Gourgand, he was so looking forward to seeing it back at work, but after the first dozen executions the wretched thing went wrong! Every time they released the blade the damn thing stuck halfway down."

"It worked well enough for me, sir," Sharpe said, remembering the harsh noise as the weighted blade slid down the grooves of the pillars. The blade had struck with a sudden crunching sound and Gourgand's head had toppled onto the floor, rolled, and then stared up at Sharpe with a reproachful look that had lasted for a few seconds before the eyes closed.

"That was the repaired machine," Fox said cheerfully, "it was only finished yesterday. And thank you for razoring the bastard's head off. He was a vile man."

"It was a vile death," Sharpe said.

"No more than he deserved! I wish I could have seen it! So off to Paris now?"

"So I'm told, sir."

"It will be good to be back there."

"You live there, sir?"

"On and off, Sharpe, on and off. Usually in London, but once the Emperor was shoveled off to Elba I bought a place in Paris."

"And didn't escape in time?"

"I rather thought they'd leave me alone. Damn silly of me, of course. Next thing I knew there were a dozen of Boney's skull-splitters arresting me! After that it was a month in the Conciergerie before they moved us all to Ham."

"What took you to Paris, sir?" Sharpe asked, suspecting that it was a question he should not have asked and prepared to disbelieve whatever Fox answered.

"Artworks, Sharpe!" Fox answered enthusiastically.

"Artworks?" Sharpe sounded dubious.

"Paintings, sculptures, the treasures of civilization! Are you an art lover, Sharpe?"

"The Baker rifle's a work of art, sir, and I love that."

Fox ignored Sharpe's comment. "I trade in artworks, Sharpe. There's money in England these days despite the damn war, and walls need decoration! I mostly bought landscapes and portraits and sold them to the nouveau riche in Britain. If you ever need a fake ancestor, then ask me, I've got hundreds of them stored in a warehouse."

"If they're still there," Sharpe commented sourly.

"There is that. Buggers have probably stolen the lot."

"So you're in Paris to buy art?"

"Why ever not? But that wasn't why I was sent there."

"Sent?" Sharpe probed.

"I was sent to do a job, Sharpe, and was damned silly to stay on when the Emperor came back from Elba. Pure arrogance on my part, but the job was only half done."

"And the job, sir?" Sharpe asked, suspecting he would get no answer.

"Over the last few years, Sharpe," Fox went on happily, "the bloody French have stolen almost all Europe's most valuable works of art. Sculptures, paintings, you name it, they stole it and crammed it into the *Musée Napoléon*. It's a treasure trove of stolen art! But a year ago, while bloody Bonaparte was cooling his heels in Elba, the allies agreed that all the stolen works must be returned to their rightful owners, and my job was to identify those works. Make a list! Works by Michelangelo, Correggio, Veronese, Titian! All the great names! And, as you can imagine, the bloody Frogs don't like what I'm doing! They believe the works should be in Paris, which they arrogantly consider to be the cradle of civilization. So the buggers arrested me!"

"For making a list?"

"For exposing their foul crime, Sharpe. Have you ever been to Paris?"

"No, sir."

"It's a splendid city! Stinks like a bad drain, of course, but what city doesn't? But when you get there make a point of going to the *Musée Napoléon* to admire the art."

"Of course, sir," Sharpe said, thinking that the last thing he would do in Paris was look at old paintings, but he was also thinking that Fox's explanation made no sense. Why send a battalion to Ham to rescue a man who had merely been making a list of stolen paintings?

"You like food, Sharpe?" Fox asked abruptly.

"I do, sir."

"Then you'll let me thank you for the rescue by buying you a meal at *Le Procope*. Boney likes to eat there, though all he ever orders is the roast chicken."

"I look forward to it, sir."

"We'll eat at the Emperor's own table," Fox said, "and damn him to eternity."

"All well, Fox?" Major Vincent, seeing the tall man deep in conversation with Sharpe, had hurried his horse to join them.

"Just inviting Colonel Sharpe to *Le Procope*, Vincent. You must join us too."

"With pleasure!"

Alan Fox spurred ahead, leaving a suspicious Vincent riding with Sharpe. "You questioned him, Sharpe?"

"I did," Sharpe confessed.

"And what did he say?"

"That he was in Paris making a list of stolen art, Major."

"That's all?" Vincent inquired sharply.

"That's all."

"And it's an important job," Vincent went on, sounding relieved. "We have an agreement with the allies to restore their stolen art."

"And that's why two of my men died at Ham?"

"There is a war on, Sharpe," Vincent answered testily.

Sharpe nodded toward Fox, who was trotting ahead of the battalion. "So why didn't the silly bugger leave Paris when the Emperor returned?" he asked. "He doesn't strike me as a fool."

"He's no fool," Vincent said quietly.

"So he was ordered to stay," Sharpe said.

Vincent rode in silence for a few paces. "Curiosity kills cats, Sharpe."

"Two of my men died, Major, and one of them was a good sergeant. I'd like to know why."

"Because their country demanded it, of course," Vincent said, then spurred to catch up with Fox.

They had retraced their steps to Péronne, reaching the town just after midday to discover that the garrison had surrendered and Wellington's army was now manning the ramparts while the Duke himself was quartered in the town's citadel. A major on the Duke's staff directed Sharpe and his battalion to a barracks in the south of the town. "I'll tell His Grace you're here, Colonel, but don't make yourselves too comfortable," he warned Sharpe, "we'll be marching tomorrow. Parade at five a.m. in the great square."

Sharpe left the battalion to settle in the barracks and walked with Harper to the square in Péronne's center. "Lucille will be here," Sharpe guessed. He had asked which was the town's most luxurious tavern, reckoning that the Countess Mauberges would take rooms there, and sure enough he found Lucille in the inn that was hard by the town's biggest church. She was finishing a late lunch, sitting in the inn's dining room that was a gloomy chamber crossed by vast oak beams onto which men had nailed the shako plates of the various French regiments that had passed through the town. Lucille stood when she saw Sharpe and held out her arms in welcome, provoking jealous glances from the many British officers who filled the tables.

"Thank God," Sharpe said.

"You suddenly believe in Him?" Lucille asked, amused.

"If He gave me you, yes." He embraced her, held onto her for a few seconds. "How's Patrick?"

"Sleeping, I hope. Jeanette looks after him, poor Jeanette, I work her too hard. And you, Richard? You look tired too."

"Been a busy few days, love." He kissed her and, despite the many men who watched, held the kiss a long time. "Won't be any easier when we reach Paris."

Lucille gently pulled away and sat. "What happens in Paris?"

"Nothing good, I suspect."

"Why?" Lucille asked delicately.

"We went to Ham to rescue half a dozen prisoners. Which we did, though it cost me two good men. Now they're going to Paris, and Major Vincent tells me he wants me there. He won't say why, but the men we freed aren't soldiers, so it's spying. Political work." He almost spat the last two words.

"But you will reach Paris before the rest of the army?"

"Well ahead," Sharpe answered.

Lucille took a scrap of paper from her small bag. "Then I must ask a favor of you."

"Anything!"

She handed him the paper. "Go there, Richard, please."

He unfolded the paper to find an address; Hôtel Mauberges, Champs-Élysées.

"Hotel?" he asked. "You want us to stay there?"

Lucille smiled. "*Hôtel* is just the word for a mansion. A very grand house! And I will stay there."

"With the Countess," Sharpe said, understanding.

"She has invited us to her house, yes, but it is occupied by brigands! Deserters from the Emperor's army. Her steward wrote and said they are beasts, and the authorities do nothing!"

"And you want me to clear the buggers out?"

"Can you?"

"With pleasure," he said.

Lucille offered him a sealed letter. "That is for the steward, if you can help."

"I'll scour the buggers out," Sharpe said, putting the letter into a pouch, "but all I really want right now is to go home."

"Home?"

"Normandy."

Lucille smiled, reached across the table, and laid a hand on Sharpe's hand. Her Englishman. She still found that strange because, like most of her compatriots, she had hated the English through the long wars that had killed both her husband and her brother, yet Sharpe had come to her and he had stayed, and now her Englishman thought of Normandy as home. "We will go home to Normandy," she told him.

"And marry?" Sharpe asked.

"Father Defoy would approve of that," Lucille said, smiling, "he believes unmarried mothers are a stain on France's honor. But you're already married."

"Father Defoy doesn't need to know that," Sharpe said. "And I imagine she's gone back to England." His wife, Jane, had stolen his money and found a protector in John, Lord Rossendale. But Rossendale was dead, hacked to pieces at Waterloo. Jane had followed Rossendale to Brussels, and the last time Sharpe had seen her she was weeping in her carriage at the battlefield. He had ignored her. "We'll marry," he told Lucille.

She squeezed his hand. "We will marry," she said.

There was a sudden scraping of chairs as men stood, and Sharpe turned to see that the Duke of Wellington had entered the dining room. Sharpe stood too, then saw that the Duke was accompanied by Major Vincent and by Alan Fox, the enormously tall Englishman, who had to stoop beneath the ceiling's thick beams. The Duke waved the diners back to their chairs, then glanced about the room. He said something to Vincent, then turned and climbed the few steps back to the inn's entrance hall. Fox followed the Duke, but Vincent walked toward Sharpe, then bowed to Lucille. "Major Vincent," Sharpe introduced him, "this is Lucille, Vicomtesse de Seleglise."

"Madame," Vincent said, "I am honored." He bowed over her hand.

"Honored?" Lucille asked.

"Your husband was a great soldier, madame."

"My next husband is too, Major."

Vincent grinned at Sharpe. "He is, madame, he is, and the Peer wants to see you, Colonel."

"Trouble," Sharpe said curtly.

"Man is born to trouble as the sparks fly upward," Vincent said airily, "and you, Colonel Sharpe, fly higher than most sparks. Madame, you will forgive me if I take the colonel from you?"

"Bring him back, Major."

"I suspect nothing could prevent his return, madame."

Sharpe followed Vincent across the room and up the few steps.

"You are indeed a lucky man, Colonel," Vincent said.

"And I want to live," Sharpe said, "to enjoy that luck."

"You shall, Sharpe, you shall!" Vincent led Sharpe across the hall to a small private parlor that looked out onto the main square. Vincent did not go in, but just opened the door for Sharpe, who discovered the Duke standing beside an empty hearth, while Alan Fox, now dressed in a dark coat and white breeches, was sprawled in a great armchair, his long legs splayed across a rug. He grinned at Sharpe, who bowed his head to the Duke. "Your Grace," he remembered to say.

"Vincent says you did well at Ham," Wellington said abruptly.

"He did!" Fox put in.

"You've met Mister Fox." The Duke sounded disapproving.

"Yes, my lord."

"Mister Fox speaks with my authority," the Duke said, "do you understand what that means, Sharpe?"

"No, my lord."

The Duke snorted. "Mister Fox is a civilian, Sharpe, but he wields my authority, which means you obey him."

"I understand, sir."

"And you, Mister Fox," the Duke stared down at the sprawling man, "will listen to Colonel Sharpe if there's any trouble. He might look like something the dog dragged in, but he understands fighting."

"Of course, Your Grace."

The Duke's eyes came back to Sharpe. "Who'll command the South Essex if I remove you?"

Sharpe flinched. He had suspected his command of the battalion would not last long, but the news still hurt. "We lost both majors, my lord."

"So you told me," the Duke scowled. "What about your company officers?"

"None I'd want in command yet, my lord. Too inexperienced."

"Then I'll find you a major." The Duke turned to a staff officer. "A draft arrived from England last week, isn't that so?"

"Yes, Your Grace."

"Tell Halkett to select a major from those men. I want the name by dinnertime."

"Of course, Your Grace."

The Duke turned back to Sharpe. "Stop looking like a dog that's lost his bone, Sharpe. You'll get your battalion back. I've written to the Horse Guards and insisted on that. They won't like it, but they can damn well swallow it. And if anyone asks where you've gone, you'll say you've joined my staff."

"I'm honored, my lord."

"Honored be damned. There's some dirty business that needs doing in Paris, Sharpe, and you excel at dirty business. Mister Fox has faith in you, so help him!"

"Of course, Your Grace."

"Then I'll leave you. Don't let me down, Sharpe! Your man, Fox." And with that the Duke left the parlor.

"He's not a happy duke," Fox said, amused, "and do sit down, Colonel."

Sharpe sat in a second fat armchair. "He's not happy?"

"Dirty business indeed. He knows it's necessary, but he don't like it." Fox spoke in a casual, almost drawling tone. "He don't like it and nor do I. But the Duke is sure you're the man for the job."

"For making a list of paintings?"

Fox smiled. "That still has to be done, Sharpe, but that wasn't all I was doing in Paris, and the rest is a deal dirtier than art. And the Duke assures me you're just the man for dirty filthy tasks. So tell me about yourself, Colonel."

"Not much to tell, sir. Born in London, raised in a foundling home, ran to Yorkshire, where I killed a man, joined the army to escape the rope, and here I am."

Fox smiled. "Born in the gutter, the Duke says?"

"I was, sir."

"And now you're Colonel Sharpe."

"Lieutenant-Colonel, sir."

"But Lieutenant-Colonel Sharpe is still at home in the gutter?"

Sharpe nodded, but said nothing. He was thinking that Normandy was home, and Normandy was very far from the filth of London or, indeed, Paris.

"Your new job, Colonel Sharpe, is to keep me alive," Fox said.

"The best way to stay alive, sir, is to stay out of range."

Fox ignored that. "I was in Paris, Sharpe, to discover stolen paintings, but by chance I discovered something more." Fox had lowered his voice, speaking now more intensely. "I found a group of men who call themselves *la Fraternité*."

"*La Fraternité*, sir?"

"A stupid name, I assume from *Liberté*, *Egalité*, and *Fraternité*. But the Frogs don't have liberty, they certainly aren't equal, so *fraternité* is all that's left to the poor darlings. *La Fraternité*, Sharpe, is a group sworn to a purpose. Think of them as the Emperor's hunting dogs."

"And do I assume, sir, that the Emperor's hunting dogs are chasing a fox?"

"They would love to catch this fox again, and they'll doubtless try, but the Emperor's hounds have much bigger game in mind, which is why we must hunt them down before they kill."

"Bigger game, sir?"

Fox sat up straighter. "So far as we know, Sharpe, the Emperor can still assemble over a hundred thousand men, but I think he's doomed.

There's a provisional government in Paris, and they've had enough of war."

"Good," Sharpe said.

Fox ignored the word. "There might be a battle. But my suspicion is that the French are tired of war and want no more of Bonaparte's adventures. If I'm right they will force him to abdicate and surrender Paris. The allies will then occupy the city. And even if there is a battle I am confident the Prussians and our troops will win, so we shall still occupy Paris."

"Yes, sir," Sharpe said, for lack of anything else to say.

"Before I left Paris, Sharpe, I became aware of *la Fraternité*. I'm told they were formed in April, just after Bonaparte arrived in Paris from Elba, and I have no doubt they received his blessing. They are men fiercely loyal to their Emperor and have sworn to protect him."

"Isn't that why there's an Imperial Guard?" Sharpe asked scornfully.

"And the Guard failed," Fox retorted sharply. "The Empire is collapsing, Sharpe. Within a few weeks France will be a monarchy again, and Bonaparte will either be dead or in prison."

"So *la Fraternité* will have failed too."

"It's a matter of pride, Sharpe. The French are being humiliated. They're defeated! So how do they recover a scrap of pride? By revenging themselves on their enemies, and *la Fraternité* is the instrument of that revenge."

"Revenge," Sharpe said, only because Fox had paused and seemed to want some response.

"The princes of Europe will be in Paris," Fox said, "they won't be able to resist a chance to gloat over their conquest. The Czar of Russia, rulers from Austria and Prussia, maybe even that fool the Prince of Wales. The Duke too, and General Blücher. *La Fraternité* want to kill them all, and your task, Sharpe, is to keep them alive."

Sharpe stared at the languid Fox. "They have armies to do that," he said.

"And you are in the Duke's army," Fox said, "and your job is to find *la Fraternité* and stop them. It won't be easy. The members of *la Fraternité* are assassins, motivated by a fierce loyalty to Bonaparte. Our job is to find them and kill them before they can inflict a single death."

"Just you and me, sir?" Sharpe asked mockingly.

"The Duke assures me you can raise a dozen men from your battalion. That should be sufficient. But they must be ready to leave tomorrow."

"The whole army marches tomorrow," Sharpe commented.

"We shall go ahead of them, Sharpe. The matter is too urgent. The Duke is at risk from the moment he enters Paris. I suspect he will be their first target. Either the Duke, or Fat Louis."

"The King?" Sharpe asked.

"Louis XVIII, by God's grace, King of France and Navarre, and he's a disgusting, gross lump of fat." Fox, who was razor thin, spat the words.

"So how do we find these killers?" Sharpe asked.

"I know one man who can tell us," Fox replied. "It won't be easy, but find them we must. You're staying in this inn?"

Sharpe had assumed he would stay with his battalion, then remembered he had been transferred to the Duke's staff. "For tonight, sir, yes."

"Then be ready with your men at dawn tomorrow. You'll need horses, I shall arrange a dozen. We meet in the stableyard of this inn." Fox rapped out those orders swiftly, then stood, towering over Sharpe. "One last thing, Colonel. It might be best if you said nothing to the Vicomtesse."

It took Sharpe a second to realize Fox meant Lucille. He still found it strange that she was an aristocrat. "She can be trusted, sir," he said defiantly.

"Her husband was a Bonapartiste. I assume she's traveling to Paris?"

"She is."

"Then she could well speak to old friends and unwittingly betray us. Women can't keep secrets! It's not in their nature, so say nothing! Dawn tomorrow, Sharpe!" Fox scooped up his coat and hat and strode from the room.

Sharpe found Lucille in the room she had taken. "You wouldn't betray me, would you?" he asked.

"Richard! How could you ask such a thing?"

So he told her everything. Then went to find the men who would go with him to Paris. To kill the Emperor's hounds.

Harper, of course. Because Pat Harper would not let Sharpe out of his sight if he could help it, and Harper picked three men who he assured Sharpe were as cunning as rats and fierce as wolves. "You'll want Rifleman Finn, sir, he's a vicious bastard in a fight. Then John Fitzpatrick from Three Company, he's a good man to have at your side. And Mickey O'Farrell from the Seven Company."

"O'Farrell? He's the small man?"

"He's a devil, sir."

"I'll take Butler," Sharpe said, "and Sergeant Weller."

"Charlie's a good man," Harper said, "but not a natural killer."

"He's steady," Sharpe said, "and I like him."

"So Weller then, and Micky Geoghegan, he's a nasty fighter is Micky." And another Irishman, Sharpe noted, but that did not surprise him. Harper was convinced that the Irish were the best fighters in the world, and Sharpe was not inclined to disagree. "But you've only one rifleman so far, sir," Harper warned.

"Three," Sharpe said, "you forget you and me. But pick me five more, all rifles."

They walked to the barracks, where Sharpe pulled the chosen dozen aside. "You're attached to me," he told them, "and you won't march with the rest of the battalion. You parade ready to march at dawn tomorrow. Sergeant Weller?"

"Mister Sharpe?"

"Come with me now and I'll show you where to meet tomorrow."

Charlie Weller was young, scarcely twenty, a farmer's son from northern Essex who had volunteered to the army out of a sincere patriotism, which made him unusual in an army that mostly depended on men who had joined to escape prison. Weller's normally cheerful face looked distraught as he walked beside Sharpe. "What is it, Charlie?" Sharpe asked him.

"We're leaving the battalion, Mister Sharpe."

"You'll be back, Charlie."

"And leaving Sally," Weller added.

Sharpe paused, understanding. Sally Clayton was one of the battalion's official wives, a married woman permitted to accompany her husband on campaign, only her husband had been killed at Waterloo and she had immediately sought out Charlie Weller's company. That made Weller fortunate because Sally was by far the prettiest of the battalion's wives. She was also cheerful, hardworking, and shrewd. "Sally will be fine," Sharpe said.

"You think so, sir?" Weller responded miserably.

Sally, Sharpe thought, would be anything but fine. She was too pretty, and Sharpe did not want Weller distracted during whatever it was he must do in Paris. "Go back and fetch her now, Charlie," he said on an impulse, "and bring her here." He pointed to the big inn next to the church across the square. "Meet me in the yard of that inn."

"Yes, sir!" Weller said enthusiastically and ran back the way they had come.

Harper had been close enough to hear what Sharpe had said. "Taking Sally with us, are we?" he asked.

"No. She can work for Lucille. Another maid."

"And Lucille stays with the army?"

"She has to, but she'll find us in Paris."

"And who looks after the ladies?"

"They'll stay with the baggage guard. They'll be safe enough." Lucille had two pistols if she needed them, and the Dowager Countess was a formidable woman. "And I'll ask Harry Price to detail half a dozen men to keep an eye on them."

The dozen men would bed down in the inn's stables, while Sharpe joined Lucille upstairs. He took Sally Clayton with him and introduced her to Lucille, who was happy to have another young woman to help with the luggage and the baby. "We'll pay you, Sally," Sharpe said, "and you get to ride in a carriage all the way to Paris."

"And you'll look after Charlie, Mister Sharpe?"

"I'll take good care of him," Sharpe promised.

Next morning the dozen men paraded in the inn's yard, where Alan Fox brought saddled horses. "We're bleeding cavalry now," Butler complained as he clambered into the saddle. "How do you make it go?"

"Kick it gently," Weller advised.

Alan Fox rode a tall black stallion that Sharpe suspected came from the Duke's own stable, while Sharpe stayed with his captured French mount, which was a docile beast. Once everyone was mounted Fox led them under the inn's archway into the square, where the first British battalions were forming. The Prince of Wales's Own Volunteers was among them, parading in front of an officer who faced them on horseback. "Who's that?" Sharpe asked.

"New major, sir," Charlie Weller answered. "He arrived last night with twenty new men."

Sharpe decided he should give the new man a wide berth and steered his horse toward the houses at the edge of the square. Then the new major turned and caught sight of him.

Sharpe checked his horse and just stared back in disbelief. Then he kicked the horse toward the major. "You," he said.

"Sharpe," the major answered, in the same tone of disbelief that Sharpe had used.

"The word you're looking for," Sharpe said, "is sir."

He waited. The major bridled, looked at the battalion, then back to Sharpe. "Sir," he said unhappily.

"Off your horse, Major," Sharpe growled, "and come with me."

He did not wait to see if the major obeyed, but swung off his horse and paced toward an alley that led between two shops. At the alley's end he discovered a small courtyard piled with broken crates. Sharpe turned there, hidden from the battalion, and watched the major approach.

He was a tall man, his uniform jacket a bright red, unfaded by campaigning. Sharpe remembered him as a handsome man, but the good looks had been dissipated by appetite and alcohol, and the major stumbled as he came into the small yard. "Charles Morris," Sharpe said the name as though it left a bad taste in his mouth.

"It's been a long time," Morris said, "Colonel."

"And the Duke appointed you a major in my battalion."

"He did."

"I'm on his staff now," Sharpe said, "and I've a mind to tell him to take you away."

"Now, Sharpe . . ."

"Sir!" Sharpe roared. "You call me 'sir.'" He paused, but Morris said nothing. "I'd been hoping to meet you, Charlie, you poxed bastard. I've been dreaming of it for nigh on fifteen years."

"There's no need . . ." Morris began, then saw Sharpe's face and went silent.

"You had me flogged, Charlie, and you knew it was for nothing. You and that bastard Hakeswill."

"Sergeant Hakeswill was a good soldier . . ."

"Hakeswill was a piece of shit, like you, and I had the pleasure of watching him die." Morris backed against the brick wall. A door opened and a gray-haired man peered out to discover the cause of the noise. He took one look at Sharpe's face and retreated swiftly, shutting and bolting the door. "Hakeswill was a lying piece of shit, and you knew it." Sharpe took a step nearer Morris.

"I didn't . . ." Morris began, then his voice faltered.

"Let me tell you, Charlie," Sharpe said, "I've been wounded more times than I can remember. Musket balls, shell fragments, swords and bayonets, but none of those wounds was as painful as that flogging. And you knew I didn't deserve it."

"I didn't . . ." Morris began again, and again faltered.

"And ever since, Charlie, I've dreamed of finding you again. Dreamed of retaliation."

Morris took a deep breath, calming himself. "Retaliation? I see that promotion has increased your vocabulary, Sharpe."

Sharpe hit him. He buried his fist into Morris's plump belly, folding the major over. "Don't patronize me, Charlie. I'm a colonel now, and you call me sir. And for the moment you command my battalion, and it's a good one." He waited for Morris to straighten. "So let me tell you the rules, Charlie. Are you listening?"

Morris managed to nod. There were tears in his eyes and his face wore a grimace of pain.

"Then listen well, Charlie. You always were a flogger because you're weak. But I won't flog men, you understand? So if I hear that one man in my battalion has been flogged on your orders I'll find you, I'll strip you to the waist, and I'll flog the skin off your back. Do you understand me?"

Morris nodded again.

"Do you understand me?" Sharpe almost shouted the question.

"I do," Morris managed to say and, after a pause, "sir."

"They're good men," Sharpe said, "and they fight well. Something you never knew how to do. One flogging, Charlie, and I'll lay your ribs bare." He took a pace back just as Patrick Harper appeared from the alley.

"Mister Sharpe," Harper said, taking in the cowed figure of Morris, "Mister Fox is wondering where you are, sir."

"He can wonder, Pat. Remember me telling you about Major Charles Morris?"

"Oh I do, sir."

"Last I heard he was in Dublin. Now he's here."

"So that's him, sir?"

"Miserable piece of shit that he is, yes."

"He had you flogged, sir? Is he the one?"

"He did, Pat." Sharpe reached out and patted Morris's cheek. "I want you to meet Regimental Sergeant Major Patrick Harper, Charlie. He and I captured an Eagle together, and if you flog one man in my battalion then Patrick Harper will wield the whip that flogs you."

"It'll be a real pleasure, Mister Sharpe," Harper said, grinning.

"Now back to my battalion, Charlie," Sharpe said, "and don't forget my promise."

Morris hesitated, as if unwilling to reappear in the town square before he had composed himself, but a threatening fist from Sharpe

96

persuaded him to move. Sharpe followed him. "What did you do to the fellow?" Harper asked.

"Thumped him once, that's all."

"He's not a happy man." Harper grinned. The blow to the belly had winded Morris and he staggered slightly as he left the alley, and then had trouble mounting his horse. The Prince of Wales's Own Volunteers watched, then recognized some of their own men among the horsemen who followed Sharpe, and jeered good-naturedly. Sharpe, mounted again, waved to them and the jeers turned to cheers, which followed Sharpe as he rode west.

Alan Fox spurred to ride beside Sharpe. "What was that about?" he asked.

"Years ago," Sharpe said, "I was a private in the 33rd and that piece of crap was my company officer. He had me flogged for something I didn't do. That was in India, Mister Fox."

"And now he commands your battalion?"

"So I just put the fear of God into him."

Fox laughed. "He looked as if he'd seen the devil!"

"Maybe he did."

They left the city through an ancient gate, now guarded by redcoats, then passed the hornwork that the light companies of the British Guards had captured, a victory that had persuaded the city's garrison to surrender. Once turned southward, Sharpe turned again to Alan Fox. "How many miles to Paris?" he asked.

"I reckon about ninety," Fox said. "Three or four days?"

"And how many troops in Paris?" Sharpe went on.

"The Duke told me there are about a hundred and twenty thousand men."

Sharpe turned and gestured at his dozen troops. "We're a small force, sir."

Fox smiled. "We will be an invisible force, Sharpe."

"Red coats and green jackets?"

"You know Colquhoun Grant, Colonel?"

"I met him once, sir." Colquhoun Grant was the most famous of Wellington's exploring officers, the men who rode in full uniform behind the French lines to estimate the enemy's strength.

"Poor Grant was captured by the French."

"I remember, sir."

"But what you may not know is that he escaped. He went to Paris and lived there for some weeks and never once took off his red coat. When challenged he claimed it was the uniform of the United States, and he was believed."

"So we're Americans now, sir?" Sharpe asked sourly.

"No, Colonel. This afternoon we should reach Roye, and there's bound to be a clothing store there. Probably not the height of fashion if that worries you?"

Sharpe plucked at his faded and stained green jacket. "Terrifies me." He paused. "Because if they capture us they'll claim we're spies and then shoot us."

"Indeed they will," Fox said, "but your job, Sharpe, is to make sure I'm not captured."

They stopped just north of Roye and Fox declared he would shop for civilian clothing. Harper was already in civilian clothing, though his green rifleman's jacket was in the pack he wore, and he accompanied Fox into the small town, leaving Sharpe with his men in a grove of trees beside the road.

"Sergeant Harps doesn't speak Crapaud, does he, sir?" Butler asked.

"Not a word," Sharpe said, "but he's Irish. He could talk himself out of the devil's lockbox."

Which turned out to be true when Fox and Harper returned with a pile of nondescript clothing. "They believed we're deserters from the Emperor's army," Fox explained, "and we're evidently not the first such men to buy clothes."

There was the inevitable hilarity as red or green jackets were discarded and replaced by homespun coats. Fox handed Sharpe a long black coat. "I'm told it belonged to a doctor. It fits too!"

"So we're deserters now?"

"I think everyone who sees us will assume that."

"And try to arrest us?"

"Once we reach Paris? Possibly. But I suspect the city will be full of deserters. The defeat at Waterloo has thrown the whole country into chaos." Fox had an insouciance that irritated Sharpe. The man dismissed all difficulties as though they did not exist, which left Sharpe to worry about them.

"And in that chaos," Sharpe said, "we have to find these assassins?"

"We do."

"How?"

"I already told you, I have a man's name, Colonel, and we start with him."

They mounted and rode on.

Toward a city of chaos.

PART TWO

The City

CHAPTER 5

Lucille had lived in Paris once and often spoke of the city in wistful tones. It was, she told Sharpe, beautiful, even magnificent. "We had a house there," she had told him, and she had been happy in the city until her father lost all his money in a foolish investment. "And all we had left was the land in Normandy." She had met her husband in Paris and had married him there. "Then he gambled his fortune away," Lucille had said, laughing. "My mother always said I had bad taste in men."

"Do you?"

"I like men to be interesting," she had said.

And now Sharpe was seeing Paris, the city he had imagined for so long, the imagination fed by Lucille's memories and love of the place. He had thought it would be a city of palaces and mansions, but as they approached he could smell the familiar stench of coal smoke and sewage. "Smells like London," he had remarked sourly to Fox.

But Fox was like Lucille, a lover of Paris, and seemed delighted to be back. He had told Sharpe that the whole city was surrounded by forts. "But they'll not expect enemies from the south, so we'll go all the way round." And that had proved true. They had passed a fort unmolested and, four days after leaving Roye, they came to a city gate. They had been riding through a suburb of small neat houses when they came to the city wall and the gate guarded by men in blue uniforms. "It's not a proper city wall," Fox explained when Sharpe expressed surprise at the sight. "It's not a defense, just a barrier, and those fellows in blue aren't soldiers, they're tax collectors."

"Tax collectors?"

"The wall is to stop smuggling. The duty on wine and other goods is much steeper inside Paris, so every road into the city has a gate and a bunch of tax collectors. They won't worry us."

Nor did they. The guards took no notice of the horsemen, even though all had either a musket or rifle slung on their shoulder. Fox called out a cheerful good morning to the sergeant of the guards, who just nodded sourly, then stalked toward a handcart laden with vegetables.

"Welcome to Paris," Fox said as they rode through the gate into a wide tree-lined street of prosperous houses and small shops. The folk seemed well dressed to Sharpe, though he noted how many beggars lined the avenue, many with a leg or an arm missing. Some had their old shakos in front of them as they called for alms. "It's the same in London," Fox said, "from soldiering to beggaring."

It seemed unnatural to Sharpe. This was Paris! He had been fighting the French for twenty-one years in Flanders, India, Portugal, Spain, then in France itself, and now he was in the first group of British troops to enter the enemy's capital, and it was nothing like his imagination. He had expected magnificence, but all looked normal, not that different from streets in some parts of London. "They're still flying the old flag," he noted. A few houses flew the red, white, and blue flag of the Empire, but Sharpe saw none showing the white flag of the monarchy.

"That'll change as our armies get nearer," Fox said.

"Which will be a while yet."

"At least a week, maybe two?" Their horses clattered across a small square, and Fox led them into a narrower street. "We shouldn't need the horses," Fox said. "I'll stable them."

"Where?"

"There are places, Sharpe," Fox said vaguely. "It just takes money." He patted the pouch where he kept the funds, evidently given him by the Duke. "I won't lose my horse and you won't lose that French nag of yours."

The streets were getting still narrower and the houses older, then they emerged onto a wide street running alongside the River Seine. "We cross the bridge and we're almost home," Fox said, turning left along the river's southern bank. Ahead, over a jumble of roofs and smoking chimneys, Sharpe could see what looked like a cathedral. "Notre Dame, Colonel," Fox said helpfully, then turned right onto a wide stone bridge. "It's called the Pont Neuf," he remarked, "though I think it's the oldest bridge in Paris." He nodded to the left. "That's the *Musée Napoléon*, and the Tuileries Palace beyond."

The small houses and shops had given way to grandiose buildings with pillared porticoes and wide entrance steps. Carriages rattled past, and Butler, who had not been comfortable on horseback since leaving Péronne, almost fell as his mare skittishly sidestepped, frightened by a large carriage passing noisily. "Bloody animal," he complained, earning a surprised look from a pedestrian walking alongside.

"Pity we couldn't have found a dozen French-speakers," Fox said to Sharpe.

"You're lucky to have found twelve who can speak English," Harper put in.

"You speak any French, Sergeant?" Fox asked.

"God save Ireland, no. Maybe a little Spanish, and Gaelic."

"So if you're challenged?"

"As you said, sir, we're American seamen. All the way from Baltimore!"

As they rode north Fox had stressed to the dozen men that they must pretend to be American sailors who were visiting Paris while their ship was trapped in Cherbourg by the Royal Navy's blockade. It was a scanty disguise, and made even more unlikely by the weapons they carried, but Harper had embraced the idea. "I have a cousin in Baltimore," he had told Fox, "and I've always had a mind to visit him. It would be a grand journey!"

"We're near the end of this journey now," Fox said. They left the bridge and he led them west along the northern bank of the Seine. There were huge anchored barges in the river, some with waterwheels clanking. "Mills, Sharpe, and laundries," Fox said, then turned north close to the Louvre. "Watch yourselves now!" he called in warning because the narrow street plunged into a slum as bad as any Sharpe had known in London. Behind him were great palaces and formal gardens, and suddenly they were in a stinking street of dark houses. A gutter ran down the street's center, flowing with filth. The smell was suddenly familiar to Sharpe, who had grown up in the London rookeries, as were the people. The women were thin and dressed in rags, the few men were sullen and menacing. Children watched them pass and called out for coins. Sharpe had to duck beneath a jutting house, and a young woman with dark hollow eyes looked at him from an alley. "Monsieur?" she asked softly.

"This is a quarter of unfortunates," Fox said.

"It looks like it."

"It's a word for whores, Colonel."

"A word for soldiers too," Sharpe said. He glanced at the decaying walls and smelled the shit in the street. "It reminds me of St. Giles."

"In London?"

"Hard by Covent Garden. A nasty place."

"As is this. They'll cut your throat for a penny." Fox twisted through the tiny streets, finally stopping at a great wooden door. "Rue Villedot," he said, "our new home."

The door was padlocked, but Fox had a key and dragged the heavy door wide. "Ride in," he said.

It was a warehouse. Rats scampered as the horses entered. "This will be home," Fox announced when the big doors were safely closed. He dismounted and paced around the huge room's edges where wooden racks were stacked with paintings. "I'm amazed no one stole them," Fox said. "If anyone does try to break in you have my permission to kill them. In this district corpses are not thought unusual."

"You lived here, sir?" Sharpe asked, surprised that Fox's lair was in such a district.

"No, I have a place close to the Tuileries Palace, but I imagine that's been emptied by the men who arrested me. This is my storeroom."

"And they left it alone?"

"I'm hoping they never learned of this place. And I'll stay here with you. We need to dispose of the horses and buy food."

"Some blankets would be good too," Sharpe said.

"Blankets, food, and wine," Fox said. "There's a water pump in the yard out the back, and a small room with a stove. We should be comfortable enough."

"Smouch!" Butler put in.

"Smouch?" Fox was puzzled.

"Tea," Sharpe translated.

"I'm sure we can find tea. There's no coffee, damn it, because of the Royal Navy blockade, but somehow the tea gets through. God knows how. I'll arrange all that, and perhaps you'd like to explore the district?" Fox suggested to Sharpe. "Turn left out the door and you're in civilization soon enough."

Fox left, and Sharpe ordered his men to stay in the warehouse while he and Harper explored the district. They left their rifles behind, and Sharpe put his cavalry sword on one of the racks. Instead he carried a rifle-bayonet at his waist and had a loaded pistol, that had once belonged to Lucille's husband, in a deep pocket.

"Christ, it's a shit place," Harper commented.

"Just like where I grew up," Sharpe said, "and you must have slums in Dublin?"

"We do, God save them, and the sooner I get back to them the better."

"You can go back now," Sharpe said. "You've no need to be here."

Harper grinned. "We've been together a long time, sir. You wouldn't want me to miss the end of the story, now would you?"

"This isn't the end," Sharpe said, "this is a bleeding mess. We're supposed to find these killers. How?"

"Mister Fox will know."

Sharpe growled, but said nothing. They were retracing their steps through the fetid streets and alleys where Harper's sheer size and Sharpe's scarred face were more than enough to deter the men who watched them pass.

"Has he told you anything?" Harper asked.

"He says he has a man's name," Sharpe answered unhappily, "but beyond that?"

They emerged from the slum into a wide and elegant street hard by a great palatial building. They turned eastward, just wandering, and Sharpe again noted the beggars who sat by every doorway. It would be the same in London, and he had a sudden yearning to be back in Normandy.

"God save Ireland, but will you look at that?" Harper interrupted his thoughts, and Sharpe looked up to see they had entered a great open square in the center of which was an enormous pillar crowned with a statue.

"Who the hell is that?"

"Has to be your man!" Harper said. "Napoleon!"

Sharpe grimaced. "They'll have him down from that."

"Up against a wall and a firing squad. Where are we going?"

"Nowhere."

"A drink might help that ambition?"

They found a small tavern down a side street and Sharpe ordered beer, which Harper condemned as horse piss, but happily drank. A legless man, still wearing his blue uniform jacket, swung himself to their table on two short crutches and held out a battered tin mug. "Where were you wounded?" Sharpe asked him.

"Spain, monsieur."

"Where?"

"Salamanca."

"I was there," Sharpe said.

"We should have won!"

"We did," Sharpe answered, and gave the man a coin.

"What was that about?" Harper asked as the man shuffled away on his short crutches.

"Poor bastard was at Salamanca."

"Christ, that was a miserable fight."

They left after Sharpe asked the barkeeper for directions, which took him farther east and north past the Élysée Palace. "I'm told that's where Napoleon lived," Sharpe said. They could see into a courtyard where men in the uniform of the Imperial Guard lounged, then Sharpe turned onto the Champs-Élysées, where he again asked directions. "This way," he told Harper, leading him to the gates of an imposing mansion. A brass plate on the gatepost announced it as the Hôtel Mauberges. "Lucille will be coming here," Sharpe said.

"Her friend the Dowager Countess?"

"It's her house."

"The old girl must have money," Harper said, "and maybe we can move here instead of that shit place in the Rue Villedot?"

"Mister Fox won't agree to that."

"Why would he care?"

"He doesn't want Lucille to know what we're doing. Thinks she might betray us."

"He thinks what?"

"I told her anyway," Sharpe said, "but we've got a problem here."

"That's a surprise."

"The old girl says some deserters have occupied the house. Wants me to get rid of them." Sharpe stared at the big house, but could see nothing untoward, but then he would not have expected to. "I'd like to help the old girl, she's been good to Lucille."

"We can fillet the buggers," Harper said, then grinned, "just you and me?"

"Christ, no. We don't know how many are there. We'll bring the lads and do the job properly." Sharpe turned to watch a half-dozen cavalrymen coming slowly down the road, heading into the city. All were cuirassiers, still wearing their steel breastplates, their tired horses smeared with mud.

"Poor bastards," Harper said, "they've ridden those poor horses close to death."

Sharpe saw the crusted blood at the horses' nostrils and saw the blood matted in their coats where musket balls had struck. Some people called out questions to the riders, but they were all too tired, too dispirited to offer answers. They had been defeated. "They're lucky to be alive," Sharpe said, remembering the vast cavalry charges that had surged up the slope at Mont-Saint-Jean to be slaughtered by the Duke's squares. The horses limped past.

Sharpe followed the horsemen, feeling a sudden fierce anger. "Twenty-one years," he snarled at Harper.

"Sir?"

"Twenty-one years since I first fired a shot in battle," he said, "and we've won, Pat! We shouldn't be here. We should be in some bloody tavern with the lads. We've earned it! Instead we're expected to kill some more, and I'm tired of it. Bloody tired of it. And I need a file."

"A file?"

"It's Dan's rifle," Sharpe explained. "It's got notches filed in the stock. I counted them. One hundred and twenty-three. And I killed that bastard in the field outside Valenciennes, so I'll add a notch. Dan would like that."

"Aye, he would. Why don't you just use a knife?"

"Dan must have used a file because the notches are smooth. Pity to change it. I'll file it, then I'll go home to Normandy and hang Dan's rifle over the kitchen hearth, and by God I hope I never take it down again."

"Farmer Sharpe?" Harper grinned.

"Why not? Worse things to be, Pat."

"Aye, that's God's truth. Hard to imagine it, though. What do you know about farming?"

"Bugger all, but I'll take Charlie Weller with me. He knows farming. You'd be welcome too."

"I'm not leaving Ireland again. Not ever. Maybe we'll visit you, though."

They retraced their steps, stopping only to buy bread and cheese to carry back to the warehouse, where they discovered that Alan Fox had sent men to take away the horses. Their authorization had been a note addressed to Sharpe that Charlie Weller had deciphered. "I didn't know you could read, Charlie," Sharpe said.

"I learned my letters long ago, Mister Sharpe, I still remember some of them. Did I do right?"

"You did right." The brief note said the horses were going to a livery stable, and added that Fox would return as soon as possible. "So we wait," Sharpe said.

It was nightfall before Alan Fox came back. "You," he pointed at Sharpe, "and me. We're going out." He was full of energy.

"Just the two of us?"

"Just the two of us."

"Where are we going?"

"Place called *Champ de l'Alouette*. The lark field!"

"And why?" Sharpe demanded.

"Because I say so, Colonel."

"Now would you look at that," Harper intervened. He had picked up Sharpe's rifle and opened the small cavity in the stock where riflemen stored the leather patches in which their bullets were wrapped. He showed Sharpe a small round file, evidently snapped from a much longer rat-tail file. "Dan was always careful."

"We should leave now, Colonel," Fox insisted.

"Do I need this?" Sharpe took the rifle from Harper.

"The man we're going to visit is a royalist and a friend to Britain. You need no weapons."

"I'll follow you," Harper said softly, "and bring some lads."

Sharpe strapped on his sword belt. Fox might believe no weapons were needed, but Sharpe reckoned it would be dark before they returned, and only a fool walked unarmed through cities after dark. "Bit dramatic, Colonel?" Fox commented when he saw the massive sword.

"My job is to keep you alive," Sharpe said, and covered the scabbard with the long black oilcloth coat. He pushed the pistol into the coat's deep pocket, then followed Fox into the street.

It was a long walk in the gathering dusk. They used the Pont Neuf to cross the river, then Fox led him into a tangle of streets going ever south and east. "The fellow we're going to see," Fox explained as he walked briskly, "has been helpful in the past. He's a royalist, though he worked for Bonaparte in the *Ministère de la Guerre*."

"Ministry of war," Sharpe offered the translation.

"Indeed! And this fellow controlled the records of officers. Who serves where and in what rank. Much the same as those inky fellows do in the Horse Guards."

"How did you meet him?" Sharpe asked.

"He wanted to sell me a portrait. It was a rather ugly daub of his grandfather that he insisted was by Boucher, but it plainly wasn't. But once he told me about his job I strung him along. Ended up paying him twenty guineas for a wretched painting that isn't worth tuppence."

"And he's expecting us?"

"I sent word this afternoon, so yes. And he'll be pleased to see us, I've no doubt. He likes our money, Sharpe. The horsemen of Saint George!" He meant guineas, the golden coin that showed St. George mounted on a horse.

Sharpe kept looking behind to see if Harper was following, but only glimpsed the Irishman a couple of times and worried that Harper and his men would get lost. Fox set a brisk pace, striding with his long legs and only occasionally pausing to decide which street to take.

The streets were muddy, and Sharpe reckoned there was rain coming. The western clouds were dark, rimmed with the sunset. Men were lighting occasional oil lamps that hung from posts, though their light was so dim that Sharpe knew they would be useless to illuminate the nighttime streets. "A thieves' paradise," he commented.

"Thieves and whores, Sharpe. Parisians! A wonderful place to live!"

They came to a wide grassy space not far from the city's southern wall and Fox led him across to the far side. "We're looking for number twenty," he said, "but the buggers jumble their house numbers."

"House numbers?"

"It's a new idea," Fox explained, "to give every house a number. They should be in order, one, two, three, four, but being bloody French they get it wrong. You'll probably find number twenty between number six and number forty-three. Clever idea, though, to number the houses!"

"You've not been here before?"

"Only in broad daylight. Ah, that looks like the place!" He pushed open an iron gate that creaked alarmingly on ungreased hinges and Sharpe found himself in a small garden facing a substantial stone-built house with dark shuttered windows. Fox rapped on the door with his stick. "Fellow's name is Collignon, Félix Collignon. Treat him with respect, Sharpe."

"Of course."

Fox rapped again. "Bugger must be asleep," he growled, then the door was pulled open by a maid who curtseyed. She seemed confused by Fox, who loomed over her, but then a middle-aged, gray-bearded man appeared in the candlelit hall. "Monsieur Fox!" he exclaimed. "Come in, come in! A pleasant surprise!"

"Surprise?" Fox asked as he took the man's outstretched hand. "I sent you a note this afternoon!"

"It never arrived, monsieur. Charlotte!" He turned on the maid. "Did you see a letter this afternoon?"

"Non, monsieur."

"These things get lost," Collignon said apologetically, "but come in, come in! With your friend."

Sharpe was introduced, then followed the two men into a comfortable book-lined parlor lit by oil lamps. "Some wine, Charlotte," Collignon called over his shoulder, then invited his visitors to sit. "Can I take your coat, Colonel?" Collignon asked in English.

"I'll keep it, sir," Sharpe said, and sat in a great leather armchair. A cat leaped onto his lap.

"Do not mind Josephine," Collignon said, amused. "She likes to be petted."

Sharpe dutifully stroked the cat, which purred happily. Meanwhile he looked around the room. The shuttered window to the small front garden was behind him, the two walls either side were filled with bookcases, while the far wall, beyond Collignon's chair, was made of doors, presumably opening into another room, which would create one long chamber the length of the house. Fox was in a chair next to Sharpe and was talking fast to their host, who nodded frequently but said little. Sharpe gathered that Collignon had offered a list of names that Fox now wanted, but it was evident that the Frenchman was reluctant to yield the list. "You know who these people are?" Fox demanded sharply.

"Maybe some of them. It is difficult to be certain."

"Why difficult?"

"*La Fraternité* is secret, monsieur."

"But you know some," Fox pressed, "who are they?"

"Soldiers."

"I want the names!"

115

"Monsieur." Collignon frowned. "I must be certain. I cannot betray men unless I am sure of their guilt."

"We can establish their guilt," Fox insisted.

"By using him?" Collignon nodded toward Sharpe. "He looks formidable." He seemed to assume that Sharpe spoke no French, an assumption Sharpe was happy to encourage.

"By questioning them," Fox said.

Collignon, Sharpe noticed, was getting ever more nervous as Fox pushed him. His hands kept gripping and regripping the arms of his chair, his eyes darted from Fox to Sharpe, back to Fox, then around the room. He seemed relieved to welcome the maid when she returned carrying a large dark bottle and three glasses on a silver tray. "It is not the best wine," Collignon said, "but alas, good wine is difficult to find right now." The maid gave each man a glass of the wine, then put the half emptied bottle on a small table to Sharpe's right. "Monsieur," she said to Sharpe, and he nodded thanks.

"You drink wine, Colonel?" Collignon asked in English as the girl left.

"I do, monsieur."

"Perhaps I should have offered you brandy." Collignon grimaced at the taste of the wine. "This wine is expensive, but . . ." he shrugged, leaving the rest unsaid.

"It's barely drinkable swill," Fox finished for him, then opened his pouch and laid ten golden English guineas along the arm of his chair. He placed each coin slowly, deliberately, and Sharpe saw the greed in Collignon's eyes. "We pay, Monsieur Collignon," Fox said, "but there will be no future payments unless you give me what you offered before I was arrested."

"And you are free now!" Collignon wrenched his eyes from the gold. "How did that happen?"

"The British army freed me, then sent me here to find you. To obtain what you promised, to obtain what you were paid to provide."

"It is delicate," Collignon said, "you do not understand."

"Colonel Sharpe is not delicate," Fox said menacingly.

Sharpe looked surprised at the mention of his name, but Collignon appeared terrified. "Non, non," he said, holding his hands out as if to ward off trouble. "I will supply what you want, Monsieur Fox."

"Names," Fox said, "I want names! You told me you had the names, so give them to me!"

"I made a list," Collignon said uncertainly.

"Then give it me!"

"I will fetch it for you," Collignon said, then stood and went to the wide doors that evidently divided the long room. "Just a moment," he said.

He opened the two center doors and Sharpe saw two men in the darkness beyond. He also saw the barrel of a musket reflect the small lamplight and he pushed hard with his feet to throw the armchair backward. A musket fired, the ball thumping into the chair's thick upholstery. The cat was hissing, clawing at Sharpe's right hand, and he hurled the beast over the fallen chair toward the far doors, then reached into his pocket for the pistol. He heard a shout of alarm, presumably caused by Josephine's sharp claws, then he was crouched behind the thick rampart of the chair's horsehair and leather. He held the pistol in his left hand and snatched the bottle of wine from the table. He planned to hurl it too, but before he could draw his arm back a mustached face appeared above the fallen chair and a pistol was pointed at his head. "You will stand, monsieur," the man said in French.

"Stand, Sharpe," Fox muttered. He had taken shelter beside his own armchair, crouching awkwardly, but now unfolded his huge height, his hands outspread to show he had no weapon.

Sharpe also stood and swung the bottle as he did. It crashed into the mustached man's head hard enough to shatter and the broken glass scored deep bloody cuts across his face. The man howled, dropped his pistol, and swiveled away. Another man leveled a musket at Sharpe, who dropped behind the chair again, took the pistol into his right hand, and edged fast about the fallen chair's right-hand side. He leveled the barrel and fired. The musket fired at the same moment, its smoke filling the room, but Sharpe saw the man stagger back, evidently struck by the bullet.

And at that same moment the window behind him shattered and the shutters bulged inward until their metal locking bars snapped out of their iron brackets and they burst open to reveal a massive Irishman holding a seven-barrel gun. "Through there, Pat!" Sharpe pointed at the open doors. "We want the fellow alive!" He tossed down his empty pistol and picked up the one dropped by the man whose face he had savaged with glass. He went to the doors, conscious he was in a well-lit room facing men in darkness who could see him while he could not see them. He heard a man panting deeply and suspected that was the man he had shot, but Sharpe wanted Collignon, who had fled. He threw the remaining doors back and saw only the panting man, who had collapsed into another chair. Sharpe snatched up the man's musket and slammed the butt into his skull.

"Ouch," Harper said.

"The fellow we want has gray hair and a beard," Sharpe said. A door was open and he went through into a hallway. Light came from a room to his right and he ran there to find the maid Charlotte in a kitchen. She screamed when she saw Sharpe.

"Quiet, girl," Sharpe said. "Where is Monsieur Collignon?"

Charlotte shivered in fear, but pointed to a door. "There, monsieur."

Sharpe opened the door to see steps going down into a cellar. "Monsieur Collignon!" he called.

Silence.

"I've killed or wounded your two companions. You want me to come down and do the same to you?" Sharpe called.

The answer was a pistol shot that thumped into the wooden stair beneath Sharpe's feet. "I have more guns!" Collignon called.

Sharpe looked at Charlotte, who nodded. "He keeps his guns down there, monsieur," she whispered.

"How many?"

"A lot, monsieur!"

The cat Josephine, none the worse for being used as a missile, stalked into the kitchen. "Give her some cream," Sharpe told the maid, "she deserves it."

Charlotte crossed to a cupboard. Sharpe heard the rattle of a ramrod in a barrel coming from the cellar. He was thinking to hurl himself down the stairs, then turn and shoot before Collignon could react, but if the man did have three or four loaded pistols then such an attack was foolhardy.

Charlotte had taken down a jug draped with a beaded muslin cover and Sharpe saw bottles in the cupboard. "What's that?"

"Brandy, monsieur."

"God save Ireland!" Harper said. "Enough for a battalion!"

"Put a couple aside, Pat," Sharpe said, "and bring me the rest."

Harper brought a dozen bottles, each corked and each bearing a small handwritten label that read "Félix Collignon. Courvoisier, Bercy, Paris."

Sharpe pulled the cork from one bottle and tasted it. "Good brandy," he said. He hurled the bottle down the stairs and it shattered on the cellar's stone floor. He threw another half-dozen bottles,

119

seeing a pool of brandy spread toward the rear of the cellar. "Get me a light, Pat."

Harper took a rag from beside the kitchen sink, opened the stove door, and lit the rag, which he gave to Sharpe, who launched it down onto the brandy. Flames immediately sprang up and Collignon called out in alarm. Sharpe hurled another bottle down the steps and was rewarded with a sudden rush of bright flame. "Non, monsieur!" Collignon called.

"Let's get the bugger," Sharpe said just as Alan Fox came into the kitchen.

"What are you doing, Colonel?"

"Burning his bloody house down. Come on, Pat."

"This first, sir," Harper said, and leveled his seven-barrel gun down toward the blue flames and pulled the trigger.

The report of the gun was immense, like firing a cannon in a closed space, and the smoke belched out to fill the cellar as the pistol balls ricocheted from the stone walls. "Now," Harper said, confident that the sound alone would have terrified the man below. Sharpe ran down the stairs, jumped into the flickering flames, and twisted toward the rear of the cellar, where Collignon was crouched behind a table on which were six pistols. Sharpe ran through the fire, reached over the table, and hauled the shivering wretch up and over. He dragged him through the shattered bottles and burning brandy, then up the stairs. Harper was reloading the volley gun. "Let me get the other fellows," he said.

"Who's with you?"

"Finn, McGurk, and O'Farrell." All Irish, Sharpe noted. "I sent McGurk and O'Farrell round the back," Harper said. "Finn's at the front of the house."

Smoke was drifting in the hallway now so Sharpe closed the cellar door then dragged Collignon into the elegant book-lined room. Finn, a lanky man, climbed through the shattered front window, and Sharpe sent him to look at the two men who had first threatened him. "One's dead, one's near dead," Finn reported.

"Savages," Collignon said, then held out his hands as if warding off evil when Sharpe looked at him.

"There's a maid in the kitchen," Sharpe told Finn, "make sure she's safe and get her out of the house before it burns down."

"We should leave," Fox said nervously. "The *sapeurs-pompiers* will be here soon."

"The what?" Sharpe asked.

"They put out fires," Fox explained.

"We'll leave when we're ready," Sharpe said. He faced Collignon and slowly drew his sword. "I guess Mister Collignon received your message this afternoon after all," he told Fox.

"So it seems."

"So question him, Mister Fox, and I'll make sure he tells you the truth." Sharpe pushed the point of the sword against Collignon's chest. "You're not going to lie to me, monsieur."

The smell of burning had thickened and smoke was seeping under the doors that led to the hallway. "We should leave, Colonel," Fox said. "Good God, man, the house is burning!"

"Question him!" Sharpe snapped, then slapped the flat of the blade against Collignon's cheek and went through into the dark half of the parlor. Doors led to the garden and he threw them open to see Harper and the remaining two riflemen in the darkness. "Pat! I need these two men searched," he gestured at the dead man on the floor and the dying man in the chair where Sharpe had clouted him with the musket's stock. "We need to know who they are."

"We must leave!" Fox shouted from the front of the parlor.

"McGurk, O'Farrell, search those two men. Pat? Make sure Collignon comes with us. Carry him if you have to. Is there a back way out of this garden?"

"There's a gate."

"Then we go that way." Sharpe suspected there would soon be a crowd at the front of the house and, presumably, men attempting to extinguish the flames that were now bright through the kitchen windows. Finn had the maid safe in the garden. Charlotte was clutching the cat.

"Coming, Mister Fox!" Sharpe called. "With me, Pat."

They hauled Collignon from his chair and Harper plucked him up and carried him to the back garden. Sharpe paused long enough to rescue the ten golden guineas that were still on the arm of Fox's chair, then followed. He pushed one of the coins into Charlotte's hand and the rest into his cartridge pouch. "Go," he told the girl. "Go home, or find another employer." She fled.

There was a brick building beside the back gate. Finn, curious, tugged open the door and, in the light of the flames that now sprang from the kitchen windows, Sharpe saw a small carriage inside. "That'll do," he told Fox.

"No horses?"

"We don't need horses." Sharpe assumed that Collignon hired carriage horses when they were needed, thus saving the expense of grooms, feed, and stabling. "Bring the bugger here, Pat."

The carriage was a small two-wheeled vehicle. "Good God," Fox said, "a curricle! Bit sporty for an old fellow like Collignon."

"Ideal for us," Sharpe said. A curricle was light. "In you get, Mister Fox, and give us directions."

Fox climbed onto the single bench-seat and Collignon was put beside him. Sharpe took McGurk's sword-bayonet from its scabbard and handed it to Fox. "If the bugger gives you trouble stick that through his ribs."

The two carriage-house doors were swung open and Sharpe, Harper, and their three men took hold of the shaft and pulled the curricle out into the night. Sparks drifted overhead and flakes of ash fell into the alley like snow. "Go left, then left again," Fox called. He had discovered a whip that he cracked over their heads. The carriage burst from the alley, turned left, then left again beside the *Champ de l'Alouette*. Collignon's house was now ablaze and a small crowd had gathered in the street to watch the destruction. "It's the books," Sharpe said with relish, "they make good fires, books."

Collignon moaned when he saw his house, then yelped as Fox pressed the sword-bayonet against his ribs. Sharpe could hear the two men talking, but as he was at the front of the shaft he could not make out the words, but it was evident Collignon was being voluble.

"It isn't right, Mister Sharpe," McGurk said beside him.

"What's not right?"

"An officer doing this. You should be in the carriage."

"No room," Sharpe said.

They made good speed. Curricles were dangerously light, much loved by young men with too much money and not much sense. They were usually drawn by two horses and could reach alarming speeds. Collignon's carriage looked old, and Sharpe suspected he had owned it a long time. "Straight ahead!" Fox called.

Folk watched them pass. The streets were surprisingly crowded and the windows well lit. Sharpe noted how many places sold meals, Lucille called them restaurants, and all he saw were doing brisk business. At some there were tables outside and the diners cheered the men hauling the curricle. Finn and O'Farrell were in their rifle green jackets, but no one recognized the uniforms for what they were and must have assumed they were French soldiers on a drunken spree.

"Left onto the river's quay!" Fox called, and the curricle bowled along the Seine's southern bank. "Take the first bridge!"

"We should take this bloody carriage into the warehouse," Finn growled.

"Why?" Sharpe asked.

"There's no fuel for that stove. We can break it up, get some hot food."

"Good idea," Sharpe said, "we burned the bugger's house so we might as well burn his carriage."

That would dispose of the curricle, but Collignon himself was another matter. Fox had questioned the man during their breakneck ride through the Paris night and reckoned he had gleaned everything there was to learn. "Do we keep him prisoner now?" Sharpe asked Fox once they were safe inside the small warehouse. "If we let him go he'll warn the others."

"What others?"

"*La Fraternité*, of course. He's one of them, surely?"

"He is."

"You want me to question him?" Sharpe asked.

"He's told me everything. I promised him his life and that persuaded him."

"So you want us to lock him up?"

"Can't think what else to do with him."

Sharpe dropped the French musket he had carried from Collignon's house and picked up his rifle. "And he was the man who betrayed you?"

"I fear so," Fox sounded regretful.

"And he's plotting to kill the Duke?"

"And the King."

"I'll look after him," Sharpe said. He primed the rifle that was already loaded.

"Colonel," Fox said nervously, but Sharpe had already walked away. "Pat?"

"Sir?"

"You and me."

They took Collignon out to the back of the warehouse, across the small courtyard, and through a gate that opened onto a dark stinking alley. Rats skittered along the walls. "Mister Fox," Sharpe said, "wants us to keep this bugger as a prisoner, but I'm not minded to do that. He wants to kill the Duke."

"That's bad," Harper said.

"And he tried to kill me."

"That's worse."

"And we've nowhere to keep a prisoner." Sharpe cocked the rifle. "And we can't release him."

Harper pushed Collignon. "Run, you bugger!"

"*Allez*," Sharpe said. "*Vite! Allez!*"

Collignon looked bemused for a moment, but released from Harper's grip he took two tentative steps toward the dim light at the alley's end. "I can go?"

"Just go," Sharpe said.

Collignon started to walk again and Sharpe shot him in the back of his neck. The sound of the rifle echoed off the walls and slowly died. "He really shouldn't have tried to escape," Harper said.

"See if the bugger has anything in his pockets."

Harper found some papers, a leather purse with coins, and a fob watch. They left the body in the alley, sure that the rats would start its disposal and that another murdered man in the alleys would cause little alarm in the city.

"I heard a shot!" Fox said when Sharpe returned.

"He tried to escape," Sharpe said curtly.

"Foolish man," Fox said, "but he did give me two more names, so it's been a good night's work! Three of *la Fraternité* dead!"

"Three?"

"The two at Collignon's house and poor Collignon himself. And I now have the two other names. A good night's work! And it means we have some hunting to do, Colonel." Fox turned as if he was dancing, and then, to Sharpe's surprise, began to sing. "A hunting we will go, a hunting we will go!" He did not finish the song, but Charlie Weller did.

"We'll catch a fox and put him in a box, and never let him go."

CHAPTER 6

"We do now have two names," Fox told Sharpe the next morning.

They were sitting at a table in the Rue de Richelieu with cups of tea. Fox had wanted coffee, but there was only tea, along with fresh baked bread, butter, and slices of ham.

"So Collignon must have betrayed you before," Sharpe said, grimacing at the weak taste of the tea, "which is why you were at Ham."

"As likely as not," Fox admitted, "yet he always seemed so reliable."

"And the names he gave you? Are they reliable?"

"It's all we have," Fox said.

"And you believe him?"

"As I said, it's all we have."

"Who are they?"

"Général Delaunay and a Colonel Lanier."

Sharpe shrugged, neither name meant anything to him.

"I know of both men," Fox said, "Delaunay is a cavalryman who commanded the Young Guard in Prussia ten years ago. He was wounded badly, recovered, given command of a division of cavalry, and went north with the Emperor. By reputation he's a capable man. As is Lanier."

"Another cavalryman?"

"Lord, no! Lanier is something of a legend. He's an infantryman, fiercely loyal to Bonaparte, and utterly formidable! He's known as the hero of Marengo and leads a battalion that the Emperor calls his devils. Collignon was plainly terrified of the man."

"And Collignon," Sharpe said sourly, "could have invented the whole story."

Fox nodded unwillingly. "It's possible. I would have liked to question him further, but you made that impossible. That was not subtle, Sharpe."

"Subtle?" Sharpe asked angrily.

"You are a soldier," Fox said, "and you employ a soldier's brutal methods. Our mission demands more subtlety. I should have stopped you last night."

"You're damned lucky I wasn't subtle last night," Sharpe said, still angry. "Those two men in the back room would have killed us both. Who were they?"

"Judging from the papers we found on them, they were both officers from Lanier's battalion, the 157th Light Infantry."

Sharpe grimaced. "The Emperor's devils?"

"Indeed. They also marched north with the Emperor."

"Then they're a beaten regiment, but what were two of their officers doing in Paris last night?"

"Depot troops?" Fox suggested. "Or perhaps the regiment is already back here?"

"The French always marched faster than us," Sharpe said, "so that's possible."

"What we have to do," Fox said, "is find this Général Delaunay. Collignon said he was *la Fraternité*'s leader, and he evidently lives in Paris. And we need to do it swiftly so I can return to my real business."

"Selling pictures?" Sharpe asked scornfully.

"Rescuing the treasures of civilization, Colonel, and restoring them to their rightful owners."

Sharpe pushed the tea away. "Mister Fox," he said sternly, "you've already walked into one trap. These people know you! If you start asking around Paris for Delaunay they'll find you again. You're not exactly unremarkable."

"Is that a compliment?" Fox asked, amused.

"You must be the tallest man in the city. *La Fraternité* knows about you, they'll be looking for you."

Fox shrugged. "I still have friends here."

"And you thought Collignon was a friend."

"I thought he was a treacherous little shit who liked our gold." Fox finished his tea.

Sharpe had a sudden thought, an instinct like the alarm a man could feel on a battlefield. "How well did Collignon know you?"

"Know me? Well, we weren't bosom friends."

"Did he know where you lived?"

"He did."

"And your business?"

"Of course he knew of it! He sold me a dreadful portrait!" Fox bridled. "Sharpe, the man is dead. He is no longer dangerous, and you fret too much. I shall discover Delaunay's whereabouts and we shall pay him a visit. You, Colonel, will stay with your men until I need you. And that is an order." He smiled as he said the last few words, evidently wanting to soften their severity.

"I'm supposed to keep you alive," Sharpe said.

"Which you did superbly last night. Trust me, Colonel, I shall be safe."

"Why?" Sharpe asked truculently.

"Why what, pray?"

"Why insist on going into danger on your own?"

Fox sighed. "I don't doubt your efficacy, Colonel, but you are a liability. Your French isn't good enough, and no one will believe you're from the *Îles Normandes*. You sound like an Englishman speaking French, which is what you are! I, on the other hand, can pass as a Parisian. Life for me is much easier when I am not protecting myself from your presence. I will find Delaunay and we will both visit him, but I will do the searching without your company."

"You won't go off on your own to question Delaunay?" Sharpe asked.

"If the opportunity arises and I deem it safe? Maybe."

"For God's sake no!" Sharpe spoke too loud, attracting glances from other tables. "And he's probably not even here, not if he went north with Boney."

"All the better," Fox said calmly. "I can search his house undisturbed. Call it a harmless reconnaissance."

"What's your job?" Sharpe asked brusquely.

Fox frowned, staring at Sharpe. "A strange question," he finally said.

"No, tell me. What are you, Mister Fox? I'm a soldier, what are you?"

Fox appeared to think about it, then shrugged. "A gentleman, Sharpe."

"And I'm not. But what kind of gentleman?"

Fox still frowned. "Does it matter?"

"It matters!" Sharpe snarled, making Fox grimace.

"I am a gentleman of private means, Sharpe. I choose to use those means to buy art, and like to think I am something of an expert."

"And you've always had money," Sharpe said, making it sound like an accusation.

"Really, Colonel, this is uncalled for."

"The Duke gave me a job," Sharpe said, "and he's a gentleman I admire and serve as best I can, but to do the job he gave me I need to know who you are."

"I think you know," Fox said coldly.

"I'll tell you what I know," Sharpe said. "You grew up privileged. You had an education. Everything in your life has come easy, Fox. You never had to struggle."

Fox looked offended, but managed to nod. "So?"

"So you think everything will still come easy. You walked into Collignon's trap without a thought. If I hadn't gone armed and with men we'd both be dead. Now you're doing it again. You think you can find Delaunay and talk him into telling you his secrets. It isn't a harmless reconnaissance, it's a bloody deathtrap."

"Oh, Sharpe, really!" Fox smiled. "I'm charmed you think I'm that capable, but truly I don't need you. I can work more swiftly on my own, and God help us if you end up killing a French general." He paused, startled by a dull rumble that echoed ominously through the city sky. "I pray that isn't thunder," Fox said.

"It isn't. It's cannon fire."

"Really?" Fox sounded dubious.

"I've been hearing guns for twenty-one years," Sharpe said, "and that's gunfire. A long way off, but those are cannons."

"So the armies are getting closer! Good." Fox reached across the table and finished Sharpe's tea. "I shall be back by tonight, Colonel."

"And if you're not?"

"You protect the Duke, you protect fat King Louis, and you pray for my immortal soul." Fox stood, attracting glances because of his height, and just then another outburst of cannon fire shuddered the sky. "Someone's busy," Fox said.

"It should be me," Sharpe said angrily. "That's my business, Mister Fox, not this . . ." He cut his words short.

"Not this nonsense?" Fox finished the sentence for him, then leaned over the table. "This nonsense, Colonel, is deadly serious, and the Duke wants it ended, and your business is to obey the Duke. I am merely going to discover where Delaunay lives. I assure you that I will want your company if I consider the situation at all dangerous. I will see you tonight." He put coins on the table, then strode off toward the river.

"And how will you know it's dangerous?" Sharpe asked, but too low for Fox or anyone else to hear. He waited a brief while, then followed the figure, an easy task because Fox loomed over the crowds. The tall man walked down the Rue de Richelieu and turned right onto the Rue du Faubourg Saint-Honoré, thus skirting the dark alleys of the slum where Sharpe's men waited. He followed the tall figure westward until Fox vanished down a small side street that ended at the Tuileries gardens. And there Sharpe lost him. He hurried to the street's end, looked left and right, saw no tall figures, and so walked back up the small street. The wide gates to a courtyard stood open and Sharpe gazed inside but saw nothing helpful. An old woman carrying a pail of water emerged from a door in the archway and looked at him belligerently.

"M'sieu?" she demanded.

Sharpe hesitated, then, "I'm looking for a very tall man, madame."

"We all are," she said, "but God is not good." She laughed, and Sharpe walked on. He supposed Fox had gone into one of the houses, but which was impossible to say.

A clatter ahead made him hurry, only to see a troop of horse artillery hurry westward along the Rue du Faubourg Saint-Honoré. Sharpe recognized two six-inch howitzers followed by their coffin-like caissons, and remembered leaning against one of the short-barreled howitzers at Waterloo while his men ransacked a captured caisson. The barrel had been scorching hot because it had been firing at his men at the top of the ridge. He shuddered at the memory of the battle. The passing artillery was going fast, forcing carriages and carts to the sides of the wide street. "Going to face the Prussians," a man near Sharpe said.

Sharpe, curious, drifted with the crowd that followed the guns, not stopping till he was beside the Élysée Palace where, he realized, folk had gathered in hope of hearing news. There were a few despondent soldiers in the great courtyard, and people shouted at them to learn what might be happening. Finally an officer came to the railings. "The Emperor is back," he announced.

"Where?" people shouted.

"Close by!"

"So are the Prussians!"

The officer shrugged. "The Emperor will protect you."

That claim provoked jeers, and Sharpe turned away, still hoping for a glimpse of Fox, though the man had vanished, which left Sharpe small choice but to return to the warehouse in the Rue Villedot.

"The bastard's gone," he told Harper.

"Do you trust him?"

"No." Sharpe accepted a mug of smouch from Charlie Weller. "And he doesn't trust me either. He says I'm not subtle."

"You're not," Harper commented.

Sharpe sipped the smouch. "Proper tea," he said appreciatively.

"So what do we do?" Harper asked.

"What he told us to do," Sharpe sipped the hot tea, "wait till he gets back."

"The lads are restless. Bored."

A burst of laughter sounded from across the wide space and Sharpe saw that Finn and Geoghegan had discovered lumps of charcoal and were adding mustaches to some of Fox's portraits. "I'm thinking," he said.

"Go on," Harper encouraged him.

"That bastard Collignon," Sharpe said, "betrayed Fox."

"And we killed him," Harper said happily.

"But he knew all about Fox. Where he lived and what he did."

"Probably."

"So assume he knew about this place?"

"Maybe he didn't."

"Fox suggested he might have known," Sharpe said harshly, "which means Collignon probably told others, and those others will eventually come looking here. And we'll be like rats in a barrel."

Harper frowned. "But not yet. The bugger hasn't been dead twenty-four hours."

"He could have told them weeks ago," Sharpe said, "and last night *la Fraternité* or whatever the hell they're called lost three men, and Collignon's house burned down. They'll know they have enemies in the city, and it's likely as not they know about this bloody place. We can't stay here, Pat."

"Jesus Christ! Where do we go?"

"We wait for Fox to come back, then we decide. He knows Paris."

"Unless the buggers come first," Harper said, and reached for his volley gun.

They waited.

*   *   *

Fox did not return, but nor did anyone else come to the warehouse. Night fell. Sharpe went out at dusk and brought back bread, ham, cheese, and wine, a meal they consumed by the light of candle stubs. Every footstep in the street made him reach for his rifle and turn expectantly toward the big doors, but the steps always went past. "I hate this," he told Harper. "That bloody fool. He's all education and no bloody sense."

"Got himself caught?"

"What else? They caught him and put him in a box." Sharpe waited as more footsteps sounded in the street. They went past. "And we can't stay here."

"So where do we go?"

"I have an idea," Sharpe said, "but getting there?"

"We walk."

"With rifles and muskets?" A dozen men walking the streets of Paris with rifles slung on their shoulders would be asking for trouble. Sharpe had no doubt that the city was filled with deserters, and the authorities would be looking for them, and men carrying weapons would be too noticeable. "We'll leave at dawn," Sharpe decided, "but we have to hide the weapons."

"And use what's left of your man's wee carriage," Harper suggested.

Much of the back of Collignon's curricle had been broken apart for fuel, but the seat and floor were still intact and would serve as a cart. Sharpe piled the weapons inside and covered them with a canvas made by slicing a huge portrait from its frame. "We haven't got far to go," he told his men, then they dragged open the big doors and Sharpe led them toward the river. It was early morning and few folk were around and no one seemed to think it odd that a broken curricle was being pulled by four men. There were other carts in the streets either bringing vegetables from the surrounding country or carrying builders' supplies, and Collignon's curricle looked little different. They pulled the curricle to the side of the Rue du Faubourg Saint-Honoré as a troop of dragoons trotted past, going west. The cannon fire was sounding again, dull thuds from the distant north. "That's where we should be," Sharpe growled, "doing our job instead of this nonsense."

"Nosey can't be far off," Harper said.

Sharpe nodded. "But that's not battle gunfire." The distant shots were sporadic and desultory, nothing like the incessant and urgent hammering of big guns in battery. Men were doubtless fighting and dying to the north, but Sharpe wondered whether the Emperor really had enough troops to make a fight for the city. Fox had reckoned that at least a hundred thousand men could be mustered, which suggested that there could be a battle before any allied troops entered Paris, but the city's mood seemed resigned to losing the war. He remembered the jeers he had heard outside the Élysée Palace and the huge numbers of maimed beggars wearing their old uniforms. Lucille reckoned the French were tired of war. "We have suffered enough," she had told him more than once, "it is time for peace. A king is a small price to pay for fewer deaths."

They followed the route Sharpe and Harper had taken on their first day in the city, looking for all the world like a group of workmen. They passed the great palaces and so into the fields, beyond which scattered houses had been built. "Here," Sharpe said, pushing open the gates of the Hôtel Mauberges.

"The old lady's house?"

"Lucille will be coming here," Sharpe said, "and whoever captured Fox won't look here."

"Nor will Mister Fox."

"He's probably dead, Pat. Silly bugger."

"He might be alive?"

"After what we did to them two nights ago? What would you do?"

"Slit his throat. Slowly."

The Hôtel Mauberges was enormous; three stories tall with elegant pillars framing the front entrance and, judging by the windows, all shuttered, spacious enough to house a whole battalion. "We go around the back," Sharpe decided, and the curricle's two wheels crunched on gravel as they followed the drive down the side of the house. There was a stable and coach house at the rear. "That'll do us," Sharpe said. The coach-house doors were open and they dragged the curricle inside and parked it next to an open carriage with plush seats and a folded leather hood. Two carriage horses were in the stable, both looking hungry. "Do you have a carriage?" Harper asked Sharpe.

"Me? A carriage?"

"In Normandy."

"We've got a dung cart. Does that count?"

Harper traced a finger over the coat of arms painted on the carriage's door. "I thought with Lucille being a proper lady . . ."

"She's poor as a church mouse, Pat. We're lucky to have a dung cart."

"The old lady must be rich enough," Harper said, nodding through the open doors at the lavish house.

"She is," Sharpe agreed. The Dowager Countess Mauberges was rich beyond his imaginings. She had inherited her husband's coal mines in the north of France, which was why she had been at Brussels before the Emperor's sudden return had turned that country into a battleground. The Dowager had been in Brussels with her man of business to negotiate the next winter's price of fuel, and there she had befriended Lucille. She had also been generous, which was reason enough for Sharpe to help her.

"Company," Harper grunted, and Sharpe turned to see that three men had just left the big house and were walking slowly toward the stables. All three were elderly, and Sharpe doubted they were deserters. The man in the center carried a cudgel, the other two were apparently unarmed. Sharpe went to meet them.

"Who are you?" the man holding the cudgel demanded nervously.

"Friends of the Dowager Countess," Sharpe answered.

"You're English?" The three men stopped and the speaker raised the cudgel threateningly.

"*Îles Normandes*," Sharpe answered. "The Dowager Countess will be here soon. She sent us ahead."

"To do what?"

"To wait for her."

"She's coming?" another of the men asked eagerly.

"She'll be here in a week or so," Sharpe said, hoping he was right. "We'll stay in the stables."

"She sent you?" the cudgel man insisted. "To do what?"

"The Dowager is worried about unrest in the city. She wants the house protected."

The man looked warily at Pat Harper, who had joined Sharpe, cradling his volley gun. The Irishman nodded. "Good day to you all!" he said in English.

The three men who were presumably servants looked terrified, and no wonder. Sharpe was a threatening figure, Harper was huge and carrying the seven-barrel gun, while Sharpe's other men were watching from the stable doors. "You will not enter the house?" the cudgel man asked.

"Not unless you need help," Sharpe said. "The Dowager asked us to come here, so here we are. And who are you?" he demanded of the man with the cudgel.

"Philippe Vignot. I'm her ladyship's steward."

Sharpe opened his pouch and brought out the crumpled letter. "Then this is for you."

The steward took the letter. "Top window," Harper muttered, and Sharpe looked up to see two men peering from a dormer window.

"The Countess says men have taken the house," Sharpe spoke to the steward.

"Deserters from the army, monsieur." The steward read the brief letter then handed it to one of his companions. "Her ladyship says we can trust you."

"You can. How many men are in the house?"

"Fifteen, sixteen? They bring their women too." He shuddered. "And, monsieur . . ." He stopped.

"What?"

"They took two of her ladyship's maids. We hear them screaming."

Sharpe grimaced. "How long have they been here?"

"Since May!"

"You fought them?" Sharpe asked.

"We have no proper weapons, monsieur," Vignot admitted miserably, "and they have muskets and bayonets."

"And plenty of powder," one of the other men put in.

"You told the authorities?"

Vignot spat. "They do nothing! I told them."

"You want us to clear them out?"

"They must be gone before her ladyship returns," Vignot said.

"Then tonight," Sharpe said. "You'll need to leave that back door unlocked," he nodded toward the door from which Vignot had come, "and leave us some lanterns."

Vignot seemed uncertain, then nodded reluctantly. He took the letter back from his companion. "Her ladyship says you are English?"

"In another week, Vignot, the city will be full of British and Prussian soldiers. Be glad you have some on your side."

"If you say so, monsieur." He hesitated. "There was a battle, monsieur?"

"A big one. The Emperor lost."

"So it is true." Vignot's face crumpled. "And the Emperor?"

"So far as I know, he lived."

"God be praised."

"So tonight, Vignot," Sharpe said, "we will come long after dark, in the middle of the night. Leave the back door unlocked and have four or five lanterns ready."

"Yes, monsieur."

"And if the men ask who we are," Sharpe said, knowing that they would, "tell them we are also deserters from the Emperor's army."

Sharpe questioned him for a few more minutes, establishing that the three servants slept downstairs, where they were expected to provide meals for the deserters who occupied the top two floors, then watched as Vignot and his companions walked back to the house. Sharpe returned to the stables. *La Fraternité* must wait and Fox's fate could stay a mystery. He had a fight coming.

The men in the house had seen Sharpe, Harper, and the others, so Sharpe had to assume they would be wary. He had told Vignot to say they were also deserters who were content to occupy the coach house, and hoped that would be sufficient to allay any apprehension, but he still waited until he was sure midnight was long past before leading all his men across the gravel to the house's back door. It was unlocked. "Boots off, lads," he said softly.

They filed into the night-dark kitchen, blundering against chairs and a table. They took off shoes and boots as Sharpe found the lanterns by feeling along the table. Harper struck a flint against steel, blew on some charred linen in his tinderbox, and Sharpe saw four candle-lanterns. "Light them all, Pat," he said softly.

The candle flames caught, illuminating the big kitchen and a door that led into a long hallway from which a grand marble staircase curved upward. The house was silent. "With me, Pat," he said, "the rest of you wait. And stay quiet!"

He had decided that taking all his men upstairs would create too much noise. Better that he and Harper made a silent exploration, and so he took one lantern that he placed at the foot of the huge curving staircase, then began to climb. The stairs were made of a pale stone so his steps were silent. He carried his rifle with a sword-bayonet fixed. Harper, the volley gun in his hands, followed. Their shadows flickered across portraits that hung in the stairwell, which made Sharpe think of Fox. The portraits showed men and women in elaborate costumes and with fantastic hair. Ancestors, he supposed, and wondered who his own ancestors were. His mother, he knew, had been called Lizzie Sharpe, but he knew he would never discover who his father was. Just another man who had sought out a whore. It was best not to know, he thought, as he reached the first landing, where another stairway led straight to the top floor, while corridors stretched left and right. In front of him was a door that, he supposed, led to the principal bedroom. There were more portraits on the walls, while an elaborate chandelier, its candles long dead, hung from the ceiling. The light was dim here. He moved to the door and put his ear against it. Harper was close behind him. "Can you hear anything?"

"Hush," Sharpe whispered. He thought he heard male voices, low and insistent, then he was certain he heard a woman moan. "Try not to use the volley gun," he said to Harper in a whisper. "We don't want to wake the bastards in other rooms."

Harper slung the volley gun and pulled out his sword-bayonet. "We kill them?"

"Just sing them a lullaby, Pat."

The door handle was a lever that Sharpe slowly pushed down, flinching as the lock's tongue grated on the socket. It freed itself with a click and Sharpe pushed the door open. His first impression was of three men, two of them naked, the third sprawled in an armchair beside an empty hearth, The naked men were on an enormous bed and, as Sharpe stepped into the room, he saw a girl was tied there, her wrists and ankles roped to the bed's corner posts. "Take the man in the chair, Pat," he said, and crossed the room, reversing the rifle in his hands.

One man bellowed in alarm, then tried to back away across the bed. Sharpe hit him with the rifle's brass butt and felt the man's skull cave in from the force of the blow. The second man launched himself at Sharpe, who managed to step back and swing the rifle so that the sword-bayonet sliced across his attacker's belly. The man fell off the bed, sprawling on a rug, and Sharpe jabbed the bayonet down at the man's ribs, then reversed the gun and hit him with the butt. "That's your lullaby," he said as the man went still.

"This bugger doesn't know whether it's Christmas or Tuesday," Harper said, and Sharpe turned to see that the third man was on the hearth, with a bloodied scalp and apparently unconscious.

"Cut the girl free, Pat, and give her a blanket."

The man on the rug suddenly tried to lunge at Sharpe's legs, then yelped as the bayonet scored a second cut across his ribs. "Stupid bastard," Sharpe said, and kicked the man between the legs. The man yelped in pain, clutched himself, and bent over in agony, which made it easy for Sharpe to thump the rifle's butt on his skull. He did it harder this time and the man fell back, unmoving.

"Poor wee thing," Harper said, and Sharpe turned to the girl, who was sitting up and covering her breasts as Harper cut her ankles free.

"Who are you, mademoiselle?"

"I work here, monsieur," she managed to answer. Harper had pulled a blanket from the bed's wreckage and she gathered it around herself. She was crying, her tears trickling silently down her face.

"Take her downstairs, Pat," Sharpe said, "then bring the others up here. Be quick, we made too much noise."

The girl staggered as she stood and Harper just tossed the volley gun onto the bed and scooped her up in his arms. "I'll be back," he said to Sharpe, and carried the girl out onto the landing and down the stairs. And as Harper went downstairs Sharpe heard footsteps from the attic floors above. He went to the bedroom door and peered up the staircase that led to the attics. He could hear voices now, men muttering in that upper darkness, and he slung his rifle and went back to the bed where he retrieved Harper's volley gun. He cocked it, hauling the stiff doghead back and flinching at the small noise it made. He instinctively ran a finger against the flint, making sure it was firmly seated, then a man called from the upper storey. "Jean?"

Back to the door. Sharpe stood in shadow, the door just a few inches ajar. The top of the attic stairs was dark, but he thought he saw movement on the landing there.

"Jean!" the man called again and, when there was no answer, the man said something and Sharpe heard muttered replies, then the unmistakable sound of a gun being cocked. He stayed in the shadows, then saw more shadows moving at the top of the straight stairway. "Jean!" a man called even louder, then started down the stairs. Others followed him. Sharpe reckoned there were five or six men, two of whom carried muskets. One of them shouted encouragement and they all started to hurry, so Sharpe kicked the bedroom door wide open, raised the volley gun, and pulled the trigger.

The gun's stock hammered into Sharpe's shoulder, while its noise was magnified by the stone walls. The house seemed to shake as the seven barrels gouted smoke and the sound hammered the walls as the seven bullets scoured the staircase. A vast gold-framed portrait shook on the stairway wall, a rip gouged across its canvas, then the whole thing collapsed onto the shrieking men who bled on the stairs. Sharpe tossed the volley gun back onto the bed and unslung his rifle. A woman screamed from the attic.

"Sir?" Harper called anxiously from downstairs.

"Come on up, Pat! All of you!"

The vast fallen portrait was canted across the staircase, trapping most of the men beneath its ruined canvas. But one man, choking and clutching his bloodied chest, had slid to the landing and now gazed in horror as Sharpe approached. "Non, non," he moaned as Sharpe got nearer, then suddenly a man stood halfway up the stairs, thrusting his upper body through the ripped canvas and leveling a musket.

Sharpe lifted the rifle, pulled the trigger, and again the hallways echoed with noise. The bullet caught the man in the upper chest, throwing him backward and spattering blood on the wall. "I hate stupid bastards," Sharpe growled.

"God save Ireland," Harper, a lantern in his hand, had joined Sharpe and stared at the carnage. The torn, bloodstained canvas moved as wounded men stirred beneath it.

"I think there are six of them under that mess," Sharpe said, "we put three down in the bedroom, so there must be others."

"Upstairs?"

"Could be anywhere, Pat. Your gun is on the bed."

Harper went to retrieve his volley gun, and Charlie Weller gazed at the fallen portrait. "Want us to move it, Mister Sharpe?"

"Please, Sergeant."

Geoghegan and O'Farrell pushed the vast portrait almost upright, then propped the heavy gilded frame against the wall while Weller and McGurk began hauling wounded men down the stairs. "What do we do with them?" McGurk asked.

"Find a window and throw them out."

"This one's hurt bad, Mister Sharpe."

"Then throw him harder."

"Where do you want this?" Harper asked, dragging one of the naked men from the bedroom.

"Downstairs, Pat."

Harper lifted the man and tossed him into the stairwell. McGurk flinched at the crunching sound of the man's fall onto the stone floor below. "He's a rapist, thief, and God knows what else," Sharpe explained. "Toss the others, Pat."

"A pleasure, sir."

Sharpe took McGurk and Butler along the two hallways that led from the landing, looking in each room, but found no more intruders, while Harper took the rest of the men upstairs. Sharpe heard two shots fired, and moments later seven men and three women were pushed down the upper stairway. All were naked or near naked. "Send them all downstairs, Pat," Sharpe said, grinning.

"This one's a maid here," Harper indicated a girl wrapped in a blanket.

"She can go to the kitchen. The rest we chuck out."

They drove the intruders at bayonet point out of the front door. Three were badly wounded and Sharpe made the others carry them. He and Harper prodded them down the driveway and out onto the road. "Come back," Sharpe told them, "and we kill you."

"Give us clothes!" one of the women demanded.

"*Va te faire foutre*," Sharpe said, and slammed the heavy gate shut.

Vignot, the steward, was waiting at the front door looking nervous. "They're gone?"

"And they won't come back," Sharpe said, "and tomorrow you start cleaning the house. It's a mess." He translated what he had said for Harper's benefit.

"And what do we do tomorrow?" Harper asked.

"We clean up an even bigger mess," Sharpe said, though how he was to do that without Fox's help he did not know. Only that it must be done. "Till then, Pat? Sleep."

CHAPTER 7

Vignot and his staff insisted on making breakfast the next morning, and afterward Sharpe took Charlie Weller on a walk through the city. "Where are we going?" Weller asked.

"Back to the warehouse, Charlie."

"We left something there?"

"We're just looking. And we need to buy some tobacco." Butler and Finn were moaning about lacking tobacco for their pipes.

Sharpe turned left onto the Rue de Richelieu. Both he and Weller were in civilian clothes and attracted no attention from the Parisians on the busy pavement. They walked up the eastern side and stopped outside a millinery store to gaze down the Rue Villedot. "Damn," Sharpe said mildly.

"Good job we moved, sir," Weller said.

There were French troops in the street and they were going in and out of Fox's warehouse, some carrying the pictures that were being hurled into a wagon. "Light infantry," Sharpe said. The soldiers' collars were red, and instead of bayonets they carried the short swords that were not unlike a rifleman's sword-bayonet. "We'd best go home," Sharpe said.

"Is that what you came to see?"

"I hoped I wouldn't see it." The presence of the troops confirmed what he feared, that *la Fraternité* knew of the warehouse and, most probably, now knew that British soldiers were already in the city.

They stopped at a tobacconist then walked back to the Hôtel Mauberges. "They're hunting us," Sharpe told Harper.

"So they must have captured Mister Fox?"

"Silly bugger wasn't subtle enough," Sharpe said, "but we should be safe enough here."

"So we just stay here?"

Sharpe was tempted to say yes, but he had his orders and the only clues he possessed were the names Fox had mentioned. Lanier and Delaunay. "Delaunay?" Harper asked when Sharpe mentioned the names.

"He's a general and Fox went looking for him."

"And I think I've found him," Harper said happily.

"Found him?"

"Follow me."

Harper led him to the back door of the house and into the kitchen. "When you were gone, sir, me and the lads had a wee look around." He pushed open a door from the kitchen and Sharpe found himself in a room racked high with wine bottles. "You found what you were looking for then?" he said sourly.

"God is good, sir, so he is, but look here."

There were some wooden crates piled at the end of the room, and Harper pointed to one of them. "Isn't that the name?" he asked, and Sharpe saw that the name Delaunay had been stenciled on the box's side. "*Vin* Delaunay," he read. "That's not our man. That's a wine-maker, our fellow is a general."

"Maybe same family?"

"Could be, I suppose." Sharpe went back to the kitchen and shouted for Vignot. "Where does the wine Delaunay come from?" he asked.

"The city, monsieur!"

"From a wine shop?"

"Non, monsieur, from the Delaunay vineyard."

"Which is where?"

"In the Rue de Montreuil, monsieur."

"That's in Paris?" It sounded unlikely to Sharpe.

"The eastern end of the city, monsieur," Vignot said. "There are four or five vineyards there, but Delaunay makes the best wine."

"And it's a family business?"

Vignot nodded. "The old *Général* and his wife, monsieur."

"Bull's eye," Sharpe said in English.

"Monsieur?"

"Thank you," Sharpe said, and looked at Harper. "You're not entirely useless, Pat."

"I wish you'd tell my mother that!"

"One day, Pat, one day. We go tonight."

"All of us?"

"All of us."

That night Sharpe wore his uniform beneath the long coat that Fox had bought him. He insisted all his men wore their uniform jackets, so that if they were captured they could claim to be soldiers, not spies, but it seemed strange to be walking the evening streets of Paris with a sword at his side. His rifle and the long guns of his men were being pushed in a handcart that belonged to the garden of the Hôtel Mauberges. They received a few curious glances, but no one challenged them as they followed the directions Vignot had given them; finding the Rue de Saint-Antoine. "If you see the elephant," Vignot had said, "you're on the right street."

"The elephant?"

"You'll see it, monsieur!"

And so they did. At first Sharpe had just seen a white mass in the distance and thought it must be moonlight reflected from a vast white wall, but as he walked closer it began to resemble a small snow-covered hill. It was not till he walked into the great open space that he saw it was a gigantic elephant, taller than a house, that stood in a pool of shallow water. "What the . . ." Harper said, gazing in awe.

"You've never seen an elephant?" Sharpe said. "I saw a lot in India."

"This isn't bloody India," Harper retorted.

"It's a statue," Sharpe said. Vignot had described it and Sharpe had not really believed what he heard, but the reality was bigger and stranger than anything he could have imagined. The vast beast loomed over the open space. "The Emperor ordered it," Sharpe said, "and they haven't had time to make it out of bronze, so that big bugger is plaster over wood."

"The man's insane," Harper murmured.

The elephant's flanks were streaked with dirt, and in places the plaster had flaked away to leave scabrous gaps. It stood on a weed-thick island in the pool, and Sharpe could see the rats moving there. Vignot had said the whole statue was a paradise for rats. "It stands where the Bastille was," he had told Sharpe, "and when it is properly built in bronze it will be magnificent!" One of the elephant's forelegs was evidently a house, because candlelight showed dimly through a window. Sharpe shook his head in disbelief. "Come on, lads, we have work."

They passed the monstrous beast and so on up the Rue de Saint-Antoine, then branching left onto the Rue de Montreuil. There were houses on both sides of the street, which led to a gate in the city wall. To his left Sharpe could see vineyards beyond the houses and then, halfway to the city gate, he found the entrance to the Delaunay estate. It was a great iron gate between stone pillars, one of which had a wooden sign on which *Delaunay* was written. The small moonlight showed a drive curving between neat vineyards toward a big house that was built hard against the city wall. The gate was padlocked.

"Who has a picklock?" Sharpe asked.

"You do," Harper said, amused.

Sharpe had to retrieve his rifle from the handcart, then opened the small brass-lidded cavity in the stock where he kept the bullets' leather patches and a picklock. "It's good for cleaning the mainspring," he said.

"Of course it is, Mister Sharpe," Butler said.

Sharpe unfolded the strongest hook and explored the padlock. It was old, simple and stiff, but he found the levers, forced them back, and the lock's staple fell open. "Easy," he said, putting the pick back in the rifle's stock. He pulled the gate open just enough to let his men file through, each now carrying either a rifle or a musket. "Don't cock them!" Sharpe warned. The last thing he needed was for a man to trip and accidentally alarm the big house by firing a gun.

Lights glowed dimly from one window on the ground floor of the house and as they started up the long curving drive Sharpe saw the silhouette of a man walk in front of the window. The man had a musket slung on a shoulder. "Into the vines, boys," he muttered.

They approached the house in a leafy corridor of grapevines that climbed gently toward the house and the city wall beyond. The grapes looked almost ripe in the moonlight, but Sharpe doubted they would be harvested for another two months. He plucked one and grimaced at the sour taste. He was crouching, watching the house as he spat the grape out, and saw two men pacing slowly in front of the building that seemed to back onto the city wall. He could see no men on the wall's top, just the two who paced backward and forward, both of them carrying muskets.

Sentries, then. He peered at the upper windows, wondering if anyone watched from there, but the windows were black and he saw nothing. Only the one window was lit, and that on the ground floor.

"They're in uniform," Harper whispered to him, nodding at the two men, whose white crossbelts showed clearly. "And there are two more of the buggers at the front door. Bloody sentries."

"We wait," Sharpe said, though in truth he did not know what they waited for nor what good waiting would do. He needed to get inside the house and question General Delaunay, but how to do that without killing the sentries he did not know, nor did he want to shoot and so wake the house's occupants. So he waited.

After a while the sentries seemed to get bored with marching up and down the front of the house and both found places to lean against the wall. One lit a pipe or cigar, the smoke drifting in the small wind. Still Sharpe waited. The two guards at the front door had retreated into a wide pillared porch. Every few minutes one would peer out, then disappear again. Sharpe remembered his own time of sentry duty, usually standing guard at some camp, and how, as the night lengthened and nothing happened, he would feel sleep creeping on him. Charles Morris had been his company commander back in those days, and Sharpe felt a surge of anger that fate had brought Morris back into his life. That was unfinished business, he thought, and his hand instinctively closed about the Baker rifle. If Morris dared flog one man in the Prince of Wales's Own Volunteers then Sharpe swore he would take the skin off the bastard's back. "Buggers are asleep," Harper whispered.

Sharpe jarred himself fully awake. He could see no one in the front door's porch, though he supposed both men were still there, while the other two were now slumped at the foot of the wall, a hundred or more paces apart. Sharpe shrugged off the stiff and heavy oilskin coat and dropped it to the ground. "Stay here, Pat," he ordered. "If I need you I'll shout, or else fire the rifle. If you hear a rifle shot, bring everyone."

"Shall I come now?"

"Stay here, Pat." Sharpe slowly got to his feet. No one shouted, the sentries did not move. Sharpe stepped from the vines onto the gravel of the driveway and slowly approached the lighted window. His boots crunched the small stones, but the nearest sentry was oblivious, his head sunk in sleep. Bushes grew beneath the window and Sharpe flinched as they rustled. Then he crouched so that only his head was above the stone sill.

He was gazing into a long parlor, an empty hearth to the right, bookshelves to the left, and the space between filled with deep sofas and elegant tables, all lit by a dozen candelabra. An elderly woman sat just beyond the fireplace, her white hair piled elaborately. She was dressed in black and was talking to someone sitting opposite her, but the man, if it was a man, had his back to Sharpe and all he could see was the top of the man's head above the sofa's frame. The man had fair hair so it was not Fox, who, like Sharpe, had dark hair. He could just hear voices, though too faint to be able to distinguish any words. A man and a woman. They laughed, then the man stood and Sharpe saw he was young and dressed in French infantry uniform. The man turned and seemed to gaze straight at Sharpe, who ducked down beneath the sill.

He waited. Then almost jumped in fright as he heard the window above him being opened. "There's not much wind, my lady," the man spoke right above Sharpe.

"It still might cool the room, *Capitaine*. Leave it open."

Sharpe froze. He sensed the man was leaning out of the window and half expected to hear a pistol being cocked. He hoped Harper was aiming his rifle at the man, but then he heard the man's footsteps go back into the room, and he dared raise his head to see the officer take his seat opposite the old woman. Sharpe gazed through the glass, confident that the candles' reflections would hide him. The open window was just to his right and he could hear the voices clearly now. The old woman was evidently asking the officer about his fiancée. "How old is she?"

"Nineteen."

"A good age. She's pretty?"

"I think so."

"So you should. What is her family?"

"Grain merchants, milady, in Poitiers."

"There's money?"

"Ample."

"She sounds like a wise choice, *Capitaine*." The old lady sounded anything but sincere to Sharpe. "I congratulate you."

"*Merci*, madame."

"But in the coming days," the old woman spoke sharply, "who knows what will happen? Is France to be conquered?"

"I fear so."

"Our enemies will wring us dry," she spoke angrily. "It is a disgrace!"

"We will make them regret it, madame."

"Indeed we will! We must!"

The captain stood and bowed to the older woman. "I must check on the sentries, madame."

"Do your duty, *Capitaine*."

"As always, madame, as always."

"And the Englishman? He is safe?"

"Sleeping with the mushrooms, madame."

"He should be dead!"

"He has more to tell us, madame." He hesitated. "He claims he is only here to take the art from the *Musée Napoléon*."

"Then he's a barbarian as well as a liar. Question him further."

"Perhaps you should question him, madame?"

"Maybe I will. He's unhurt?"

"A little bruised and very hungover, madame."

"A waste of good brandy," she said, then waved the captain from the room. She sat in thought for a moment, stood, and paused to gaze at a portrait above the mantel. She looked sad, then abruptly turned and followed the captain from the great parlor.

Sharpe stood, stretching cramped muscles. So Fox was here, a captive, and he was "with the mushrooms?" What the hell did that mean?

There was the noise of a door opening and a sudden shuffle of feet on stone and Sharpe realized the officer had come from the front door, where the sentries were presumably straightening up and pretending to have been alert. The noise was sufficient to stir the two men at the front of the house, who scrambled to their feet and started pacing again. Sharpe realized he was outlined against the candle-glow through the big window, and ducked down again. He was hidden by two thick bushes. Laurel? He did not know. Lucille would know, he thought. She was amused by his inability to tell an elm from a beech, an oak from a sycamore. He wondered where she was, where the armies were. Surely they must reach Paris soon? Cannon fire had punctuated the sky all day, sounding nearer and always from the north. Fox had told Sharpe that the forts defending Paris were thickest to the north, and he wondered if the Emperor planned a defensive battle somewhere close to those ramparts.

And if there was no battle, or if the Emperor lost, then the allies would be in Paris and *la Fraternité* would want their revenge, which Sharpe had been ordered to stop. And crouching between two laurel bushes, or whatever they were, would not help. He turned and saw that no sentries were in sight and so, carefully, slowly, he stood again. The parlor was empty, the door ajar, and he leaned his rifle against the wall and clambered over the open window's sill. His metal scabbard clanged on the stone and he froze, but no one seemed to notice, and he half fell into the room. He leaned from the window and retrieved his rifle, then crossed toward the open door. The portrait above the empty hearth caught his eye and he stopped to look at it. The painting showed a good-looking man in a cuirassier's breastplate mounted on horseback. There were French cavalrymen behind him and he seemed to be gesturing them forward. It was a striking portrait.

"That was my husband," a voice said in English behind him, "and you must be Colonel Sharpe."

He turned. The elderly woman was in the doorway, her face resolute, and in her hand was a horse pistol. "Sit down, Colonel," she said, twitching the gun, "now!"

Sharpe sat.

CHAPTER 8

"My name," the old woman said, "is Florence Delaunay. And you are Colonel Sharpe."

"Yes, madame."

"You look dangerous, Colonel," she said, evidently amused. She spoke in faultless English. "Be assured I can use my husband's pistol."

"A cuirassier's pistol, madame?"

"My husband's." She nodded at the handsome portrait. "He carried two into battle, but preferred using his sword."

"Most cavalrymen do."

She crossed the room toward a chair, but always holding the gun steadily, aiming it at Sharpe's chest. She was a small, thin woman, dressed in a black fabric that had a glossy sheen. "Have you ever been shot, Colonel?"

"More times than I can remember, madame."

"But never by a woman?"

"Indeed, madame. She very nearly killed me."

"A Frenchwoman, I hope?"

"Indeed she was, madame."

"Good for her! So she drove you off?"

"For a time. I hope we'll be married soon."

"Married! Who is this woman?"

"Her name, madame, is Lucille Lassan."

The pistol faltered and she looked astonished. "Henri and Marie's girl?"

"I believe so, madame."

"A very pretty girl, I remember."

"Your memory is good, madame."

"She married well! The Comte de Seleglise. Then he died, poor man."

"In Russia, madame."

The pistol was held firmly again. "I met her in '12, and liked her. I was sorry about her husband, then last year I heard a rumor she'd taken up with an Englishman. I hoped it was not true."

"Happily, it is."

"Yet she shot you. Why?"

"She believed I had killed her brother."

"And had you?"

"No, madame, it was a Frenchman who killed him."

She snorted, evidently unwilling to believe the story. "There's an estate in Normandy, isn't that right?"

"Indeed, we live there."

"So you speak French?"

"I'm learning it as well as I can, madame," Sharpe answered in French.

"Which is not very well, apparently," Madame Delaunay said in English.

"Unlike your English, madame," Sharpe said politely.

"I am English, Colonel. I was born and grew up in Hampshire. My father was in the Royal Navy." She plainly enjoyed the surprise

158

on Sharpe's face. "I was English," she corrected herself, "but by marriage and after living here for almost forty years I count myself French. And fortunate in that."

"Fortunate, madame?"

"You fight for king and country, Colonel?"

"I do, madame."

"Then you fight for a lunatic! A mad king! And you would foist a gross fat man onto the throne of France! It's disgusting. At least the French had the sense to decapitate their king. You should do the same! Or perhaps Lucille will civilize you." She looked at the portrait above the mantel. "Just as Lieutenant Delaunay civilized me."

"By teaching you French?"

"And he plainly taught me better French than young Lucille has taught you, Colonel!" She paused to sit, though the pistol never left Sharpe. "I thought English gentlemen imbibed French with their mother's milk?"

"I'm no gentleman, madame, and never knew my mother."

Madame Delaunay snorted again. "Then who raised you?"

"A foundling home, madame."

"From which you joined the army?"

"Indeed so, madame."

"As a common soldier?"

"Very common, madame."

"Yet you are a colonel?"

"A lieutenant-colonel, madame."

"You must be a remarkable man, Colonel Sharpe."

"Thank you, madame."

"It will be a pity to shoot you."

"You have no reason to shoot me, madame."

"You break into my house!"

"The window was open."

"Uninvited! Unwanted! Why are you here?"

"To see your husband, madame."

"My husband is dead!" She almost spat the words. "Slaughtered by you English two Sundays ago!"

So General Delaunay had been at Waterloo? Why had Fox not known that? Or Collignon for that matter? The man's widow was now holding the pistol higher, aiming it at Sharpe's face, and he was watching it like a hawk. He had handled French cavalry pistols, and remembered how stiff the action had always been, which meant that Madame Delaunay would need a deal of strength to pull the trigger. She was a slight woman and he wondered if he would see the effort and have time to throw himself sideways. He doubted it, but on the other hand the pistol was heavy and was wavering slightly as she aimed it, and even as he watched she lowered the gun so it rested on her knees. "I am truly sorry, madame," Sharpe said. "The *Général* was a cuirassier?"

"He was."

"They were brave men," Sharpe said, remembering the heavy horsemen in their breastplates and helmets charging the British squares again and again, only to be cut down by canister and relentless musketry. The breastplates had looked good, but a musket bullet spat a hole in them easily.

"Of course they were brave." She half raised the pistol, immediately pointing its huge dark muzzle at Sharpe's chest again. "His aide brought this from the battlefield. This, his sword, and his *Légion d'honneur.*" She let the pistol rest again. "And why did you wish to see my husband?"

"To question him, madame."

She snorted. "He would have answered you nothing! He was a patriot."

"Which is why I wished to speak with him."

"Explain yourself," she demanded peremptorily.

Sharpe thought for a few seconds. His search for *la Fraternité* seemed hopeless if General Delaunay was dead, and he doubted any mention of Alan Fox would prompt a helpful reply. "The Duke of Wellington, madame, is concerned that Paris does not become a battleground."

"Why would he care?"

"I believe he has a fondness for the city, madame."

"I met him when he was ambassador here a year ago, a charming enough man." The compliment was grudging.

"And he wishes to know whether the French forces in the city will yield peaceably. He has no wish to unleash artillery in the streets."

"So you were sent to spy, Colonel?"

"Spies do not wear their country's uniform, madame," Sharpe said, plucking at his green jacket.

"What uniform is that?"

"The Rifles, madame."

"It's ragged," she said disapprovingly, then frowned. "Rifles? Is that a rifle?"

The rifle was leaning close to Sharpe on the sofa. He moved a hand toward it and she jerked the pistol up. "Do not touch it, Colonel." She waited till his hand had gone back to his lap. "Our army does not use rifles, is that right?"

"They don't, madame. It's said the Emperor disapproves."

"My husband did too. We did try them years ago, and Charles said they took too long to reload. Yet he much disliked facing riflemen."

"Good to know, madame," Sharpe said, earning a frown.

"Stay where you are, Colonel," Madame Delaunay said, standing. She was keeping the pistol aimed at his chest again as she moved

161

toward him. She came within two paces, stopped, and reached out with her left hand to take the rifle's barrel. She lifted it, evidently surprised by its weight, and shuffled backward to her chair. Sharpe did not move. Rather awkwardly she laid the rifle across her knees, still keeping the pistol pointed toward Sharpe. "Is it loaded?"

"It is, madame, but not cocked."

"My husband said they were accurate."

"He was right, madame."

"Maybe I should find out." She laid the pistol on the sofa's arm and lifted the rifle, pointing it toward Sharpe. "So you are here, Colonel, to discover whether there will be resistance to your army inside Paris?"

"I pray not, madame."

"Or did you come in an attempt to rescue your compatriot?"

"My compatriot?"

"Mister Fox," she spat the name.

"Do you have him, madame?"

"He says you're a nuisance, Colonel."

The rifle was wavering, its weight too much for Madame Delaunay's thin arms. "My task, madame, was to keep Mister Fox alive."

"To do what?" she demanded.

Sharpe hesitated, but decided that the story of the *Musée Napoléon*'s stolen paintings was harmless enough. "His job is to recover the stolen paintings in the *Musée Napoléon*," he said.

"They are not stolen," the widow snapped, "they belong to humanity! And Paris is the best place for such treasures."

"The Italians and Dutch might disagree, madame."

"Lesser races, Colonel Sharpe. Paris is the center of Europe, and Europe the repository of civilization."

"Nevertheless, madame, Mister Fox would only restore those treasures to their rightful owners."

"And your job is to keep him alive?"

"Indeed so, madame."

"It seems you've failed."

"He's dead? I'm sorry to hear that."

"He lives, Colonel." She paused to cock the rifle, needing all her strength to haul back the doghead. Sharpe was tempted to rush her while she grimaced at the effort, but stayed resolutely still. He did not believe she would kill him, not while he still had answers to her questions.

The doghead clicked into place and she aimed the rifle again, the brass buttplate against her right shoulder. "The rifle kicks, madame," Sharpe said, "I'd advise caution."

"You are impertinent, Colonel. I have used guns since I was a child."

"But not a rifle?"

"There is a first time for everything, Colonel," she said. She was aiming the rifle at Sharpe's chest, though the weight of the gun was causing the barrel to waver. Then, quite suddenly, she raised the barrel, sighted, and pulled the trigger.

The gun fired, the noise huge in the room, the smoke spewing out to fill the parlor with its stink as the bullet seared over Sharpe's head to vanish through the open window. Madame Delaunay cried aloud in pain, her shoulder either broken or badly bruised by the rifle's mule-like kick. Sharpe had seized a cushion, which he threw at her, and she dropped the rifle and raised her left hand to fend off the missile, which gave Sharpe more than enough time to stand, cross the room, and pick up the horse pistol. "I did warn you, madame," he said, standing back from her.

"You will not dare shoot me," she said, her voice sounding pained.

"Where is Mister Fox?" Sharpe asked.

She gasped, not in pain, but because a flurry of shots sounded

163

outside the house and Sharpe realized Harper had taken the rifle shot as his expected signal. "You are a fool, Colonel," Madame Delaunay said.

"I'm the fool with the gun, madame. Where is he?"

There was a stampede of footsteps beyond the parlor door, which was thrown open to reveal the officer who had supposedly gone to inspect the sentries. He stopped abruptly when Sharpe swung the pistol toward him. "Madame!" the man said.

Madame Delaunay kicked Sharpe's leg, but so feebly he hardly registered the blow. "Come in," Sharpe told the officer, "and sit next to Madame Delaunay."

"Are you all right, Mister Sharpe?" Pat Harper called from the window.

"Never been better, Pat. Come on in." More shots sounded outside. "What's happening, Pat?"

"There's a dozen Crapauds running around, sir. No need to worry."

Sharpe turned the pistol on the French officer, who had long fair hair falling across his face. "Madame?" he said nervously.

"You," Sharpe spoke in French, "go to the mushrooms and bring Mister Fox here. Go!"

The man looked for confirmation at Madame Delaunay, who was staring at Sharpe. "I said go!" Sharpe snarled. "So go!"

"Go," Madame Delaunay said resignedly.

Before the Frenchman could leave, the parlor door was pushed open and Rifleman O'Farrell stood there. "You need help, Mister Sharpe?"

"Are you alone?"

"Four of us here, Mister Sharpe."

"Go with this fellow," Sharpe pointed to the French officer, "and bring Mister Fox here."

Sharpe was left alone with Madame Delaunay. "I should have killed you," she said bitterly.

"You broke your collarbone?" Sharpe guessed.

"You did warn me. You will permit me to send for a doctor?"

"Of course."

She used her left hand to ring a bell, which brought a maid who was instructed to fetch Doctor Joseph. "And bring me brandy," she added, then looked back to Sharpe. "I just wanted to fire the rifle."

"And aimed at the open window?"

"I did. If I had wanted to kill you, Colonel, I assure you that no doctor could have saved your life."

"Then I thank you, madame."

"And do put that pistol down. A harmless old lady is no danger to you."

Sharpe sat, keeping the pistol close, and decided to be more honest about his visit to the house. "Tell me about *la Fraternité*, madame."

She laughed. "So that's why you're here! You fools."

"Fools, madame?"

"*La Fraternité*, you idiot, is nonsense! Medieval claptrap!"

The scornful answer surprised Sharpe. "Claptrap encouraged by your husband?"

"Charles was a patriot, Colonel, and a strong supporter of the Emperor. He feared for the Emperor's life in battle and recruited men who would avenge his death. If, indeed, such a tragedy happened."

"In battle?"

"The ancient medieval fraternities were companions in battle, Colonel. They vowed to protect and avenge each other. I fear my husband's brotherhood died with him, yet you have come all this way to discover it?"

The parlor door opened and Pat Harper came in. He was carrying

Sharpe's discarded coat and the volley gun. He bowed to Madame Delaunay. "Madame," he said.

"My friend, Sergeant Patrick Harper," Sharpe made the introductions, "and Madame Delaunay."

"The widow Delaunay," she put in. "You're another rifleman?"

"From Ireland," Harper said proudly.

"And God alone knows why you fight in the British army, Sergeant! The English have been nothing but trouble to Ireland."

"And we've been a rare trouble to them too, madame," Harper retorted.

"Good for you. Don't stop."

"No danger of that, madame."

Madame Delaunay's eyes widened at the sight of the volley gun. "What is that weapon, Sergeant?"

"Mister Nock's volley gun, madame. A wicked thing, so it is."

"With a kick," Sharpe added, "that makes a rifle's recoil feel like a sparrow's kiss."

"I will resist trying it," Madame Delaunay said. "Do sit down, Sergeant, you're making the room untidy."

"Thank you, madame."

"So!" Madame Delaunay stared imperiously at Sharpe. "You came all this way to discover the truth of *la Fraternité*."

"Indeed, madame."

"What credulous fools you all are! A group of men takes a vow to protect the Emperor in battle and you assume they will start another war?"

"If they kill the allied leaders, madame, they could well provoke a revenge."

She shrugged and immediately flinched as her shoulder hurt. "You foresee slaughter in the streets? A national uprising of vengeful Frenchmen besieging your troops?"

"I foresee nothing," Sharpe said, "but the Duke desires order, madame, and an assurance that French forces will accept the war's outcome."

"And you believe my husband could have provided that assurance?"

"His opinion would have been valuable."

"He would have told you to go to hell, Colonel. But for what it is worth I can assure you that the French are tired of war. They have had enough."

"Thank you, madame."

"And you, Colonel? Have you had enough of war?"

"More than enough, madame."

"Enough of what?" a familiar voice asked, and Alan Fox came from the hallway, with Rifleman O'Farrell following. "You found me, Sharpe!" Fox declared in a slurred voice. "Well done." He bowed to the widow Delaunay. "It seems I no longer need your hospitality, milady." Fox, still in the clothes he had been wearing when Sharpe last saw him, looked ragged and tired.

"You're well, Mister Fox?" Sharpe asked.

"In need of a bath and a good meal. These wretches took me to a bloody great cellar they use as a mushroom farm! Can you believe it?"

Sharpe ignored the question, turning to Harper instead. "All quiet outside, Pat?"

"There were eight of the buggers, sir. Four have joined their ancestors, and the others are locked in a room off the hall here."

"Then we can go," Sharpe said. He stood and bowed to Madame Delaunay. "I am sorry for your injury, madame."

"Self-inflicted," she said tartly, "and it will heal."

At that moment the maid returned with a tray on which were two glasses and a decanter of brandy. Fox seized the tray, put it on a table, and poured two generous measures. He handed one to the widow, then drank the other. "We can go," he announced.

Sharpe picked up the pistol, opened the frizzen, and blew the powder from the pan so the gun could not fire. He tossed it back onto the sofa. "Madame," he said, bowing again.

"Remember me to Lucille," Madame Delaunay said.

"I shall, madame."

"And Colonel?" For the first time Madame Delaunay seemed uncertain. "I am hoping my husband's body can be brought back for burial. Is there any hope of that, you think?"

Sharpe remembered the fires in the valley, the great fires on which the naked French corpses blackened and shriveled. "I would not hold out high hopes, madame. I'm sorry."

"He will have been buried already?"

"With his men," Sharpe lied, unwilling to confess that the General must have been burned.

"Sharpe! We can't wait all night!" Fox snarled, and strode from the room.

"Obnoxious man," Madame Delaunay said quietly, then watched as Sharpe, O'Farrell, and Harper left.

Sharpe gathered his men at the front porch, where two French soldiers lay on the flagstones. "Back home, lads," he said.

"Home?" Fox asked. "You mean the warehouse?"

"That's gone," Sharpe said curtly, "and your paintings too. Place was swarming with Crapauds when we looked."

"Damn," Fox said mildly, "and there were some fine canvases there! A Fragonard, among others."

Sharpe neither knew nor cared what a Fragonard might be, but hurried down the drive to recover the handcart that would hide the rifles and muskets. "You're fit enough to walk?" he asked Fox.

"Fit as a fiddle! A bit bruised, and a little too much brandy, perhaps, but I can walk."

Harper went to open the gate and a shot sounded behind them, the ball striking one of the gate's iron bars. "Buggers don't give up," Sharpe grumbled, and began reloading his rifle. "Riflemen!" he called. "See them off."

What small moon there was had vanished behind cloud, but Sharpe could see figures on the big house's forecourt. Men were coming down the slope, evidently eager to stop their escape, and musket flames flashed from the house's upper windows. The balls were mostly flying high, but some ripped through the vines. "How many of the buggers are there?"

"I counted eleven men in the cellar," Fox answered.

Sharpe rested the rifle on the handcart, waited, then saw a movement among the vines to the right. He aimed, fired, the rifle's muzzle flash sudden and bright. He doubted he had hit his man, but the rifle fire would distract and delay the attackers. "Keep firing!"

"Gate's open!" Harper called.

"Time to withdraw, boys," Sharpe said. He rammed a bullet down the barrel and fired up the drive, hearing his ball ricochet from the stones. A musket ball, fired in return, thumped into the handcart as Sharpe helped drag it out to the road. They turned right. Folk peered from windows, curious about the sudden noise, but the pursuers had given up their chase. Sharpe pulled on the long black coat to cover his uniform and tossed the rifle onto the handcart.

"They were going to kill you," he said to Fox.

"Oh, I doubt that! Madame Delaunay assured me otherwise."

"Why did you go without me?" Sharpe demanded angrily.

"I admit it turned out to be unwise," Fox said, "but it seemed worth the risk. I was told General Delaunay had died, so I thought I'd question the widow. To be honest, Sharpe, I thought she might be a bit low on cash, and offered to buy her portraits. You saw the one above the mantel? I swear it's by Jacques-Louis David."

"And she recognized you," Sharpe guessed, "because members of *la Fraternité* all know what you look like."

"She accused me of being a spy!" Fox protested.

"And questioned you."

"A rather unpleasant sergeant questioned me."

"And you revealed my name."

"I did. Always best to give the scoundrels something, Colonel. It keeps the thumbscrews at bay."

"They tortured you?"

"Good Lord, no! They hit me a few times, and when that didn't work they plied me with brandy. Rather good brandy too. They thought it would loosen my tongue, but I only told them about the paintings in the *Musée Napoléon*. I said nothing of *la Fraternité*."

"I did," Sharpe said.

Fox stopped abruptly. "Good God, man, you did what?"

"I asked her," Sharpe said calmly. "Besides, Collignon knew what you were after, and he would have told them."

"So what did the old woman say?"

"That it was medieval claptrap. Just a group of soldiers sworn to protect the Emperor and each other on the battlefield."

"Ha! Didn't work, did it?" Fox said. "Delaunay died."

"Maybe," Sharpe said.

"You think she lied about that?"

"For a widow," Sharpe said, "she seemed to be enjoying herself too much."

"She's a tough old bird," Fox said, then paused. "She's English, of course."

"So she told me."

"Father was a naval captain, rather a good one. He captured a French troop ship in the American war and brought one of the captives home, and young Florence fell for him. Good God, perhaps you're right? The General is alive?"

"The other fellow too," Sharpe said, "Lanier? Or maybe Collignon just fed you two dead men's names." Fox did not answer, just looked disappointed. "We should have searched the house," Sharpe said ruefully.

"Too many infantry there," Fox said. "We were damned lucky to get out!"

"You only saw eleven?"

"There could be more," Fox said vaguely, "it's a damned big house."

"To protect a vineyard?"

"And there's a tunnel, Sharpe."

"A tunnel?"

"The walls of Paris have dozens of tunnels, Sharpe. Smugglers' tunnels. The duty on wine is prohibitive, so smugglers bring the wine in through tunnels, more than a hundred of them, I'm told. And I heard them talking about a tunnel. That old woman is cheating her government by smuggling wine, and she has soldiers to protect her. They're up to no good, Sharpe!" Fox announced this in a loud voice, startling some late-night pedestrians leaving the cafés on the Rue de Saint-Antoine. "No good at all! Good Lord, man, yes! Suppose the old boy is alive! How better to hide him than pretend he's dead? Where the hell are we going?"

"Home," Sharpe said.

It was well past midnight when they reached the Hôtel Mauberges, but Vignot was still awake, sitting on the front porch with one of the evicted deserters' muskets over his knees. "They didn't try to come back, Colonel," he told Sharpe.

"They won't," Sharpe said, "and we'll sleep in the stables."

"If there's a proper bed?" Fox suggested.

"Straw," Sharpe insisted, "in the stables."

"This is not a good idea, Sharpe," Fox hissed as they circled the house.

"And why not?"

"The Countess Mauberges is a supporter of the Emperor! We're like mice living in the cat's house!"

"There'll be a lot of mice here soon," Sharpe suggested.

"They can't be far off," Fox said airily, "and the Frogs are considering surrender."

"They are?"

"That's what the old lady told me. She didn't approve, of course. Called the politicians lily-livered scum."

"And what happens to the Emperor?"

"Up against a wall, take aim, fire! I hope."

Sharpe stood guard once the others had settled to sleep. He was tired, but did not want to inflict sentry duty on any of his men, who were just as weary. He walked the grounds of the Hôtel Mauberges, seeing nothing except a cat prowling in some shrubbery. The Champs-Élysées stretched off to his left and there were fires smoldering among the crude shelters. Vignot had said that French soldiers, bereft of orders or battalions, were camping there. He stared at the northern sky, hoping to spot the glow of an army's campfires reflected from the clouds, but saw nothing.

Did *la Fraternité* really exist? He doubted it. The idea was too fanciful, yet there was something equally strange about the Delaunay vineyard. Why were soldiers there? General Delaunay had been a cavalry officer, yet his house was infested with infantry. "You should sleep," Harper's voice startled him.

"Morning, Pat."

"Go and sleep, sir. I'll keep watch."

"We have to go back, Pat."

"Go back?"

"To that damned vineyard."

"Later, sir. Get some sleep."

"Wake me when they brew some tea."

"I will, sir. Now go!"

Sharpe went. Fox had commandeered the carriage with its plush bench-seat, where he was snoring loudly, so Sharpe settled for a straw bed. And slept.

Fox had vanished again by the time Sharpe woke. "He said he was going for a bath, sir," Charlie Weller told him.

"In the house?"

"No, sir. He said Paris was full of public baths. He said we should all go."

"Bugger that."

"He said some are full of naked women," Weller said coyly.

"You can go, Charlie, but I'll tell Sally."

"I've never had a bath, sir. Too late to start now."

"Women are strange about taking baths," Sharpe said, "Sally would probably like it if you were clean."

"She might, sir," Weller answered uncertainly.

"There's a pond in the grounds here," Sharpe said. "Have a swim and a good scrub."

Damn Fox, he thought. The man had gone off alone again! Then Sharpe would go too.

He left Charlie Weller with his men and with orders to stay hidden in the stables, while he and Harper went back to the east of the city, both covering their riflemen's jackets with coats, which looked strange on what was proving to be a hot day. Sharpe carried a pistol, but no other weapons, while Harper had his rifle's sword-bayonet hidden under his coat. "I'm tired of this, Pat," Sharpe said.

"I know you are, sir."

"Fox is like a bloody child! Needs a clout around the head."

"He seems a nice enough fellow," Harper said, "you know his father is a bishop?"

"I didn't."

"He told me, said he was supposed to go into the church himself, but preferred dabbling with pictures."

"And that's what he is," Sharpe said vengefully, "a dabbler. I had words with him yesterday."

"Words?" Harper sounded amused.

"I told him he'd had life too easy. He thinks everything comes easy, and it doesn't. Now the bugger's gone off on his own again!"

"You think he's really gone for a bath?"

"He's gone to look at naked women if what he told Charlie is true."

"Lucky man. And what are we looking at?"

"I want to know what's going on at that vineyard."

"And they might be expecting us," Harper pointed out, and proved to be right because as they walked up the Rue de Montreuil Sharpe saw that there were now infantrymen guarding the stone-pillared gate.

"Keep walking," Sharpe said. One of the city gates was ahead, but just before they reached it Sharpe saw a footpath between two houses that seemed to lead toward the vineyard. He followed it to find a gate in a wooden fence. The gate was not locked, and they went through to find the city wall rearing up to their right and the rows of vines stretching ahead. "Keep low, Pat."

There were soldiers on the wall, though none seemed to notice as the two men crawled between the vines. Sharpe had his telescope, not the fine one that had been a gift from the Duke, but a cheap replacement he had bought in Normandy, and he aimed the glass at the ramparts and saw that the blue-coated infantry had red collars and were armed with short swords as well as muskets. "Light infantry again," he muttered to Harper.

"Buggers will see us, sir."

"Not if we stay low."

They crawled up the row of vines, reaching a high spot from where Sharpe could gaze at the house. He saw the sentries on the forecourt. Four men. Two at the pillared porch and two pacing up and down the forecourt. There was a second large stone building beyond the house, one without windows, and Sharpe assumed it was a warehouse or maybe where the wine was made and, as he stared, he saw the big doors open and a wagon being hauled into the sunlight by a pair of horses. "Fox says he saw eleven men yesterday," Sharpe said, "but there has to be more." There were guards on the gate, at the house, and on the wall behind the house.

"We only saw a half-dozen."

"There's more than that on the wall right now," Sharpe said, glancing up at the ramparts, then pausing. He turned awkwardly and trained the telescope on the wall beyond the gate, where it curled away to the south. "That's odd."

"What?"

"It's just a wall, Pat. No firestep. But up here?" He looked again at the wall behind the Delaunay estate and saw that the firestep was made of timber and reached by stout wooden steps.

"They didn't build the wall to defend the city," Harper said, "just to raise taxes."

"And I'm guessing the General wanted to see over his part of the wall," Sharpe said, "so he built his own firestep."

"A military man might do that."

They waited as the sun moved around the city. Harper fell asleep midafternoon, and Sharpe let him doze while he continued watching the house through the clumsy glass. By evening, he thought, the sun would reflect from the glass and he would have to collapse it. The sentries were changed in the late afternoon and he saw how the men going off duty went to the warehouse. Others came from the same big doors, four to take over guarding the front of the house, four more to watch at the gate on the Rue de Montreuil, and a dozen who climbed to the city wall.

"Seeing anything?" Harper woke up.

"Bugger all, just a sentry change."

"And horsemen," Harper said.

"Horsemen?"

"Look at the drive."

Sharpe turned the glass left and saw six horsemen trotting toward the house. All were in uniform, all officers, judging by the glint of braid on their blue uniforms. Through the glass they appeared to be laughing as they spurred up the drive, and one kicked his horse into a canter. Young men, Sharpe thought, in high spirits. Servants came from the house to hold the horses, and the widow Delaunay appeared in the porch to welcome her visitors.

"Sir," Harper said.

"What, Pat?"

"Look at the wall."

A group of men and women were walking on the timber ramparts behind the General's house and more were joining them. Children ran there. A few of the women carried parasols against the setting sun, others led dogs. "It looks as if anyone can stroll up there," Harper suggested. "So maybe we can too?"

"Looks like it," Sharpe agreed. He collapsed the glass. "Let's try."

The guards at the city gate were there to enforce the tax laws and took little notice of the two men following other civilians up the timber steps onto the wall's broad walkway. "It's permitted?" Sharpe asked one of the guards.

"You're allowed till sunset."

They climbed the stairs and ambled north along the wall's wide top. The Delaunay vineyard lay to their left, while beyond the wall to their right was a rough-grassed slope leading to a scatter of houses, a church and, next to the church, a large building with a garden where folk were sitting at tables. "Lot of infantry down there." Harper was looking at the same building.

Sharpe pulled out the telescope. "Light infantry again," he said. "It's a tavern." Through the glass he could see soldiers and women sitting at the tables with wine or ale. It looked like a pleasant place to spend a summer evening.

"Why drink outside the city?" Harper asked. "Plenty of taverns much closer."

"The tax," Sharpe guessed. "The wine will be cheaper there." He still gazed through the glass and saw the tavern's back door open and a group of officers appear. Six of them, gold braid glinting in the sun's sinking light. "Good God," he said, "I swear those are the men we just saw ride up the drive."

He could not be sure, of course, but the six, still laughing, found a table, where they were joined by three young women. "They went through the tunnel," Sharpe guessed, and explained to Harper how the city wall was notorious for the tunnels that smugglers had driven beneath it to evade the high duty on wine. "Fox claims he heard men talking about the tunnel," he added.

"Dust," Harper said, then added, "over there." He was pointing east, and when Sharpe looked around, he saw that many of the folk on the wall were staring in the same direction. He aimed the glass and saw the army, or rather he saw, in the wavering circle of the lens, a mass of dark shapes above which dust hung in the air. He was gazing almost due east, which suggested the approaching men were circling the city.

"Bloody hell," he said, "it's either our lot, or the Prussians." He gave the telescope to Harper. "And the sooner they get here the better."

"Think the buggers will fight for the city?" Harper asked.

Sharpe gestured at the wall. "Fox tells me they want to surrender, but God help them if they don't. A parish choir could capture this wall."

They walked on, staring down at the back of the Delaunay house, where yards were piled with firewood and rubbish heaps. Beyond it the warehouse was built hard against the wall, with a walkway from an upper story onto the timber ramparts. A dozen infantrymen, wearing the red collars and cuffs of a light battalion, were crossing the walkway. "Far enough," Sharpe said, and stopped to gaze over the rampart. He trained the telescope again, this time seeing horsemen in the distance.

"May I, monsieur?" a voice said close to Sharpe, and he looked up to see a young French officer gesturing at the telescope.

"Please." Sharpe held him the glass.

The young man gazed for a few seconds. "The Prussians," he said in a tone of disappointment.

"Not the British?"

"They are on the city's west. You sound English, monsieur!" It was not an accusation, more an expression of curiosity.

"I'm from the *Îles Normandes*," Sharpe said.

"Ah, I have never been, but one day?"

"You should go," Sharpe said, sounding awkward to himself. "They are beautiful islands!"

"I hope I can visit." The officer looked through the glass again.

"You're stationed here?" Sharpe asked.

"For the moment. Our depot is at Péronne, so alas, we cannot go there, and our colonel brought us here. And you, monsieur? You served?"

"The navy," Sharpe said, "but if there is a fight for the city?" he left it as a question.

"I am told there will be no fighting," the young man said, sounding disappointed, then swerved the glass to the right and trained it at the tavern garden. "My colonel told us that. He says the politicians have no guts."

"You marched north with the Emperor?" Sharpe asked.

"We did, monsieur," the young man sounded proud, "and we beat the Prussians at Wavre! We took the Bridge of Christ! What a fight that was! The colonel led the charge, of course."

"Would that be Colonel Lanier?" Sharpe risked asking. He knew that the battle at Wavre had been fought on the same day as Waterloo and had been between a Prussian force and a French corps that should have marched to Napoleon's aid. Instead it had wasted its efforts, and the Emperor, bereft of their support, had lost.

"Ah! You have heard of him! Who has not, eh? And he prays for a fight! Poor man, he suffers from this disgrace." He was still gazing at the tavern's garden. "He is a great soldier, the Colonel! We call him *le Monstre!*" He said the last two words with admiration. "He's a monster in a fight! A killing machine!"

"The monster," Sharpe said under his breath, then nodded toward the tavern, "and he brought your battalion safely back to Paris?"

"He did! We are all here and eager to fight, but alas, the politicians?"

"Alas," Sharpe agreed.

"But our colonel has not given up hope," the young man said, nodding toward the tavern beyond the wall.

"He's there?" Sharpe asked.

"*Le Monstre* can afford his pleasures, monsieur, which are women, wine, and death to his enemies. I, alas, cannot afford the wine or the women. I thank you for the glass."

"I must bid you good evening," Sharpe said, taking the telescope back, "because we must leave before sundown."

They strolled toward the gate, but halfway back Sharpe trained the glass on the tavern again and saw two officers sitting with two young women at a small table. One was the fair-haired captain he had met the night before, but the other, he was certain, had to be Lanier. He was older than the other soldiers, a man perhaps in his forties with dark hair going gray at the temples and drawn back to a long queue that was held by a black ribbon. The thin face, Sharpe thought, was savage, a soldier's face, darkened by sun, scarred by war, confident and even cruel. "I'm guessing that's Colonel Lanier," he told Harper, giving the Irishman the telescope. "Table farthest right by the house."

"Who's Lanier?"

"Another of *la Fraternité*."

Harper trained the glass. "Christ, he looks a bloody handful." He stared a moment longer. "He looks like you, sir, except for that fancy tail of his hair."

"Very funny, Pat."

"He does, sir! Just like you, except his hair is tidier. Let's hope we don't have to fight him. He looks like a right bastard."

"Just like me, eh?"

"Could be your twin, sir."

They walked on, and Sharpe had the soldier's premonition that before this nonsense was done he would have to face the killing machine, *le Monstre*.

CHAPTER 9

"General Delaunay is dead, Sharpe," Fox boomed. "Gone to meet his maker, and good riddance."

"You know that, sir?"

"I spoke to two officers who saw him fall."

"You shouldn't have gone off on your own," Sharpe said.

"Oh do stop being an old woman, Sharpe." Fox had returned to the Hôtel Mauberges, where he now strolled in the garden with Sharpe. He had inspected the Dowager Countess's pictures and declared them to be dross. "Just the kind of daubs you'd expect from a coal merchant's taste," he said dismissively.

"And who were these men who saw Delaunay fall?"

"Cuirassiers. They were exercising their horses just up the road." Fox gestured westward. "Have you seen the arch there?"

"Only from a distance."

"The arch of triumph, they call it! It's not even stone! It's wood and canvas! A fake! But the Emperor ordered it made. I think we should burn it."

"And I think we must find *la Fraternité*," Sharpe offered sourly.

"It doesn't exist, Sharpe! That old bitch was right, it was medieval claptrap! And with her husband gone? Forget it."

"Colonel Lanier lives. I saw him."

"Bugger Lanier, from what I heard he's a mere adventurer."

"So probably the right man for medieval claptrap."

"Where did you see him?"

"At the Delaunay vineyard."

"Then your job, Sharpe, is to make sure he stays there. Can't do any damage with a bullet in his filthy heart, can he? I want him dead, then I can get on with my proper job."

"Listing paintings?"

Fox sneered at that. "Saving paintings, Sharpe. That may sound trivial to you, but we have an agreement with our allies to restore the stolen works, and that's important!"

"More important than *la Fraternité*?" Sharpe asked harshly.

"Bugger *la Fraternité*! A piece of romantic balderdash, Sharpe, and with Delaunay dead the balderdash died too."

"Except for Lanier."

Fox sighed with exasperation. "Lanier is a brute. But yes, maybe you're right, maybe he's a danger, but if it makes you feel safer, kill the man. You're good at that."

"Is that an order?"

"As if from the Duke himself. Who must be here soon! Maybe tomorrow? You know the craven little buggers are surrendering?"

"They are?"

"It was settled this morning. Our troops will occupy Paris, and all French forces are ordered to scuttle off to the far side of the Loire. Bonaparte has abdicated and given the throne to his four-year-old son. Shouldn't have much trouble eviscerating that little bastard, should we? But it's all flim-flam."

"Flim-flam?"

"Pure show, Sharpe, circus tricks. No one takes Bonaparte's wishes seriously. They've lost and they damn well know it. The four-year-old can concentrate on his toilet training, and Fat Louis will be king again, peace is restored, and we can all go back to sleep."

"Where is Bonaparte?"

"Skulking somewhere. Licking his wounds and hoping he isn't put against a wall and filleted. The provisional government want no part of him. Except, perhaps, his head!" Fox thought this a great joke and laughed heartily.

"So who's in charge?" Sharpe asked when the laughter subsided.

"This is France, Sharpe, no one is in charge. They're like headless chickens, a lot of clucking, feathers everywhere, and broken eggs. Don't concern yourself! Just make sure none of the bastards takes a shot at the Duke."

Fox had expected the Duke to march the British army into Paris the next day, but it was three days before Sharpe heard a band playing and recognized the tune as the "Female Drummer"; a song celebrating a girl who had marched with the British army at the very beginning of the wars. "That must be our boys," Harper said.

"Unless the Frogs use that tune."

"Let's see!"

They walked to the gate of the house where, to Sharpe's pleasure, a battalion of British infantry was marching westward. Horse artillery followed, then a long column of cavalry on tired horses. More infantry came behind. Sharpe, emboldened by the music, wore his green jacket and was greeted by a company of riflemen who saw him at the road's edge and gave him a cheer. The infantry was marching with colors flying, the flags protected by sergeants carrying halberds.

184

"It's a grand sight," Harper said.

"It is?"

"From Portugal to the heart of France, sir. We deserve this."

"But you wouldn't celebrate them in Dublin."

"Christ, no." Harper grinned. "Unless they were marching out."

A crowd of Parisians watched the soldiers, their faces dull, even sad. Some looked askance at Sharpe and Harper, doubtless wondering why they were not marching with the rest of the British. A provost must have thought the same thing because he marched to confront them. "You men don't know the Duke's orders?" he demanded brusquely.

"What orders would they be, Sergeant?" Sharpe asked mildly.

"No one, but no one, is to leave the line of march on risk of punishment."

"And you wish to punish us, Sergeant?"

The sergeant looked Sharpe up and down, seeing a tattered rifleman's jacket, French cavalry overalls, and scarred boots. Sharpe was not wearing his officer's sash, though he did have the heavy cavalry sword at his side. "Who's your commanding officer?" the provost sergeant demanded.

"The Duke, Sergeant."

"Don't be funny with me! What's your name? Both of you."

"I'm Patrick Harper, Sergeant," Harper said happily.

"A bog Irishman?"

"I crawled out of the bog over twenty years ago. And your name?"

"I'm a provost, that's all you need to know."

"I think not," Harper said. "I'm a regimental sergeant major and he's Lieutenant-Colonel Sharpe, and the only man we answer to is the Duke of Wellington. Maybe we should flog you?"

"What is your name, Sergeant?" Sharpe demanded.

"Cullen, sir." He stepped back, looking frightened.

"Back to your duty, Sergeant," Sharpe said quietly.

"Sir!" Cullen stood briefly to attention and then happily fell in with a passing battalion.

"Poor wee man," Harper said.

"This might be our lads." Sharpe was looking to his right and could see a battalion approaching with yellow facings on their red jackets.

"It is!" Harper said happily. "I can see Pigface Malone! Bugger never could keep step."

Major Morris, mounted on a black horse, led the battalion. He pretended not to see Sharpe, but Captain Jefferson, leading the Grenadier Company immediately behind Morris, made sure the pretense failed. "Grenadier Company!" he called. "Eyes left!" Jefferson saluted with his sword and Morris turned, annoyed.

"Stop that noise, now!" he snarled as the grenadiers gave a cheer.

"Good morning, Major," Sharpe called, startling Morris, who grimaced and spurred his horse on without answering. The cheering, Sharpe noted, did not subside.

One by one Sharpe's companies marched past, all saluting him and all cheering. Sharpe waited for Harry Price to appear and fell in beside him. "How are things, Harry?"

"Dire, sir. We're the worst-disciplined battalion in the history of the British army."

"Morris's opinion?"

"Frequently expressed, sir, and I'm the disgrace of the battalion."

"You are, Harry?"

"Indolent, insolent, and impudent, he told me."

"He got that right," Harper put in.

"Thank you, Sergeant," Price said cheerfully.

"Any floggings, Harry?"

"Two, not yet carried out, sir, both my men."

"Who?" Sharpe felt a surge of anger, but tried to control it.

"O'Neill and Flaherty, sir, accused of being asleep on sentry duty."

"Were they?"

"They were probably dozing, sir, but Christ! We were exhausted, and they'd marched all day. And we hadn't seen an enemy for days! Their real offense is being Irish. He hates the Irish."

"He hasn't flogged them yet?"

"Says it will wait till we're in our cantonment here, sir."

"Which is where?"

"The Bois de Boulogne, sir, wherever that is."

"Not far off," Sharpe said, "so tomorrow, probably?"

"Or tonight, sir."

"I'll stop it, Harry."

"I hope you do, sir."

"Have you seen Lucille, Harry?"

"She's fine, sir, not far behind us. And . . ." he paused.

"And?"

"Major Morris has been paying her attention, sir." Price grimaced. "Unwelcome attention, sir."

"Meaning?"

"He can't take his eyes off her, sir, and thinks she'll welcome his company."

"But nothing—" Sharpe began asking, then stopped.

"Nothing at all, sir. Of course not, sir!"

"You heard all that, Sergeant Harper?" Sharpe asked.

"Every word, sir."

"Have you ever seen a major flogged?"

"Not had that pleasure, sir."

Sharpe touched Harry Price's arm. "I'll see you soon, Harry."

Sharpe let the rest of the battalion march past him, then greeted the wives who drew up the rear just behind two baggage wagons. He was still talking to them when a rough-coated dog sped up the avenue and leaped at his chest. "Nosey!" The women laughed to see their colonel being assaulted by the big dog, who was finally calmed as the Dowager Countess Mauberges's carriage rolled to a stop. Sharpe bowed to the women in the carriage, then climbed to join them while Harper pulled himself up beside the coachman on the box. "Keep going, Pat!" Sharpe called. "Stay with the battalion."

"All the way, sir."

"Richard!" Lucille reached for him. "Thank God."

Sharpe embraced her, suddenly feeling tears in his eyes. "I hate this city," he said.

"But it's beautiful!" Lucille protested.

"Now you're here, it is."

"We'll go home soon." Lucille smiled.

"Can't be soon enough." Sharpe nodded to Sally Clayton, who was holding the baby, Patrick. "How's the boy, Sally?"

"He's your son, Mister Sharpe! He's boisterous."

"There is my house, Colonel!" the Dowager said brusquely, wondering why the carriage was not turning into the entrance.

"And we kicked out the men who invaded it, milady," Sharpe said, "and it's been cleaned up, but forgive me, I really need to stay with the battalion for a while. We'll come straight back."

The Dowager sniffed disapproval, but silently yielded and the carriage followed the Prince of Wales's Own Volunteers past the monstrous arch that the Emperor had ordered built in the Champs-Élysées. There had been no time to make a proper arch from stone, so a wooden frame had been made, then covered with canvas painted as stone. "It celebrates the Emperor's victories," the Dowager said proudly. Torn scraps of canvas fluttered in the fitful wind and birds nested at the arch's top. "You have nothing like it in London?"

"Can't build an arch big enough," Sharpe said, and was rewarded by a dig in the ribs from Lucille.

"There is news of the Emperor, perhaps?" the Dowager asked.

"I'm told he's abdicated, milady, and no one is sure where he is. And Paris has surrendered to us."

That news was greeted with another disapproving sniff. "So no more war?" Lucille asked.

"It's over, thank God," Sharpe said. "All the French troops in and around Paris have been ordered to withdraw beyond the Loire. Only allied soldiers here now."

Though that was not quite true. He had spent the last three days watching the Delaunay mansion and had seen that the soldiers camped inside the warehouse had stayed. He had looked for Lanier, but had not seen the colonel, only his men, who now mostly wore civilian clothes, though the sentries at the house still retained their uniforms. The walls beyond the house were unmanned, a place now for civilians to walk whenever they wished. Sharpe had strolled the length of the wall behind the house and had seen no soldiers on the ramparts, but plenty of evidence that the battalion of light infantry was still occupying the vineyard. He had used the telescope to gaze at the tavern beyond the wall, but the man he thought was Lanier seemed to have vanished. "Will you really shoot him?" Harper had asked one evening.

"Those are my orders."

"But would you?"

Sharpe had shrugged. Alan Fox seemed convinced that any danger posed by *la Fraternité* had evaporated with General Delaunay's death, yet insisted that Lanier must follow the General into oblivion. Sharpe instinctively disliked the order. Lanier was a soldier, and, if his reputation was accurate, a good one. Fox had admitted as much. "He was the hero of Marengo, Sharpe!"

"Hero?"

"The battle was lost, Sharpe! Austrians were advancing everywhere, and Lanier's men made a last stand that they turned into a rout. Broke half the Austrian army and turned defeat into victory. Splendid stuff! It was a makeshift battalion too, but the Emperor called them his devils!"

And Sharpe reckoned such a man deserved better than a rifle bullet fired after peace had been declared. He had carried the rifle to the vineyard every evening, but had been happy that Lanier had not shown his face. On their most recent visit to the wall above the vineyard, Sharpe and Harper had seen the smoke of the British campfires to the southwest of the city, and Sharpe had reckoned there were fewer soldiers in the courtyards behind the Delaunay house. Maybe most of the battalion had retreated beyond the Loire as the agreement between the allies and the French had demanded? And perhaps Lanier had retreated with them.

The land around the shabby arch was scrubby and dotted with crudely built shelters that made it look like an army's encampment, except there were no sentries, and too many of the folk crawling in or out of the shelters were women. "They're taking refuge here," the Dowager lamented. "Deserters and frightened folk! They should be cleaned out!"

The same sad shelters were built in the Bois de Boulogne, a half wooded area that lay beyond the Champs-Élysées and in the embrace of a sharp curve of the River Seine. Harry Price came back from his company. "We're to billet here, sir," he called up to Sharpe.

Axemen were already attacking trees to make shelters. The Dowager sighed again. "This was a royal hunting preserve and rather beautiful. I suppose that ghastly fat man is on his way back?"

"He is the King," Sharpe said.

"He is a gross disgusting creature, Colonel. He wobbles when he walks! He's a sack of offal on legs the size of tree trunks! An offense to the eye."

Harry Price had led a work party that was struggling great canvas bags from the supply wagons. "What are those, Harry?"

"His lordship likes to sleep in a tent, sir."

"His lordship?"

"Bloody Morris, sir. Best not watch them unpack his tent."

"Not watch?"

"The boys like to piss in the bag before they unpack it, sir, so it stinks."

"Carry on, Captain," Sharpe said very formally, then walked toward the growing encampment.

He found Morris sitting on a fallen tree trunk from where he contemplated the growing shelters. The major stood as Sharpe approached. He looked nervous. "Are you resuming command, Colonel?" he asked.

"I never relinquished it, Major," Sharpe said. "How are the men?"

"Spry, Colonel, spry! Tight discipline!"

"They've always had discipline," Sharpe said, "as you'd have seen at Waterloo."

"I shall always regret missing that," Morris said. His eyes flicked right to see Lucille, who had left the carriage and was now watching just out of earshot.

"Look at me, Major!" Sharpe snapped, and waited for Morris to obey. "Strange, isn't it," he went on, "that I was with them through the Spanish war and they never lacked discipline. Never lost a battle either, and I never flogged one of them."

"Ah." Morris shifted uncomfortably.

"Tell me, Major," Sharpe said, "after you had me flogged, did you find I was more disciplined?"

"It was a lesson to the company," Morris muttered.

"So I was the last man you flogged?"

"No," Morris admitted.

"Then the company didn't learn your lesson that day, did they?" Sharpe lowered his voice. "I promise you, Major, that if one of my men gets flogged then you follow them. As a lesson. And I'll flog you myself. Do you understand?"

"Discipline must be maintained!" Morris managed to find some courage. "There has to be punishment!"

"Your choice, Major, but I warn you that a flogging hurts. Hurts like hell. You won't like it."

"You wouldn't dare," Morris said.

"Sergeant Harper!" Sharpe called. "Would you say I was daring?"

"You're a mad bugger, sir, so you are."

Sharpe looked back to Morris. "There is a convention in this army, Major, that men who perform well in battle are forgiven punishment. The Duke does it, we all do it. I watched O'Neill and Flaherty in battle. They stood, Major, against the worst the enemy could throw against us, and they carried their bayonets against the Imperial Guard. I think they deserve forgiveness for that, don't you? How many lashes did you order?"

Morris looked uncomfortable again. "Just a hundred."

"And if they receive even one lash," Sharpe said, "I will personally give you two hundred."

"And I shall watch," Lucille put in. She had come closer. "Good morning, Major."

"Your ladyship." Morris bobbed his head toward her.

"And I'm taking the Light Company from you," Sharpe said.

"Taking the Light Company!" Morris sounded alarmed.

"If you don't like it, Morris, talk to the Duke."

"Come, Richard, we must take the Dowager home." Lucille held out her arm and led Sharpe away. "Will you really flog him?"

"I bloody well will."

"He's a frightened man," Lucille went on, "frightened of his own soldiers. But he's even more frightened of you." She stopped walking and turned toward him. "You are a frightening man, Richard, but you know what is strange? You are also a kind man, a good man." She stood on her toes and gave his cheek a lingering kiss, which provoked a cheer from some of the watching men. "That annoyed him," Lucille went on, amused. "Now we shall take the Dowager home."

Sharpe ordered Harry Price to muster what was left of his company. The decision to detach the Light Company had been a sudden one, but Sharpe needed another officer, and the extra men would be useful. He now led forty-three men, all of whom would have to sleep in the Dowager's stables and coach house. "Make sure they know the rules, Pat," Sharpe said when they reached the house. "No one goes into the main house, no one leaves the grounds without permission, and no fires in the stables. I'll be back later."

"You're taking time with Lucille, sir?"

"I'm taking Captain Price to the Delaunay estate."

"Shall I come, sir?" Harper asked eagerly.

"Just the captain and me," Sharpe said. He slung his rifle, made sure the sword was loose in its scabbard, and walked with Price toward the city center. Now that the allies had entered Paris he no longer needed to cover his uniform with a long coat and could wear the sword openly.

"Doesn't seem possible, does it, sir?"

"What's that, Harry?"

"We're in bloody Paris! Think how long we've fought them, and here it is! Bloody marvelous!"

"Just be glad it isn't the Crapauds in London."

"Christ, no!" Price was gazing at everything, unable to take it all in. "Beautiful buildings, sir. And the women! Oh my God."

"You've been away from women too long, Harry."

"That's true, sir. Christ, but there's money here."

"This is the smart part of the city."

"And I'm allowed here?" Price laughed. He was notoriously careless about his uniform and appearance. "That bloody man kept telling me to smarten up! I told him, sir, I've worn this uniform ever since the battle of Salamanca, and it ain't my fault it got dirty."

"You have a servant?"

"He's tried brushing it, sir, but I like this uniform. It's kept me alive. It was blessed."

Sharpe smiled. "Blessed? You, Harry?"

"It was a village priest in Spain, sir. Sprinkled it with holy water and said I'd never die wearing it."

"You went to church? You!"

"Best place to find women, sir, and they liked it if they saw you saying a quick prayer."

"And were your prayers answered?"

"Couple of times, sir." Price grinned.

"And did you explain to Major Morris that you have a holy uniform?"

"He told me to stop being stupid, sir, and have it properly scrubbed, but I don't want to wash the holy water off it."

"Keep wearing it, Harry. I like you alive."

"Me too, sir." Price brushed down the front of his red coat that bore the yellow facings of the Prince of Wales's Own Volunteers. The red coat was attracting glances, far more than Sharpe's green jacket, which could have been mistaken for a French dragoon's coat. There were plenty of other uniforms in the streets, some of them Prussian, many British, and a surprising number of French officers. "I thought they'd been told to piss off, sir?" Price remarked.

"I suppose some live here, Harry."

"They don't much like us, do they?"

"Can you blame them?"

"I suppose not. Oh my God!" Price stopped abruptly, staring at a young woman. "God in his heaven, sir, but you can see clear through that skirt!"

"It's a fashion, Harry."

"It's a bleeding miracle!"

Sharpe pulled him onward. "The French army is supposed to be on the other side of the Loire," he said, "but I'm worried a battalion might have stayed in the city. We have to keep an eye on it, and you'll be commanding a picquet to do that."

"A picquet against a battalion, sir?"

"Think of it as an opportunity, Harry."

He showed Price the massive elephant, which, in the daylight, looked even more dilapidated and sad, with chunks of plaster fallen away and streaks of dirt down its pale flanks. "Why did they make it?" Price asked.

"The Emperor ordered it."

"But why a bloody elephant?"

"God knows."

Price was distracted by another pretty girl and Sharpe drew him on to the Rue de Montreuil, past the gate to the Delaunay estate, and so to the city wall. A guard tried to stop them, saying the wall's fire-step was private property, but Sharpe growled that the allies now commanded Paris and were free to go wherever they wished. The guard reluctantly stepped aside, and Sharpe and Price climbed the steps. "That's new," Sharpe said.

"New, sir?"

"Trying to keep us off the wall." He thought about it. "It's because they've got something to hide," he went on, "and they didn't need to hide it before the city fell." That explanation made sense to him. "I believe there's a battalion of light infantry in those buildings." Sharpe pointed to the house and the huge warehouse, "and they're here to make trouble." There was little sign of any men, but in one of the yards between the warehouse and the wall there were a dozen blue coats hanging out to dry. "And there's a tunnel under the wall," Sharpe went on, "that we think goes to that tavern." He pointed and saw that the tables in the inn's garden were crowded. He took out his telescope and trained it, seeing men drinking and eating. He moved the glass to the table nearest the door and stiffened. "Look," he gave the glass to Price. "Look at the table nearest the door on the right. There's a man I want you to recognize." It was the man he supposed was Lanier, no longer in uniform, but unmistakable.

"You mean the fellow with the queue?" Price asked, meaning the horsetail of dark hair that Lanier wore.

"That's him."

"Christ, he looks unpleasant," Price said.

"I think his name is Lanier, he commands a battalion."

"Horrible-looking bugger. He reminds me a bit of—"

"Don't say it, Harry."

"I was only going to say he reminds me of the devil, sir. My aunt had a picture of Satan in a book, and that fellow has the same eyes. And oh my God, now he's looking at us!"

Sharpe took the glass back, trained it, and saw that Lanier also had

196

a telescope, which was aimed directly at him. The Frenchman raised a hand. He could have been brushing a scrap of dirt from his coat, but Sharpe suspected it was a greeting. He collapsed the glass, troubled that Lanier had noticed them, and he supposed he and Harper had been too obvious in the last three days. "Bugger," he said softly.

"Sir?"

"I have a feeling the bastard knows who I am, Harry, and he might even have sent men to follow Pat Harper and me home."

"That wouldn't be difficult, sir. Can't miss Pat Harper. Built like a prizefighter."

"Cheer me up, Harry."

"We could go to a public bath, sir? Sergeant Weller says there are naked women in them."

"So I'm told, Harry, so I'm told."

They walked back to the gate, down the steps and then back through the city. "I want the house watched, Harry," Sharpe told him, "just a small picquet, and I also need a picquet on the gate of the Mauberges house. Six men. Just to guard against intruders."

"Of course, sir, but you think that's necessary?"

"I hope it isn't, but that bastard Lanier worries me."

"Anyone who looks like Satan should worry you, sir. What do we do if they try to get in?"

"Shoot the buggers."

No one tried to enter the grounds that night. Sharpe relieved Price some time in the middle of the night and later in turn was relieved by Harper. Sharpe went to the house and wearily climbed to the bedrooms to find Lucille. "You were standing guard?" she asked, surprised.

"Half the night, yes."

"Are we in danger?"

"Officially no, but possibly. Do you know of an officer called Colonel Lanier?"

"The hero of Marengo! Everyone knows of him."

"It's possible he's kept some troops in the city."

"Because of *la Fraternité*?"

"Which you know nothing about," he reminded her.

"Which I know nothing about."

"And yes," Sharpe said, "*la Fraternité*. And I suspect he knows about me."

"And will kill you?"

"If I frustrate him, yes."

Lucille shuddered. "Lanier is a dangerous man."

"So am I," Sharpe said lightly.

"You will take care, Richard!"

"I always do. That's why I'm still alive. But right now I'm going to sleep." He had undressed and had just climbed into the bed when there was a sudden commotion downstairs, starting with a pounding on the front door. Sharpe instinctively sat up, and Lucille put a calming hand on his shoulder. Sharpe heard Vignot shouting to ask who hammered on the door. "If it's one of my men," Sharpe said, "I'll kill him."

He heard the door open, then another voice boomed in the great hallway. "Oh, the west wind doth blow, And the small rain down doth rain. Oh that my love were in my arms, And I in my bed again." It was Alan Fox, who paused briefly. "Sharpe! Get up! I need you!"

Sharpe groaned. "I must go." He turned and kissed Lucille.

"Go," she said.

He started to dress, pulling on his shirt and then the French cavalry overalls.

"Sharpe!" the voice boomed. "Get your duds on, we have business! Dalliance must wait!"

"Bloody man," Sharpe said. He pulled on his boots, slung his coat, sash, sword belt, and scabbard over his shoulder, paused to kiss Lucille again, then went out to the corridor.

Fox, grinning, was waiting in the downstairs hall. "Did I interrupt you, Colonel?"

"Go to hell, Fox."

"My passage thence is booked and paid for, Sharpe. The Peer wants to see you."

"The Duke?"

"You know another peer?"

"At this time of the morning?"

"Time and tide wait for no man, Sharpe. Ah! Good man!" The last words were to Vignot, who had evidently been commanded to bring a glass of brandy, which he did with an ill grace. Fox drained it, tossed the glass back to the steward, and dragged the front door open. "It ain't far, Sharpe. The Peer, like you, prefers his luxuries."

"He didn't in Spain and Portugal."

"We are back in civilization, Sharpe. Come."

A light rain had started, which did not improve Sharpe's mood. He dragged on his green jacket, buckled the sword belt, and followed Fox's long strides up the drive. "Have you killed Lanier yet?" Fox demanded.

"Not yet."

"You think he's left Paris?"

"I thought he had. Didn't see him for three days, but he was there last night."

"And you didn't shoot him?"

"He was too far away. I saw him through a telescope."

"The Peer won't be pleased," Fox said, then hailed Pat Harper, who was in charge of a six-man picquet at the gate. "You were quite right, Sergeant! Up in the bedrooms!"

"Bastard," Sharpe growled.

"A pleasure to serve you, Mister Fox," Harper said. He was grinning, but his face suddenly changed to anxiety. "You remember that officer who borrowed your telescope, sir?"

"I do."

"I think I saw him." Harper gestured through the barred gate at the rough grassland beyond. "Him and three men, sir."

"In uniforms? Armed?" Sharpe felt a cold shiver.

"No uniforms, sir, but they were carrying a long bundle. Could easily have been muskets."

Sharpe looked at the picquet. "McGurk?"

"Mister Sharpe?"

"You know where my rifle is kept?"

"Yes, Mister Sharpe."

"Run and get it, would you?"

"Sharpe! The Duke is waiting!" Fox insisted.

"Where is he?"

McGurk had already left and Sharpe turned to see Fox was pointing north across the grassland to where some evidently lavish houses were protected by a high brick wall and tall stands of trees. "He's in one of those houses," Fox said, "and we need to leave now."

"Not without my rifle," Sharpe said.

"I'll come too," Harper offered.

"Follow us, Pat," Sharpe said, "but stay back. You're sure it was the same fellow?"

"Positive. Floppy hair."

"That was him."

"Sharpe—" Fox began, but got no further.

"We'll leave in a moment, Mister Fox," Sharpe interrupted him, "but not without a rifle."

McGurk brought the rifle and Sharpe frustrated Fox a further moment by insisting on loading it. He took his time, wrapping a bullet in its leather patch and, once the weapon was primed, he pulled the cock all the way back so the rifle was ready to fire. "We can go," he said.

"Thank the good Lord," Fox said, and pulled the gate open. "It's not far! There's a back gate to the Peer's house. He has coffee!"

"Is that why you're in a hurry?"

"I like my coffee hot," Fox snapped. "This way!" He headed off across the grass, which was dotted with the crude shelters put up by the homeless and by the scared folk who had fled from the advance of the allied armies. "Most of these folk fled the Prussians," Fox explained.

"Not from us?"

"The Duke enforced discipline, Sharpe, but the Prussians behaved like beasts. They treated the civilians badly."

"As revenge for what the French did to Prussia?"

"So they say. Do keep up, Sharpe."

Sharpe was looking ahead, trying to find the men Harper had seen, but there were far too many places to hide. Each shelter, most of which were made from branches covered with turf or sometimes canvas, was a shadowed cave in which a man could find concealment. Sharpe was carrying the rifle low in his right hand, ready to bring it to his shoulder, and he felt that prickle of apprehension that he knew from the battlefield. Fox was following a well-worn path through the grass, and Sharpe plucked his left elbow. "This way," he said, steering Fox off the path into the longer grass between the shelters.

"We're in a hurry, Sharpe!" Fox protested at the detour. "The Duke will not be happy if we keep him waiting."

"You want to die fast? Trust me."

Fox looked disgruntled, but reluctantly stayed with Sharpe as he wove a random course through the shelters. The enemy, Sharpe knew, would be watching the path, and he had been walking directly toward their ambush, if indeed there was an ambush. But how had they known he would cross this ground? And was there even an enemy? He paused, searching the land to the north. There were about three hundred yards between his position and the high garden walls, and if Pat Harper's suspicion was right there were four men from Lanier's battalion somewhere in that space. "Can we move, Sharpe?" Fox asked impatiently. "It's raining and you're dawdling!"

"Stay with me, Fox."

"If I must," Fox grumbled.

Sharpe started walking, only to be checked by Fox's hand. "That's the way we want to go, Sharpe," Fox insisted, pointing to the large houses.

Sharpe looked that way, seeing a gate in the far wall, but he also saw the glint of light reflected from metal as a man moved in one of the closer shelters. The man must have thought Fox was pointing directly at him because he was aiming a musket. Sharpe shoved Fox hard to one side, making him stumble, and brought the rifle to his shoulder. Rifle versus musket, he thought, and damn the man. A shot sounded and a billow of smoke obscured the man in the shelter, but Sharpe's rifle was already aimed and he pulled the trigger. A woman screamed nearby and children started crying. Fox was sprawled on the turf as Sharpe started running. He slung the rifle and drew the sword. He had seen one man whose hasty musket shot had evidently gone wide, so where were the others? Harper was shouting at his men to advance and had shaken them into a loose skirmish line. Sharpe was running toward the man who had fired and who now appeared to be dead, or at least unmoving in the mouth of the shelter from which the smoke had cleared, then the sharp crack of a rifle made him look to his right and he saw three men running back toward the city. Two more rifles fired and one of the men stumbled, but was helped by his companions. "Let them go, Pat!"

The man who had first fired was indeed dead, struck messily in the head by Sharpe's bullet. Fox peered at the corpse, then turned away, retching. "That was a good shot," Harper said.

"You sound surprised, Pat."

"Astonished, sir."

"What worries me," Sharpe said, "is why they ambushed this place. Almost as if they knew we'd be on this path."

"They must know where you're quartered," Fox said, "and it's no secret where the Duke is staying. They must have assumed you'd go to see him."

McGurk dragged the corpse from the shelter and began searching the man's pockets. "Look at the seams of his coat too," Sharpe said, knowing that many soldiers concealed small valuables in the seams.

"What do we do with his body, Mister Sharpe?" McGurk asked.

"Leave it here, but take his musket and cartridge pouch. And Pat, thank you."

"Shall we see you the rest of the way?"

"We'll be fine. Just guard the Dowager's house. Mister Price will relieve you. And thank you all, lads!"

"We can go?" Fox asked impatiently.

"We can go," Sharpe said.

To meet the Duke.

CHAPTER 10

The Duke was at a dining table that was covered in papers. He was, as Fox had said, in a bad mood. "That firing just now," he demanded curtly, "was that you?"

"The second shot was," Sharpe said.

"And the first?"

"Missed me, Your Grace."

The Duke grunted almost as if he regretted that news. "And the second shot?"

"Killed the man who fired the first shot, Your Grace."

Another grunt. The Duke, Sharpe thought, looked older. There were flecks of gray hair at his temples and his face was lined. Maybe it was tiredness. Suddenly he looked directly at Sharpe, his eyes as keen as ever. "It's your belief there's a French battalion still in the city?"

"I was told it was a battalion, Your Grace," Sharpe said carefully, "but it could be fewer men."

"Where?"

"An estate on the Rue de Montreuil. A vineyard, Your Grace."

"Delaunay's estate?"

"Yes, Your Grace."

"The Prussians tell me you're dreaming, Sharpe."

"The Prussians, Your Grace?"

"They're now occupying the eastern part of the city. Mister Fox told us of the Delaunay estate, and the Prussians sent men to search the place. They found nothing."

"They certainly were there," Fox put in.

"And it's your belief that General Delaunay headed *la Fraternité*?" the Duke asked Fox.

"I'm certain of it, Your Grace."

"He's dead," the Duke said curtly. "His body was identified at Waterloo."

"His widow," Fox went on, "seems to have inherited his ambitions."

"I met her a year ago," the Duke said, "English, yes?"

"From Hampshire," Fox said.

"Daughter of Rear Admiral Sir Philip Latimer, Your Grace," an aide offered.

"Unpleasant woman," Fox said.

"I rather liked her," the Duke said, looking at his aide. "Maybe a dinner invitation?"

"Surely unwise, Your Grace?" Fox suggested. "The woman's an avid Bonapartiste."

"Her father," the aide put in diffidently, "was snubbed at court. I believe the family felt the insult was grievous."

The Duke dismissed the explanation brusquely. "The woman's hardly likely to assassinate me at dinner. She has manners, Fox." He picked up a cold slice of toast and spread it with butter. "So who was the man who shot at you just now, Sharpe?"

"One of Colonel Lanier's men, sir, from the battalion the Prussians claim doesn't exist."

"You're sure of that?"

"Certain, Your Grace."

"How can you be sure?"

"I've been watching them, Your Grace. We recognized the officer leading the men."

"There was more than one?"

"Four of them, Your Grace."

"A prisoner would have been useful."

"They fled, Your Grace. And a pursuit through the city might have meant a running fight."

"Which we do not want," the Duke said heavily. "Parisians are excitable, so let's keep them calm. Gordon," he was talking to the aide, "Request the Prussians to keep a close watch on the Delaunay place."

"There's a tunnel, Your Grace," Sharpe said, "from the Delaunay cellars to a tavern outside the wall."

"Those damn tunnels," the Duke growled. "Tell them that, Gordon."

"Of course, Your Grace."

The Duke bit into the toast and grimaced at the taste. "So does *la Fraternité* exist still?"

"Yes," Sharpe said.

"No," Fox said at the same time.

"No? Yes? Which is it?"

"It's medieval claptrap," Fox said.

"Medieval claptrap can kill you, Fox."

"Delaunay's dead and *la Fraternité* died with him, Your Grace."

"You know that?" the Duke demanded.

Fox hesitated. "I surmise it, Your Grace. The man Collignon promised me a list of *la Fraternité*'s members and there were just two names on the list. Delaunay and Lanier."

"Not much of a fraternity," the Duke said caustically.

"Their purpose," Fox went on, "was to protect the Emperor in battle and avenge his death if that should occur."

"And he's alive," the Duke said, "somewhere. Any news on that?" The question was addressed to the aide, who shook his head.

"Somewhere to the south of Paris, Your Grace, but we still have no definite news."

"So what you're saying, Fox," the Duke looked back to the tall man, "is that *la Fraternité* was never the conspiracy we believed it to be?"

"Indeed. We exaggerated its potential, Your Grace, for which I must take the blame."

The Duke grunted at that, then looked at Sharpe. "You concur, Colonel?"

"I believe *la Fraternité* is a danger so long as Lanier is alive."

"I know of Lanier," the Duke said, sounding disapproving, "one of their more capable officers."

"His battalion was in Delaunay's corps," Fox said, "and from what I understand he took a few men to help at the widow's estate. They're smuggling wine, not trying to start another war."

"Then why shoot at Colonel Sharpe?" the Duke asked.

"Colonel Sharpe, Your Grace, has a talent for aggravating people. I ordered him to watch Lanier, and I suspect Lanier resents that."

"You agree, Sharpe?"

"I think Lanier's a dangerous man, Your Grace, and that so long as he's in the city he must be watched."

"Then we'll let the Prussians aggravate him," the Duke said. "They must watch him. We have other fish to fry."

"The *Musée Napoléon*?" Fox inquired eagerly.

"The Louvre, indeed. That's your responsibility, Fox?"

"Indeed, Your Grace."

"And if we clean it out we're likely to cause resentment?"

"I'm sure of it, Your Grace."

"Yet the Foreign Office insists it must be done." The Duke glared at Sharpe. "An order, Sharpe. Resume command of your battalion and assist Mister Fox. You will keep order at the Louvre."

"The Louvre, Your Grace?"

"The damned French," the Duke snarled, "stole half the paintings of Europe and hung them in the Louvre, which they insist on calling the *Musée Napoléon*. We have a treaty obligation to return those paintings to their rightful owners. Your men will remain at the Bois de Boulogne, but you will take them to the Louvre every day, dawn to dusk, and keep order. There will doubtless be protests, maybe even attempts to stop us, but your battalion will keep order."

"Yes, Your Grace, but . . ." Sharpe broke off.

"But?" the Duke demanded coldly.

"If we're to guard the place, sir, wouldn't it be easier if we billeted there?"

The Duke grimaced. "The Parisians, Sharpe, consider the Louvre a temple to man's highest achievements. If I quarter a battalion of redcoats in their damned temple they will be offended, and we are doing our utmost to keep Parisians calm. So try very hard not to start a war, Sharpe. Break some heads if you must, but I don't want the streets of Paris running with blood."

"I understand, Your Grace."

"Do you, Sharpe?" The Duke's tone was now distinctly unfriendly. "You know what order is?"

"I hope so, Your Grace."

"Threatening to flog Major Morris is not conducive to good order, Sharpe."

"No, sir." Sharpe was standing to attention now, his eyes fixed just above the Duke's head.

"Did you really promise to flog him?"

"I did, Your Grace."

"You won't, that's an order. You understand?"

"Of course, Your Grace."

"If majors can be flogged, then colonels can be hanged, and I will have order!" The Duke sounded angry. "There will be discipline! No thieving, no rape, no provocation! We will give the Parisians no reason for insurrection!"

"Other than stripping the Louvre," Fox muttered.

"Then what do you suggest, Fox?" the Duke demanded brusquely.

"Make sure the theatres reopen," Fox said, "slash the duty on wine, and start importing the goods the Parisians have been missing. Coffee, for a start."

"We are not the civil power, but we shall lean on them. By God, we shall. Now go!" Sharpe followed Fox from the room into the hall, where the tall man stopped. "No coffee left for us!" he complained. "But at least we can get on with cleansing the *Musée Napoléon*. You've been there, of course?"

"No," Sharpe said, collecting his rifle from the corporal serving as the doorkeeper.

"Good God, Sharpe, how long have you been in Paris? At least a week and you haven't visited the greatest art collection in Europe?"

"It skipped my mind, Fox."

"Well, we're going now." Fox strode down the garden, through the gate, and followed the path southward. Sharpe followed, but when he reached the Dowager's house he called out to Pat Harper. "Come with us, Pat! We're going to look at art."

"Oh joy," Harper said. He hefted his volley gun.

"You won't need that!" Fox insisted.

"I never leave it behind, sir," Harper said, "on account of this town being full of Crapauds."

They followed the river eastward, past the Élysée, the Tuileries gardens, and so to the Louvre. "It was a fortress once," Fox said, "then became a palace, now it's a museum."

"*Musée Napoléon*," Sharpe said, reading a sign on the wall.

"We'll change that soon enough."

They climbed steps to a grand pillared entrance hall and Fox led them confidently on into the museum, then abruptly stopped in front of a statue. "Isn't that sublime?" he said in awe. The statue showed a woman sitting with her young son standing between her knees. She had a long, sad face.

"Looks like a mum and her son," Harper said. "Pity she couldn't afford to buy him any clothes."

Fox ignored the remark. "That," he said, "is the Madonna and child by Michelangelo."

"Who?" Sharpe asked.

"Michelangelo. Surely you've heard of him?"

"Never," Sharpe said.

"I have," Harper said proudly.

"Good man," Fox said enthusiastically.

"Who is he?" Sharpe asked.

"You must remember him!" Harper said. "Spanish lad who joined the second battalion of the Rifles after Talavera. Miguel Angelo."

"Miguel did that!" Sharpe gazed at the statue. "Bloody hell! He was a damned fine shot, I do remember that."

"Poor bugger was gut-shot at Salamanca," Harper went on, "and died. And by Christ he could use a chisel!"

"Michelangelo," Fox said patiently, "was an Italian genius of the Renaissance. He painted the ceiling of the Sistine Chapel."

"So not the same man, sir?" Harper inquired.

"Not the same man, Sergeant. And the statue will have to be returned. They stole it from a church in the Kingdom of the Netherlands."

He paced on, making notes as he went and calling out enthusiastically to Sharpe. The names meant nothing to Sharpe. Caravaggio, Titian, Rubens, but Fox became ever more excited. "Look at that!" he said, stopping in the largest exhibition hall and pointing up to a vast painting. "Raphael!"

"Is he the one at the top?" Sharpe asked, gazing upward.

"That is Christ, Sharpe," Fox said, still patiently. "Raphael was the painter. It shows the Transfiguration." He gazed up at the canvas in rapture and Sharpe suddenly understood that this was the task that truly interested Fox. *La Fraternité* was doubtless important, but had distracted Fox from his real passion. Was that why he had insisted *la Fraternité* no longer existed?

"She's got a great bum." Harper was gazing at a woman in the lower part of the painting.

"Bit too big for my taste, Pat," Sharpe said.

"You always did like them skinny, sir."

"That might well be the most famous painting in the world," Fox pointed out indignantly.

"And no wonder!" Harper said reverently.

"And it was stolen, from Rome." Fox waved a hand around the immense gallery. "Half of these works are stolen, and they all have to be taken away and sent back home."

"The Frogs won't like that," Sharpe said.

"They will not, which is why your battalion will guard the work."

Fox walked to the massive Raphael and fingered the frame. "Bolted to the wall. We'll need ladders, trestles, and tools. I'll find the workmen, Sharpe, and you protect them."

"Might need more than one battalion," Sharpe commented. "It's a bloody big place, and has a lot of entrances."

"The Duke will provide," Fox said airily, then turned as an indignant man with a beard strode toward them.

"Weapons are not allowed in the galleries!" the man shouted.

Harper unslung his volley gun and pointed it at the approaching man. He might have spoken in French, but his tone was unmistakable. "Don't shoot, Pat," Sharpe said quietly.

"You will leave." The man confronted Fox. "Now!"

"*Barrez vous!*" Fox retorted. "You are no longer in charge of this museum. I am!"

The loud voices had attracted a small crowd, who started shouting encouragement to the bearded man, who was insisting that the English soldiers leave the gallery. Sharpe unslung his rifle and, during a pause in the argument, cocked it. The sound echoed from the high stone walls. "You," he spoke to the bearded man, "will do what he says. *Foutez le camp!*" He rammed the rifle's barrel into the man's belly.

"What are you doing here?" the man asked, but in a quieter tone.

"Looking for stolen art," Sharpe said.

"Dear God, this is the greatest collection of art in the world! It is civilization! You cannot spoil this . . ."

Sharpe prodded the rifle. "We can do what we like. We have the guns, you don't."

"The art belongs here." The man was almost in tears. "Paris is the center of civilization, monsieur! It is only right that the world's greatest art should be assembled—"

"Should be returned to their rightful owners," Sharpe snarled. "Now bugger off!"

"I must protest—"

"Pat! If he says one more word," Sharpe was speaking in French, even though Harper would not understand, "put seven bullets into that woman's bum."

"Sir?"

"Sharpe!" Fox protested.

"Aim the volley gun at her bum," Sharpe said in English.

"Sir!" Harper grinned and turned the gun to the enormous painting, and the threat was enough to make the bearded man back away. The growing crowd pressed forward, but Harper's size and Sharpe's face held them at bay.

"Go!" Sharpe snarled at the bearded man. "Go! Now!"

"We should go too," Fox said as the indignant man beat a hasty retreat. "Lunch, I think."

"You're finished here?" Sharpe asked.

"For the moment." Fox plainly feared the crowd's hostility. Sharpe did too, but the threat of the cocked rifle and Harper's volley gun kept them away. Some followed the three soldiers as they left the museum, shouting that the artworks belonged in France.

Fox led them east, stopping shortly after they left the museum to point at a great stone arch that stood on the far side of an open space. "Bonaparte's *arc de triomphe*," he said.

"I thought he was building that in the Champs-Élysées?"

"That's a new one. Twice the size of this one. See the four horses on top? They were stolen from Venice and have to go back there. We shall be busy!"

Sharpe gazed up at the four horses. "What are they made of?"

"Bronze. And they're ancient." Fox strode off, forcing Sharpe and

213

Harper to follow him. "The Venetians stole them from Constantinople," Fox called back.

"Why don't we send them back there?"

"Because we like the Venetians and we don't like the Turks, of course. Lunch!"

"You'll want a crane for those horses," Sharpe said, following Fox down the street, "so I suggest asking the Royal Engineers."

"Engineers? Why?"

"Those horses must weigh a couple of tons each."

"Royal Engineers, good idea! You can arrange it?"

"Better that you ask the Duke, Fox. He has an engineer on the staff."

"Dear God! You're a lieutenant-colonel, can't you just give the fellows an order?"

"Not without the Duke's sanction. You'll need wagons too, and draft horses."

"If you say so, Sharpe. Ah, this place serves splendid food. Capital!"

Harper stopped before Fox could enter the restaurant. He was staring across the street with a look of pure joy on his broad face. "God save Ireland," he murmured, "but would you just look at that!" He was gazing at a long wagon that had a high cage filling its bed. The wooden side of the wagon was painted with the word *scimmie*, which meant nothing to Sharpe, then he saw movement inside the cage and a shape darting up a ladder. "It's a monkey!" Harper exclaimed, delighted, then crossed the street to join the small crowd around the wagon. Sharpe followed, to see there must have been twenty monkeys in the enormous high cage. They were scampering up and down a half-dozen long ladders, all of the little beasts dressed in small red waistcoats. One snatched a hat from a bystander, which provoked a cheer, dragged it through the bars, then carried the hat to a high beam where it rubbed the hat between its legs.

"Trained monkeys." Fox had followed Sharpe. "Vulgar little beasts."

"They're funny."

"Oh, look at him!" Harper said in delight as the monkey peed into the stolen hat. "Oh, that's marvelous!"

"You've surely seen monkeys before?" Fox demanded.

"Never a one, sir," Harper said.

"Too many," Sharpe said, "in India."

"They're good little fellows," Harper said, laughing.

"Thieving little bastards," Sharpe said, remembering how the monkeys at Gawilghur had loved to steal whatever they could lay their hands on. Gawilghur! Morris had been in command of the company then, and he had shirked the attack on the breach. Sharpe just remembered the savage fighting, the shrieks of the enemy hacking at him with curved blades, the hammering of muskets as he clambered up the breach, the thump of the howitzer shells sending scraps of stone and shards of iron through the flame-shot air. He remembered too the terrified monkeys sheltering in the casemates, gibbering in fright. He had pitied them. "We should get some lunch, Pat."

"I could watch these little fellows all day!" Harper said.

"You can stay and watch," Fox said, "but we're eating."

"They'll be here after lunch, Pat," Sharpe said.

"You think so?"

"Look at the size of that wagon! Must be a bastard to move."

"I suppose you're right, sir."

Sharpe hesitated as he followed Fox into the restaurant. For a start it was plainly expensive, with linen-covered tables beneath glittering chandeliers. It was crowded too, the diners all dressed expensively and a number of them, Sharpe noted, wearing gold-braided French uniforms. A hush descended on the large room as the three entered. "They don't like us," Sharpe murmured to Fox.

"I'd be surprised if they did!" Fox said, then summoned a waiter with a click of his fingers. "A table for three," he demanded. "They know me here," he added to Sharpe, "and the food is excellent."

A table was found, though Fox complained it was too near the door leading into the kitchen, but there was no other, so the three settled on spindly chairs. Sharpe propped his rifle against the wall, while Fox ordered wine. "A Sancerre to begin, I think? Will that suit you, Sharpe?"

"Thank you." Sharpe had his back to the wall and could see the hostile glances that were thrown their way. There were no other British soldiers in the room, while at least a quarter of the diners were in French uniform. Sharpe assumed they lived in the city and so had not retreated beyond the Loire.

"And I shall order," Fox went on. "Is there anything you particularly like, Sergeant?"

"Black pudding," Harper suggested enthusiastically.

"They do a very decent *boudin*, we can start with that," Fox said, "does that suit you, Sharpe?"

"Whatever you suggest, Fox." He was uncomfortable. He and Lucille had eaten in restaurants in Caen, but never in any place as delicately sumptuous as this, and he was aware of the animosity in the room, especially from a nearby table, where six men sat, three of them in uniform, who made no attempt to hide their scorn.

"Roast chicken would be good," Harper said. He seemed to be enjoying the restaurant, looking eagerly at the paintings and the pillars. "This is grand," he added.

Wine was brought, and then a second bottle, and Fox ordered food. "You don't mind garlic?" he asked his companions. "The dish is rich."

"Garlic's fine," Sharpe said.

"I'll eat anything," Harper said, "so long as there's a lot of it."

"You'll like it," Fox said. "*Poulet Marengo*."

"Marengo?" Sharpe snarled.

"It's said Napoleon's cook devised the dish after the battle. There weren't too many ingredients available, so he used what he could find. Chicken, oil, garlic, eggs and crayfish."

"Sounds horrible," Sharpe said.

"We should have Chicken Waterloo," Harper said happily. "Bloody great chickens roasted with potatoes."

Sharpe was thinking of Lanier, the so-called hero of Marengo. "At least the Prussians will have to deal with the bastard," he said.

"What's that, Sharpe? Deal with who?"

Sharpe had not meant to speak aloud and he shrugged as he answered. "Lanier."

"And you're right, the Prussians will cook his goose. He's not our problem anymore."

"He was this morning," Sharpe said.

"And he failed." Fox tasted the second bottle of wine. "Splendid!" He gestured for the waiter to pour. "*La Fraternité* is dead, Sharpe. It died at Waterloo. My impression was that Lanier has a handful of men at Delaunay's house and they're there simply to protect the widow while she cheats the revenue agents."

"Your impression?"

"I was in that cellar. I saw eleven men at most. The Prussians are more than capable of containing them, while our problem now is to remove thousands of paintings and sculptures from the Louvre without sparking an insurrection. Paris labors under the misapprehension that it's the city of civilization and that they deserve to have the world's treasures, and they won't like us taking some away."

Harper was not listening. Instead his face had reddened and he was gazing blankly at the wall, looking furious. "What is it, Pat?" Sharpe asked.

"Just listen," Harper said. His fists were clenched.

The men at the next table were talking loudly, and one of them, a tall man in a French infantry jacket, louder than the rest. It was plain he wanted to be overheard, yet the language he spoke was strange. Fox was listening too. "I speak seven languages," he said, "but I don't know that one."

"Gaelic," Harper said angrily.

A burst of laughter sounded from the table, and Sharpe saw that the tall man was interpreting his words for the benefit of his companions. He caught one word of the translation, *traître*. "Traitor?" he asked quietly.

"The bastard is saying I'm a traitor to Ireland," Harper growled, "that any true Irishman should be fighting the British."

The tall man had plainly overheard Harper's accent and could see that his words had infuriated the big man in his rifleman's jacket. "Calm down, Pat," Sharpe said.

"Oh, I'm calm, sir."

"A fair number of Irish rebels are in France," Fox said.

"You'd think they'd want to be a long way from our army," Sharpe suggested.

"I doubt the Duke cares about them," Fox said, then turned to look at the neighboring table where the tall man was again speaking too loudly. Most of the restaurant had gone silent, aware of the small drama, and ready to be entertained.

"Jesus Christ!" Harper swore. He pushed his chair back.

Sharpe put a restraining hand on Harper's arm. "I'll shut him up, Pat."

"My battle, sir," Harper retorted. He stood, and the tall man, maybe surprised by his victim's sheer size, fell silent.

Harper crossed to the table and stood over the tall man. "Hunger, you bastard," he growled, "drove me to this army, and you're spoiling my meal."

The man appeared to be about to answer, but Harper leaned down and seized his head. He held the man's skull with a massive left hand and pulled his jaw wide open with his right. He tipped the man's head back, then spat into his open mouth. "One more word," he added, "and I'll pull your tongue out." He closed the man's mouth and came back to the table, where he sat, looking pleased with himself. "The trouble is," he spoke quietly, "that he's right. We should be fighting against the British."

"Pat . . ." Sharpe began, though he was uncertain of what he could say to console the Irishman.

"So it's hunger that drives you?" Fox intervened.

"Have you ever been hungry?" Harper retorted. "Tried to live on a tenant farm with a bastard landlord and too many children to feed?" He paused to watch the table of six men leave. "It's all right for him." He nodded at the tall man's back. "He was no country lad out of Donegal. He had an education. He's an officer. But for most of us? There's no escape, sir." He was staring at Fox. "You starve or you serve. And we're bloody good at serving."

"True," Sharpe said vehemently.

"When the Duke's in trouble," Harper said, "he calls on the Irish. He knows who fights hardest."

"I thought he called on Sharpe," Fox said lightly.

"Mister Sharpe's probably Irish, sir." Harper looked at Sharpe. "Just doesn't know it."

"My father could have been Irish, I suppose," Sharpe said.

"You didn't know him, Sharpe?" Fox asked.

"Not sure my mother did either, Fox. But I hope she got paid for his pleasure."

"Ah." Fox looked embarrassed, and was saved by the arrival of the *boudin*.

Harper stood and looked through the window. "Monkeys are still there," he said, cheerful again. "What does *scimmie* mean?"

"Italian for monkeys," Fox said, "I suppose the fellow is Italian?"

"Do they have monkeys in Italy?" Harper asked.

"They have beautiful women, Sergeant, fine painters, and good opera, but monkeys? Alas, Italy is bereft of monkeys, so I suspect the fellow imported them."

As they left the restaurant Sharpe gave Harper a handful of small coins. The Irishman looked surprised. "What's that for, sir?"

"There are two fellows collecting monkey-money, Pat." Sharpe nodded at the crowd still crammed about the great cage. "Drop those in their hats."

"Ah, you're a grand man, sir, for an officer."

"Then join us in the Louvre. No more than an hour, Pat."

Harper went happily to watch the monkeys, while Fox led Sharpe back to the huge museum. "What I must do, Sharpe," Fox said, "is note down which paintings we take, then your fellows can take them down. We can start tomorrow?"

"We'll have to close the museum."

"Is that necessary?"

"It's necessary," Sharpe said. He suspected there would be a riot if Parisians knew that their plundered riches were being taken from the Louvre's walls. "How many paintings are we talking about?"

"That's what I'll determine this afternoon," Fox said, "but I suspect thousands."

"Thousands!"

"Maybe two thousand paintings? And God alone knows about sculptures, but maybe another two thousand. I'm told the Prussians

220

are sending a delegation to discover items stolen from the German states, and doubtless the Austrians and Russians will identify more when they arrive, but we'll begin with everything stolen from Italy."

They were standing beside the painting Fox had called the *Transfiguration* and Sharpe looked up at the vast canvas. "Do we send back the frames?"

"Good question, Sharpe!" Fox said enthusiastically. "I think with the big ones we can take them from their stretchers. We still have to get them down, though. Can you find the museum's ladders?"

"I need to alert my battalion."

"Find me ladders first, there's a good fellow."

Sharpe wandered the marble halls for a time, marveling at the sheer grandeur of the museum with its pillared walls, sweeping stairways, and painted ceilings. He finally discovered a door that led into a drab passageway and from there a staircase that went into the cellars. There was no gilding down here, just gloomy stone walls dating from the time when the Louvre had been a fortress. The vast space was now crammed with storage rooms and workshops. He asked a man where he could find ladders. "There aren't any," the man replied.

"You must have ladders. How do you hang the pictures?"

"We did have ladders! But the director ordered them turned to firewood."

"When?"

"This morning." The man flung open a door and pointed toward a heap of splintered timbers. "There." He gave Sharpe a triumphant look. "Every ladder, firewood now."

"Why?" Sharpe asked.

"Because the director ordered it, monsieur." The man grinned, plainly happy that the perfidious British had been thwarted. Sharpe shrugged and left him, climbing back to the marble halls to discover

Harper gazing enthralled at the *Transfiguration*. Fox was wandering the gallery and making notes.

"No ladders," Sharpe told him. "The director had them broken up."

"Then find ladders, Sharpe!" Fox said absently.

"I'm bringing the battalion here first."

"The battalion? Why?"

"To protect you while you make a list of the bloody pictures."

"Good thought, Sharpe. And ladders! Can't do a damn thing without ladders."

"Ladders cost money," Sharpe said, "and I'm skint." He was far from skint, but he would be damned if he spent his own money. He held out a hand. "The Duke must have given you some cash?"

"He did," Fox admitted, "for necessary purchases."

"Ladders are necessary."

"I suppose so," Fox said reluctantly and felt in a pocket. He brought out a handful of gold coins, all of them twenty-franc pieces. "One should be enough," he suggested, "more than enough?"

Sharpe reached out and took three Napoleons, the gold coins showing the Emperor's head. "This will do," he said, "you'll have your ladders." He put the coins in his pouch and beckoned Harper. "We have to go back to the battalion, Pat."

The two men walked westward through the city. Sharpe grumbled most of the way, ignoring Harper's enthusiastic tales of monkey mischief. "It's a bloody waste of time, Pat. We shouldn't be wasting time with paintings, we should be killing Lanier."

"You think the Italian fellow would give me a monkey?"

"You'd have to feed it, and the bugger would shit everywhere."

"Sounds like a recruit. We could give him a green jacket!"

"Lanier's not going to give up. I should talk to the Duke."

"Why don't you?"

"Because he'll tell me to do what I'm told and leave Lanier to the Prussians."

"Sounds sensible to me. Corporal Collins's wife would do it."

"Do what?"

"Make a small green jacket! She's handy with a needle."

"You do not need a monkey," Sharpe growled. They were passing the Dowager's house. "Go in there, Pat, and have Price bring the Light Company to the battalion. We're moving out."

"Going where, sir?"

"The bloody Louvre."

He walked on alone, brooding. Lanier had dared send men to the Champs-Élysées with orders to kill Sharpe! And if he tried once, Sharpe thought, he could try again. And doubtless Lanier knew where Sharpe was quartered, and Sharpe had just stripped away the men guarding that house. And all for some goddamned paintings!

There were pictures in Lucille's house in Normandy. There was a drawing of the church where she had married her late husband, and two paintings of the river meadows that her mother had done, while up in the bedroom, there was a gloomy picture of the Virgin Mary that Sharpe hated, but Lucille would not move. She claimed it was very old and very precious, and Sharpe had pointed out that the château needed a new roof, in which case . . . ? That suggestion had gone nowhere and the Virgin Mary stayed, looking down disapprovingly on the bed. Sharpe had seen the excitement on Fox's face as he noted down which paintings to remove, and he suspected Fox was hoping to remove a couple for his own benefit. Was that true? And could one of them pay for roofing slate? He bridled at the thought. He had been a thief in his youth, but now? It's just loot, he told himself, but still the thought repelled him. Lucille, he knew, would never approve of it and, damn it, he was an officer now.

223

Sergeant Reddish was with the sentries guarding the battalion's encampment. He grinned at Sharpe. "Good to see you, Mister Sharpe."

"Thanks, Lennie. It's damn hard being honest, don't you think?"

"Sir?"

"Never mind." Sharpe paused. "Any of your men speak Italian?"

"Most can't speak English, sir."

I asked for that, Sharpe thought as he strode toward Morris's tent. The major was seated at a camp table going through papers, but stood nervously as Sharpe approached. "Colonel," he said warily.

"We're moving," Sharpe said, "pack up, be ready to go in an hour."

He left Morris looking astonished and walked to the tables where at least half the battalion's officers were seated over the remnants of a long-ago lunch. "We'll be moving," he said, "one hour! And do any of your men speak Italian?"

"Italian?" Captain Brown said, as if he'd never heard of such a language.

"Pat Bee does," a lieutenant said.

"Pat Bee?"

"Patrick Bee, sir. He was in the draft that arrived after the battle, with . . ." he paused and jerked his head toward Morris's tent.

"I know Private Bee," Sharpe said, "send him to me and start packing up."

"He's in Harry Price's company, sir."

"Then he'll be back here soon."

"Where are we going, sir?"

"The Louvre."

One hour later the battalion paraded and Sharpe walked their ranks, noting that though their uniforms were shabby, the muskets were clean. Harry Price had brought the Light Company back and Sharpe kept most of them, but sent Price and fifteen men back to the Dowager's house with orders to guard it. "Tell Lucille I'll be in the Louvre," he told Price, "and for God's sake keep her and the boy safe."

"I will," Price said.

"And you can forget about posting a picquet to watch the Delaunay estate," Sharpe went on, "the Prussians will do it instead."

Morris was mounted, and Sharpe wished he had his own horse back. "Pat," he said to Harper, "did Fox tell you what he did with our horses?"

"He said they were safely stabled."

"I want mine."

"Me too!"

"I'll talk to him," Sharpe said, then turned as Harry Price approached with the frail-looking Private Bee, who looked terrified as he approached Sharpe. "Sir?"

"You speak Italian, Bee?"

"Yes, sir."

"Good Italian?"

"Yes, sir."

"When did you learn it?"

"My mother's Italian, sir," Bee said. "Irish father and Italian mother, sir."

"Good boy," Harper put in.

Sharpe took one of the twenty-franc Napoleons from his pouch and gave it to Harper. "You'll go with Sergeant Harper," he told Bee, "and tell an Italian we're buying his ladders. He's using them to show off some monkeys, but we need the damned ladders more than the monkeys do." He looked at Harper. "You'll need men to carry the things, Pat, so you can take the rest of the Light Company. And you do not, repeat not, bring back a monkey."

"Wouldn't dream of it," Harper said.

"Come with us to the Louvre, Pat, and then take Private Bee and get the ladders. Nothing else!"

"Nothing else, sir," Harper said solemnly.

Sharpe called for Captain Jefferson, his most aristocratic officer, and sent him to tell General Haskell that he was moving the Prince of Wales's Own Volunteers to the Louvre. "I'm buggered if we bivouac here," Sharpe explained, looking around the damp woodland, "so we'll billet ourselves in the museum." The Duke had expressly forbidden such a move, but Sharpe reckoned there was little sense in leaving the galleries unguarded during the night. "Tell Haskell it's at the Duke's request, and then find the Duke and tell him it was Haskell's idea."

Then the battalion marched. Sharpe led, with Harper and Bee beside him. "The funny thing, Private Bee," Sharpe said as they marched eastward, "is that less than twenty years ago I was a private too. Now I'm sending messengers to the Duke of Wellington."

"And buying monkey ladders," Harper put in.

"And my point, Bee, is that you can do the same!"

"Me, sir?"

"If you're smart, keep your nose clean, why not? Become a sergeant, learn to read. The army needs good officers."

"I can read, sir."

"You can?"

"My mother taught me, sir."

"You're halfway there," Sharpe said. "Is there still a pub called The Saracen's Head on Bow Road?"

"Yes, sir."

"I was told my mother lived there," Sharpe said.

Bee was no fool. He looked surprised, even blushed. "She . . ." he began, then tactfully stopped.

"She was, Bee. And one day you and I will have a drink in there. You're buying."

"Yes, sir."

Sharpe made sure Price and his few men went back to the Dowager's house, then marched on into the city. He heard the crisp sound of marching boots behind him and knew the battalion was putting on a show for the Parisians. They were proud. They might carry battered weapons and wear ragged uniforms with mud-spattered shoes, but by God they had defeated the best the Emperor could throw against them.

Sharpe remembered the morning of the battle, when stray shafts of wan sunlight had slanted onto the southern ridge where the Emperor had paraded his army. It had been a glittering mass of uniforms, of breastplates and lances, of cannon and bayonets. That parade had been designed to terrify the waiting redcoats; a display of an Empire's magnificence, plumes, blades, banners and glory, while the massed drums hammered out their threat of imminent death. Even Sharpe, who had fought the Emperor's men more often than he cared to recall, had been awed by the sight, by the massed pennants of the lancers, the rows of huge cannons, the horde of infantry shouting *Vive l'Empereur* whenever the drums paused.

But when that glittering mass of men had crossed the valley, they had met the ragged battalions from London's slums, from the English shires, from Ireland, from the Scottish wastes and the Welsh hills, and the ragged men had hammered the glory of Napoleon's Empire into the mud, and now Paris was seeing their conquerors. And those conquerors were still ragged and dirty, but Sharpe was proud of them. They were soldiers, and they had fought through hell itself to reach their enemy's capital. He turned to watch them and saw they were marching proudly behind their battle standards, their steps driven by a half-dozen drummers. "God," he said to Harper, "they look good."

"They look horrible, sir, so they do, but I wouldn't want to fight them."

"I pray you don't, Pat."

"So long as you're not one of them," Harper said, "be a pity to kill you, sir."

Sharpe half smiled, then turned the battalion in to the courtyard of the Louvre. He halted them, climbed the few steps of the entrance, and looked out at his men. "This is the *Musée Napoléon*," he said, "and the Crapauds will tell you it's the most important museum in the world. Our job is to guard it! The bloody Frogs stole paintings from all over Europe and we're sending them back where they came from. It's possible that will make people angry and they'll try to stop us. You stop them! You do not fire at them unless they shoot first! Musket butts and bayonets should be enough. You'll live and sleep in the museum, where you will light no fires! Nor will you use charcoal to put mustaches on paintings! You will behave your bloody selves!" He saw there were several civilians listening to him. "You treat this place with respect!"

"They won't," Morris said dourly as they went into the vestibule.

"You like discipline," Sharpe growled, "so keep it. And put a half company on every door out of the museum. The rest can meet me in the *Salon des Empereurs*."

"Which is where?"

"Where you'll find me," Sharpe said.

He knew he was being both rude and obdurate, but for years he had nursed a hatred of Morris. Even as a private Sharpe had recognized the falsity of the man, the fear that lurked behind the bravado. Many officers feared their own men, but Morris was terrified of his redcoats, and responded by trying to make the men fear him more. Instead they just hated him, and Sharpe found himself wishing that Morris did demand another flogging, because then he would scour

SHARPE'S ASSASSIN

the flesh off Morris's back and leave him screaming. He could almost feel the pleasure.

"Ladders are here, sir!" A cheerful voice interrupted his thoughts and he turned to see Harper striding through the vestibule. "But your man wants them back, so we're just renting them."

"Well done, Pat."

"Nice fellow, that Italian!"

"Private Bee spoke to him?"

"They jabbered away like a pair of monkeys, sir. Good as gold, that lad."

A burst of laughter sounded from the museum's entrance and Sharpe walked toward it.

"So where do you want the ladders, sir?" Harper asked loudly.

"Just stack them somewhere, Pat," Sharpe said, then stopped.

Private Bee was surrounded by half the Grenadier Company, who had been posted to guard the main entrance, and on Bee's shoulder was a monkey.

"Sir . . ." Harper began.

"For God's sake, Pat!"

"Just a wee monkey, sir."

"Didn't I tell you not to get one?"

"I didn't, sir! That's young Patrick's monkey!"

"God help us," Sharpe said, "what do you feed it?"

"The fellow says vegetables, fruit, and nuts. And Charlie will eat bugs too. The little bugger loves a cockroach!"

"Charlie?"

"That's what we call him."

"After Major Morris?"

Harper grinned for an answer, then snapped his fingers. "Hey Charlie! Come here!"

The animal looked at Harper then leaped, not to obey the summons, but evidently in a bid for freedom. Private Bee made a lunge for the leash, failed, and the monkey scuttled across the floor, pursued by yelling redcoats. Sharpe tried to step on the leash, missed, and the animal raced into the galleries. Sharpe followed to see Charlie leap and scamper up the ornate gilded frame of the painting by Raphael. Reaching the top he edged to the center of the frame, from where he gazed down at his pursuers. Then, apparently deliberately, he peed copiously.

"God save Ireland," Harper said, "but the little bugger just peed on Jesus."

"I'll pee on you—" Sharpe began, but just then a shot sounded from beyond the museum's entrance. "Oh, Christ!" he swore and ran back to the big doors, pushed through, and saw horsemen milling in the courtyard. "Who fired?" he bellowed at the men of the Grenadier Company at the top of the steps.

"Not us, sir," Sergeant Reddish said, looking anxious.

"Sounded like a rifle," one of the men said.

"But he missed, Colonel Sharpe," another voice said coldly, and Sharpe turned to see the Duke of Wellington had dismounted and, accompanied by staff officers, was coming toward him.

"Your Grace," Sharpe said, coming to attention.

"It seems you are right, Sharpe, someone wants me dead." The Duke was not pleased.

Sharpe looked to his left and saw a patch of thinning smoke drifting northward at the top of a tall building. "Sergeant Reddish!"

"Sir?"

"A dozen men, there!" he pointed.

"A little late, Colonel?" the Duke asked sarcastically.

"Don't want the buggers waiting for you to leave, Your Grace."

"Carry on, Sergeant," the Duke said, then grimaced at Sharpe. "You have some explanations to make," he spoke as he strode into the vestibule, and then stopped, staring for a second or two at the monkey, which was now perched on the head of a statue and was busy scratching itself. "You are fond of disobeying orders, Sharpe?" He started walking again.

"I am, Your Grace?" Sharpe asked, lost for anything else to say.

"I gave no orders for your battalion to billet itself here."

"Mister Fox is eager to move the work on, Your Grace. It seemed sensible to work around the clock."

The Duke grunted, strode on. "Yet the permanent presence of a redcoat battalion in this building is likely to provoke discontent."

"They're already discontented, Your Grace."

Another grunt, then the Duke stopped and rounded on Sharpe. "The Prussians insist there is no battalion hiding at the Delaunay place."

"They might have moved, sir," Sharpe said uncertainly.

"And the man who just took a shot at me? He's one of them?"

"I wouldn't know, Your Grace. But I believe Colonel Lanier will keep trying."

"So find him, Sharpe, these damned pictures can wait. Your only task now is to find Lanier and his men. Kill them, Sharpe. Put an end to this nonsense. That's an order you will not disobey."

"I can use the battalion, Your Grace?"

"It appears I can't stop you." The Duke walked back toward the vestibule, then suddenly stopped. "I almost forgot. You're to dine with me tonight, Sharpe. Seven of the clock. Bring your lady."

"Yes, Your Grace."

And Sharpe felt a sudden quick joy because, just like Charlie the monkey, he was off the leash.

PART THREE

The Fight

CHAPTER 11

"Bleached linen," Lucille said, buttoning the white shirt at Sharpe's neck, "brand new and clean."

"You bought it here? In Paris?" Sharpe asked.

"In Lisieux. Monsieur Ballat made it. He made this too." She handed him a jacket cut from a cloth so dark green that it almost looked black. "I had it made from the measurements of your old jacket. Monsieur Ballat made all the uniforms for the Count. He's a very good tailor."

"And doubtless not cheap," Sharpe grumbled as he pulled on the jacket.

"Good clothes are never cheap." Lucille stepped away and looked at Sharpe. "It looks so good, Richard! The cloth is English! Lambswool!"

Sharpe looked at himself in the bedroom's full-length mirror. The jacket did look good; tight fitting and, above all, clean. "I don't need a new uniform," he grumbled. "I've worn the old one for the last five years. Longer, probably."

"Yes, dear," Lucille said, "and you cannot wear it for dinner with the Duke."

"There's no oak leaves," he complained. His old jacket, now strewn across a chair, had a wreath of oak leaves sewn onto one sleeve. They denoted that Sharpe had been in a Forlorn Hope, and he was proud of it.

"Jeanette will take them from your old coat. Now try these on." She held out a pair of trousers made from the same sleek cloth.

"I'm wearing these overalls," Sharpe insisted. He had stripped the leather-reinforced overalls from a dead French cavalry officer, and the bloodstain down the right thigh had never been wholly washed out.

"They're baggy and threadbare!"

"And they're mine," Sharpe said stubbornly, "they're comfortable."

"And they need mending," Lucille said patiently. She stepped to him and undid the twelve silver buttons of the coat. "Take that off, and your overalls, and try them on."

The trousers fit just as perfectly as the coat. "I feel like an idiot," Sharpe said. "I don't want to go to his bloody dinner anyway!"

"But I do," Lucille said, "and we will. The Countess has said we can use her carriage, and Pat says he'll be coachman."

"You don't like mutton," Sharpe pointed out.

"It's not my favorite."

"And it will be mutton," Sharpe said, "it always is. With a vinegar sauce."

"And I will eat it and be grateful," Lucille said placidly. "It's kind of the Duke to invite us!"

"He's never kind," Sharpe snarled, "he's planning something, and these trousers are too tight."

"They're supposed to be tight, but you can't wear those boots!"

Sharpe pulled on the boots anyway and stamped his feet. "Dead man's shoes, darling," he said, "best for a soldier."

"Even dead man's shoes can be cleaned."

"They just get dirty again."

"You can't dance in them!"

"I can't dance anyway," he said, then looked alarmed. "There won't be dancing tonight!"

"I doubt it," Lucille said sadly, "just dinner."

"Mutton and vinegar!" He pulled on his new coat, secretly rather pleased with it. "Jeanette will sew on the oak leaves?"

"She'll do it right now."

"And put it back on the old coat before tomorrow?"

"Of course." Lucille sighed, then handed Sharpe an officer's scarlet sash. "It is silk," Lucille said, "and I sewed it myself."

Sharpe looked at himself in the mirror, seeing a stranger; a man in a smart tailored uniform with the epaulettes of senior rank, and he thought about his very first uniform, the red coat of the 33rd over white breeches that had slowly turned pink as the red dye of the coat leaked in the rain. "In a month or two," he said, "I'll never wear a uniform again."

"Of course you will! There will be dinners and parties to attend!"

Sharpe grunted at that, then unwound the sash, unbuttoned the jacket, and gave it to Lucille. "And what are you wearing?"

"Something you will like," Lucille said. "We don't need to leave for another hour, which gives you time to shave."

Sharpe muttered something about having mislaid his razor, then dressed in his old uniform, less the oak wreath badge that Lucille had snipped from the sleeve, then toured the grounds to check on the picquets. He found Harper washing the Countess's carriage. "Must look smart for you!" the Irishman said. The carriage was a barouche with seats for four, a high box for the driver, and a leather hood that could be raised over the back seat. "The leather's all rotten," Harper said, "so pray it doesn't rain."

"All bloody nonsense, Pat. And why does the Duke want us at dinner anyway?"

"He probably doesn't want you, sir, I expect he wants Lucille there. The man's no fool."

And Lucille, whom Sharpe found when he went to dress, looked like a vision, in a tight-fitting dress of gray silk, cut low. "I've got a better idea," Sharpe said, "we stay here."

"Dress, Richard," she said patiently, then hung a string of pearls around her neck. "The Countess loaned me the pearls," she explained.

"The Duke should have invited her."

"She wouldn't accept. She is loyal to Bonaparte."

"Silly old bat."

"Richard! She has been so kind!"

"And you?" he asked. "You're not missing Bonaparte?"

Lucille sighed. "He was always very gracious to me, and he was a clever man. Is a clever man. But so many died, Richard, and he always asked for more men, more deaths. I am sad for France, but the Emperor has killed enough men. We must have peace. Now are we ready?"

Sharpe dressed in the new uniform that Lucille had ordered made in Normandy, and he wondered what small treasure she had sold to pay the tailor's bill. "This was good of you," he said, patting the faded oak wreath on his upper sleeve before hanging the massive sword on its slings.

"It was my pleasure, Richard." She raised a hand and stroked his cheek. "You haven't shaved!"

"No time," Sharpe said.

"Stubborn man," she said, then handed him his shako. "I brushed it," she said, "and polished the badge. And we should leave."

"God save Ireland!" Harper exclaimed as they came down the big curving staircase. "I didn't recognize you!" He gave an ironic bow. "Your carriage awaits."

238

Harper sat on the box, the seven-barrel gun beside him. "I should have brought my rifle," Sharpe grumbled.

"I have mine," Harper said.

"There's no danger, is there?" Lucille asked.

"Not with me here, madame," Harper said happily, patting the massive volley gun, then taking the reins. "Nice evening for a drive!"

The sun was low in the western sky, a cloudless sky, as the carriage rolled smartly eastward. Folk watched them pass, and Sharpe could not resist a secret pleasure in riding in an open carriage with a beautiful woman at his side. "I used to envy folk in carriages," he said.

"And steal from them too!" Harper put in, turning the horses north. "Not far now!"

"We could have walked," Sharpe grumbled.

"In these shoes?" Lucille lifted a foot to show a delicate pair of silver shoes.

"Rue du Faubourg Saint-Honoré," Harper announced as he turned left again.

"When did you learn to drive?" Sharpe asked.

"Never did, sir! But how hard can it be?"

Redcoats stood guard outside the Duke's house, which was another mansion, even larger than the Countess's house. "Ah," Lucille said, recognizing the house, "the Hôtel Grimod de La Reynière. The Duke likes his comfort."

"He deserves it," Sharpe said. The carriage rattled past an ornamental pond where two fountains played, then the wheels made a crunching sound on the driveway's gravel and Harper hauled on the reins to stop under a high portico, where a corporal of the 1st Foot Guards stepped forward to open the door and lower the steps. Sharpe jumped down first to assist Lucille. "God help me," he muttered. He thought he would rather fight a battle than face this evening.

"You'll enjoy it, Richard!" Lucille said brightly, then put her arm in Sharpe's and drew him to the front door that was held open by a redcoat.

"I'll be waiting for you, sir!" Harper called, moving the carriage away.

Sharpe took a deep breath and stepped into a hall of senior officers in laced and braided uniforms. Almost all had sashes bearing bejeweled decorations, and one man, in the severe dark blue uniform of Prussia, wore a star with more diamonds than a Piccadilly whore could have earned in a lifetime. The Prussian was talking to the Duke, who looked as if he was not enjoying the conversation. There were perhaps a dozen men in the room, almost all of whom Sharpe recognized and almost none of whom he felt comfortable with, but then a door at the room's far end opened and Major Vincent entered and, seeing Sharpe, raised a hand in greeting. Vincent's entrance evidently gave the Duke a chance to break off his conversation with the Prussian and cross to Vincent's side. They spoke briefly, then Sharpe heard the Duke's great neigh of laughter, which prompted Vincent to beckon Sharpe. "You'd best come with me," Sharpe said to Lucille.

"I'll wait here," Lucille said, entirely at home in a room of beautifully uniformed officers.

Vincent left the Duke and led Sharpe into a small parlor. "It's good to see you, Sharpe! How are you?"

"Confused."

"As are we all. The Emperor has abdicated, the King is coming, but no one really knows what the hell is happening. But you've done well!"

"I have?" Sharpe sounded dubious. "*La Fraternité* still exists."

"Does it?" Vincent was equally dubious. "We're inclined to believe that Fox is right, and that *la Fraternité* died on the battlefield with

General Delaunay. And the Duke wants to reward you for rescuing Fox from Ham. With this." He opened a flat black case no bigger than a cavalryman's sabretache and took from it an enameled red cross that hung from a length of red ribbon. "Stand still, Colonel." He hung the cross around Sharpe's neck, then took from the case a glittering silver star that he pinned to Sharpe's left breast. "Congratulations, Sharpe."

"For what?"

"The Czar of Russia has just awarded you the Order of Saint Vladimir, second class."

Sharpe had to laugh. "The Czar? He doesn't know I exist!"

"He will."

"And why me?"

"You want the truth?"

"Please."

"The Czar sent the order requesting the Duke to give it to a worthy recipient, so the Duke offered it to Colonel Lygon, who refused it."

Sharpe could not resist glancing in the mirror above the mantel to see the medal reflecting the candlelight from his breast. "Why would he refuse this?"

"Because it's second class, and the colonel thought it degrading. Lygon, of course, is a cavalryman, so you can't expect much sense from the man, and the star of the second class is a much better-looking decoration than the first, but Lygon was insulted, so the Duke said to find another recipient. I suggested you and the Duke agreed. Are you insulted?"

"Far from it, Major. Lucille can wear it."

"It's a tawdry thing, of course, but it gives you certain privileges in Russia. You can whip the serfs and piss in the Volga, that sort of thing."

"I'll manage without those."

"Then I suggest we join the others and, by the way, the widow Delaunay is invited tonight."

"Bloody hell," Sharpe responded. "Is Fox here too?"

"Good Lord, no! This is military men only."

Sharpe, curiously pleased at the star of Saint Vladimir, followed Vincent into the reception room, where a knot of officers had gathered around Lucille. He was going to join them, but the Duke caught his eye and beckoned. "Congratulations, Sharpe."

"On the medal, Your Grace?"

"You deserve it."

"I hope the Czar agrees."

"He said to give it to a brave man, so yes, he'll be pleased." The Duke snapped his fingers and a passing orderly swerved with a tray of champagne glasses. "Take one, Sharpe," the Duke ordered.

"Thank you, Your Grace."

"I particularly want you to meet Colonel Kippen of the Prussian army. If you operate in the east of the city you'll need a liaison officer, and Kippen's your man."

"Very good, Your Grace."

Lucille had managed to detach herself from her admirers and, seeing the silver glitter on Sharpe's chest, glided across the room to join them. "Your Grace." She curtseyed to the Duke, then fingered the star. "Richard, what is it?"

"It's a bauble, milady," the Duke answered, "but a well-deserved one." The last five words were spoken in what sounded to Sharpe like perfect French. He also noted that the coldness had gone from the Duke's voice.

"Yet I am told your army does not award medals?" Lucille stayed in French.

"It's not our custom, milady, but I am thinking that every man at Waterloo deserves one, so perhaps we will change the policy."

"Oh, you should, Your Grace! Soldiers are simple souls who like baubles that reward their valor," Lucille said mischievously, "and Richard is very proud of his oak leaves."

"Those, milady, are not awarded for bravery, but for insanity." The Duke gave Sharpe a harsh look. "Why don't you introduce yourself to Kippen, Colonel?"

"Of course, Your Grace."

Colonel Kippen was the Prussian with the elaborate star on his broad chest. He had a scarred face, a large mustache, and a nose that had evidently been broken. "I am an infantryman," he told Sharpe, not bothering with any formal greeting.

"As am I, Colonel."

Kippen leaned closer to Sharpe. "That is the Duke's woman?" he spoke heavily accented English in a hoarse whisper.

Sharpe looked back at the Duke, who was smiling as Lucille spoke. "She's my woman," Sharpe said.

"Ah! So you are a lucky infantryman! She's English?"

"French."

"The spoils of war, eh?"

Sharpe had no idea what to say, so sensibly said nothing.

"I am to be attached to you," Kippen said, "perhaps you find me a woman like that?"

"She's one of a kind," Sharpe said coolly.

"And you are Colonel Scharf, yes?"

"Sharpe," Sharpe said, still cool.

"*Scharf* is our word for sharp," Kippen said, evidently amused, "and you are the man who says there is a battalion of infantry in that vineyard?"

"I believe so."

"Then I must tell you we searched the house and found nothing except an unpleasant old woman."

The unpleasant old woman chose that moment to arrive, her right arm in a sling made from black cloth on which she had pinned her dead husband's red ribbon from which hung the glittering badge of the *Légion d'honneur*, and, in case anyone misunderstood her allegiance, she also wore an enameled brooch of violets, Napoleon's favorite flower. She paused in the doorway, her gaze scornful. "Oh good," she said loudly, "no fat man here. I feared you would invite him."

"Fat man?" the Duke asked stiffly.

"The gross Louis, supposed King of France."

"I believe His Majesty arrives in two days' time," the Duke said, "and welcome, madame."

The widow Delaunay sniffed at that. "The last time I dined with Your Grace," she said, "the wine was atrocious. Undrinkable!"

"I trust you will enjoy this evening's selection, madame."

"I've brought you a gift of wine," she said, "my people are unloading it now. There is a cellar?"

"You are too kind, madame," the Duke said, discomfited. He nodded at Captain Burrell. "Do show madame's men the way to the cellars, Captain. And the rest of us, I think, can go through." He offered his arm to Lucille and led the way through newly opened doors to a candlelit dining room where a long table glittered with silver and crystal. There were small cards with names indicating who should sit where, and Sharpe found himself between Kippen and General Halkett. Lucille was seated to the Duke's right, and Madame Delaunay to his left. "The Peer always prefers women's company," Halkett murmured to Sharpe.

"Can you blame him, sir?"

"He deserves the best, though I'm not sure I'd wish that widow woman on him." Halkett, a decent man, grinned suddenly. "Did you really threaten to flog your new major?"

"I did, sir."

"He complained to me!" So that, Sharpe thought, was how the Duke had discovered his threat.

"I'm sorry, sir."

"But why, Sharpe? Fellow seemed harmless enough."

"A long time ago, sir, he had me flogged for something I didn't do, and he knew it."

"Good Lord, Sharpe! You were flogged?"

"I was, sir, and it hurt."

"Rather the point of it, yes? But it doesn't seem to have hurt your chances of promotion."

The conversation paused as an orderly placed a soup plate in front of Sharpe and another ladled a dark transparent liquid into the bowl. A third poured a glass of white wine into one of the three glasses in front of Sharpe.

"Consommé of pheasant," the Duke's steward announced, "accompanied by Muscadet."

That provoked a snort from the widow. "No dumplings?" she asked.

"Dumplings, madame?" the Duke inquired.

"Sparrow dumplings. Very good with consommé. Larks are better if you can get them. You wrap them in batter, then boil them. Delicious."

"Would you really flog Morris?" Halkett asked in a low voice.

"Happily, sir."

"Yes, I told the Duke I thought you would. He was amused too."

"He didn't sound amused to me, sir."

"He wouldn't, would he? I say, this soup is good."

Sharpe was just lifting the first spoonful when an enormous crash resounded through the house, startling the diners. "What the devil?" The Duke looked up, frowning.

A splintering sound followed, as if a door was being broken down, and then an ominous rumble that sounded like thunder. There was another, smaller crash, a shout of alarm, and a moment later Captain Burrell appeared at the door, hurried to the Duke's side, and stooped to his ear. The Duke listened, grimaced, then looked at Sharpe. "Colonel, I hate to disturb your dinner, but men have broken the outer cellar door. Tell them to stop their damned noise!"

"With pleasure, sir," Sharpe said, standing. Lucille looked alarmed, but Sharpe was secretly pleased to escape the formal dining room and pleased too that the Duke had again turned to him in an emergency. He beckoned to Captain Burrell. "You can show me the way?"

"Yes, sir."

Burrell led him into the hallway. "They're delivering wine, Colonel, and decided to use the outer cellar door, but it was locked. They just hammered it down!"

Sharpe followed Burrell to the side of the house where a wagon and two horses stood. The men, he could see six of them, were rolling barrels down a plank ramp from the bed of the cart. Two more men were then rolling the barrels down more planks laid over the cellar steps, and the crashing sound was repeated as each barrel landed on the stone floor. "Stop it!" Sharpe shouted, seizing a man's elbow. "You carry the barrels down to the cellar."

The man whose elbow he had seized simply turned and tried to drive a fist into Sharpe's belly, but Sharpe moved into the man, making him miss, and brought up his knee. The fellow collapsed, groaning, and Sharpe hammered a fist down onto his head. "I said stop it!"

246

A second man took a pace toward Sharpe, then a hard voice sounded. "Enough, Sergeant!" The man stopped. The man who had spoken was at the foot of the cellar steps and now climbed toward Sharpe. "There is a problem, monsieur?" he asked.

"The Duke wants the noise to stop. So stop whatever you're doing."

"We are bringing the Duke a gift of wine!" the man said, now standing on the driveway.

The man was dressed in a plain brown coat over black breeches, but there was no mistaking his military stance. His face was in shadow, but Sharpe had no trouble recognizing the saturnine face he had seen so often through his telescope. It was Colonel Lanier. "Twelve barrels of the finest red wine," Lanier said, sounding amused. "The Duke does not want the gift?"

"The Duke wants the gift given in silence," Sharpe said. "Your men can carry the barrels down the steps."

"Ah! We disturb the Duke's dinner?"

"Carry them!" Sharpe ordered. "Carefully!"

"You heard him," Lanier said, "so tiptoe down the steps, boys, and be careful!"

Sharpe pushed past Lanier and went down into the cellar where three barrels lay on the stone-flagged floor. A lantern gave small light. Sharpe rolled one of the barrels close to some racks filled with wine bottles and heaved it upright. Something struck him as strange as he heaved the barrel, but there was no time to think about that because Lanier had followed him. "You would like the barrels there, monsieur?" He spoke in English.

"Here," Sharpe said. "And you are?"

"I am Henri Fellion, one of Madame Delaunay's vintners. And you, monsieur?"

"Sharpe, Colonel Sharpe."

"This wine is four years old, it should be drunk now. Madame was generous. 1811 was a very good year for wine!"

"You broke the door down," Sharpe said accusingly, still trying to identify what had struck him as odd about the heavy barrel.

"I am sorry, monsieur, but no key was available. We can send men to make a repair?"

Captain Burrell had come down the stairs and now watched as the planks were taken from the steps and the next barrels were carried down into the cellar. "He is a boy," Lanier said to Sharpe, nodding at Burrell.

"You have the same boys in your army."

Lanier half smiled, as if recognizing that Sharpe was not such a fool as to believe his tale of being a vintner. "We have them. They're decorative, brave, and useless. They die fast."

"So who is useful?"

"Men who know their business, Colonel. Give me officers who fought in the ranks."

"So you served, Monsieur Fellion?" Sharpe asked.

"We have no choice, Colonel. We have conscription."

"And let me guess," Sharpe said, "you were a good sergeant."

Lanier laughed. "I was an excellent sergeant! Even the generals were scared of me."

"The Emperor too?"

"We were all scared of him, Colonel. And you, Colonel? You haven't been scared of sergeants?"

"Only when I was in the ranks, and I killed that bugger."

Lanier checked. "You were in the ranks?"

"Just like you."

"I thought the English did not promote men from the ranks?"

"Only the mad ones," Sharpe said.

"Mad?"

"The ones who fight like monsters," Sharpe said.

Lanier smiled, recognizing his own nickname. "And you are a monster, Colonel?"

"I kill monsters, monsieur, it's what they pay me to do."

The two had moved closer to the lantern. Lanier's men had finished bringing the barrels to the cellar and now watched them alongside a very uncomfortable-looking Burrell. Sharpe decided he had pretended long enough. "So tell me about Marengo, Colonel," he said.

Lanier smiled again. "My moment of glory, Colonel." He mocked the word *glory* with his tone. "But in truth we fought well that day. And you? You had a moment like that?"

"Talavera," Sharpe said.

"I missed the Spanish war. What did you do?"

"I took one of your Eagles."

For an instant Lanier looked offended, then he nodded. "I salute you, Colonel." He sounded sincere. He turned to glance at his men, and Sharpe saw that his long queue had been wrapped tightly with black ribbon and hung down beneath his neck. For a heartbeat Sharpe was tempted to take hold of the queue, haul it down, and slam his other hand hard onto Lanier's exposed throat, then Lanier turned back and Sharpe had the odd thought that the Frenchman had recognized that impulse and was amused by it. Lanier touched the star on Sharpe's breast. "They gave you that for your bravery?" he asked.

"You do know you're supposed to be on the far side of the Loire by now?" Sharpe ignored the question and spoke harshly.

"I resigned from the army and stayed to help madame work the vineyard," Lanier said. "Believe it or not I know the trade. My father grew grapes in Burgundy. The war is over, Colonel."

"It is?"

Lanier gestured at the wine barrels. "We bring you the best Pinot Noir instead of bayonets." He turned to a small table beneath the lantern where there was a half full bottle of wine and a tray of glasses. He crossed to the table, uncorked the bottle, and sniffed the wine. "I assume this is what the Duke is drinking tonight?" He poured wine into two of the glasses and handed one to Sharpe. "One day we must tell each other the tales old soldiers tell, Colonel."

"I'd like that," Sharpe said.

"Your health, Colonel." Lanier lifted his glass.

"Yours, Colonel," Sharpe said.

"Vinegar," Lanier said, having tasted the wine. "My work here is done and the gift delivered. *Au revoir*, Colonel Sharpe."

"*Au revoir*, Colonel Lanier," Sharpe responded, and was rewarded with a chuckle.

Damn it, he thought, I like the man! He's a lying, untrustworthy bastard, but I like him! He watched the men climb from the cellar and heard the wagon being driven away. "That was nice of them, sir," Burrell said.

"Nice?"

"They brought a gift, sir."

Sharpe frowned. "They brought barrels," he said, "not bottles. Why?"

"Not unusual, sir. My father always buys his claret in barrels. We decant it."

A door opened at the top of the stairs leading into the house. "Colonel Sharpe?" a voice called.

"Coming!" Sharpe said. He looked around the cellar and saw some tools on a bench. He found a chisel and hammer. "What happens when you roll a barrel of wine, Captain?"

"No idea, sir," Burrell said.

"It makes a noise! The stuff sloshes around. Did you hear it sloshing?"

"No, sir."

"Exactly." Sharpe hammered the chisel into the top of a barrel, then levered up the shattered piece of wood. He sniffed and grimaced at the smell. "I knew something was wrong."

"Oh my God." Burrell had gone pale.

"It's safe enough," Sharpe said, "but they plan to come back later, don't they." He pushed a hand through the gap he had made and brought out a handful of gunpowder.

"I'll call out the guard," Burrell turned away.

"Don't bother," Sharpe said, "the buggers have gone."

"What do we do?" Burrell asked.

"You get a squad of men to take the barrels into the garden. There's a pond here?"

"An ornamental lake, sir. With fountains."

"Drop them all in the lake. Then put a guard on the cellar to see who comes back later tonight."

"Dear God," Burrell said. "I should tell the Duke, sir."

"Don't spoil his dinner! I'll tell him later. Just get rid of the stuff."

"Sharpe!" It was Major Vincent's voice, peremptory from above.

"Coming!" Sharpe clapped Burrell on the shoulder, then climbed to the kitchen, where Vincent waited. "They can't serve the main course till you return," the major complained.

Sharpe went back to the dining room and took his seat. "All well, Sharpe?" the Duke demanded.

"Madame Delaunay has been very generous, Your Grace," Sharpe said, "a dozen barrels of the 1811 vintage. I'm told it's excellent."

"It is," the widow put in.

"You tasted it, Sharpe?" Halkett asked.

251

"No, sir, we just left the barrels in the cellar." He said that loud enough for the widow to hear.

"There was a comet in 1811," the widow said, "and years with a comet always give the best wine. I hope Your Grace enjoys it."

"I shall, madame, and am most grateful for your generosity." The Duke scowled at Sharpe, then clapped his hands. "Roast leg of mutton and vinegar sauce," he announced happily.

"Of course," Halkett grumbled. Sharpe liked roast mutton, but as he sat he suddenly wondered if he had been right. Supposing Lanier was not planning to return? Suppose there was a slow match in one of the barrels? Dear God, that is how he would have ignited the powder. He would have made a separate compartment in one of the barrels and secreted an artillery shell attached to a slow match that could even now be burning in the cellar. He had not smelled burning powder, and a slow match would be extinguished if the barrel was airtight, but he could not lose the suspicion, nor the fear that at any moment the whole house would be engulfed in a vast explosion. "You'll forgive me," he said to the table at large, stood, and dashed back to the kitchen. Down the stairs and into the cellar where a half-dozen guardsmen were manhandling the last three barrels up to the garden. Sharpe followed to watch them rolling the barrels across the lawn to the ornamental pond with its two fountains. Captain Burrell stood watching. "That's the last barrel," he told Sharpe. "All safe now."

The barrel was rolled into the pond.

"Well done, Captain. Keep a guard on them."

"I will, sir."

Sharpe went back to the house, knowing he would have to explain his sudden exit. Sure enough the Duke gave him an unfriendly look. "You had a more pressing engagement, Colonel?"

"I forgot to thank the men who delivered the wine, Your Grace. I thought they deserved some thanks."

"Even though they destroyed something?"

"The outer cellar door, Your Grace, rather than trundle the barrels through the house. They couldn't find the key."

The Duke grunted. "Sensible, I suppose. Sit down, Sharpe. What did you give them?"

"Twenty francs, Your Grace."

"Good God, that was generous!"

"They assured me it is very good wine, Your Grace."

"It is excellent wine," the widow put in, and Sharpe dared not meet her gaze.

"I'll reimburse you, Sharpe," the Duke said ungraciously, then sawed at the mutton with his knife. Lucille, Sharpe noted, was eating with feigned enjoyment. He winked at her and she half smiled.

"You're really planning to settle in Normandy, Colonel?" Halkett asked him.

"Already have, sir. Can't wait to get back there."

"Understandable," Halkett said, looking at Lucille, "but if you stayed in the army there'd be advancement for you."

"I doubt it, sir. There'll be too many colonels and not enough war."

"There's always war, Sharpe, it's the natural state of mankind. Are you sure this is mutton? Tastes like goat."

"Long time since I ate goat," Sharpe said, "probably not since Portugal." And he thought how far he had come since those first battles in Portugal. He looked across the table at Lucille, who was speaking animatedly to the Duke. Would he really be happy in Normandy? Maybe he should stay in the army as Halkett suggested. Now he was a colonel the promotions would come without effort; no purchase needed, just seniority. Live long enough, he thought, and he would be General Sharpe, and that thought made him smile. General Sharpe! That would be an achievement for a gutter-born boy from East London, but the thought was also ridiculous and he knew that as long as he lived he would always be the officer who had come from the ranks, and whose back was scarred by a flogging. In Normandy he had nothing to prove, except perhaps that he could farm Lucille's acres as well as any other man. And he remembered the Duke at Waterloo, amid the din of battle, under the thick powder smoke that hung over the ragged infantry, the trumpet calls and the drumbeats of the approaching French, and every man in that thin abraded line at the crest of the ridge had known that death was coming up the slope; death by musket fire, by bayonet lunges, by canister or by round shot, and in the center of that dread the Duke had called out that the reward for standing and surviving was peace, and for Sharpe that meant Lucille. "I'll not stay in the army," he told Halkett, who looked slightly surprised at the sudden words. "The army's been good to me, sir," Sharpe went on, but did not finish the thought. The army, he thought, had guided him to Lucille, so the army had done its job, as he had. He had fought on the ridge at Waterloo, and now he would take the Duke's promised result; peace.

Except Lanier would break that promise. Fox had reckoned *la Fraternité* could start another war, a war of vengeance for the deaths of dukes and princes, and if Fox was right then there would be no sanctuary in Normandy, just another campaign and more battles. "I've fought long enough," he muttered.

"Few have fought better," Halkett said. "You know you're something of a legend, Sharpe?"

"I doubt that, sir."

"Truly!" Halkett insisted.

"I remember in India, sir, a cavalry officer told me what I was. I was a sergeant then." He paused.

"What did he say?" Halkett insisted. "Tell me!"

"A lump, sir. He said I was a lump. Not sure he wasn't right."

The mutton was cleared away, the wine glasses refilled, then dishes of strawberries were put on the table with bowls of lemon ice cream. A clock in the hallway struck ten and the widow stood. "I must cross the city," she said, "so I hope you will excuse me?"

"It was good of you to come," the Duke said, "and I thank you for the wine."

"I know you will enjoy it, Your Grace." She moved to the door, then looked back. "Colonel Sharpe! May I have a word?"

The Duke nodded permission and Sharpe followed the widow into the hallway. "Madame?"

"Do you still persist in believing that silly story?" She spoke in English.

More than ever, Sharpe thought, then realized that there could not have been a slow match concealed in the barrels while Madame Delaunay was in the house. So men were coming back to finish the treachery. "We're assured that there's no truth in the tale, madame," he said, "and my job now is to clear the stolen paintings out of the Louvre."

"Sheer vandalism! The *Musée Napoléon* is the most important repository of culture in Europe! In the world!"

"I'll do my duty, madame."

"Always the soldier's excuse," she snarled, then calmed down. "The world changes, Colonel, and it's not good. The Emperor was a clever man and a good ruler. You know the Prussians want him executed?"

"They do, madame?"

"They're savages! But the Duke assures me he will plead for his life."

"Then we must hope the Duke lives to make that plea," Sharpe said. She gave him a very hard look. "Did you taste the wine, Colonel?"

"There wasn't time, madame, and besides we like the wine chilled. We put it all in the fountains."

"You . . ." she began, then nodded as she understood what he had done. "You are a clever man, Colonel Sharpe. But it's no matter, I rather thought that fat fool the King might be here. He wasn't."

"And you planned to send men here later to fire the barrels?"

"I planned to rid France of an obese wobbling monarch, Colonel. What kind of world allows my husband to die and Fat Louis to live?"

"A world that allows my Lucille to live."

"I would have regretted that," Madame Delaunay said. "I like her. She deserves better than you, of course, but look after her."

"I intend to, madame."

"Then good night, Colonel." Hoofbeats and carriage wheels sounded from the portico and she swept out of the door with what Sharpe thought was indecent haste.

Coffee and cognac were being served in the great parlor, where Lucille had attracted a small crowd of admirers. Sharpe ignored them and headed for the Duke, who was standing by a curtained window evidently having been trapped there by Colonel Kippen, who was talking earnestly and emphasizing his words with a pumped fist. The Duke looked rather relieved as Sharpe approached. "Colonel Kippen," he interrupted the Prussian, "assures me that the Delaunay property is free of enemy."

"Your Grace," Sharpe said, "a word?"

"You'll excuse us, Colonel?" The Duke turned away from the Prussian. "What is it, Sharpe?"

"I have to commend Captain Burrell, Your Grace."

"Jack's a fine fellow. I'm glad you approve of him."

Kippen had followed them and Sharpe lowered his voice to tell the Duke of the attempt to fire the mansion. The Duke's eyes widened as he listened. "You didn't think to warn me!"

"And interrupt your dinner? Captain Burrell had the situation well in hand, Your Grace."

"And that damned woman was my guest!" The Duke was angry now, but it was a cool anger. "And Lanier was here?"

"I spoke with him, Your Grace."

"I thought you were under orders to kill the man?"

"A fight in the house would not have been a good idea, Your Grace. He had men, I had none."

"Not like you, Sharpe! Learning discretion are you?" The Duke gave him no chance to answer. "So we're safe now? You're certain?"

"Quite certain, Your Grace. Captain Burrell put all the powder in the pond here."

"Then damn the Prussians," the Duke went on, loud enough now for Kippen to hear. "Tomorrow you clean out that nest of vipers, and that's an order."

"Yes, Your Grace."

"Colonel Kippen," the Duke turned to the Prussian, "you will be good enough to inform your masters that a British battalion will be active in the east of the city tomorrow."

"But—" Kippen began.

"No buts!" the Duke snapped. "If your fellows can't do it, mine will. Your fellows will do it, Sharpe." He prodded Sharpe by poking the star on Sharpe's chest. "If you want to help, Colonel," he was talking to Kippen now, "then bring some troops, but Colonel Sharpe is in command. You understand?" He did not wait for an answer, but stalked across the room, leaving Kippen and Sharpe by the empty hearth.

"They are not there!" Kippen pleaded to Sharpe. "We searched!"

"The cellars too?"

"Nothing there but, what do you say? *Pilze?*"

"*Pilze?*"

"They grow in the forest. Under the trees."

"Mushrooms."

"*Ja!* Mushrooms."

"And the tunnel, Colonel?"

Kippen looked flustered. "There is a tunnel?"

"There is a tunnel," Sharpe said, "and tomorrow we search it."

"There is no tunnel! We would have found it! There is nothing but a mushroom farm. My men were thorough!"

"Tomorrow," Sharpe said, tired of the man. "If you want to be part of it, Colonel, meet me in the Louvre at midday."

"This is madness," Kippen protested.

And it had been madness, Sharpe thought, since the moment he had marched his men onto the ridge at Waterloo. And damn it, the war was over, the victory won! But tomorrow he must face *le Monstre* and his devils. Damn it, Sharpe thought, but Kippen was right, it was madness.

CHAPTER 12

"Midnight," Sharpe said firmly, putting a finger on the map of Paris. "You have to be here ten minutes before," his finger prodded the map, "at the elephant, you can't miss it, and here," he moved his finger to the Delaunay estate, "when the church clocks strike midnight."

"And the Prussians?" Major Morris asked.

"We will be waiting at the gate," Kippen said. "When you arrive, Major, we all go to the house." Kippen had promised three companies of troops. "And my men will lead," he insisted, "but they will find nothing. We were there two days ago and the house was not occupied."

"And if it is?" Morris asked.

"Then you get rid of them," Sharpe said.

"But the Prussians go first?" Morris asked anxiously.

"You all go," Sharpe said. "If there's a battalion of French Light Infantry in Madame Delaunay's house then three companies of Prussians won't be enough."

"We will go first," Colonel Kippen assured the nervous Morris.

Sharpe slapped the table hard. "No one goes first! You attack together. I don't give a tinker's cuss who's first into the house, so long as you get there fast and go in fast."

"The doors will be locked," Morris pointed out.

Sharpe looked at Captain Jefferson. "Get some axes from the Pioneers."

"I will, sir."

Sharpe looked back to Morris. "The Grenadier Company will break the doors down, and the other companies can smash the windows and get in that way."

"But no windows on what you say is the storehouse," Morris said, pointing to the rough sketch Sharpe had made of Madame Delaunay's house and warehouse.

"So you go through the bloody door!"

"But you think most of the French will be in that warehouse?"

"Which is why you go in fast and hard!"

"We searched that warehouse two days ago," Kippen said, "and there were no men there. Just a wine press and barrels."

"If there are no men, why—" Morris began.

"Because the Duke insists, and so do I," Sharpe snarled.

"The warehouse," Kippen said slowly, "is the more formidable building. My men will assault it."

"That seems sensible," Morris said, unable to hide his relief.

"And we'll put two companies of my men with you," Sharpe said to Kippen.

"You've already detached the Light Company," Morris began complaining.

"And now I'm detaching two others. That leaves you seven companies, more than enough."

Sharpe could almost smell Morris's fear, and he remembered the man's cowardice from India, where he had refused to assault the breach at Gawilghur. Sharpe could not blame a man for fearing to assault a breach, it was perhaps the most dangerous duty any soldier faced, but there were moments when a man just had to block the terror and do his duty. But Morris had hung back, sheltering behind a sepoy ladder party rather than climb into the guns protecting the broken stone ramp, and in the end the Scots had done the work Morris was supposed to do. So why, Sharpe wondered, was he refusing to lead the battalion against the Delaunay house himself? Because he had another idea, which meant Morris had to command. He looked at the captains who were gathered in the office. "I don't know what's waiting for us," he told them, "but unlike Colonel Kippen, I expect a battalion of Crapauds. A good battalion! The Emperor called them his devils, but you're better. You don't hold back, you understand? You get in the house and you kill the bastards. Hunt them down and kill them. Don't give them time to stand!"

"I think there will be none there," Kippen said unhelpfully.

"In which case I'll find them," Sharpe said, "and you all find me." He looked at Harry Price. "We leave at ten thirty, Harry."

"Yes, sir."

"No later," Sharpe went on, "because we have a longish march. And we'll have some artillerymen with us."

"Artillery?" Price asked. "We'll have a cannon?"

"Just men," Sharpe said, "three or four of them."

"Why artillerymen?" Morris wanted to know.

"Because I asked the Duke for their help," Sharpe said, and though he knew they all wanted an explanation he was in no mood to offer one.

"We can have some artillery too?" Morris asked hopefully.

"You've got one of the best battalions in the British army," Sharpe snarled, "and that's enough."

"And if you're not on time?" Morris persisted with his questions.

"We'll be on time," Sharpe said, "and so will you."

"Of course," Morris said uncertainly.

"We will be at the house as the clocks strike midnight," Kippen said, then glanced at Morris. "All of us."

"Then I suggest you all get some rest this afternoon," Sharpe finished.

The battalion officers filed out of the room that was some kind of office. Kippen stayed. "Your Major Morris . . ." he began.

"He's not mine."

"He is frightened."

"He's scared out of his wits, Colonel, but the captains know their duty. So do the sergeants."

Kippen hesitated. "Perhaps you," he began.

"Should lead them?" Sharpe finished for him.

"Yes, Colonel."

And maybe Kippen was right, Sharpe thought. In essence his plan was simple; just assault the house and warehouse, and root out whoever was hiding in the buildings, but Sharpe knew it would not be that simple. Lanier would surely know the assault was coming. The Frenchman was no fool and would certainly have men watching the streets around the vineyard, and by the time Kippen and Morris reached the gate Lanier would have his defenses ready. Sharpe's only response to that was to encourage the attackers to go fast, and while they swarmed up the vineyard toward the house he would approach from the rear to stab Lanier's men in the back. Or, if he was unlucky, to confront Lanier's retreating men with an entirely inadequate force. "Lanier believes we don't know about the tunnel," Sharpe explained, hoping he was right, "and I believe that's where he hid his men two days ago. We have to take the tunnel, Colonel."

"If you say so." Kippen sounded unconvinced.

"You still believe there's no one there?"

"I do."

"Then your task will be easy and I'll look like a fool."

Or he would be dead. Sharpe was still convinced that Lanier's battalion was concealed in the house and his only explanation for the failure of the Prussians to discover them was to assume that Lanier, forewarned by his sentries, had concealed his men in the tunnel. And if Lanier did the same again, then the Prince of Wales's Own Volunteers' Light Company would find themselves trapped in the tunnel against an overwhelming force. And if Lanier knew the assault was coming, which he surely would, then why wouldn't he repeat the trick? The tunnel, Sharpe suspected, would be a deathtrap, yet he had to capture it, and he would lead the men who would meet the enemy in that underground darkness. He had thought of giving the task to Harry Price, but suspected that was only because he did not want to risk his own life. That thought had shamed him. He would lead the Light Company into the darkness because that was where the greatest danger lay.

A bellow of rage sounded from the vast halls of the Louvre beyond the office door, followed by a single shot. "For God's sake . . ." Sharpe snarled and ran to the door.

He went into the gallery where a cloud of powder smoke lingered. "What the hell?" he shouted.

Major Morris had fired the pistol. "I'll kill it!" the major shouted.

"Kill what?" Sharpe demanded.

"That damned monkey!"

Sharpe looked to his left and saw Private Bee was crouching beside a statue. The monkey, evidently unscathed by the pistol ball, crawled into Bee's arms and nestled inside his red coat. "I warned you!" Morris shouted at the boy. "You do it on purpose!"

"Do what?" Sharpe shouted. The gallery was full of redcoats who were watching the scene. "Major Morris! Private Bee! Over here, now!"

He took both men back into the office. "Now what the hell is happening?" he demanded.

Bee just looked frightened, as did the monkey, whose small face peered anxiously at Sharpe from inside the red jacket. Bee murmured to the creature and stroked its head. Morris pointed at them. "He encourages the bloody animal to shit on my bed! He does it on purpose!"

"Do you, Bee?"

"No, sir." Bee's voice was almost too faint to hear.

"He controls the animal," Morris spat, "no one else can!"

"Is that true, Bee?"

"I speak to him in Italian, sir," Bee muttered, "because he under-stands Italian."

"This is the third time it's happened," Morris complained.

"Where's your bed, Major?"

"In a small room down there," Morris pointed.

"And the door is locked?"

"There's no lock. I warned him!"

"Warned him of what?"

"That if it happened a third time I would shoot that damned monkey and," Morris hesitated, then found what small courage he possessed, "flog him."

"Go, Private," Sharpe said to Bee, and the boy fled. "Flog him?" Sharpe asked Morris.

"You don't frighten me, Sharpe," Morris said, "I talked to General Halkett."

"Whined to him, did you?"

"If you lay a finger on me, Sharpe, you'll lose your commission and face punishment."

"And if you lay a finger on Private Bee or his damned monkey,"

Sharpe said, "I'll flog the skin off your back, Major. And tonight, Major, you lead the attack and you'll do it as I said. Fast!"

"I know my duty," Morris said.

"I somehow doubt that," Sharpe retorted. "I've seen you in a fight, Charlie, and you don't fight. You look for somewhere to hide. But you won't do that tonight. You get to the house fast and you get inside fast. And there'll be no flogging! None!"

"And if that Prussian is right," Morris said, "it will all be a waste of time."

"Then you'd best hope he is right," Sharpe said, "because then you'll be safe. And Private Bee is also safe now, as is his monkey."

"You know what they call that damned animal?" Morris asked indignantly.

"The damned animal is called Charlie. Now go, Charlie. Go!"

Morris stalked from the room and Sharpe sank into the chair behind the table. The door opened and a grinning Pat Harper came in. "He didn't look happy."

"He's not. Did the boy tell the monkey to shit on his bed?"

"Probably. The wee thing speaks Italian, can you believe it?"

"Tell him to stop it."

"The men encourage Charlie," Harper said, "they open the major's door and give it a slice of apple."

"Then tell them that the next man to do that will be flogged. By me!"

"And they won't believe you. But not to worry, I'll stop them." Harper looked down at the map spread on the table. "So your man didn't go back last night?"

"No one did," Sharpe said. "I told the widow we'd ruined the powder."

"Why?"

"I don't think the Duke would be happy if there was a firefight at his mansion in the middle of the night."

"Aye, true enough. But you think Lanier will try again?"

"Unless we stop him. And the next attempt won't be so clumsy."

"What if your Prussian is right? And they're not there?"

"Then we find them, Pat. They haven't gone."

"You're sure of that?"

"Lanier isn't a man to give up. He's here and so are his men."

Harper sank into a chair and laid the volley gun across his knees. "So we'll need this tonight," he said, patting the seven barrels.

"You should stay here, Pat."

"Save your breath, Colonel Sharpe."

"It could be nasty, Pat."

"Could be? It will be! It'll be a bloody horror! That's why they're sending us. And I'm coming."

To face Napoleon's devils, led by the Emperor's monster.

The elephant loomed in the moonlight, its pale skin streaked with soot and dirt. Sharpe gazed at the monstrous beast, wondering what madness had demanded its construction. Even as he watched, a lump of plaster fell from the belly and crashed into the thick weeds growing between its vast legs. "They're mad, so they are," Pat Harper said.

"Everything's mad," Sharpe said curtly. He had paused to let the Light Company gape at the elephant. "Can you imagine that in Dublin? Or London?"

"I think it's kind of wonderful," Harper said enthusiastically. "You think they'll finish the beast?"

"It's supposed to be made from bronze. God knows where they'll find it."

"A pity. Folk would travel miles just to see it!"

"Keep going!" Sharpe called, and headed past the elephant. "The Bastille was here."

"Their prison, yes?"

"Now it's got a bloody elephant, and the world has gone mad."

It was dark, though the moon was bright enough, even if frequent strands of cloud obscured it. The Light Company, forty-three strong, followed Sharpe, their rifles and muskets slung on shoulders. Parisians watched them pass. "Lanier will know we're coming," Sharpe said.

"You think so?"

"Wouldn't you have sentries watching the roads?"

"I would."

"Which means they'll see the battalion approaching."

"So your bloody man will run into trouble."

"He will," Sharpe said grimly. The "bloody man" was Morris, and Sharpe had no faith in him at all.

"The kipper will have to lead them," Harper said. The whole battalion now called the Prussian "the kipper."

"If the bloody man lets him." Sharpe brooded for a few steps. "Men are going to die, Pat, and that makes me angry. The war's over, for Christ's sake!"

He ignored the Rue de Montreuil, which led to the Delaunay estate, instead slanting right onto the Rue de Vincennes. He suspected Lanier's picquets had seen the Light Company, but by turning away from the Delaunay estate he hoped they would be persuaded he was no threat.

Sharpe felt irritable, nervous. There had been a time when he welcomed a fight, but this night's madness had made him apprehensive. It would be such a stupid time to die. The war was won, the Emperor was defeated, and still Sharpe was marching to battle. It was Lucille, he knew, that made him so nervous. In the past he had little or nothing to lose, but now he had everything to lose; a woman, a son, and a life. He remembered the countless men who had experienced a premonition

267

of death before a fight, and how many of them had fallen, and he touched the brass buttplate of Dan Hagman's rifle and rubbed the notches in the stock as though it were a talisman against his fear. Lucille! He said the name to himself, and marveled that she was his woman. We'll marry, he promised himself, and he imagined being in Normandy again, yet somehow that vision would not take shape in his head. This night's work was all he could see.

He turned and watched a pair of artillerymen pushing a garden cart. "Doing all right, lads?" he asked.

"Much further, sir?"

"Another half hour or so."

The cart, meant for light loads of cuttings or manure, held three long wooden boxes. The two men pushing the clumsy vehicle were commanded by a lieutenant dressed in a suspiciously clean blue jacket, suspicious because it suggested he had seen little action. His name was Anderson and he came recommended by his commanding officer.

"Waterloo was your first battle, Lieutenant?" Sharpe asked as they headed on down the Rue de Vincennes.

"I was at the fight two days before, sir, and the next day."

"And you brought me six-pounders?"

"Six of them, sir. Two to a crate."

"And your watch is working?" Sharpe had requested not just the artillery's assistance, but a man with an accurate watch too. "It's a Breguet, sir!" Anderson sounded excited. "Took it off a dead French officer after the battle. It looks brand new, too! It has an eccentric dial!"

"Is that good?"

"It's amazing, sir! Probably worth more than my commission!"

"We'll need it," Sharpe said, "but I'm hoping I won't need you."

"And I'm hoping you do," Anderson said enthusiastically, and Sharpe remembered when he had been just as impatient to join a fight.

"Just stay alive, Lieutenant," he said, knowing the words were meaningless. But Sharpe feared the tunnel simply because a tunnel, any tunnel, was easy to defend. However inaccurate a musket was, a tunnel would serve to guide the bullets as they ricocheted from its walls, and a group of determined infantry could fill a tunnel with a deadly hail of lead. Lieutenant Anderson was Sharpe's answer to that fear.

Sharpe had half expected an argument at the city gate that lay at the end of the Rue de Vincennes, but the guard there simply hauled the gate open and sullenly watched them pass. The street beyond had small houses that petered out into scrubby fields where goats and cattle grazed in the moonlight.

They turned north just as the city clocks started a jangled chiming to mark eleven. They were following a paved road. To Sharpe's right was countryside, to his left he could see houses, beyond which was the city's wall. Ahead was a sprawling village and Sharpe stopped well short of it. "We wait here," he said, turning off the road into a small orchard. "The cart goes no further," he ordered. "Pat? You and I will take a look ahead."

He left Harry Price in charge of the company with orders to lie quiet while he and Harper made their way through the rough fields to the east of the village, which was dominated by a church and, next to it, a big building with two high gables. Sharpe settled into a ditch and nodded at the big building. "That's the tavern," Sharpe said.

"Whorehouse too, sir."

"Probably."

"And it's busy enough," Harper grunted. They could see lamplight showing through the big building's windows. They could also see moonlight glinting from the bayonets of two sentries posted on the firestep of the city's wall.

"Busy drinking and whoring," Sharpe said.

"Lucky people, then. Do we go look at them?"

"No, let them drink. We'll move a few minutes before midnight. Lieutenant Anderson claims his watch is accurate enough."

Sharpe watched the tavern for a few more minutes, unable to shift the dread from his thoughts. He tried to think of Lucille, tried to imagine a wedding service in the château's old chapel that he had done his best to restore, but the more he thought of that hoped-for day, the worse his anticipation of this night's madness. He was fairly sure the battalion could get into the house, and he was equally sure that Lanier's battalion was there, but once the firing started there was a good chance of chaos, and a fight inside a large house would be difficult to control. Lanier must be warned already of a battalion of British troops moving through the city, but had he detected Sharpe's presence behind him? And if so, would the tunnel be barricaded? Dear God, he thought, but I should have led the battalion in the main assault, because this was madness. "Let's fetch the others, Pat," he said, and then, after a pause, "and thank you."

"Thank me?"

"For everything. From Portugal onward."

Harper was silent for a moment. "Is that how you're feeling?"

"Terrified, Pat."

"Then let me lead."

"Christ, no. It's just nerves, Pat. I was the same before Toulouse."

"And we won that."

"We always win," Sharpe said, hoping he spoke the truth.

He waited until Lieutenant Anderson's watch said it was a quarter hour short of midnight, then he led the Light Company and the artillerymen back through the fields to the ditch at the edge of the village. He dared not use the road because they would be seen by the sentries on the wall's firestep, but trees and hedgerows hid their approach. An owl hooted somewhere to the east as Sharpe crouched behind a thorn bush. "Time, Lieutenant?"

Anderson tilted the watch to catch the moonlight. "Eight minutes to midnight, sir."

"We wait," Sharpe said. Beyond the tavern he could see the loom of the city wall and the roof of the Delaunay buildings beyond. There were at least two sentries on that wall, the pale moonlight still reflecting from their fixed bayonets, but Sharpe was confident his men had not been seen. "Tell me when it's three minutes to midnight," he told Anderson.

Because then he would go where every instinct told him not to go.

Damn it, the war was over! And Sharpe was going to war.

There was singing in the tavern as Sharpe approached, a raucous singing by men who had plainly been drinking, and the sound persuaded Sharpe not to use the big door at the building's front. The last thing he wanted was a drunken brawl, and so he swerved to the right and found a smaller door at the building's side. It opened into a lantern-lit kitchen where a big man was stirring a pot on a stove and two women were sitting at a table jointing chicken carcasses. The big man just gaped as Sharpe's men filed into the steamy room. "Where's the tunnel?" Sharpe demanded of the man.

"Monsieur?"

"The tunnel," Sharpe snarled. "*Le tunnel. Où est-il?*"

The man looked from Sharpe's scarred face to Harper's eyes and seemed to shiver. "In the cellar, monsieur."

"And where's that?"

The man was holding a big ladle that he dumbly pointed at a door. Sharpe wrenched it open and found himself in a hallway where a second door opened onto a dark flight of stairs leading down. "This way!" he called, and ran down the steps. "Harry!"

Captain Price caught up with Sharpe in the cellar that was stacked with barrels and with racks of wine bottles. "Sir?"

"Three men, Harry, stay here and make sure the bastards upstairs don't follow us."

"Sir," Price said.

The cellar was dimly lit by lanterns, and in their light Sharpe could see a big wooden door on the far side. He dragged it open and there were more steps going down into darkness. "Time, Lieutenant?" he asked.

"A minute to midnight, sir," Anderson answered after a pause.

"Then let's go. You stay behind me, Lieutenant."

Sharpe ran down the stone steps to find a tunnel some six or seven feet wide and low enough to make him stoop. Harper had brought one of the lanterns and Sharpe could see that the tunnel seemed to be hacked through a pale limestone. Harper paused beside him, the lantern in one hand, his volley gun in the other. The Irishman peered into the tunnel's darkness. "Christ, it's a lot of bloody work just to get cheaper wine."

"According to Fox it started as a gypsum mine," Sharpe said.

"Gypsum?"

"Plaster, Pat. The stuff the elephant's made from. Are we all here?"

"All but Harry Price and his three men."

"Then let's go." The tunnel sloped down for the first few yards then tilted upward. The lantern gave a feeble light, barely illuminating more than a few feet of the stone walls. "If your man's expecting us," Harper began and did not finish the thought, nor did he need to because Sharpe was wondering the same. If Lanier had men guarding the tunnel then it would be a bloody business to get through.

He reached the foot of the downward slope and now the tunnel seemed to stretch straight and slightly upward. "I hate tunnels," Sharpe said.

"What's that?" Harper had seen a faint red light far ahead. "Oh God, no."

"Down!" Sharpe shouted and dropped to the floor.

Then the world ended, or it seemed to. There was a gout of brilliant flame at the tunnel's distant end and a noise that sounded as if the earth itself had exploded. Smoke obliterated the flame as devils clawed and screeched at the tunnel's walls. Something struck Sharpe's right shoulder and a lance of pain streaked down to his arse. Behind him a man cried out. "Cannon," Harper said.

Lanier was guarding his tunnel and had somehow managed to get an artillery piece underground and the wretched thing had just fired a round of canister. The small red glow had been the portfire about to touch the powder charge on the gun's vent. "Are you hit, Pat?"

"No."

Sharpe moved his right arm. He suspected one of the musket balls from the canister had struck his back just behind the shoulder, but the ball had not pierced. It still hurt though. He pulled his rifle forward, ignoring the pain, and fired a shot down the tunnel. "Lieutenant!"

"Sir?" Lieutenant Anderson was crouched behind Sharpe.

"This is why you're here. Those bastards are reloading. Stop them."

The tunnel would be impassable if the French had a cannon firing canister, a weapon all infantrymen feared. A canister was simply a tin tube crammed with musket balls and, fired from an artillery piece, the can disintegrated as it left the barrel and the musket balls spread out like duckshot. The tunnel could only concentrate that deadly blast, bouncing the balls off the stone roof and sides to form a concentrated blizzard of death. "Anyone hurt?" Sharpe asked.

"I think Potter's dead, Mister Sharpe," McGurk called. "Hit in the head."

Three men were wounded. Sharpe's shoulder was stiffening and he could feel blood on his back, but he rolled aside to let Anderson's men lug one of their rockets past him. Sharpe had first seen rockets in India where his enemies had used them, then he and Harper had tested them in Spain after the artillery claimed great things for the outlandish weapons, which were copied from the Indian models. Anderson had brought a half-dozen six-pounders, the smallest of the rockets, each one a thick stick over a man's length trailing from a cylinder that contained the gunpowder that propelled the rocket with its explosive head. Sharpe had seen a handful of the rockets fired at Waterloo, tracing their erratic course through the gray sky, and that memory had prompted him to ask for the artillery's assistance here. He feared meeting Lanier's men in the tunnel, perhaps having to face most of the French battalion with just his small company, but the rockets would be fearful weapons in the confined space.

Sharpe started reloading his rifle as Anderson peered down the smoke-obscured passage to estimate the range. All that was really visible was a red trace where a gunner was swinging a portfire to keep it alight, but Anderson grimaced at how close the enemy appeared, then cut the fuse at a rocket's base. He knelt and struck flint against steel, then blew the charred linen into a flame that he put to the weapon's fuse. It fizzed to life and Anderson pushed the stick to move the rocket farther up the shallow slope. "Careful," he said, and then the rocket lit up, its base flared noxious smoke and a searing flame, and the weapon leaped up the tunnel, struck the roof, bounced down to the floor and up to the roof again.

The problem with rockets, Sharpe remembered, was that they

hardly ever went where they were aimed. They were as likely to turn in the air and come back at the men who had fired them as hit the enemy, though on the day before Waterloo he had seen one rocket explode right on a French gun team. Lieutenant Anderson's first rocket might want to wander anywhere, but the tunnel acted as a gun barrel and the rocket flamed and seared its erratic path, slamming against the tunnel's walls to leave a trail of sparks and smoke, then exploded at the tunnel's far end. "Well done, Lieutenant," Sharpe said, "now give them another."

"Sir." Anderson was already trimming another fuse.

The second rocket behaved like the first, scraping along the wall, bouncing from ceiling to floor and back again, but always channeled by the tunnel to its target where it exploded. The explosion was like a shell, bursting scraps of iron, and Sharpe hoped the two weapons had gutted the cannon's crew. His ears were still ringing from the noise as he stood. "Let's go!"

"You're bleeding," Harper said.

"A scratch."

Sharpe had to stoop as he ran. The lantern had gone out so the tunnel was utterly dark, the smoke noxious and thick. If the bastards had survived Anderson's rockets then another blast of canister would come soon and in the tunnel's confines it would prove murderous. Best not to think of it, and then ahead, through the dense smoke, Sharpe saw a flickering red glow. Something was on fire there. Still the cannon did not fire. His shoulder was hurting now and the pain slowed him so that Harper pushed past him. Sharpe tried to keep up, stumbled on a rough patch and struck his head on the roof as he recovered, then heard Pat Harper bellow with rage as he reached the French gun. Sharpe noted it was another old six-pounder, the smallest cannon in the French arsenal, and he realized he had not seen many of the small guns since the early days of the war in Spain. The gun had been replaced by the larger eight-pounder, but presumably Lanier had found this weapon in a Paris arsenal and brought it to protect his precious tunnel. Sharpe reached the gun and leaned against the barrel as his riflemen streamed past. The French crew, there were three of them, were all dead, blasted by Anderson's rockets. Behind the cannon was a wooden ramp sloping up. It was smoldering. And Sharpe could just hear the thorn-crackling sound of musketry. So the battalion had reached the estate and, with Kippen's men, were advancing on the house. Sharpe had hoped that by attacking through the tunnel the Light Company would be a stab in the back to Lanier's men who would be concentrating on the larger assault, but that had not worked. Lanier had guarded his tunnel, and now men were at the top of the ramp firing down into Sharpe's company. One of Anderson's artillerymen was crawling by the gun, spewing blood from his mouth, while a Frenchman was shouting for other men to join the group at the ramp's head. Then a great crash sounded as Harper fired the volley gun, and the half-dozen men above Sharpe were snatched backward. The smoke thickened in the tunnel. "Up the ramp!" Sharpe called, and pushed off the small cannon.

"You're hurt, sir!" Anderson was beside him.

"I'm fine." He was not. He could feel blood wet on his back, and his right shoulder was flaming with pain, but speed was everything. He drew his sword, flinching at the agony, and hurried up the ramp. A musket fired, the ball plucking at Sharpe's left sleeve, then Rifleman Finn was past him and his sword-bayonet sliced into the man who had fired. Sharpe had expected to emerge into a vast cellar, instead he was in a small room lit by lanterns that hung from stone arches. A door was to his right. He tugged it open and there was the large cellar filled with trays of growing mushrooms.

"You're bleeding badly." Harper was beside him.

"Just a scratch, Pat." He nodded at the volley gun. "Is that thing reloaded?"

"Not yet."

"Load it. We might need it."

The larger cellar appeared to be empty except for the mushrooms. Sharpe suspected Lanier had left a small squad of men with the cannon, confident that the canister would prove enough to defend the tunnel against any intruders. Harry Price appeared at Sharpe's elbow. "Are you all right, sir?"

"Never better, Harry. I thought you were guarding our rear?"

"Sergeant Miller's there, sir. Which way do we go now?"

"We find the stairs up to the house. Lieutenant Anderson!"

"Sir?"

"You did well, Lieutenant. Can your men load and fire that cannon?"

"Of course, sir."

"Bang some more canister down the tunnel, quick!"

Anderson looked puzzled. "You want us—"

"Lanier will hear it and think the tunnel's still being defended. Quick, Lieutenant."

Anderson went back down the ramp as Sharpe headed toward the cellar's far side. The crackle of musketry was louder here, an incessant noise that had the familiar rhythm of platoon fire. Then the small French six-pounder fired again, the report almost deafening Sharpe, but it was followed by another monstrous crash from above. "That's another cannon," Harper called from where he was ramming the balls down the volley gun.

Sharpe swore, knowing he had underestimated Lanier. Sharpe was reading the battle by sound, and the platoon volleys were closer than the rest of the musketry, which told him Lanier had trained his men to be as efficient with their muskets as the British and, worse, the Frenchman did not have one cannon, but two. "Three," he said, as yet another cannon fired from above. He imagined the canister flensing across the vineyard, shredding the advancing ranks. It was a mess, and his fault. But then there was a stone stairway and Sharpe pounded up the steps, the Light Company following, and crashed through a door into a vast kitchen. A woman screamed, but went silent as Sharpe turned on her with his sword. "Stay here," he told the woman, who crouched beside the stove.

"This way." Sharpe headed for a door that evidently led into the main house. He paused before opening it. "Make sure you're all loaded," he told the Light Company. He waited till the last man had rammed a rifle or musket, then opened the door. The hallway stretched in front of him and it was empty. The noise of the battle was much louder now and it spoke of bad news. Sharpe could hear the disciplined fire of the defending French and could tell that the return fire was sporadic and, worse, ill-disciplined. Windows were shattering as the men under Morris's command fired too high. God damn it, he should have led the battalion's main attack, which had plainly stalled under the defending fire. "McGurk!"

"Mister Sharpe?"

"Go and tell Lieutenant Anderson to stop firing the cannon and bring me his last four rockets. You'll find me upstairs." There was no point in Anderson keeping up the six-pounder's firing because any moment now Lanier would learn that Sharpe and his men were already in the house. McGurk went back into the kitchen while Sharpe led his men up the big stairway. He kept expecting to meet defenders, but the house seemed deserted. He went into the first room he found, a dark bedroom, and went to the shattered window from where he could look down onto the wide forecourt.

Lanier's battalion was in line and, astonishingly, only a line of two ranks, which, Sharpe guessed, Lanier had copied from the British. They were kneeling, presumably to make it harder for the redcoats down the slope to hit them, but each company took turns to stand and fire. And they were good, reloading as fast as any redcoat battalion. A musket ball hammered above Sharpe's head to hit the wall behind him. He stepped back from the window, not wanting to be killed by his own men, then peered out again as one of the cannons fired. There were two, one on each flank of Lanier's battalion, and they were sending gouts of canister fire to shred the grapevines and shatter the men who sheltered in the rows. Harry Price appeared beside Sharpe and looked down at the carnage. "Christ," he said.

"He won't be much help, Harry, but split your riflemen into two squads. One to the right and one to the left. Each squad to find a window and kill the gunners."

"Yes, sir."

A loud volley crashed from the vineyard and Sharpe saw that Kippen's Prussians had fired and were now advancing in a line of three ranks. He could see the cannon on the right of Lanier's line being slewed around to face the threat. The two guns had been firing diagonally across the slope, but now that right-hand gun would aim straight down the rows of vines to eviscerate Kippen's men. He could see a gunner swabbing the barrel, another carrying the powder charge ready to be rammed down the cleansed gun, while a third had the canister ready. "Hurry!" Sharpe muttered to his riflemen, who would be finding a room from which to shoot. He sheathed his sword, flinching at the pain in his shoulder, and unslung his own rifle. It was loaded, but in his haste at the tunnel's far end he had not wrapped the bullet with its leather patch, which meant this shot would be inaccurate. He raised it to his shoulder and aimed at the man holding the canister. Pain was racking his back, but he forced the gun's butt into his shoulder and lined the sights on the man, raised the rifle's barrel a half inch, and pulled the trigger. Smoke billowed from the barrel, Sharpe cried aloud at the pain, then stepped to one side of the window. The smoke cleared slowly and he saw that he had missed. The man had fallen, but appeared uninjured and was picking up the canister that he slammed into the muzzle, and a second man rammed it down the tube. The Prussians were getting closer, their bayonets reflecting the moonlight.

The cannon to the left of Lanier's line fired, evidently aimed at the redcoats among the vines. They should have been attacking along-side Kippen, but it was plain the remaining companies were farther down the slope and sheltering between the rows of vines. Sharpe had given Kippen two of his companies, but there was no sign of them, and he suspected Morris had somehow held them back. "I'm going to kill the bastard," Sharpe said aloud.

"Sir?" Private Bee asked nervously.

"Never mind. Talking to myself." Then Sharpe flinched as the French cannon fired and he saw the center of Kippen's line reduced to mangled men. The Prussians closed ranks and kept coming as the right-hand end of Lanier's line stood and aimed muskets.

Then the riflemen started firing from the upper story, and the gunners went down. The Prussians were cheering and running. More fell as Lanier's men fired into their ranks, but Kippen's Prussians, their bayonets fixed, stormed through the two-deep line and had reached the warehouse where his men were streaming through the big doors. Kippen and his Prussians had done well, but Sharpe's battalion were still far from the house, sheltering among the bullet-riddled vines. "The kipper will be trapped in there," Sharpe said. It was shameful. His men were cowering, while the

Prussians had captured the warehouse, only to be faced by a company of Lanier's superbly trained men who now blocked the warehouse's single entrance. Sharpe was reloading the rifle, this time using a leather patch, and it hurt like hell to ram the bullet down the barrel. And Lanier now knew an enemy was behind him, because he was already sending a company into the house.

"God save Ireland." Harper found Sharpe and was looking down onto the forecourt. He raised the volley gun to fire down at the men jostling to get under the entrance portico, but Sharpe touched the Irishman's elbow. "Save it, Pat. Back to the stairs, use it there."

Because Sharpe was also trapped. He had brought his men upstairs so they could look down on the fight, but now Lanier's men were filling the hallway below and firing up the stairway to where a dozen redcoats of the Light Company shot back. "Have you seen McGurk?" Sharpe asked Harper.

"He's here somewhere, sir."

"Find him. Harry!"

"Sir?" Price's voice called from the end of the long passageway that ran the width of the house.

"Bring all your men here! And hurry!"

Because there was a stairway to defend and a monster to kill. And Sharpe was trapped.

CHAPTER 13

More men were gathering in the hallway, firing their muskets up the stairway, while Harry Price was ordering furniture to be dragged from the bedrooms to make a barricade at the top of the flight of stairs. Sharpe was reloading his rifle when McGurk appeared with the last four rockets. "Lieutenant Anderson says he's no more ammunition . . ." he began.

"Just break off the sticks," Sharpe said, "and give them to me. And McGurk, how did you get here?" McGurk could not have used the main stairs that were blocked by the French troops in the hallway.

"Back stairs, Mister Sharpe," McGurk said.

There were always back stairs in a house like this, stairs for the servants to use, and Lanier would know where they were, which meant that a squad of his devils could already be climbing. "Harry!"

"Sir?"

"McGurk will show you the back stairs! Take half a dozen men and block them. Take these!" He tossed two of the rockets to Price. "And hurry!"

"Sir!"

Butler and O'Farrell had discovered some heavy vases that they were now tossing over the upper balustrade. The vases crashed down

282

into the crowd of men below, each crash greeted with cheers from the redcoats, who reveled in destruction. They began throwing furniture as well, and a chest of drawers appeared to crush two Frenchmen, which provoked a concerted charge up the stairwell.

"Make way!" Harper bellowed, aiming the volley gun and pulling the trigger. The leading Frenchmen were snatched backward and blood streaked up to spatter the stairwell's wall. A chamber pot followed, hurled by Butler, which struck a French officer on the head. The sound of the volley gun, let alone the destruction it had caused, prompted a moment's stunned silence from the enemy, then the muskets started firing upward again.

Sharpe was kneeling behind the crude barricade. He took out his short knife and cut the fuses of the rockets as short as he dared, then opened his tinderbox. He struck the steel with the flint, blew on the charred linen to encourage a flame, and lit the first fuse. He waited a heartbeat, then tossed the rocket's carcass over the balustrade down into the hallway. The rocket ignited halfway down, but without its long stick it had no guidance. Instead it spun crazily, bouncing off men and walls, searing a four-foot tail of flame, and then exploded.

Sharpe reckoned there had been at least thirty men in the lower hallway, but now there were only a dozen still standing, and two of those fled back through the front door. An officer shouted at a sergeant to lock the door, and the man threw the two heavy bolts before a rifle shot took him down. The stone floor glittered with blood. Sharpe fired his rifle down into the smoke-wreathed horror, then heard a crash of musketry coming from somewhere inside the house. "Pat! Find out what's happening!"

Before Harper could leave, Rifleman McGurk returned and knelt beside Sharpe, who was crouching behind the upper balustrade. "Mister Price has blocked the back stairs, sir."

"Does he need help?"

"He says not, sir. He stuffed a bed down the stairwell. No one can get up now."

Or get down, Sharpe thought, and cursed himself. He had led his men upstairs so they could look down on the fight outside, and now he could not see a way out. More of Lanier's men had come to reinforce the men in the lower hallway, and Sharpe reckoned there was the best part of a company summoning the courage to assault up the staircase. Kippen, as far as Sharpe knew, was in the warehouse, but he too was trapped there by the companies out on the forecourt, and the one man who could destroy those companies was bloody Morris, who would not fight.

There was no sign of Lanier, and Sharpe assumed the Frenchman was on the forecourt where his men were dominating the fight with their disciplined musketry. And that was where Sharpe should have been. If his Light Company had attacked Lanier's men from the rear, using the rockets to create chaos and their muskets and rifles to kill as many as possible, then the rest of the battalion could have advanced up through the vineyard while Lanier's men were distracted. If Morris would have led them, Sharpe thought, but surely even Morris would see the opportunity? None of that had happened because Sharpe had climbed the stairs so his riflemen could deal with the two cannon. And now he was trapped.

Long ago he had suffered a recurrent nightmare. It had started after the battle at Fuentes de Oñoro, which had been a nasty fight in a small village on the Spanish frontier, a fight in tight alleyways where men had clawed at each other like animals, screamed like devils, and died like beasts.

In the dream, which often left him awake, sweating and shaking, he had been trapped in a narrow alleyway. Behind him and to either side were high stone walls, while in front was a mass of French soldiers. He had told Lucille of the dream and she had smiled. "Dreams mean things, Richard," she had said.

"So what does that one mean?"

"Stay out of blind alleys, of course."

The vestibule below him was now apparently empty except for the growing pile of broken furniture to which his men were still enthusiastically adding tables, chairs, chamber pots, paintings, and chests of drawers. The French had pulled back so they could not be seen from above, but Sharpe could hear them, and when he took a few exploratory steps down the wide staircase he was greeted with a blast of musketry, most of which ricocheted off the marble banisters. "They're not giving up, the buggers," Harper commented.

"There's at least a company back there," Sharpe said ruefully. Any attempt to reach the front door would expose him to their volleys, yet every instinct told him he needed to escape the house and reach the rest of his battalion that was somewhere in the vineyard. Damn it, he thought, but he should have led the main attack, but he had been seduced by the thought of using the tunnel to erupt into his enemy's rear. Now he was trapped upstairs in this damned house and Lanier controlled the night.

"Keep them busy, Pat," he told Harper, and went along the corridor into the farthest bedroom, where two riflemen were making sure none of the French tried to use the cannon at the right-hand end of Lanier's line. The bedroom was dark except for what small moonlight came through the shattered windows. Sharpe peered over a sill.

"Bastards are good, Mister Sharpe," Rifleman Godwin said.

"They're well trained," Sharpe muttered. Lanier had advanced his line to the forecourt's edge, from where they still fired platoon volleys down into the vines. The response from his men was desultory, which angered him. Was there no officer there who saw what needed to be done? "Where are the Prussians?"

"All in that big building." Godwin jerked his head toward the warehouse. "A company of Crapauds followed them."

Which meant, Sharpe thought, that the Prussians were safe enough in the warehouse, but faced by a well-trained company of French Light Infantrymen who guarded the one door.

Sharpe used the hilt of his sword to knock out shards of glass sticking up from the window's frame, then leaned out into the night. He could drop to the ground, but reckoned the chance of a broken or turned ankle was too high. He was in enough pain already, and landing behind Lanier's battalion with a broken ankle was suicidal. He swore.

"You're bleeding, Mister Sharpe," Godwin said, worried.

"I've had worse." He pulled back from the window, troubled by what he had seen. The French were in two ranks and he had counted one company, then multiplied it by the six companies he could see. Lanier had over five hundred men on the forecourt! "Just make sure none of the bastards get that cannon working. And try to pick off the officers and sergeants in their line."

"A pleasure, Mister Sharpe," Godwin said, ramming a ball down his rifle's barrel.

Sharpe went back to the stairhead. Nothing had changed. If any man crept down the stairs he was greeted with a fusillade of musketry. Harry Price was still guarding the back stairs, and Butler and O'Farrell were still hurling Madame Delaunay's furniture into the vestibule, making a crude barricade across the wide space. "We still have one rocket?" Sharpe asked.

"Here." Harper held up the cylinder. The rocket's stick had been tossed down onto the shattered furniture.

Sharpe turned and looked at his men. He had thirty, and what he planned was insane, yet he was deep in the alley, the walls were high, and the enemy winning. "Load," he told them, "then fix swords."

Two men staggered from the right-hand corridor somehow carrying a gilded wardrobe. Sharpe let them tip it over the balustrade. It crashed into the furniture heap, turning valuable chairs and tables into matchwood. "Is there another like that?"

"Yes, sir."

"Fetch it."

He loaded his rifle, pushing two balls down the barrel. "We're going down, lads," he told his men, pitching his voice low so no one below could hear him. "Save your shot till we get outside the house, and when we go we go like the devil's on our heels."

"Where?" Harper asked.

"Straight through Lanier's line," Sharpe said. He could think of no other way to reach the rest of his battalion, and his whole godforsaken idea had been to attack Lanier from behind, so damn it, that's what he would do. Five hundred Frenchmen against his thirty men, four of whom staggered into sight again with another huge wardrobe on their shoulders. "Just put it on the balustrade and wait for my order. Pat? Give me the last rocket. And send for Captain Price, tell him to bring his men." Sharpe had crept four steps down the stairs, hugging the wall and staying low so that he would not be a target for the mass of Frenchmen crowded behind the crude barrier of splintered furniture. He could see the front door, which was locked by two iron bolts. The dead French sergeant lay on the mat just inside the door, his blood still slowly spreading across the marble floor. "Private Bee?"

"Sir?"

"When we go down, your job is to pull that dead Frog out of our way."

"Yes, sir," Bee said nervously.

"Don't worry, lad," Sharpe said, "he's too dead to fight back. And where's the monkey?"

"He's safe in a crate in the museum, sir."

"I daresay he'll be glad to see you."

"He will, sir. He's a good monkey, sir."

A Frenchman had heard the mutter of voices and shot his musket up from the lower hall. The ball slammed into the wall just over Sharpe's head, then ricocheted up to the ceiling, where it knocked a lump out of the molded plasterwork. Sharpe retreated up two steps. "Ready?" he asked.

"What are we doing?" Harry Price asked.

"Attacking the bloody Frogs out front," Sharpe said, "and listen lads, we go fast! We go through them and join the battalion! Just run like the devil, kill anyone who tries to stop you, and follow me!"

He struck the flint on the steel and puffed the tinderbox into a flame. "When I throw this thing," he spoke to Rifleman O'Farrell, "push that thing over the edge."

"Pleasure, Mister Sharpe." The wardrobe teetered dangerously on the balustrade. "Not yet," Sharpe said, then held the rocket's shortened fuse to the flame. The paper caught light. He waited two heartbeats, then tossed it toward the crowded Frenchmen at the back of the vestibule, and at the same moment O'Farrell heaved and the wardrobe slammed down with another almighty crash. "Now, lads!" Sharpe said, and started down the stairs, his rifle slung on his shoulder.

Panicked shouts sounded at the back of the hallway as the rocket began searing its crazy way among the Frenchmen's legs. Some muskets fired at the men following Sharpe down the stairs, but most of the Frenchmen had been scared by the splintering crash of the wardrobe and now by the fizzing mad rocket that spewed its flame tail until it lodged in the heap of broken furniture and exploded just as Sharpe reached the door. He pulled back the two bolts as Pat Bee hauled the corpse to one side.

"Fast, lads," Sharpe said, and drew his sword. "Fire at them as we run! Now come on!"

The oak wreath had been sewn back onto his old faded jacket and he remembered the Duke saying it had been given for insanity rather than bravery, and now he was doing something equally insane. Lanier had over five hundred men on the forecourt, and Sharpe was attacking them with just thirty, but as he erupted from the portico he saw that the company immediately in front of him was still reloading their muskets. So maybe there was a god who looked after lunatics.

Pat Bee was shouting in a high voice, though Sharpe could not make out any words. Pat Harper was beside Sharpe, the volley gun held at his waist. Sharpe had his sword drawn, his loaded rifle banging against his hip as he ran. "Kill them!" he shouted, and Pat Harper pulled the volley gun's trigger and the balls hit the two-deep French line like a blast of canister. Bee's musket hammered. The French were turning, some falling as more shots hit them, then Sharpe backswung the sword at an officer who just stood with mouth open in surprise. A man with his ramrod halfway down a barrel stopped to unsheathe his bayonet and Sharpe rammed the sword at him, twisted the blade, and was past him. There was a strip of flower bed at the vineyard's edge and Sharpe leaped it and started running down one of the alleys between the vines. "South Essex!" he bellowed as he ran. "On your feet!" He kept running. Shots came at him from the left, the balls making a flickering noise as they whipped through the vines. None hit him and he was still shouting. "South Essex! On your feet! Stand! Fix swords!"

He saw them standing and saw too that they were a long way down the shallow slope, but at least they were on their feet and forming into companies, though the files were too far apart because of the vines. Another French volley gouted smoke and balls that snatched some of the men back from the crude line. "To me!" Sharpe bellowed. "South Essex! To me!"

A voice shouted from behind the ragged line, though Sharpe could neither identify who had shouted nor make out the words, but he suspected it was Morris ordering them to stay where they were because he saw men look around uncertainly, saw them hesitate. "To me, now! Move your bloody selves!"

He turned left and forced his way across the vines, tearing and trampling the plants from their chestnut stakes. "Captain Jefferson!"

The Light Company, having broken through the French battalion, had stopped where Sharpe had turned to his left. "Fire at the bastards!" Harper shouted, unslinging his rifle. The shout reminded Sharpe that he had a loaded rifle and he slid it from his shoulder, pointed it up the slope, and pulled the trigger. "Captain Jefferson!" he bellowed again, and suddenly Jefferson was in front of him. The French had started their platoon volleys again, and the balls shredded the vines or whipped overhead. "What the hell is happening?" Sharpe snarled.

"Those volleys are happening, sir," Jefferson said.

"So? We can fire just as fast, if not faster. Beat the buggers down."

"The cannon didn't help," Jefferson muttered. "My company took a full load of canister."

"I told you to attack fast. If you stand around and give the buggers targets they'll fillet us. Get up there and kill them!"

"The major thought that was a bad idea, sir."

"Morris said that?"

"Yes, sir."

"Well, bugger Morris, I'm in charge now." He slung the rifle on his shoulder and drew the sword again. "South Essex!" he shouted. "We're going to kill those bastards. We'll do it fast! Follow me! Now!"

The old anger had come back to him, the same anger that had driven him through Flanders, India, Portugal, and Spain. For a time he had thought the anger was gone, calmed by Normandy and Lucille, by having a place he could call home, but it was still there. It was a fighting anger that went back to the streets of East London, to the callous brutes who had run the foundling home, who had called him a common bastard, unwanted, a guttersnipe. Well, the unwanted guttersnipe would show the bastards who could fight harder, and at the top of the vineyard was a man who reckoned he was Sharpe's equal as a soldier, if not his better, and Sharpe would bloody well show him that a decent county regiment from England led by a guttersnipe could hammer the Emperor's precious devils into bloody ruin. "Come on!" he bellowed and began to run. He did not look around to see if the battalion was following him, he did not need to, he could hear they were behind him, trampling up the slope, some shouting incoherently, and he could see Harper leading the Light Company to his left.

The madness was on him, the madness that had driven him at Talavera to snatch an Eagle, or at Badajoz, where he had crossed the ditch of death and climbed the breach in a welter of blood and rage. A hundred paces to go, and a small part of his mind knew that the nearer he went to the French line the greater the risk of death, and he had a sudden vision of Lucille, so kind, so beautiful, so loving and so much a hater of the war that had killed her husband. And Sharpe had a son too, and that thought almost checked him, almost made him stop, but he kept running. "If I die," he told Jefferson, who had kept pace with him, "tell Lucille she's the best woman ever."

"There's not a Crapaud alive who can kill you, sir."

Fifty paces to go, and the company immediately in front of Sharpe fired a volley and he sensed the musket balls all around him and heard the thump of them striking men behind him, but somehow they had missed both him and Jefferson. It was the vines, he realized, and that thought gave him a new energy, helped him forget the searing pain in his shoulder and down his back. Volley fire worked against massed troops, but the South Essex was advancing between the vines, in the alleys between the thick rows. One file to an alley, and that meant the battalion was double spaced and the enemy's muskets, inaccurate at the best of times, were wasting most of their shots on those empty spaces. "We're going to bloody win," he said to no one, and watched the company in front start to reload. Lanier had trained them to be fast, as fast as the redcoats, but they were nervous now and he could see men fumbling with cartridges, dropping ramrods. "They're ours!" he shouted. "Fast, you buggers! Fast!" He tried to run faster, to reach the French while they were still reloading, but his breath was coming hard now, his back was agony, and the ground was uneven. Jefferson saw him stumble and, in the moonlight, saw the blood darkening Sharpe's back. "Careful, sir."

But this was no time to be careful. This was the time to let the madness drive him. This, he suddenly thought, was probably the last fight of a long war, a war that had seen both Washington and Moscow burn, that had scorched the fields of India, and soaked the Spanish plains, and drenched the German and Austrian fields with blood, and if this was the last battle, then Sharpe was bloody well going to win it. "Keep going," he told Jefferson. The company to his front was mostly ramming their musket barrels, so they were close to being ready to fire, but he also noted that none had fixed bayonets. A bayonet fixed on a musket made it slower to load, so Lanier had kept the barrels clear of the obstruction. "We'll kill them all!" Sharpe shouted, and found a new release of energy that took him up the last few yards, across the dainty flower bed, and the Frenchman immediately to his front dropped his ramrod, pointed the musket, and pulled his trigger.

A misfire. The powder in the pan flared, but the musket did not fire. God had to love a guttersnipe, and Sharpe hammered the musket to one side and lunged with the sword. Captain Jefferson fired a pistol and the ball hit the man just as the sword pierced his belly. Sharpe was still moving forward, twisting the blade so it did not get stuck in the clinging flesh, and using his left shoulder to hit the man in the second rank. The sword came free and Sharpe swept it in an ugly haymaking swing that sliced across a man's face and let Sharpe stumble into the open space behind. An officer was there, carrying one of the slim elegant swords of the French infantry, and the man lunged at Sharpe, who had tripped and was falling. The blade flashed over Sharpe, who, sprawled on the ground, snatched up a handful of gravel and hurled it into the young officer's face, then swung the heavy sword onto his assailant's nearest ankle. The man recoiled from the pain, then lanced his narrow sword at Sharpe's chest. Sharpe could see the man's grimace, expressing effort as much as pain, and a regret seared through him. What a stupid way to die, killed by a stripling enemy when the war was as good as over, and he rolled fast toward his attacker, whose sword slid over him to strike the gravel. Sharpe hooked the man's ankles with his left arm, heaved, and the boy went backward, falling, and Sharpe was on his feet, the sword in his right hand. "Bloody fool," he told the French officer, and slashed the heavy cavalry blade across his throat.

The Prince of Wales's Own Volunteers had reached Lanier's men and the bayonets were doing their work. The French, those who lived, were retreating toward the house and Lanier was bellowing at them to stand and fight. Sharpe could hear him, but not see him.

Sharpe had gone through the defenders' line, which was now breaking into retreating groups harried by the redcoats' long bayonets. A tall man came at him with a musket, planning to smash the stock at Sharpe's head, but it was simple to step inside the wild swing and hammer the heavy hilt of his sword into the man's face. Blood spewed from the blow, then the man went down with a bayonet in his back. Private Carter tugged the bayonet free and grinned. "Bugger was trying to kill you, Mister Sharpe!"

"I knew you'd be close, Jem."

Carter looked past Sharpe. "Bloody house is on fire!"

Sharpe turned. The widow Delaunay's house was indeed burning, or at least the big hallway where he had been trapped on the staircase was well ablaze, the flames bright beyond the shattered windows through which smoke was now boiling. A Frenchman tugged open the front door and recoiled from a blast of flame that gushed bright. Lanier's line had re-formed with their backs to the house, and Sharpe could see men loading their muskets. "South Essex!" he bellowed. "Don't give them time! Follow me!"

Let the bayonets finish it, he thought. They had already thinned Lanier's soldiers, most of whom had not fixed bayonets and who were now caught between a burning house and Sharpe's vengeful redcoats. "Kill them!" he heard himself scream as he ran across the forecourt.

"Stop! Halt!" An even louder voice bellowed in English, and Sharpe's men, confused, checked their charge. "South Essex! Halt! Cease fire!"

It was Lanier who had shouted and who now walked calmly between the two lines toward Sharpe. "Brave Englishmen!" he called. "You have fought well! But the war is over and there is no need to die. I wish you only to go to your homes, to your wives, to your children."

Sharpe, astonished and offended that Lanier had given orders to his battalion, and that, moreover, the battalion had obeyed the commands, turned on the Frenchman. "South Essex!" he shouted. "This fight's not over!"

"But it will be soon!" Lanier called. He turned to look at Sharpe's men. "You have fought well! But no more men need die. Your colonel and I will decide this fight." He looked at Sharpe, smiling. "And if I win, Colonel, your men go back to their billets."

"And if I win?"

"My men will withdraw beyond the Loire, of course." Lanier drew his sword, a blade as heavy and long as Sharpe's crude sword. The man sounded annoyingly calm and supremely confident, and Sharpe could only admire the way Lanier had taken command of the night. "That is fair, is it not?" Lanier appealed to Sharpe's men. "Too many good men have already died in this war, and there is no need for more men to die. One death will decide the night."

"Kill the bugger, Mister Sharpe!" a voice called from the red-coated ranks and was greeted by a cheer.

Sharpe turned his back on Lanier so he could face his men. He turned slowly so that the growing flames from the burning house lit his back that he knew was soaked with blood, though he was not sure whether that would show clearly against the dark green of his uniform. "Quiet, lads!" he called. "Load your muskets! And rifles!"

"You wish the fight to go on?" Lanier asked mockingly.

"I don't trust you," Sharpe said. "You win and you could still massacre my men. I'm making sure they're not defenseless."

Lanier came a few paces closer. "I give you my word that your men are safe. Whoever wins, Colonel, your men will live. Can you say the same about mine?"

"Your men will live," Sharpe said, and knew that with those words he was accepting Lanier's challenge. He did not want to, he had wanted to destroy the French battalion, but Lanier appeared to have control, and now Sharpe must fight despite the stabbing pain in his shoulder and back.

"Let me speak to my men," Lanier said and, without waiting for an answer, turned and addressed his battalion. He told them what he had told Sharpe's men, that too many had already died in the war, that no more needed to die, and therefore this fight would be between the two colonels. That provoked a cheer from the blue-coated ranks, some of whom were edging away from the heat of the burning house. Lanier let the cheer die, then ordered his men to ground their muskets. "You might do the same?" he suggested to Sharpe.

"Sergeant Major Harper!" Sharpe called.

"Sir?"

"Once the men are loaded they can lay their muskets on the ground."

"Very good, sir." Harper sounded dubious. He walked to Sharpe, the volley gun low in his right hand. "Are you sure about this?" he asked.

"I'm not, but if I beat the bastard we'll keep our word."

"And your back is fair messy with blood."

"I'll live," Sharpe said.

"Let me fight him, sir."

"I doubt he'd agree to that, Pat. Besides, it's my fight."

"You're a mad bugger, sir, so you are."

"Tell Lucille . . ." Sharpe began, but could not finish.

"Oh, I think she knows." Harper clapped a hand on Sharpe's left shoulder. "And I'll have no need to say a word to her. Just kill the bastard, sir."

Some of Lanier's men had gone into the house, using windows to get access, and were evidently trying to extinguish the flames that must have started when the rocket hit the broken furniture in the big hallway. Sharpe wondered what had happened to the men he had left in the cellar, and hoped they had had the sense to escape back through the tunnel, then he turned to face Lanier, who was standing five paces away. "So, Colonel," he said, "you and I fight the last battle of the war?"

"And only my second against the English," Lanier said.

"The first?"

"A small fight in Italy," Lanier said, "at a place called Maida. My battalion came late to that fight, but I remember the carnage caused by your volleys, and I trained my men to fight with equal speed."

"And you lost at Maida," Sharpe said.

"You have never been in a losing battle?" Lanier asked, amused. Sharpe said nothing and Lanier smiled. "Until tonight, perhaps?"

"And tonight," Sharpe said, "when I kill you. Who commands your battalion?"

Lanier shrugged. "My major *en second* is called de Brosse. I assure you he will keep our agreement. And who do I look for in your battalion?"

"Major Morris," Sharpe said, and looked along the South Essex to see Morris standing close to the Grenadier Company. "Morris! Come here!" Morris hesitated. "Here, Charlie! Quick now!"

Morris came slowly, ignoring the sniggering from the ranks. He stopped short of Lanier and Sharpe. "Colonel?" he said to Sharpe.

"The word you want, Morris, is 'sir,'" Sharpe snarled, "and let me introduce you to Colonel Lanier, a famous French killer."

"The word you want, Colonel Sharpe, is '*soldat*,'" Lanier said, still amused.

"A famous French soldier, Morris, the hero of Marengo. His men call him the Monster. He's good, very good. He had you skulking in the vineyard."

"He . . ." Morris began, then decided courtesy would be better. "I am honored to meet you, Colonel," he said to Lanier.

"The honor is entirely mine, Major." Lanier had looked from Sharpe to Morris and back again, and his amusement was plain. He sensed their hatred. "You summoned Major Morris to instruct him in his duty if I kill you, Sharpe?"

"No, Lanier. I summoned him because he's my deputy. Are you my deputy, Charlie?"

"I am," Morris said stiffly.

"And the thing is," Sharpe said, turning around, "that I'm wounded. That's blood on my back, Charlie, in case you've never seen it except at a flogging. Won't be a fair fight, will it? A wounded man against a monster, so why don't you fight Lanier for the honor of Britain?"

"Why don't I . . ." Morris stammered and looked appalled.

"Colonel Lanier won't mind, will you?"

Lanier understood precisely what Sharpe was doing and smiled affably at Morris. "It will be a pleasure to fight you, Major, and an honor. I have killed sixteen men in single combat, but no Englishmen," he paused, "yet."

God damn it, Sharpe thought, but I like this man. "So, Charlie, want to use my sword? It's heavier than yours." He held the cavalry sword hilt first toward Morris. "It's a right butcher's blade, but you need something like this to slaughter a monster."

"Monsieur?" Lanier sheathed his sword as if to encourage Morris, and gestured for the major to come and take Sharpe's blade.

"This is ridiculous, Sharpe," Morris protested.

"So what do you suggest we do?" Sharpe asked. "Come on, now, tell me! You're a proper officer, Charlie, not some jumped-up gutter-snipe from the ranks. Tell me what a proper officer should do?"

"Do?" Morris asked faintly.

"That's a Crapaud battalion, and that's a British battalion. It's a fight, Charlie. Maybe the last fight of the whole war, and Colonel Lanier and I have seen enough slaughter to last a lifetime. So we've agreed to settle it man to man, only I'm wounded. I'm weak, Charlie. So what do we do?"

"You . . ." Morris began, then fell silent.

"I? I what? I picked the fight? Aye, I did. Because I've never backed down from a fight, Charlie, and you've never fought properly. Are you refusing to fight Colonel Lanier?"

"It's a preposterous idea," Morris said, taking a backward step.

"You're refusing?" Sharpe demanded.

"I'm . . ." Morris began, then fell silent again. Jeers sounded from the battalion.

"Captain Jefferson!" Sharpe bellowed to stop the noise.

"Sir?" Jefferson ran along the ranks.

"If Colonel Lanier kills me," Sharpe said, "you will command the battalion and you will obey Colonel Lanier's orders, which will be to take the battalion back to the Louvre. You will also take Major Morris under guard."

"Under guard, sir?" Jefferson inquired.

"Cowardice in the face of the enemy," Sharpe said, "that's the charge. Lock him up and report the incident to General Halkett in the morning."

"Of course, sir."

"Take him away, Captain."

Morris looked as if he was about to protest, but Sharpe stepped toward him, raising the sword's bloody blade, and Morris just stumbled backward. The battalion cheered. "Quiet!" Sharpe roared. He looked at Lanier. "Sorry about that, Colonel."

Lanier watched Jefferson escort Morris away. "You do not like this Charlie?"

"I despise him."

"And humiliate him. You are cruel, Colonel Sharpe."

"And you're not?"

"When necessary," Lanier said.

"And it's necessary now," Sharpe said, and stepped toward the Frenchman, who slowly drew his sword again.

"We fight with swords, yes?" Lanier asked.

"Swords," Sharpe agreed and noted that Lanier carried a long blade, equal in length to his own, but with a very slight curve, which suggested it was designed for slashing rather than stabbing. Lanier held it low, evidently content to let Sharpe begin the fight. "This is a Solingen blade," Lanier said.

"And this is cheap Birmingham steel," Sharpe responded. He knew of the reputation of Solingen swords; they were forged in Prussia and reputed to be the best in Europe.

"How old are you, Colonel?" Lanier suddenly asked.

"I don't know," Sharpe said, "does it matter?"

"Forty maybe?"

"About that, I reckon."

"I like to know something of the men I kill," Lanier said, then took a half pace backward as if he would rather continue the conversation than begin the fight. "You used a word to Charlie," he invested the name with scorn, "guttersnipe. What does that mean?"

"It means I was born in the gutter, Lanier. *Je suis un bâtard.*"

"I salute you, Colonel," Lanier said, and swept his long blade up in a salute. "I like bastards, they fight hard." He lowered the blade again. "How bad is your wound?"

"I've had worse."

"Then we fight," Lanier said, "but if you yield you will live. You agree?"

"Are you here to talk or fight?"

Lanier acknowledged the question with an inclination of his head, then raised the sword. "*En garde*, Colonel."

Sharpe raised his own blade and touched Lanier's sword. Behind him the fire roared, its glare illuminating the forecourt, where the two battalions watched in silence. "I would regret killing you, Sharpe," Lanier said. He twitched his blade, presumably to test Sharpe's reaction, but Sharpe stayed motionless. He was thinking that this was all wrong. It was supposed to be a fight to the death, yet Lanier was offering friendship, even sympathy, and Lanier was *le Monstre*, famous throughout France for his exploits, and Sharpe realized the man was deliberately soothing him to take away his anger.

And that anger had been Sharpe's fuel since childhood. Anger at the people who had raised him, at the sergeants who had tried to break him, at the men who had flogged him, and at the officers who despised him. Anger had driven him into breaches reeking of blood, across fields littered with the dead, and into the command of a battalion, and Lanier had seen that in him and so wanted to take away the anger. So damn Lanier, Sharpe thought, and the familiar anger surged into his blood and he twitched his sword as Lanier had done, and the Frenchman responded with a parry and stepped back.

"Bastard," Sharpe spat at him and let the anger loose. He attacked, provoking an instant cheer from his men who watched as he savaged the heavy blade at Lanier. There was no subtlety in his assault, only massive cuts that he hammered hard at the Frenchman, who parried them all with an instinctive ease. The two blades rang together so hard that Sharpe feared his own cheaper sword would break, but the Birmingham steel held firm as he drove Lanier backward with the sheer ferocity of his slashing assault.

And Sharpe realized within seconds that the crazed attack would not work. True, Lanier was being driven backward and the slight alarm in his eyes showed his appreciation of Sharpe's strength and speed, but he was parrying each blow skilfully, and after the fourth or fifth slashing attack he began to smile. That smile enraged Sharpe, knowing he was being mocked, but instead of changing his attack he redoubled the blows, trying to batter Lanier's obstinate blade aside and slam the heavy cavalry sword into his head or neck. Sharpe's men were cheering, Lanier's troops looked downcast, though Lanier himself now appeared unworried and content to block each wild slash.

"My mother," Lanier said, "first taught me to fight with a sword," he paused to parry a blow, "'and always remember, Philippe,' she told me, 'that the point beats the edge.'" He smiled, then looked startled as the next swing of Sharpe's sword slid down his blade and struck the hilt's crossguard hard and pushed his arm across his body. Sharpe lunged, driving the point of his sword toward Lanier's belly, but the Frenchman moved aside fast and threw Sharpe's blade off. "Your mother didn't teach you to fence, Colonel?" the Frenchman inquired.

"I never knew her," Sharpe said. His back was a sheet of pain, the muscles protesting at the exertion needed to swing the heavy blade. He was breathing hard. Lanier had stepped back after eluding his lunge, and Sharpe did not press forward, but let his sword arm drop as he caught his breath.

"So your mother will not mourn your death?" Lanier asked.

"From the grave, Colonel. She's long dead."

"Time you met her then!" Lanier raised his sword and made a half-hearted lunge toward Sharpe's right-hand side. Sharpe parried, but the Frenchman's blade seemed to dip under his stroke and flashed toward his left, striking him on the hip. He felt the sword's tip pierce his skin and strike bone. Lanier recovered his blade to block Sharpe's counterstroke, beat the sword hard to Sharpe's right, and thrust again,

302

this time his sword piercing Sharpe's jacket just above the belt and again breaking skin. "Two," Lanier said.

The bastard is playing with me, Sharpe thought. He could have pushed the thrust harder and his damned sword would have been in my belly. His back was a streak of fire now, every movement of his sword arm a lance of pain. The blood was warm on his skin, but not as hot as the fierce fire that was spreading through the roof and bursting through the rafters to flame in the sky. "Are you ready to yield, Colonel?" Lanier asked. He had lowered his sword so that the tip rested on the gravel.

"Go to hell," Sharpe said.

Lanier raised his sword slowly, the polished blade reflecting the bright flames. "My mother taught me first," he said, "but the village priest was my real tutor. An extraordinary man! He had been a soldier, but found God. He taught me to pray in the words of the psalmist. '*Béni soit l'Eternel qui dispose mes mains au combat, et mes doigts à la bataille.*'" He smiled mockingly. "A good prayer for a soldier, don't you think?" He suddenly lunged with the sword and Sharpe stumbled desperately backward, his parry missing Lanier's blade altogether.

"You are clumsy, Colonel," Lanier said. He had pulled the lunge back at the last moment. "Sword fighting is an art, Colonel. It should be graceful, even subtle."

"Like putting gunpowder in a cellar?" Sharpe asked. Lanier had taken a backward step and Sharpe let his sword's tip rest on the gravel.

"It was *Madame* Delaunay's notion," Lanier said. "A bit crude, I admit, but it might have succeeded." He suddenly raised his blade, lunged it to Sharpe's left, swerved it low, and kept lunging until the tip of the slightly curved blade was at Sharpe's belly again. He pressed, forcing Sharpe back. "You really should yield, Colonel. I would regret killing you. You're in pain, yes?"

"I've had worse."

"We all have, I suppose." Lanier kept the pressure on Sharpe's stomach, still forcing him backward. Sharpe had his sword held low, but knew that the moment he moved it the Frenchman's blade would slide forward fast. The French troops were calling to their colonel to kill Sharpe, while Sharpe's men were now silent. "It is a pity about the house," Lanier said, glancing to his right where the fire was rampaging through the widow's house. The glance was swift, too swift to give Sharpe an opening. Lanier prodded the sword, its sharp tip breaking skin again. "Yield, Colonel," Lanier urged him, "there is no dishonor in defeat."

"And what honor is there in assassination?" Sharpe asked harshly.

"A nation's honor," Lanier replied, "a consolation in defeat, and a lesson to the victors."

"A lesson?"

"That victory has a price."

Sharpe nodded. "And if I defeat you now," he asked, "is that the end of *la Fraternité*?"

Lanier hesitated, then nodded. "It is. I am the last one alive."

Was that true? Sharpe suspected it was, but then he was disposed to believe Lanier, a man he liked, but still had to defeat. He winced and bent slightly forward as if trying to ease the pain in his back, then suddenly turned to the right and used his wrist to sweep the sword up. Lanier, taken slightly by surprise, was slow to lunge, and by then Sharpe's turn had pushed the sword's needle-sharp tip away from his belly and the lunge merely scored a cut across his stomach. Not deep, but Sharpe felt the warm blood as his sword knocked Lanier's blade aside. For a heartbeat the Frenchman's sword was held wide and Sharpe sprang. He dropped his own sword, using both hands to seize Lanier's epaulettes. He pulled the Frenchman toward

304

him and head-butted him hard. The blow hurt like hell and momentarily blurred his vision, but if it had hurt him he knew it must have half blinded Lanier with pain and dizziness.

Lanier staggered backward and Sharpe kicked him hard between the legs. The Frenchman bent over and Sharpe's fist caught him as he went down and there was suddenly blood on Lanier's face. He tried to bring the sword around to defend himself, but Sharpe was too close and had his hands around Lanier's neck and was squeezing. "Your mother taught you to fight with a sword," he said, "but mine gave birth to me in a gutter. And that's where I learned to fight."

Lanier could not speak, but tried to saw at Sharpe with the sword, and Sharpe kept squeezing. The sword was cutting at the back of his thighs, but the force of it was weakening as he choked the Frenchman. Lanier's nose was broken and bleeding, the blood trickling down to Sharpe's wrists. Then Sharpe suddenly released his grip and used his left hand to seize Lanier's black-ribboned queue of hair. He yanked the Frenchman's head back hard, then slid his right hand onto Lanier's face. He used his index and little fingers to push beneath his eyeballs. "I'm going to blind you next," he promised Lanier, "and when I've gouged your eyeballs out I'm going to pick up my sword and cut off your right hand and your left foot. You understand? You can be a blind cripple or you can yield."

Lanier made an incoherent noise and Sharpe pushed his fingers harder, feeling the pressure of the eyeballs. "*Non, non!*" Lanier managed to gasp.

"Do you yield?" Sharpe snarled, pressing harder.

Lanier croaked unintelligibly. His sword still scraped at Sharpe's legs, but feebly, and his left hand gave Sharpe's arm two taps. "Is that a yes?" Sharpe asked and felt the taps on his arm again. He let go of Lanier and stepped back. Lanier immediately swept the sword at him, but Sharpe had half expected the cut and seized Lanier's sword wrist in his right hand and took the Frenchman's elbow in his left. He brought his knee up and his hands down and heard the crack as he shattered Lanier's forearm. Then he let go and stepped away, stooping to pick up his fallen sword.

Lanier had somehow held onto his sword, but his broken arm had taken away his ability to fight. Sharpe cut at him and saw the Frenchman flinch as he tried to parry. Sharpe stopped the cut just short of Lanier's neck. "Yield," he said. His men were cheering, shouting at him to cut the Frenchman into ribbons. "Yield," Sharpe said again.

"I yield, monsieur," Lanier said hoarsely.

"You may keep your sword," Sharpe said, then on an impulse, "and in Normandy there is a farm called Seleglise. You will always be welcome there." He thrust his sword into its metal scabbard. "Captain Jefferson!"

"Sir?"

"Collect our wounded. There's a wagon and horses in the warehouse and we'll carry them back in that. We need surgeons. Colonel Kippen!"

The Prussian had come from the warehouse with his men to watch the fight, and now came to Sharpe's side. "Colonel?"

"You will stay here to make sure Colonel Lanier marches away. He's going to the River Loire."

"Of course," Kippen said.

"And treat them well, Colonel," Sharpe growled, "they're brave men." He turned back to Lanier. "You have surgeons?"

"Two."

"They can tend your wounded. Those who can't march I'll have taken to a hospital tomorrow. The rest of you must be gone by dawn."

There was an almighty crash as half of the house roof collapsed, the burning rafters tumbling bright into the lower fires, which sprang up anew to dazzle the night. A huddle of servants stood by the gun, which had been firing from the left-hand side of Lanier's defensive line, and Sharpe saw the widow was there. He walked toward her. "I apologize, madame," he said.

She spat at him. "You are a barbarian, Colonel."

"The word you are looking for, madame," Sharpe said, "is *soldat.*"

He turned his back on her and walked away. Sharpe's war was over.

EPILOGUE

Sharpe sat with Lucille beneath the willows that edged the stream that marked the western edge of the estate. "The bugger won't be back," he said.

"Richard!" There was remonstrance in her voice. "You should not have shot him!"

"The buggers can just steal our sheep?"

"They're hungry. And you could have killed him!"

"I wish I had."

It was a rare fine day, scarce a cloud in the sky, and Sharpe, dressed as ever in cavalry overalls, sprawled at the water's edge. Nosey, his dog, lay beside him. "Maybe the weather's turned," he said hopefully.

"Too late for the harvest." Lucille sighed.

The summer of 1815 had been the coldest and wettest in memory, but this year's promised to be as bad. France was hungry. The price of bread was dangerously high. There was unrest in the cities, while the countryside was threatened by bands of discharged soldiers who had learned how to live by pillage. Sharpe was fairly certain that the thieves who had stolen three sheep from his land were such men.

Charlie Weller had purchased the sheep in Dorset. They had cost a pound apiece and another three pounds to pay for their shipping from Lyme Regis. Twenty-five sheep, of which twenty-two still lived. The small flock was in the pasture behind Sharpe, and next to him on the stream bank was the rifle that protected them. "It was no one from the village," he said. "We'd have heard if it was."

The night before he had waited in the beech wood at the top of the pasture and seen a man coming from the northern hedgerow. He had eased Dan Hagman's rifle forward, aimed, and shot. He had aimed to kill, but the bullet had merely wounded the trespasser, who had turned and fled with the rifle bullet embedded in a thigh. "He won't be back," Sharpe said, "and next year we'll have mutton and wool."

"We can make cheese."

"You can," Sharpe said, "and Charlie wants to put a trap in the stream. Reckons we can live on salmon and sea trout."

Hiring Charlie had turned out to be a huge success. He was energetic, knew his business and, better still, was popular in the village. His wife Sally was pregnant, Charlie was happy, and the estate, despite the weather, looked as if it might turn a small profit. "Poor Charlie," Lucille said, "he works so hard."

"He's happy."

"And you?" Lucille asked pointedly.

Sharpe took her hand and squeezed it gently. "You know I'm happy."

"You miss the army," Lucille said, almost accusingly.

"No," Sharpe said, knowing he lied. He did miss some parts of it; the joy of outthinking an enemy, the elation of victory, the energy that came from constant danger. But he did not miss the stench of death, the sound of men weeping as they died, the agony of wounded horses. It had been a year since the fight at Waterloo, but Sharpe still woke some nights sweating and shivering, his mind racked with the images of suffering and horror.

"You can go home," Lucille had said.

"This is home," Sharpe had insisted, and so it was, and it was the first home Sharpe had ever known, even if many of the local people distrusted him. He was *l'Anglais*, a word spoken with vinegar on the tongue, and though folk nodded in greeting, there was little friendliness in their eyes or manner. And Lucille was right, he thought, about the sheep-stealer. If the man had come from the village then the unfriendliness would have turned to hatred, maybe even revenge, for there were a score of men back from Napoleon's army who still possessed their muskets. And many of those folk wished Napoleon was back, instead of being marooned on St. Helena.

France was an occupied country now. There were 150,000 allied troops stationed in Bonaparte's old garrisons and the Duke commanded the occupying forces, who were fed from the French treasury. Sharpe had been summoned to the Duke's presence at Mont-Saint-Martin, to a country house the Duke had commandeered north of Paris. "So you're leaving the army?" he had peremptorily greeted Sharpe.

"I am, Your Grace."

"To go home?"

"To Normandy."

The Duke grimaced. "Strange fate, Colonel. You fight them then live with them."

"Indeed, Your Grace."

They were walking across a wide, damp lawn where a half-dozen of the Duke's foxhounds were romping. "Had them sent from England," the Duke explained. "There's decent hunting here, even boars." He paused. "So, peacetime army has no appeal to you?"

"Never known a peacetime army, Your Grace."

"What will you do in Normandy?"

"Farm, Your Grace."

A grunt, which suggested Sharpe was ill-equipped to be a farmer. "We'll miss you, Sharpe."

"Thank you, Your Grace."

"You have had a remarkable career. I assume that if we need your services we can call on you?"

"Of course, Your Grace."

"I've confirmed your rank, which should help."

"Thank you, Your Grace," Sharpe said fervently. Almost all of his promotions had been brevet, which meant his official rank was probably still a captain, but the half-pay of a lieutenant-colonel would go a long way to help replacing the château's roof.

"Captain Burrell tells me you have a dog?"

Captain Burrell, Sharpe thought, should keep his bloody mouth shut. "I do, Your Grace."

"Called Nosey?"

Sharpe blushed. "He is, Your Grace."

The Duke snorted, which Sharpe supposed to be laughter. "Morris told me you were an insubordinate bastard."

Sharpe said nothing. He knew that Morris had resigned in disgrace rather than face a court-martial for cowardice. "You should have told me when I appointed him, Sharpe," the Duke said, "I had no idea there was a history there."

"I didn't want to speak ill of a fellow officer, sir."

"I remember him from when I commanded the 33rd. He seemed full of promise. But you approve of the new fellow?"

"Peter d'Alembord will make a fine battalion commander, Your Grace."

"Even with a gammy leg?"

"He may not be able to dance, Your Grace, but he can fight."

Peter d'Alembord, recovered from the wound he had taken at Waterloo, had been given command of the Prince of Wales's Own Volunteers. "Let's pray there's no more fighting," the Duke had said, then glanced up at the sky. "More rain coming," he grumbled, "never known weather like it." He had looked awkward for a moment, then held out his hand. "I summoned you, Sharpe, to thank you," the Duke said, letting go of the handshake. "You served me well for many years."

"Thank you, Your Grace." Sharpe was almost as embarrassed as the Duke.

"I wish you well, Colonel, and if you're ever in England then I hope you will let me know."

"And if life takes you to Normandy," Sharpe said, then faltered.

"You'll stay for lunch? It'll be a cold collation."

"Mutton, Your Grace?"

The Duke snorted again. "You heard the news of Colonel Lanier?"

"No, Your Grace."

"Brigadier Lanier now, and in the royal service. They've made him the commandant of a military training establishment."

"He's good," Sharpe said.

"So were you, Sharpe. You were a damned fine rifleman." The Duke had started strolling back toward the house, driven by the first few drops of rain.

"I liked the Rifles," Sharpe said.

The Duke began to hurry, but then stopped at the lawn's edge. "Tell me," he said, "did you intend to kill or just to wound?"

Sharpe hesitated. He knew exactly what the Duke was talking about, but still suspected his answer could get him into trouble. Then decided he would part from the Duke with the truth. "I meant to kill, Your Grace."

"Thought so. But it was a damned fine miss. Well done, Sharpe.

You know the bloody fool now claims he won the battle?" He was talking of William, Prince of Orange.

"I heard that, Your Grace."

"And he's thinking of putting a damn great monument at the place where he was wounded." The Duke started across the gravel toward an open door. "Do you know what won the battle, Sharpe?"

"You did, Your Grace."

"No," the Duke said sharply, "it was you, the finest infantry in the world, and God knows how many times that infantry got me out of trouble."

A dozen men had shared the lunch, and insisted on hearing Sharpe's recollections of old battles, which accounts were interrupted when a message arrived for the Duke. He tore open the ornate envelope, read the contents, and looked at Sharpe. "The Pope thanks you, Sharpe. Maybe he'll make you a cardinal?"

"Me, Your Grace?" Sharpe said, flustered.

The Duke gestured with the message, which had an elaborate seal at its foot. "It seems Mister Fox sent his holiness a list of the paintings that have been recovered, and which we'll now return. You had a hand in that, did you not?"

"A very minor part," Sharpe said.

Major Vincent, seated to Sharpe's left, shook his head. "Poor Fox," he said, "not much of a spy."

"Clever fellow, though," the Duke said, his tone suggesting that was not a compliment.

Sharpe had left feeling flattered and pleased, and wealthier too. Major Vincent had walked him to the stables, where Sharpe discovered the big black stallion that Fox had ridden south from Péronne. "The Duke is eager you should have him," Vincent said. "He's called Tempest."

"Good God," Sharpe had said, looking at the magnificent beast. "I'm happy enough with my old nag."

"Take your old horse back too. And if you sell Tempest don't take anything less than two hundred guineas."

Now Tempest was in his Normandy pasture. Charlie Weller reckoned there were too many horses for sale and prices were unnaturally low. "Keep him a year or two, Colonel, till the price recovers. He's still young!"

Pat Harper would be jealous of the horse, but Harper was two countries away in Ireland. Once in a while a letter would come, evidently dictated to a young priest, which gave news. Isabella had given him a son. "We're calling him Richard and I'll murder the little bastard if he joins the British army."

"We must go to Ireland," Sharpe told Lucille. "Patrick can meet Richard Harper."

"I'd like that." She had taken off her shoes and was trailing her feet in the stream. "When I was first married," she said wistfully, remembering her dead husband, "I would swim here."

"You can now. No one's watching."

"You are!"

"And I always will." He stripped off his boots, overalls, and shirt, then leaped into the water. "Come on, girl," he said, and waited for Lucille to join him in the chill pool of the stream where he floated, unaccountably happy, and home at last.

HISTORICAL NOTE

The Battle of Waterloo was fought on 18 June 1815. Three weeks later the British and the Prussians were in Paris, Napoleon had abdicated, and his troops were ordered to retire southward beyond the River Loire. Those three weeks were not peaceful. The Prussians had fought a number of small actions against the French rearguard, while the main Prussian army, remembering the atrocities committed by the French on Prussia in 1806, sought revenge by ravaging France. Wellington, advancing south to the west of the Prussians, marched more slowly and fought only two minor actions, to capture the fortress towns of Cambrai and Péronne. The Duke insisted on strict discipline, fearing that any thefts or assaults committed against the French population would result in *guérilla* warfare against his troops. On 3 July 1815, the Convention of Saint-Cloud ended the conflict. French forces were ordered south of the Loire, the Provisional Government recognized Louis XVIII as King of France, and Paris was yielded to the victorious allies. There was no action at Ham. The château in that small town had once been a formidable fortress, with outer works designed by the famous military engineer Vauban, but by 1815 those outworks had gone. The château was used as a prison for much of the nineteenth century, but was largely destroyed by the Germans in the First World War, and all that remains today is the great square gatehouse.

La Fraternité is a novelist's invention, though there were plots to assassinate the Duke of Wellington while he was in Paris. Probably the best known was an attempt to shoot the Duke by an ex-soldier named Marie André Cantillon, who narrowly missed his target. He was imprisoned, but doubtless consoled by the bequest of 10,000 francs left to him in Napoleon's will. A far more dramatic attempt occurred in June 1816, when Wellington gave a ball in his Paris mansion and a fire was discovered in the cellars. Servants extinguished the blaze, but discovered stashes of gunpowder and cartridges, which had happily failed to ignite, but which inspired the story in this book. The house, the grandly named Hôtel Grimod de La Reynière, was on the site of what is now the American Embassy.

The "prayer" that Private Pat Bee said over Hagman's grave is an ancient Latin Christmas carol taught to Italian children, while Lanier's quotation from the Psalms is a slightly edited version of Psalm 144, verse 1: "Blessed be the Lord who trains my hands for war and my fingers for battle."

Sharpe's claim to having seen proof of a guillotine in Halifax is quite possible. There had been a guillotine in the town since medieval times, though the last execution is thought to have been in 1650. It was not the only guillotine in Britain, there was another in Edinburgh and, though Dr. Guillotin is popularly credited with the invention of the device, there were evidently other guillotines in many European countries long before Dr. Guillotin's machine was first used in 1792.

The *Musée Napoléon*, now the Louvre, was indeed filled with works of art stolen from all across Europe. I have anticipated the restitution of the artworks, which were mostly removed much later in the year. Not all were returned, and some, like Veronese's stunning canvas of *The Wedding at Cana*, which had been stolen from Venice, still hang in the Louvre. The British had some difficulty in taking many of the pictures down because of a lack of ladders, and replacements were indeed borrowed from a traveling showman who displayed monkeys.

I took immense pleasure in giving Sharpe the Order of Saint Vladimir, second class, which I am sure appealed to his well-hidden vanity. The story is based on truth. The Czar sent the order to the Duke of Wellington, asking him to find a worthy recipient, but Colonel Lygon refused it on the grounds that it was second class, so Wellington ordered that it be given to "Colonel Somebody-Else!" Why not Sharpe? He deserves it. At the time, the British army awarded no medals, but Wellington had a silver medal struck for every man who had been present at Waterloo.

There are still small vineyards in Paris, but there were far more in 1815, many of them just north of the Rue de Montreuil. There were also scores of tunnels beneath the city wall, almost all of them devoted to smuggling wine and spirits, which were heavily taxed when they entered the city.

The Arc de Triomphe in the Champs-Élysées, like the elephant in the Place de la Bastille, was a model built of wood. The wooden arch was covered with painted canvas, while the monstrous elephant was finished in plaster. The arch, of course, was finally built, but the elephant decayed until it was demolished in 1846. It was supposed to be constructed of bronze melted from cannons captured by the Emperor and, had it ever been completed, would surely have become a famous landmark.

One of the delights of writing novels is to discover that the characters insist on creating their own destinies. Pat Harper, I knew, would always return to his beloved Ireland, but Sharpe astonished me by settling in Normandy, where, for the moment, I shall leave him. I am grateful to the many readers who have accompanied us on the journey, and especially to my wife, Judy, who has endured Sharpe's many battles. Thank you!

ABOUT THE AUTHOR

BERNARD CORNWELL is the author of the acclaimed *New York Times* bestsellers *Waterloo*, *1356*, *Agincourt*, and *The Fort*; the bestselling Saxon Tales, which include *The Last Kingdom*, *The Pale Horseman*, *Lords of the North*, *Sword Song*, *The Burning Land*, *Death of Kings*, *The Pagan Lord*, *The Empty Throne*, *Warriors of the Storm*, *The Flame Bearer*, *War of the Wolf*, *Sword of Kings*, and, most recently, *War Lord*; and the Richard Sharpe novels, among many others. He lives with his wife on Cape Cod and in Charleston, South Carolina.